DIAMOND DEVIL

ZAKHAROV BRATVA
BOOK 1

NAOMI WEST

Copyright © 2023 by Naomi West

All rights reserved.

No part of this book may be reproduced in any form or by any electronic or mechanical means, including information storage and retrieval systems, without written permission from the author, except for the use of brief quotations in a book review.

❦ Created with Vellum

MAILING LIST

Join the Naomi West Mailing List to receive new release alerts, free giveaways, and more!

Click the link below and you'll get sent a free motorcycle club romance as a welcome present.

JOIN NOW!
http://bit.ly/NaomiWestNewsletter

BOOKS BY NAOMI WEST

Zaitsev Bratva
Ruby Malice

Ruby Mercy

Aminoff Bratva
Caged Rose

Caged Thorn

Tasarov Bratva
Midnight Oath

Midnight Lies

Nikolaev Bratva
Dmitry Nikolaev

Gavriil Nikolaev

Bastien Nikolaev

Sorokin Bratva
Ruined Prince

Ruined Bride

Box Sets
Devil's Outlaws: An MC Romance Box Set

Bad Boy Bikers Club: An MC Romance Box Set

The Dirty Dons Club: A Dark Mafia Romance Box Set

Dark Mafia Kingpins

Read in any order!

Andrei

Leon

Damian

Ciaran

Dirty Dons Club

Read in any order!

Sergei

Luca

Vito

Nikolai

Adrik

Bad Boy Biker's Club

Read in any order!

Dakota

Stryker

Kaeden

Ranger

Blade

Colt

Tank

Outlaw Biker Brotherhood

Read in any order!

Devil's Revenge

Devil's Ink

Devil's Heart

Devil's Vow

Devil's Sins

Devil's Scar

Other MC Standalones

Read in any order!

Maddox

Stripped

Jace

Grinder

DIAMOND DEVIL
ZAKHAROV BRATVA BOOK ONE

It's my first time meeting my sister's fiancé.

I knock on the door, and who do I see with his arm around her?

The man who got me pregnant.

Three months ago, I almost got hit by a car.

The guy behind the wheel was gorgeous as they come.

We got to talking and… well, things got a little carried away, if you know what I mean.

But when it was over, we went our separate ways.

Except, not quite.

The little plus sign on this pregnancy test that tells me our story isn't over.

But that's a problem for another day.

First, I have to go to my sister's engagement party.

When I see who she's marrying, my jaw hits the floor.

This… This cannot possibly be real.

But it *is* real.

So is the attraction I felt when I first met Ilarion Zakharov.

So is the hatred.

And so are the bullets that start flying when Ilarion's enemies attack the party.

Turns out Mr. Not So Nice Guy is a big, bad Bratva don.

And now that he knows I'm **pregnant with his heir...**

He's not letting me out of his sight.

DIAMOND DEVIL *is Book 1 of the Zakharov Bratva duet. The story continues in Book 2,* **DIAMOND ANGEL.**

NOTE: This is a light mafia contemporary romance. No cheating.

1

TAYLOR

I'm crying and running and running and crying. At this point, I'm mostly just curious to see which one will give out first: my tears or my legs.

Sixty minutes into my run, though, both are going strong. Turns out it's easy to run when you're putting your whole sordid, nasty, terrifying past behind you. When you're turning your back on your family and your sins, running actually comes kinda naturally.

As for the tears?

Well, those come naturally, too.

My dad's handprint on my cheek burns like he branded me there. He's never hit me before, but he sure didn't hold anything back from this one. And for a first timer, he did a damn good job. He slapped me right across the face as if he's been waiting my whole life to do exactly that.

He regretted it as soon as it happened, of course. I could see that much in his eyes: fear, hot shame, the instant surge of self-hatred.

But no matter how much he regretted it, the damage was already done.

It's kind of ironic that it's a beautiful evening in Chicago. Shouldn't terrible things happen on terrible days? It ought to be pouring buckets down from the gray heavens so that fat raindrops mix with my tears. Locusts should be descending on the suburbs like Moses and the Pharaoh just got into their little tiff. Someone I love should cut their own bangs.

None of that is happening, though. The sun is shining, the birds are chirping, and the park I'm circling on my broad running loop is full of children and mothers laughing.

It's not just Dad's slap that's seared on my skin—it's also the things I said to him right before that. Things that crossed the line, that broke the thin ice we've been living on for the two long years since Mom's diagnosis.

I wish I could take those words back, just like Dad wishes he could undo the slap. But like I said: the damage is done.

No turning back now.

So I parrot the words I said out loud to myself between painful gasps of breath. Why? Maybe because I'm a masochist and I like it. Or maybe because I just think I deserve to be punished. But not even punished in a cool, cosmic, *God-strike-me-with-a-bolt-of-righteous-lightning* kind of way. Just a petty, cruel kind of way.

"'If only Mom's cancer were contagious. Then all of us could be trapped at home, too. Miserable just like you are.'"

Diamond Devil 3

That's what I said to him.

Even now, I can't help but cringe. I've repeated my own words back to myself a thousand times since I ran out of the front door of the home I grew up in, and they aren't getting any easier to hear.

My sister Celine didn't know what to do when she heard me say that. She came downstairs in the middle of the fight, trying to play the peacekeeper as always.

"Stop!" she screamed. "Both of you, please, stop!"

But there wasn't any stopping after that. I said what I said, Dad slapped me, and from that point forward, we were all stuck on the same nightmarish rollercoaster with no way off.

I wonder what Celine is doing right now, as I begin my third lap of the track encircling the neighborhood park. She's probably still slack-jawed and staring at the door I ran through like I'll come back any moment bearing flowers and cake and apologies.

Old Taylor might've done exactly that.

New Taylor just can't.

Two years of watching your mother wither to a husk of herself will do that to a woman. She's the one dying, but I feel like I'm losing parts of myself, too, with every pound that evaporates from her too-thin frame.

We almost avoided this fate. One year in, we were told that the treatments were taking. The chemo was working. The tumors were shrinking from golf balls to pinheads to nothing at all.

Then—*Whoops,* the doctors said. *Scans were wrong. We made a mistake. Looks like you're dying after all.*

Those tears were some I'll never forget.

It got worse after that. Mom shrank faster; her skin grew pale and thin like tissue paper. Her eyes were the most haunting bit of all: gray and almost unseeing, like one of those cave fish at the Shedd Aquarium she used to take us to on rainy days when Celine and I were little.

She's still here. For how much longer, none of us really know. I wonder how much of tonight's fight she heard from her bed upstairs.

You know what I can't get over most of all, though? That the shame in my dad's eyes *preceded* him actually hitting me.

It started as a silly little bickering over my curfew. Yes, I still live at home—but I'm twenty years old now, and a midnight curfew for a grown-ass woman is almost a slap in the face in its own right.

If only Mom's cancer were contagious. Then all of us could be trapped at home, too, miserable just like you are.

It felt disturbingly good to say that to Dad when he tried to tell me where I could and couldn't go. Those words have been bubbling up in my gut for almost two years of his overprotectiveness and paranoia.

But it's more than that, too.

Dad is *afraid*.

And he's been afraid since *before* Mom got sick.

I first noticed it when I caught sight of him making dinner in the kitchen one night and realized with a jolt just how skinny he'd gotten. He was never a big man, but the beer-gut dad bod I'd always known was gone. In its place was a skittish man, badly shaven, paler than he had any right to be.

His eyes never stopped moving, either.

Like he was waiting for a shadow to lunge out and strangle him.

Why would that be? I have no earthly idea. Archie Theron is a travel agent, for crying out loud. Not exactly a high-stakes profession. He's a father of two, married to his high school sweetheart, living in the quiet, tree-lined suburbs of Chicago. There are no shadows out here who like to strangle people. The obscene property taxes pay for some very nice streetlights, actually, so there aren't many shadows at all.

But you wouldn't know that by looking at Archie Theron. He was the kind of scared that makes you scared, too, just by happening to glance in his direction.

I should've asked then what was frightening him. But the next day, we found out about Mom, and everything else dimmed in importance.

I wonder what he would've said if I did.

I snap myself out of my reverie and look up to realize the sun has sunk behind the trees. The park has emptied, too, and my legs are starting to quiver from exhaustion. My tears dried up at some point while I was thinking, though I'm not quite sure when.

With a sigh, I turn toward home.

Home. What a concept. It's supposed to feel safe, isn't it? You should never be scared to go home. You should never be afraid of what monsters are waiting for you in the corners of your room. You should never hate the people who also call it home.

But all those things are true right now.

Still, where else would I go? I've got nowhere else. No *one* else. I know better than anyone what happens when you dare to believe in a future or in other people, and as foolish as I may be sometimes, I'm not about to make that same mistake twice. I did that once, and it almost cost me my sister. I won't do it again.

I take an easy pace around the final bend. Home is a few blocks away now. My thoughts have quieted, though I wouldn't say they've exactly sorted themselves out. More like they've just agreed to take a breather. They're as exhausted as I am.

I can see the Theron household way down at the end of the road. The rose bushes under the windowsills have gotten a little raggedy without Mom tending to them every day, and the yard has begun to outgrow its boundaries. But it's still cute. Still peaceful.

For now.

I'm crossing the street when several things happen at once.

First, a blinding light appears in the corner of my vision.

Second, I look up to realize that a car is barreling towards me, and it isn't stopping anytime soon.

Third, I do the only thing I can do: close my eyes and pray that death doesn't hurt as bad as life has lately.

2

TAYLOR

I only open my eyes again when I realize I'm not dead.

The car I thought was being driven by the Grim Reaper comes to a screeching halt about two inches away from my bare legs. I can feel its exhaust on my skin like it's a wild animal breathing on me.

But the windshield is tinted dark, so I can't see who's actually behind the wheel. I just stand there, frozen with fear, and try to remember how to breathe.

The sun has extinguished itself over the horizon. Night is reclaiming Evanston. All the sidewalks are empty and, except for the purring engine and my racing heart, everything is quiet.

Then the driver's door swings open.

A foot hits the ground.

A giant's foot. Booted, huge.

A leg follows, just as massive. I watch, transfixed, as a man unfurls himself from the vehicle.

When he's out, my mouth flops open. To call him "gorgeous" is a disservice to the word. Honestly, calling him a "man" is kinda rude as well. He's the kind of man who makes you want to reserve that label exclusively for him. He's *that* big, *that* stunning, *that* chiseled from marble.

But my god, he is *terrifying.*

His jaw is clenched so tight it's a wonder that his teeth don't shatter like sugar glass. Those eyes are roiling storms, black whirlpools that function like an express lane to Hell.

And when he speaks, his voice comes out like The Devil himself.

"What the *fuck* is wrong with you?"

I know what you're thinking: this is the part of the story where I quip something witty and go about my way. Back to my miserable house and the miserable family that lives there. This is the part where you admire the heroine's tenacity and you kinda sorta maybe start to girl-crush a little bit, maybe put yourself in her shoes, maybe start to wonder how she'll mend her relationship with her daddy and nurse her mommy back to health and finally go about solving the mysteries of all those past sins she vaguely alluded to before.

This is also the part of the story where none of that happens.

What happens instead is that I open my mouth to unleash a clever, devastating retort on this six-foot-six titan, but all that comes out is…

"Big."

The man pauses. Of all the things he expected me to say, that couldn't have been in the top hundred.

Finally, he says, "What?"

My cheeks flame. "You're big," I mumble stupidly. "Like, tall."

"And you're a fucking moron," he snaps back. He rakes a huge hand through his thick, dark hair. "It's after sundown, and you just sprinted blindly across the street, a hundred yards from the nearest crosswalk, without even pretending to look to see if anyone was coming to murder you with a car."

He's not, strictly speaking, *wrong*. But he *is* being a humongous douche about it. I've never had someone talk to me in a way that made me feel this small.

"Is that what you were doing?" I answer, finally remembering how to patch a subject and a verb together. "Coming to murder me? Honestly, great timing. I won't even put up a fight."

"So you're reckless *and* insane," he mutters. "Fantastic."

He pauses and surveys me as if finally seeing me for the first time. I can't help but blush under his gaze. He's got this way of looking at me that makes me feel like I'm in one of those bad anxiety dreams where you go to deliver the most important speech of your life and the whole crowd sees you naked. I wish I was wearing something less revealing than tiny pink Spandex running shorts and a black sports bra. Like a parka, maybe. Whatever it takes to conceal as much of me as possible from this man's sinful eyes.

"I'm not insane," I say. "Just casually having the worst day of my life. Well, one of them, at least. There's a lot to choose from."

He remains quiet for a long time. "Someone hit you," he says at last. His eyes are locked on the cheek where Dad slapped me. I don't even know how he saw the mark through the darkness and the flush from my running, but he did.

Something tells me this man doesn't miss much.

I cover it up with one hand, while I simultaneously say, "No one hit me; what are you talking about?"

The man rolls his eyes. "I'd call you a terrible liar, but I'm pretty sure you're already aware of that."

"And I'd call you a terrible driver, but I'm pretty sure *you're* already aware of *that.*"

"Bold words from Blind Bambi in a sports bra," he drawls.

"Don't you have somewhere else to go be an asshole?" I ask him. "Or were you just flying around the neighborhood, looking to smear someone across your grille like a new hood ornament?"

"If I was, I wouldn't have chosen such a mouthy one."

I frown. "Maybe I was wrong. Maybe your schedule isn't that busy, if you have time to sit here and banter like the hotshot you so clearly think you are."

He pauses, taking his time to drink me in again before answering. That's how it feels: like he's drinking me in. Slurping a little bit more of me up with every pass of his eyes, whether I like it or not.

Spoiler alert: I do.

"You weren't kidding. You *are* having a bad day."

"No shit, Sherlock. Is it written on my forehead?" I've got my fists balled up and planted on my hips, face screwed up in anger. The fact that he's so obnoxiously calm after his initial bellowing outburst is irritating me.

I'm in one of those moods where I'm like, *My world is shit, so everyone else's should be, too.* It's not fair for him to be so cool and collected.

"No," he murmurs. "It's written in your eyes."

I shiver involuntarily. "Are you a fortune teller or just a run-of-the-mill creep?"

"Neither. I'm a businessman."

That makes me snort. "And your business brings you to the most boring suburb in the country at—" I check my watch—"ten p.m. on a Tuesday?"

"As a matter of fact, *tigrionok,* it does."

"Sounds like you need a new line of work." I blink. "Also, what did you just call me?"

"*Tigrionok,*" he enunciates in a cool, dark rumble. "It means 'little tiger cub.' Because you've got your claws out, but I don't think you have the faintest idea how to use them."

I back up a few steps. I'm suddenly, painfully aware of how isolated we are. This stretch of Evanston isn't exactly the big city. It's silent and still everywhere I look. The thunder clouds overhead seem to be pressing down on us like a big, flat palm smushing me into the earth.

"Is that a threat?" It takes everything I've got to keep my voice from trembling.

The man chuckles and spreads his hands wide as if to show me he's unarmed. "I have better things to do than threaten feisty little girls who don't know how to look both ways before they cross the street."

"You came barreling out of nowhere! This is Evanston, not the Daytona fucking 500."

"Excellent reminder. Let me get the fuck out of here then." He turns to go back to his car, which is still growling and vibrating.

But just before he gets in, he stops and looks up at me again. It sends goosebumps racing down my spine. "Someone did hit you." It's not a question, so I don't bother denying it. "Did you hit them back?"

I can't help but let out a bitter bark of laughter. "Slapping your own dad is pretty unforgivable."

"Slapping your own daughter is worse," he lashes out, so viciously that my breath catches in my throat for a moment. "Any man who does that is a coward."

I think about my dad's frail, trembling hands. The way the skin hangs loose on his neck these days, so gaunt he almost matches Mom.

"Yeah," I admit. "Maybe he is."

Then, to my everlasting horror, a tear leaks down my cheek.

I clap my hand over my face almost as soon as I feel it. But, to pile horrors on top of horrors, the man sees it, because of course he does.

"I—I'm sorry," I stammer, as more tears follow the first. "I don't know why I—"

The words die on my tongue.

Because the man has slammed his door shut.

Crossed the distance between us.

And, with one swipe of his rough thumb, wiped the tear off my face.

I'm looking up at him, speechless and bamboozled and all the synonyms that go with this situation that cannot possibly be real.

He's even more beautiful up close. But it's a harsh kind of beauty. Like a profile carved out of stones that have been around for a long time and seen a lot of hideous people do a lot of hideous things.

Sharp jawline. Wicked chin. Eyes hard as ice.

Only his lips are soft, and the image of them tracing up my inner thigh flashes through my mind like a comet before I snuff that shit right out.

"I'm sorry," I blurt again.

He rests his thumb on my closed lips. "Don't apologize. You are not the one who has done something wrong."

I sniffle and try to stop the flow of tears. But my cheeks keep getting wet. It takes me an embarrassingly long time to realize that that's because the clouds overhead have opened up.

I turn my face to the sky and get rewarded for my curiosity with a fat raindrop directly to the eyeball. More rain comes after, plastering my already-sweaty hair to my scalp.

"Do you have somewhere to be?" the man murmurs. Somehow, his voice slices right through the growing cacophony of the storm.

I hesitate, then shake my head. "I... I don't really want to go home, actually." I know my dad and sister are probably worried about me, and if Mom heard the argument or the slamming doors, then she probably is, too.

But I just want a minute. Maybe two. Just three calm, quiet, silent minutes for me to pretend that my life isn't in shambles.

"Why not?"

"Why not? Gee, let me count the ways. My dad is a wreck and my mom is really sick and my sister is just overwhelmed. I feel like I'm the only one holding it all together and I'm doing a worse and worse job of it with every day that passes," I whisper. The words fall from my lips as easily and heavily as the rain. "They all hate me and I don't want that, because they're my family, you know? But part of me is so angry with every single one of them, too. I'm angry with my sister for trying to pretend like everything is just so fucking peachy all the time. I'm angry with my dad for, for... for hitting me, of course, but also for being so paranoid. The world isn't out to get us, you know? But he acts like it is. He acts like if he doesn't keep us locked up in this miserable little cage, that some big bad wolf is gonna come swallow us whole. Hell, I'm even angry at my mom for getting sick. How messed up is that? And then, most of all, I'm angry with myself. I should, for once in my life, just do what *I* want. No one's ever asked me what that is. I don't even ask me what that is. I just put my head down and hold onto this crumbling fucking family with my bare hands. And I'm failing at it. I really am. I'm failing so bad and I don't know how to stop."

My voice dies only because I'm doing my damndest not to burst into tears. At the end of this torrent of completely unasked-for word vomit, I risk a glance up. The man's face is wet and his hair is dripping, just like mine, but you wouldn't know it from the calmness in his eyes. Those haven't changed one bit since he got out of that car.

He doesn't seem to care that he's wearing what I would guess is an extremely expensive suit in the middle of a thunderstorm.

He doesn't seem to care that he's holding a strange, blubbering girl he just met who's telling him way, way too much about her personal life.

He doesn't seem to care that none of this, not one bit of it, makes any goddamn sense.

He just puts that rough, soft, strong, tender thumb under my chin, lifts it up so I'm forced to meet his gaze, and he whispers a few little words that change the course of my life.

"So tell me then, *tigrionok*. What do you want?"

3

ILARION

The doors slam shut in unison. Rain thunders on the roof of the car, but in here, it's dry and warm.

I kill the engine so that the only sound is the crackling of thunder and the girl's quiet inhalations.

"I probably shouldn't get in cars with strangers," she remarks suddenly. "Not unless I want to end up on a true crime podcast, and believe me, I do not."

"You just told me your whole life story without pausing for breath. We might not be friends, but I don't think we're strangers."

She laughs for a second before she kills it nervously. "Sorry for that."

"I told you once not to apologize. I'm not the kind of man who repeats himself."

"What kind of man are you then?" she asks. "I wouldn't have pegged you for the white knight, lay-your-jacket-over-a-puddle-so-the-lady-doesn't-get-her-feet-wet kind of dude."

Diamond Devil

It's my turn to laugh. "I'm certainly not that, either."

I glance out the windshield. The heavens are really letting loose now. It suits my mood. Dark and powerful.

On my way out of the meeting I just attended, I was ready to break something. Anything. This little tiger cub sprinted in front of my car, and for one wild second, I thought, *Maybe I'll even break her.*

I didn't, of course. Obviously. I stopped the car and got out to read her the fucking riot act.

But something in her made me pause.

In my line of work, I don't see unvarnished fear in people's faces that often. They always try to hide it. Try to hide everything, actually, like I don't see everything there is to see. They think it'll help them to hold their cards close to the chest.

But this girl? It didn't even cross her mind not to wear her heart on her sleeve. It didn't occur to her that I could use that weakness against her. She was surprised when she started crying, but I wasn't. I saw the cracks skittering across her surface long before the first tear fell.

I *will* admit that things getting carried this far away is somewhat surprising, though. We're in my car, just the two of us.

I wonder if she knows how dangerous a place this is.

"Are you from here?" she asks.

I shake my head. "Russia."

"Russia. That explains the accent and the, uh… the…"

"*Tigrionok,*" I supply with a subtle smirk. "Yes, that is Russian."

"*Tee-gree-oh-knock.*" She wrinkles her nose as she echoes it.

I press a mocking hand to my chest. "Awful. You're butchering my native tongue. I ought to put you back out in the rain for your crimes against my people."

Laughing, she slaps me on the arm. "I'm trying my best!" Then, remembering herself, she lets her hand fall back in her lap. That uncertainty crawls over her face.

Pity. I like it better when she is unbridled. The nickname started as a joke, but it is more on the nose than I realized. Her wildness, her rawness—it speaks to me.

You live long enough in a world of deceit and lies, and that shit starts to rub off on you. It feels like being cloaked in mud from the moment you open your eyes in the morning until you close them at night. There's never any clawing it off.

Her, though? It's like she's never even seen the stuff.

"You said business brought you here. What kind of business do you do?"

I blink and turn my gaze back on her. "Murder. Drug trafficking. Despicable sins of all kinds—the more profitable, the better."

She rolls her eyes. "Hilarious. I bet you're here all week."

"No, actually. Just tonight," I reply with a straight face. "Someone betrayed me, so I came to warn them what would happen if they did it again. If you ever see me back here, it means that person is dead."

A stunned silence swallows up the car. In the half-dark, the girl's eyes are bright. Her cheek still blooms with that handprint. It makes me angry. Very fucking angry. I meant what I told her—any man who strikes his daughter isn't fit to live.

My hands twitch. My father is already dead, luckily for him.

But if I wasn't so sure he's currently burning in hell for what he did to our family, I'd dig him up and kill him again.

"Ha … ha?" she ventures, uncertain. Her throat bobs as she swallows. "Let's pretend I know you're kidding, because otherwise, I'm going to have a nervous meltdown, and I've already had enough of those today to last a lifetime."

"Sure. Let's say I'm kidding."

"Good." She sighs with relief and slumps back in her seat. "Can I ask you a question? Is it nice, not giving a shit?"

My mouth curls up with amusement. "Is that the impression you have of me?"

"One hundred percent. I'm pretty sure your watch costs more than I could make in a lifetime of swinging from a pole with my tatas out, but you stood out in the rain with me, a complete and total stranger—and a lunatic of a stranger at that—for no good reason."

"Don't forget the shoes. Those are expensive, too."

She rolls her eyes again, but she laughs as she does it. That sound does something to me. Zaps a jolt of electricity straight to my cock.

A jolt I haven't felt in a long, long time.

It crosses my mind out of nowhere how long it's been since I fucked. I didn't choose celibacy; it just hasn't occurred to me in months to do anything different. Nothing called to me. No one spoke to me.

Until her.

But now, every cell in my body is suddenly screaming bloody murder. It wants to ravage something.

I have to hold back, though. Ravaging a girl like the one in my passenger seat will ruin one of our lives—but it sure as fuck won't be mine.

And I've left enough damage in my wake tonight.

"To answer your question, I don't know if it's nice or not. I've never been any other way."

"Sounds nice to me," she answers at once. "All I do is give a shit. About my—well, you already heard the whole spiel." She blushes and glances away from me like I won't notice her shame.

"What else would you like to not give a shit about?"

She scoffs. "You name it, I'd like to not give a shit about it. I just want something that feels like mine, you know? Something I chose because I wanted it, not for any other reason." She starts to tick things off on her fingers. "I mean, I go to a college I don't like to take courses I don't care about. I hate running, but I do it anyway, because I don't want to be home any more than I have to. It's just… tiring, that's all. I'd just like to set it all down for a sec."

"So do it."

She laughs again, high and mocking. "You say that like it's easy."

"It is. It's exactly as easy as I'm saying. The way to stop doing something is to just… stop."

She tilts her head as she regards me from a new angle. I can't see anything past the windows; the rain is still relentless. It looks cold and foreboding out there. But in here, the air is suddenly crackling. It's alive—*I'm* alive—in a way I haven't been in a very long time.

And the chains holding back my lust are growing weaker by the second.

"When you say it like that," she croaks, "I almost believe you."

I don't know if she knows it, but she's leaning in toward me. Closer and closer. With every inhale, she freezes—but with every exhale, she inclines like I'm a black hole sucking her in.

Fuck, maybe that's exactly what I am. I'm something she's never experienced and, after tonight, she'll never experience me again. It's best that way.

For both of us.

Because nothing good can come of mixing my world with hers. She's sad about college and Daddy; I have blood on my hands and skeletons in my closet and sins in my past that would make her fucking weep.

This close encounter is bad enough. Anything more than that would be devastating.

But here she comes anyway.

Closer.

Closer.

And I'm getting closer, too. She smells like jasmine and sweat and rainwater. Her eyes are bright. Her skin, soft and clear.

"I'll ask you one more time," I growl. We're inches apart now. She sucks in my words and makes them her breath. "What do you want? Fuck all the other people trying to get you to submit to their desires, to live according to their fears, to paint inside the lines they set out for you. What do *you* want?"

Her answer comes after the slightest moment of hesitation, and it couldn't be better if I wrote it on her lips myself.

"I... I want you."

4

TAYLOR

Who just spoke?

It couldn't have been me. I, Taylor Theron, would never get in a stranger's car, blab my entire sob story without taking a single break to inhale, and then beg him to kiss me.

Except that there's a weight in my chest the size of Chicago, and a need sitting on top of it that's twice as big. He told me to stop thinking about everyone else. He told me to tell him what I wanted.

And apparently, what I want is a kiss.

No, not just a kiss. A kiss from *this* man. A man who's so unlike anyone I've ever met before. A man who my father would take one look at and lock me up in the tallest tower he could find.

That's me. A golden-haired Rapunzel with a sailor's mouth and a fear of heights.

His eyes bore into mine, holding me there like a captive. The waiting makes it feel like he's deliberating. To kiss the girl or not to kiss the girl? I can practically see the wheels in his head turning. *She seems like a basket case, but maybe her kissing isn't as sloppy as her crying.*

"That's a dangerous request."

"You asked me what I wanted."

"I thought you had a small modicum of self-preservation."

Is this rejection? Or is he just trying to make sure I'm not so vulnerable that he'd be taking advantage?

I strike that thought almost immediately. He really doesn't seem like the type of guy who'd have any moral qualms about taking advantage of anyone.

"I'm tired of being careful all the time," I explain. "It's exhausting."

He smiles cryptically. "I'm warning you right now. If I kiss you, I doubt it'll stop there."

A shiver ripples down my spine. But it's not just nerves; it's excitement. Honestly, my dad is to blame. He's tried so hard to keep me safe that it's made me want to run right into danger.

And this man…he's danger personified.

"You asked me what I wanted," I say, sucking in a breath. "And I told you. If you don't want to kiss me, then just say that instead of—"

I gasp when his lips come down on mine. He tastes like whiskey and smoke, the kinds of heat that singe your nerves and remind you that you're alive.

There's no awkwardness, no flailing, no sense of uncertainty.

He knows exactly what he's doing.

His tongue traces over my bottom lip and I part for him. I've never been more eager to deepen a kiss in my life. I've never been more lost in one, either.

I can't feel my legs or hands. I'm too focused on our fused lips, our entangled tongues. His touch is a lightning bolt cracking through the darkness of my life.

When he pulls his lips from mine, I draw in a hungry breath of air. I'm surprised to see that it's still thundering and pouring outside. Somehow, my world had gone quiet in the sparse few seconds of that kiss.

Something occurs to me. "W-wait…" I gasp.

He pulls back just far enough that I can see his lips glistening. "Scared, *tigrionok?*"

"I just realized that we don't even know each other's names."

He arches one dark, thick eyebrow. "I'm—"

"No!" I blurt. "Never mind. I don't want to know."

He hesitates, breathing slowly for a moment, the lust blowing his pupils so wide open I feel like I could fall into them.

But I meant what I said. I don't want to know his name, because if I don't know his name, then none of this is real. It's all a figment of my imagination and it can stay there forever. It'll be just a dream I had, one wild night. A moment untethered in time.

"Very well," he says at last. "No names."

"I've never done this before," I whisper, even as my hand curls around his neck again.

"And you probably won't do it again after this," he responds confidently. "So make this count."

"What makes you so sure?"

"Because you're looking for a memory. Something that you can look back on when you're old and say, 'I did that. It was dangerous and stupid and reckless, but I did it anyway.'"

My eyes flare as he talks. He's right. I've spent my whole life walking the line, listening to my parents, existing meekly within the confines of the box they've built around me.

But tonight, with him, I'm taking my power back. Because all those doubting voices at the back of my head, telling me to be careful—they're not mine.

The real me has only two words to say: *Do it.*

I haul myself into the back seat. Then I grab the edges of my sports bra and pull it off over my head. It's a half-assed striptease, clumsy and fumbling, but it doesn't matter. His gaze is hungry all the same the moment his eyes land on my breasts.

And then he comes toward me.

It's a marvel that a man so huge can maneuver so gracefully in such a tight space. Everything seems effortless for him. It's the most attractive quality to me, a girl for whom everything feels like an effort more often than not.

The way he crawls on top of me takes any apprehension I might have possessed and coils it low and warm in my belly. The corded muscles in his arms ripple as he braces himself over me.

Breathe, Tay. Remember to breathe.

He cups the side of my neck. I get the sense that those hands are capable of both beautiful and terrible things, and I'm not sure which he's about to do to me.

What does it mean if I want both?

He guides my lips back to his. In the same breath, his other hand grabs my hip. I instinctively wrap my legs around his waist and that must be what he wanted, because suddenly, we're rolling and shifting until I wind up straddling his lap.

Not once has he stopped kissing me. His warm tongue sweeps between my lips and tangles with my own, and it's the way he pulls the moan from me that also banishes the annoying voices from my head.

Celine's.

Mom's.

Dad's.

They disappear, one by one. Until the only voice left is mine.

Do it, it says again. *Do it.*

I lift my hips so that he can slide down my jogging shorts.

"Fuck," he snarls angrily. "I've always liked how tight these things are until now."

I giggle deliriously as he tugs them down my legs, yanking my panties down with them. When I'm bare, he hauls me against him with another reverberating growl that sends shivers straight to my core.

Then he dips his head low and kisses a fiery trail to my breasts. Now that he has me naked and pliant in his arms, he's taking his time to savor the taste of me.

It's torture.

His lips are even softer than I imagined they would be. His tongue flicks and glides over my skin. Warm breath and cool air tease my nipples into painfully rigid peaks.

When he sucks one into his mouth, I buck on his lap and nearly unravel right then.

"Oh, fuck…" I gasp, letting out another wordless cry that's immediately swallowed up by the rolling thunder above us.

I rest my chin on the top of his head as he suckles and tugs. Every pull into his mouth sends a wave of pleasure straight to the ache building between my legs. When I feel his fingers stroke my slit, my body jerks violently as electricity speeds up and down my spine.

I've never felt this much, and we haven't even gotten to the actual sex part yet.

He arches back and stares at my face while he presses two fingers inside me. I'm so wet that there's next to no pressure. Just a whole lot of soft bliss that works its way into my body and irons out all the knots I've been carrying around with me for the past two years.

We're gazing into each other's eyes, which only makes this hotter. More intense. More intimate.

But it's more than that.

It's *jarring*, too.

In my (admittedly limited) experience, men tend to focus on everything below the neck when you're sleeping together. Like they'd prefer if you were a blow-up doll instead of, like, an actual human being with thoughts and feelings and eyeballs.

But this man? *This* man gazes at me with an intensity that's equal parts predatory and hypnotizing—like he can't decide if he's going to devour me or possess me. I'm inclined to believe "both" with the way he strokes and presses inside me, his thumb massaging until I'm on the edge of begging him for mercy.

Instead, I shatter. And it's more, so much more, because he's not satisfied with simply letting me ride it out on his fingers. He fists his other hand in my hair at the nape of my neck so I have nowhere to look but at him—and instead of letting me ride to my own completion, he thrusts his fingers and coaxes me to new heights.

If someone's feelings are going to be dragged through the mud here, it won't be his. He's the one in control. I'm the one losing what little ground I had to begin with.

And even still…

"Fuck me."

The words fall out of my lips like a whispered prayer. I've never in my life uttered those words. I've never even dared to consider it.

But it's hard to be aware of the rules right now, even my own self-made ones. I feel like I'm in a suspended reality where anything goes.

I feel strong, and I almost never feel strong.

I feel confident, and I'm not a confident person.

I feel sexy, and I've always been scared of my own sexuality.

But not now. Not with him. Not like this.

His hands glide to my hips and raise me up. At this angle, it's easier to rest my brow against his, and *oh my god* is it intimate. I more than half-expect him to push me away, but instead, he only flicks his gaze low long enough to undo his pants, pushing down the zipper to release his erection.

Our lips are only inches apart, our breathing nearly synchronized, and instead of closing the distance, he teases me by making me want it more.

I take one look at his cock and it all makes perfect sense to me. There's no way he could be anything but confident and charismatic when he's packing a beast like that.

"You're gonna break me," I whisper fearfully.

Something wild flits across his face. His eyes are a mesmerizing misty blue with deep hazel that almost glows around his irises. They're the one part of him that betrays just how close to losing control he really is.

"I don't break anything I have no interest in fixing," he says as his cock rubs against my slit.

I'm still afraid. But the moment he pushes himself inside me, I no longer care.

There's no room to be anything but alive.

5

ILARION

I have to stop waiting so long between fucks.

That's the only reason why this would feel so destructive.

So intense.

And so goddamn incredible.

My cock sinks inside her, and for a moment, I hear music playing in the backs of my eardrums. I know this isn't some slow-motion movie scene with fireworks exploding around us, but that doesn't stop every nerve in my body from feeling like exactly that.

And I know she's not some special unicorn of a woman who's going to enter my life and save me.

First, I don't need saving.

Second, I don't need another distraction.

Fuck knows I've let enough slip through my fingers. That's the whole reason I'm in this nauseating suburb with this mess of a woman bucking on top of me.

It's just her lips, I tell myself. I've always been a sucker for lips like hers. The kind that beg to be kissed and sucked and tasted. They've been distracting me since the moment she threw herself in front of my car.

And now, they're wet from my tongue and swollen from my kisses, parted as she gasps and moans on my lap.

She has this way of throwing her head back and exposing her neck to me when I push into her. It's almost like she wants me to take a bite out of her.

And fuck if I don't want to do exactly that.

Every time I thrust into her, she cries out, a little more desperate each time. I know she's close to another orgasm. So am I.

But I find myself holding back, drawing out the moment for every single second I can. I want to—no, *need* to squeeze just one more squeal from those deadly lips of hers. So that I can watch her breasts bounce in my face just one more time. So that I can lock onto those fuck-me eyes for another breath longer.

She explodes on my cock, and the way she ripples around me, milking me into her, is enough to shove me over the edge. I can feel my toes curl as every surge of pleasure rockets straight from my brain down through my shaft. I have to close my eyes so she doesn't see them roll back inside my head.

Fucking hell. This was supposed to be quick. Just getting my dick wet.

It wasn't supposed to be a fucking revelation.

Her breath mingles with mine, and she falls limp against my chest, her head tucked perfectly under my chin. *Goddammit.* If I don't do something, and quick, this is going to become something way more than a backseat fuck.

I wait until I can actually control my breathing again. Then I push her off me.

She doesn't seem to mind the unceremonious dismount. Her eyes are hazy and lost in thought. Her hair is strewn wildly around her head, and I swallow back the satisfied growl that threatens to escape from knowing I'm the one who did that.

Ridden hard and put away wet. If there was a poster for such a thing, she'd be the perfect model.

She glances out the window, noticing that the storm has now subsided. It's still raining, but there's a calm settling over the skies. Apparently, they're just as tired out as we are.

She looks on the verge of sleep as she picks up her shorts off the car floor. I don't want her to get dressed yet. I haven't yet had my fill of looking at her naked body.

But I'm not about to give her the impression that I want more time with her. Or that my fingers are already twitching to touch her again.

Even if both things are true, I've already stolen enough from her mundane little life.

She wiggles her clothes back on patiently, and I watch as she maneuvers into the tight fabric. "I think you're right," she remarks suddenly. "I will look back on this memory when I'm old and gray."

I was the one who initially suggested that. But now, somehow, the idea of becoming just a distant memory to her doesn't sit well with me. I chalk that up to lingering resentment from the evening I've had, and I manage to suppress the snarl that wants to twist my face.

The sinking feeling in my gut is just late-night hunger. That's all. I'll grab some tasteless fast food after this and prove that the discomfort has nothing to do with knowing I'll never see this little *tigrionok* ever again.

She glances at the ugly, white watch on her wrist. "Oh, shit!" she gasps, jerking upright and paling visibly. "Shit. Shit. Shit. Shit. Shit. Shit."

"What's wrong?"

She starts pulling at the car door, trying to get it open. "It's two in the morning! I'm so…" She trails off and starts patting herself down. "Oh my god, where's my phone?"

I find it on the car floor next to her foot. "Here."

She checks the screen and I notice seventeen missed calls, all from "Dad."

"He realizes you're an adult, right?" I drawl.

"Why isn't this stupid door opening?" She's completely flustered by the lock, which she's trying to twist in the wrong direction.

I take my car keys and press the unlock button. She throws the door open and jumps out, right into the drizzling rain as though she's on fire. Gritting my teeth, I find myself following her.

Maybe she *is* on fire. Maybe we both are. I can't ignore the way the raindrops feel like they're sizzling on my skin.

I don't like knowing *she* did that to *me*.

"Stop."

I didn't yell, but she freezes and twists around as if I'd bellowed at her. She stands perfectly still, doe eyes wide, seemingly oblivious to the drizzle hazing over the neighborhood. "Yes?"

"I can drive you back home."

She frowns and glances down the road as though she's scared someone is watching us. "No, I, uh—that's okay." It's amazing how she's transformed from a sexy, independent woman to a scared, skittish child in a matter of seconds.

"Don't be stubborn."

"I'm not. Listen, it's… it's complicated, okay? My dad worries a lot, and—"

"And you're a grown-ass woman," I cut her off. "Who should be standing up to him."

"I did."

"And you got slapped for it."

She bristles indignantly, and I watch as those dark green eyes turn cold. "Just because I told you a couple of things about my life doesn't mean you know me."

"Doesn't it?" I ask calmly. One of us needs to at least pretend to be calm. "What's the matter? Scared you broke curfew? Scared that Daddy will ground you if he sees you with a big, scary monster like me?"

Her face flames with shock, then with anger. "I'm walking away now."

She starts stomping off in what must be the direction of her home. I roll my eyes, but instead of chasing after her, I get in my car and shift into Drive, then accelerate slowly until I'm cruising alongside the girl at her pace.

"You're a stubborn one, *tigrionok.*"

She twists toward the car and comes to a grinding stop. "Stop calling me that. You don't know me."

"Oh, I think I do. I see you for what you really are."

I've lit the match. Now, I'm about to throw it onto the fire, and I don't care. I don't fucking care—just as long as I get to sit here and watch her burn.

"And what's that?" she snaps.

I meet her icy gaze. "Trapped."

Her eyes flare like twin torches. The only reason she's this mad is because I'm right about her. But instead of admitting as much, she flips me off and starts stalking away again.

I watch her go. I can hardly blame her—I would've done the same thing.

I stay where I am until she rounds a corner and disappears from sight. Then, when the night is silent and still again, I rev my engine and make a U-turn.

I speed away from this entire neighborhood and the tormented people who call it home.

If they're lucky, I'll never be back.

6

TAYLOR

It hurts more than it should to hear his engine fade into silence.

It's ridiculous that I should feel so judged by a stranger. Because he *is* a stranger. He may have a cute yet annoying nickname for me. He may have finished inside me. He may know more about my feelings than my own family does at the moment.

But he's still a stranger.

And his opinions don't matter.

I repeat that mantra to myself right up until I reach the house. It used to be that I would see the old bricks and the yellow curtains at the window and feel comforted.

But this is my *childhood* home. And I'm no longer a child.

It doesn't help that, despite the late hour, the curtains are still thrown open. Which means Dad is waiting up for me, ready to unleash the rant of a lifetime the moment I walk through the doorstep.

Except that it's eerily silent when I walk in. I pass the threshold and peer into the living room.

Dad is there, just like I thought he'd be. Sitting in his recliner, shoes still on his feet. But his chin is slumped to his chest and his eyes are closed. There's a cold mug of tea at his side and a book flopped open in his lap.

He must've been waiting all night for me to come home.

I close the curtains and lean against the wall, just gazing over at him for a moment. It's so much harder to be mad at him like this. When he's asleep, it's impossible to avoid the fact that he's gone so deathly gray. His mouth is a mess of worry lines and his crows' feet stand out like cracks between tectonic plates. Those age spots on his hands—were those there before? I can't remember.

I hate what I said to him tonight. I hate how he reacted. But at the end of the day, I still love him., just like I know he loves me.

That's what they don't tell you about cancer: the disease spreads to everyone *around* the one who's sick. It depletes them of their patience and hope and reduces them to the worst versions of themselves.

My worst version came head to head with Dad's worst tonight.

And I'm starting to realize that if I stay here…it'll keep happening again and again. We'll be caught in a Groundhog Day version of what happened tonight. More cruel words. More vicious slaps.

Which is why I came to the conclusion that's been waiting for me all night. The obvious choice that I refused to make until I stepped out of that stranger's car and into the cold and rainy night.

I have to leave.

I felt brave about that choice at first. It's the right thing to do, I know that. I knew it would be hard.

But now that I'm here, actually doing it, it's a trillion times harder than I ever could've imagined. Tears stud my eyes as I scoop up a yellow blanket from the basket at Dad's side and drape it over his legs.

Guilt pulls at my heart as I turn my back on him and sneak upstairs. It takes me only a few short minutes to get my stuff together. When I'm packed, I sling my duffel bag over my shoulder and creep back down the corridor towards the staircase.

I'm almost at Celine's door when it opens. She glances out into the hallway and catches sight of me immediately.

"Tay?"

I sigh and set the bag down on the floor. I want to hem and haw, but there's no beating around the bush now. "I'm leaving, Celine," I say. "I can't stay anymore."

She rushes over to me, soft blonde hair spilling from her messy bun. "Oh, Tay, it was just a fight! A bad one, yes. He never should've hit you. But you were both emotional and tired. And after what the doctor said yesterday... I'm—I'm not trying to justify what he did. But...well...you know that Dad loves you—"

"I know that," I cut in. "I do. But he's suffocating me, Cee. I feel like I can't breathe in this house anymore."

"He just wants us to be safe."

"I'd rather be unsafe and happy than safe and sad."

Celine winces. "I just think you should—"

"Don't do that," I interrupt again. "We can't all be selfless martyrs like you." As soon as the words are out of my mouth, though, I grimace. I'm just walking around spreading happiness wherever I go tonight, it seems. "I'm sorry, Cee. I'm just not like you."

"What does that mean?"

"It means that you have this big heart. You're kind and patient and giving. But me… I don't think I can do it anymore. It's too much—living here, taking care of Mom, dealing with Dad and his overprotectiveness. He's getting worse in his own way, just like she is. And I… I can't do it anymore."

"So you're just gonna skulk out into the night with your things?"

"I wasn't skulking. I was gonna leave a note."

"How considerate," she mutters with uncharacteristic sarcasm. She immediately flushes and backtracks. "Sorry. That was unfair."

"No, it wasn't. I'd understand if you hate me for this."

She shakes her head. "You have the right to do what's best for yourself. It's one of the things I've always admired about you: you're not afraid to go after what you want, even if it's hard. Maybe even *especially* when it's hard."

There's not an inkling of resentment in her tone when she says that, and it makes me love her even more. It would be so easy to be petty. Celine has more than enough ammunition, given what lies in our past, but she doesn't use it. She never does.

I throw my arms around her and hug her as tight as I can. "I'll be back as often as I can. I don't want you to feel like I'm abandoning you. I don't expect you to look after Mom or deal with Dad alone."

"Duh. I know that."

She's giving me the benefit of the doubt, because of course she is. She always does. The only exception was years ago, when…

No. I stop the thought in its tracks. We agreed to put that behind us and we did.

Mostly.

She gives me another hug and I pick up my duffel bag. She doesn't ask me where I'm going. She doesn't pepper me with questions the way that Dad would have.

But that's because Celine has always known what Dad refuses to accept: that I can take care of myself.

7

ILARION

There's a gentle breeze drifting through the garden. It's quiet. Tranquil. Soothing. Still. It'd be easy for a man to relax in a place like this. After all, no one anticipates a murder when the stars are shining and the lilac is fragrant.

The man who's about to die certainly doesn't.

I turn to him. "Armond, you know Bruno Domi well, don't you?"

Armond Ivanov, one of my *vors*, frowns. He looks mystified by the question. "Bruno? Sure, I know Bruno."

"Known him a long time?"

"Couple of years," Armond says with a shrug. "Decent guy."

Next to him, Slava, one of the Bratva's newer recruits, is squirming as though he's got a nail up his ass. He keeps looking over at Armond, probably waiting for him to wise up.

He might; he might not. It doesn't matter either way.

It won't save him in the end.

Armond is still blathering on. "He runs some fenced electronics. Sells 'em cheap. I got a grade-A stereo system at home for a fraction of the price 'cause of him."

"So you know that Bruno Domi is a Bellasio man?" I say. The shift in my tone is subtle, but it's enough for Armond to finally notice the noose tightening around his throat.

His eyes widen when he realizes where I'm going with this. "I… Listen, boss, Bruno and I talk cheap electronics. Nothin' else. He's selling and I'm buying. That's as far as our relationship extends. And as far as I know, he's not high in the ranks."

"So the answer is yes. You do know what he is."

He gulps, but he stands his ground and looks me in the eye. "I got nothin' to hide, boss. I'm loyal to you. Bruno may be a Bellasio, but I'm Zakharov through and through."

He's convincing. But then again, so was the other bastard who swore his loyalty to me and then stabbed the Bratva in the back. Fool me once, shame on you. Fool me twice…well, that's not an option. For anyone.

"It's funny," I muse. "Someone else said the same thing to me not too long ago."

Slava and Armond exchange a glance. "We heard about that, boss," Armond stammers. "Through the grapevine. Are…are you sure?"

"No, I just blindly rampage into things without making sure." The back of my teeth clench as I take a deep breath. It sounds more like a growl than a sigh. "Are you accusing me of making this up, Armond? Of not doing due diligence?"

"That's not what I was trying to—"

"Then choose your words more carefully." I brandish the knife that I've had concealed in my waistband all this time. "Where were you last Friday night?"

Armond blanches. "I was at a—a—a—"

"Spit it out," I snarl.

"A strip club!" he cries out. "The Lucky Slipper on 58th. I swear to God I was, Ilarion, I swear it."

I nod. That confirms my intel. Then I steer my gaze towards Slava. "And you?"

"I…I would never betray you, boss—"

"Answer the question, Slava."

He flushes scarlet. "I was…was at my mother's."

"*That* was convincing," I drawl sarcastically. "Are you sure you were trained under me?"

"Boss," Slava croaks, his color darkening from scarlet to off-purple. "*Pakhan*, listen—"

"No," I spit, "*you* listen." I stride right up to him, dwarfing Slava in my shadow. "Tell me where you were right now, or I'm going to carve the name 'Bellasio' into your forehead so that everyone who sees your head on a spike knows what you did to deserve it."

Slava shakes his head. "I'm serious! I was at my mom's place. She insists I have dinner with her twice a week."

"Should we call her and confirm?"

Slava's eyes bug out. Even Armond is looking disgusted at his cowardice. "Boss, my mom ain't got no clue what I do. She doesn't even like toy guns."

I grab him by the collar of his shirt and drag him towards me, placing the knife right at his Adam's apple.

"How about knives?" I muse. "Does she like knives?"

He swallows, and his throat bobs up and down against the blade, nicking it enough to draw a single bead of blood. He cringes, but he doesn't swallow again.

Repulsed, I shove him away from me and flick the blade between my fingers.

"I'm going to clean up my house if it's the last thing I do," I intone. "Armond, get out of the way."

"Boss…?" Slava gasps, looking around wildly.

I remember thinking the kid had potential. He still might.

But I can't take that chance.

My fist hits the side of his face before he even realizes what's happening. I don't know if it's the shock or the blow itself that sends him toppling backward. Maybe both. What I do know is how fucking satisfying it is to watch him eat grass and cough up blood.

I've been chasing ghosts for a week.

It feels good to hit something.

Armond stands rooted to the side, looking like he wishes he was anywhere else. I'm not about to give him a pass, though. Maybe I'll spare their lives tonight; I haven't fully decided yet. But both of these motherfucking *mudaks* need to understand the consequences of disloyalty.

I'm closing in on Slava again when I hear shuffling on the stone path behind us.

"For God's sake!" an unwelcome voice calls impatiently. "What's going on here?"

I glance over my shoulder to see Mila standing there in her usual tomboyish clothes, her hair pulled back into a tight ponytail. Dima is standing right behind her, surveying the scene with wary eyes.

She walks over to me and braces her hands on her hips. "When are you gonna be done with this?"

"When Slava stops breathing," I answer grimly.

"For God's sake, Ilarion," Mila hisses, "the kid's not a mole." She glances over at Slava, who's still spitting out blood and grass. "He's got nothing to do with the ugly business from the suburbs."

"You seem awfully confident, oh sister of mine. Know something you're not telling me?"

"I conducted background checks on all the men with access," Dima interrupts, stepping in for my sibling. "Both Armond and Slava came out clean."

"I told ya, boss," Slava splutters through broken teeth. "I would never betray you."

Where have I seen that song and dance before? It's still too fresh. Too familiar. But with a grimace, I turn away and wipe my knuckles on my pants.

Fine. These bastards will live—for now.

"Get on your feet," I tell Slava without looking at him.

He's shaking when he manages to straighten up. I've broken his nose and cracked two of his front teeth, and I don't feel the least bit sorry about it.

"Tell the rest of them that if they even think about double crossing me, I will end them. Am I understood?"

Slava nods over and over. The way he sniffles, with tears in the corners of his eyes, only reminds me of just how young and new to this world—this fucked-up hellscape—he really is. I tell myself we need the manpower. My not killing him has nothing to do with the sudden sting of pity in my gut.

"Get out of here," I sigh. "Both of you."

They don't wait around to be told twice.

"Well, *that* was smooth," Mila grumbles the moment both men disappear around the corner.

"It was necessary." I tuck the blade back in its sheath.

"Was it?" she asks. "What are you trying to do, exactly? Alienate the rest of your men by accusing them of treachery one by one? Not all of them will do what—"

"Don't say his name in my presence," I growl. "Not today."

Mila stops short and sighs. Then she glances at Dima as though he has the power to talk some sense into me. But I don't need sense; I need results. I need fucking *answers*. My sister always feels like she needs to "manage" me. It's what makes her a fantastic second-in-command—and also a fantastic pain in my ass.

Thank fuck for Dima. He has a habit of balancing us both out by being the honorary third sibling we never knew we needed.

"Listen, Ilarion," Dima begins in that old-man voice he uses whenever he's trying to inject reason into a conversation between my sister and me. "This whole business with—" he catches himself and rephrases, "with 'the rat', it caught us all off-guard. But you may be taking it too far."

"'May'?" Mila interjects.

Dima shoots her a warning look. "All I'm saying is that you might be overreacting."

"You almost killed a loyal man just now! Two of them!" Mila cries out. She's never had very much diplomacy. "You're seeing traitors wherever you look, Ilarion. It's not healthy."

"You're not exactly the poster girl for mental health."

She takes half a threatening step towards me before Dima deftly inserts himself in the middle of us.

"What happened yesterday, by the way?" he asks.

For one insane moment, I think he's talking about the little hellcat that I nearly ran over. My *tigrionok*. But he can't know that; I haven't breathed a word of our encounter to anyone.

Mostly because I'm still trying to forget it.

"Is he dead?" Mila asks.

Of course—they're talking about the rat. As far as they're concerned, he's the only reason I'd be in Evanston in the first place. "No. Luckily for him, he's not dead."

Mila and Dima exchange a meaningful glance. "That's... unlike you," he says. "What changed?"

"Inspiration struck," I reply vaguely. "I'm not going to kill him so long as I can use him."

"'Use him'?" Mila exclaims. "He betrayed you! He betrayed all of us! We have no use for him."

"That's what I thought, too. But then I realized that I haven't played my last card yet." I take out my phone and scroll to the picture at the bottom of my gallery, then present it to them. "*This* is my last card."

Dima's eyes go wide. Mila's narrow.

"This?" she breathes. "It… Shit, Ilarion, it seems like a long shot."

But Dima shakes his head. "Actually… I think this will work."

"If she falls for your bullshit," Mila scoffs.

Dima and I lock eyes. Then we both start to chuckle.

Mila rolls her eyes and turns her back on the both of us. "Fuck you both. Not every woman is so easily won over."

Dima glances at me and shrugs. "I wouldn't be so sure, Mila. You're his sister; you're immune to his powers. But I've seen Ilarion in action. No woman can resist the smolder."

"Oh, I know," I say with an arrogant smirk. "I'm counting on it."

8

TAYLOR

FOUR WEEKS LATER

"Sorry I'm late!" I lean over so I can hug Celine. It feels so good to hold my sister again. Has it really only been four weeks? It feels like a lifetime has passed. I forgot her smell, the shape of her face, the freckles on the back of her neck.

"It's okay. I already ordered drinks for us. I got you an iced tea."

"Bless you."

"Also, you're choking me."

Grinning sheepishly, I let go of her, shrug off my coat, and dump it and my bag in the empty chair next to me. Then I drop down and try to catch my breath. It was a mad dash to get to the restaurant on time. Well, almost on time. Punctuality has never been my strong suit.

"You look like you've just rolled out of bed," Celine remarks.

I wince and immediately reach up to pat down my hair. When my fingers get caught in the knots at the back of my head, I pull off my ponytail and start from scratch.

"That would be because I did just roll out of bed," I admit.

Celine glances at the elegant blush wristwatch on her hand. "It's 10:30, Tay."

"Yes, yes, spare me the lecture. I pulled a double shift at the restaurant last night, and then I headed straight to the library for a study session that ended at two in the morning. Slept right through my alarm."

Celine purses up her lips. "I walked by your new apartment building yesterday."

I cringe inwardly. I can already tell where this is headed. "Oh?"

"You couldn't find a better place?"

"It wasn't like I had a lot of time to look for a place, and I couldn't stay on Tiffany's couch forever. It's just temporary anyway. Until I save up enough to afford something a little better."

"That explains the double shift."

I curse myself internally for sleeping through that stupid alarm. I wanted to show up confident and breezy, looking like a competent adult for once in my life. Instead, I'd thrown on the clothes I'd been wearing the night before in my haste to get out the door. My mouth still tastes like sleep scum—gross, I know.

The waitress appears with our drinks and reads out the specials. My stomach roils when she mentions the crab benedict with hollandaise sauce. It's a splurge for me, considering the one plate will run me twenty-two dollars, but I haven't eaten since yesterday morning. They could serve me Flounder from *Little Mermaid* and I'd gorge myself on that cute little fella.

"You know, there's a perfectly decent spare room at home," Celine points out when the waitress walks away. "And it's rent-free."

I sigh. "Can we not, Cee? I haven't even eaten yet."

"You're being stubborn."

"Yes, as a matter of fact, I am. In case you missed it in the twenty years I've been your sister, I am stubborn." I sip my iced tea and give her a cheeky grin.

Celine shakes her head. She's frustrated, of course, but I know her well enough to see how she's biting down a wry smile. It's how we are—she does the right thing all the time, I do the wrong thing all the time, and we both look at the other one like, *What were you thinking?*

It's funny—we're only separated by two years, but you wouldn't believe it if you really looked at us. She's an "old soul," as they say, which I always used to mentally substitute for "boringly responsible." Less so now, though. I'm starting to admire her willingness to simply take what life gives her and not ask for more. Kinda jealous of it, really.

Even now, she's sitting across from me in luxe black leggings and a white linen button-down just loose enough to be chic and stylish. When I wear oversized clothes, I look like I ransacked Dad's closet.

"Things didn't go great when you left," she says.

I groan and bury my face in my hands. *As if I needed that reminder.*

"Celine," I protest, "for the length of one breakfast, if nothing else, I'm begging you to—"

"Dad was just hurt that you left in the middle of the night."

"I left a note!"

"You should have stayed and spoken with him. Face to face."

I sigh and look up at her through my parted fingers. "We don't communicate well. You know that. I try to talk to him, but he just ends up yelling at me." She snorts quietly into her lemonade, and I raise my eyebrows. "Something you'd like to share with the class?"

She shrugs. "Well, it's just that he says the same thing about you."

I roll my eyes. "Of course he does."

"Maybe it's fair to say that you're both at fault here?" she suggests gently.

I lean back in my chair and cross my arms over my chest. We're treading on old, familiar territory here. Reading back lines we've read a million times before.

Just listen to him!

Why can't he *listen to* me?

Aaand, scene. Repeat 'til you puke.

"Are those real pearls?" I quickly change the subject, admiring the way the teardrop earrings compliment her pristine white shirt.

"Tay!"

"Guess not."

She sighs, but I notice that she gets a little fidgety. I frown. My sister is the picture of Zen calm ninety-nine percent of the time. She only starts to get the itchy-butt face (yes, I did come up with that name when I was six years old, and yes, it does perfectly capture her lowkey anxiety) when she's holding back a secret she really wants to let out.

"They were a… gift."

"Wait, so they *are* real? Hold on. Who's the guy?"

"Nuh-uh." Celine shakes her head. "We're talking about Dad right now."

I groan. "Please don't make me."

"He loves you. He misses you. He's miserable without you."

"Oh, come on," I scoff. "You still live at home."

"Yes, but I'm not the favorite daughter."

That one almost makes me spit out my tea. "Excuse you. I am *not* the favorite."

Now, it's Celine's turn to roll her eyes. "Oh, for crying out loud, Tay. Stop acting clueless. It doesn't suit you."

"He loves us both equally. They both do."

"Oh, yes, of course. Everybody loves everybody and our family is perfectly peachy."

"That's not what I—"

"Fine. We'll table it for now." She folds her hands in front of her and leans forward. "Either way, I just want you to talk to Dad. And I mean, *really* talk to him. No yelling."

"I don't yell until he does. And if I move back in, there's definitely going to be yelling."

"I'm not asking you to move back in. But the least you can do is come over to the house."

"The last time I came over, he yelled at me and called me a 'selfish brat.' Mom didn't mind that I moved out, so I don't know what his problem is."

Celine falls silent, twirling her hair absentmindedly with one finger as she looks at nothing and everything at once. "You know what? Sometimes, I don't, either."

"Come again?"

She glances at me distractedly. "Dad's been so jumpy lately," she whispers. "It's like he's spooked or something. He's always looked at Mom as though he's scared she'll disappear on him. But now, he looks at me that way, too."

"Should we suggest a therapist?"

"I did. This morning, actually," Celine admits. "He told me that no shrink could save him, and then he went back to staring out the window."

"You… you don't think…?" I shake my head and abandon the thought mid-sentence. "Never mind."

"Tell me," she insists.

"You don't think he's going senile, do you?"

Celine shakes her head. "No, I just think he's getting more and more paranoid the older he gets. I think maybe taking care of Mom as long as he has is taking a toll."

"I don't think that's it. He's been scared for longer than Mom's been sick. I remember looking at him, right before we got the diagnosis. And he just looked… I don't even know. He looked like something was eating him from the inside out." I set my jaw stubbornly. "But if he won't ask for help, that's on him."

My sister scoffs. "That's the pot calling the kettle black if I've ever heard it."

"I'm not like that at all! He's got demons in his head? Well, join the freaking club. At least I'm doing something about it. Dad's just gonna have to accept that he can't control us forever."

"I don't think he's trying to control us. I think he just wants to protect us."

"Do you ever get tired?" I suddenly blurt.

"Of what?"

"Of defending everyone all the time."

Celine recoils and her face falls. She looks at me for a long moment, breathing heavily. Then she sighs and just like that, the tension goes whooshing out of her. "You know what? Sometimes, I do."

She does suddenly look exhausted. There are lines in her face that didn't used to be there, and when the sun catches her head from behind, I see grays in her hair I've never noticed before.

I reach out and cup her hand between mine as I give her the warmest smile I can muster. "I've got an idea," I suggest. "For the next hour, how about we forget the fact that our mother's sick, and our father's losing his marbles—" She tries to interrupt me, but I hold up my hand and barrel ahead. "And let's just have a nice brunch and talk about stupid things that don't matter at all and have some quality, one-on-one sister time."

Celine smiles, truly *smiles,* for the first time since I sat down. "Okay. I can agree to that."

"Great! Now, tell me about the guy who gave you the pearls."

She laughs and shakes her head at me. I don't miss the subtle blush creeping up her cheeks. "You're relentless."

"You made me this way. You never tell me anything about your personal life."

"Because up until recently, there hasn't been much to tell. I mean, not that there's much to tell now," she overcorrects.

But that blush on her cheeks is here to stay. "Nothing much to tell?" I echo. "Cee, he gave you pearl earrings, and they look pretty damn real from where I'm sitting. I think there's a whole lot of something to tell. I'm all ears."

Her eyes fall into her lap and she unconsciously reaches for the pearls at her ears. A soft, shy smile plays over her lips.

"Yeah… he's a good guy," she murmurs. "He makes me feel… Well, anyway. It's really new."

I want to be happy for her, I really do. And I am. I just wish that she trusted me enough to believe that I'd be happy for her. That I'd root for her the way I've always tried to.

I want her to believe I love her.

The waitress brings over our food. I take a moment to rearrange my face and thank her.

"So," Celine says, grabbing her fork and knife and clearing her throat, "what about you? Any romantic prospects on the horizon?"

I'm glad I gathered my composure right before she asked that question, because if I hadn't, she would've seen the guilt written all over me. My mind goes straight back to the perfumed leather seats of his car. His rich, smoky, whiskey scent.

Sometimes at night, when I concentrate hard, I can still feel heat in all the places he touched me.

"No," I tell her soberly. "None at all."

"Hm." She glances at me over her avocado toast. "By the way, before I forget, would you mind taking the chemo shift with Mom tomorrow evening?"

"Of course not. I'm on it."

"Thanks. I made plans for dinner and I'm cutting it close as it is. Don't want to be late."

"Ah-ha! It's a date?"

She smiles coyly. "I'll tell you about him when I know it's gonna turn into something. I promise."

I don't have the right to be annoyed. It's not like I'm being honest with her about my little roll in the hay with Adonis. Everyone's entitled to their little secrets.

Celine's got hers.

And I've got him.

9

TAYLOR
SIX WEEKS LATER

There should be a more graceful way to determine if your life is about to fall to pieces than squatting down to pee on a stick.

Terrifying things shouldn't also be humiliating.

As if that weren't bad enough, my phone vibrates right when I start peeing. I jerk forward on instinct like the Pavlov-conditioned Gen Z'er that I am—and promptly feel pee running over my fingers while I try to keep the stick at the right angle.

Oh, you have got *to be kidding me.*

I'm forced to sit there and soak until the job is done. Only then can I deposit the test on the bathroom counter in my premade nest of paper towels before lunging to the sink and washing my hands three times over.

"Fantastic," I mutter to my reflection. "Really dignified. This'll be a great story to tell my future kid one day. 'I ended up peeing on my hand while I was waiting to find out if I was pregnant with you. It was a sacred and beautiful moment of motherhood.'"

The moment the words are out of my mouth, though, I feel a wave of nausea, followed by a wave of fear. Suddenly, nothing is funny.

"Oh God. Please, please… This can't be how it happens…"

I button my pants and pace around the tiny bathroom. I pointedly avoid looking at the pregnancy test. Instead, I pick up my phone to see who rang.

I've got a missed call from Celine and one from Mom. I decide to call Mom first.

"Hey, sweetie," she answers. She sounds tired today. "Did you talk to Celine?"

"No, should I have?"

"She called me twice and I missed both calls, then didn't pick up when I rang her back. I was just wondering if everything was okay?"

"I missed Celine's call, too. I was, uh…busy."

I don't add that I was busy peeing on a stick. And my hand. And questioning my life choices.

"Find out if everything is okay and then call me back."

"Mom," I say patiently, "doesn't Celine live with you?"

"She hasn't been at home the last two nights."

Whoa. That's news to me. "Really?"

"It's that new boy she's dating," Mom says, oblivious to the shock in my voice. "I think things are getting serious between them."

I glance towards the test stick, but I can't see anything from here. I push it out of my head for the duration of this call. For the next few minutes, I decide to believe that I'm not pregnant. I'm pretty sure this is what all the woo-woo TikTok girlies mean by "manifesting."

"Why do you say that?"

"She's just in such a good mood all the time," Mom explains. "Plus, she's spending more and more time over at his place. She basically only comes home for a change of clothes."

I frown. It's very unlike Celine to do anything new so quickly. She makes life changes the same way she gets into a swimming pool: one tippy toe at a time.

"What do you know about him?" I ask.

"Next to nothing." Mom sighs. "But he seems very impressive. He inherited his father's business and now, he runs it on his own. Has a really nice house in The Valley, too."

I don't know what I'm more annoyed by: the fact that he's clearly a trust fund kid or that Mom knows a lot more about him than I do.

"Celine hasn't really told me anything about him, either."

"Oh." I've never heard an 'oh' said with so much weight behind it. Of course, Mom being Mom, she jumps right into Diplomat Mode. "I'm sure she just wants to keep things private for a little while. You know her."

I sigh. "Yeah. I'm just saying—"

"I'm sure it has nothing to do with Alec."

Oof. Those words land like a punch to the gut. I close my eyes for a moment, thinking about how simple things were back then. Back when Mom was healthy and Dad wasn't so scared. Back when summers were long and worries were short-lived and no blue-eyed demons came barreling through my neighborhood when I was crossing the road.

My phone starts beeping, alerting me to an incoming call. "Mom, can I call you right back?"

"Better yet, why don't you come over this evening?"

"Oh, Mom, I—"

"Please, Taylor," she says. "Your father misses you. I do, too."

"Okay," I sigh. "I'll come by later. Bye, Mom. Love you."

I end the call with her and accept Celine's. The pregnancy test is still lurking on the counter like a grenade with the pin missing, but I choose to put that off a little longer. Give it time to change its mind, y'know?

"Hi, Cee. Sorry I missed your call."

"It's okay. Just wanted to share some news."

I hear the verbal equivalent of her itchy-butt face. An anxious, lip-chewing excitement. "Something you'd like to tell me, sister dearest?"

She draws in a deep breath before launching into it. "Okay, here goes: I know this is going to come as a huge shock, but I want you to know that I've thought this through."

"I'm not sure I like the way this is starting…"

"You know what a cautious person I am. You know I never do anything without thinking it through first."

"Of course. I've always said you're well on your way to becoming Dad. Why do anything when you can just worry about how it will go wrong instead?"

She fakes a sarcastic laugh. "Ha. Ha. Do you want to hear my news or not?"

"Yes, sorry. Proceed."

Another deep breath. This one makes me catch my own.

Suddenly, I'm less concerned with the pregnancy test than I am with whatever Celine is about to tell me. I get the same sense I got the night the man almost ran me down outside of the park: a feeling of something huge and violent and unavoidable hurtling in my direction. A feeling that everything is about to change forever, and the person I was before this moment is not the same as the person I will be after.

"I'm…engaged."

I blink. "What?"

"Like I said, I know it's fast—"

"Fast?" I gasp. "*Fast?!* Celine, how long have you even been with this guy?"

"Two months as of last night."

"You just heard yourself right now, right?"

"I warned you it'd be a shock."

"Of course it's a shock! Celine, I know nothing about this guy! He could be a—a—a—"

"A what?"

"A murderer! A psychopath! A K-Pop fan! Shit, I don't know!"

"You will get to know soon enough," she assures me. "I'm calling to invite you to our engagement party tomorrow."

I hold the phone away from my ear to double-check that it is in fact Celine Theron I'm talking to. "*Tomorrow?*" I repeat into the mouthpiece. "Now, I *know* I'm hallucinating."

"Yes, we're having a luncheon in the garden. At noon. I'll text you the address."

"A 'luncheon.' In 'the garden.' Sweet Jesus, Cee, what is even happening? I don't even know this guy's name!"

"His name is Ilarion," she fills in. "And he makes me happy. Isn't that all you really need to know?"

All I want to do is scream, *No.* There's a hell of a lot more I'm dying to know. But that road is paved with the thinnest ice imaginable. We've been down it, she and I, and it almost cost us our relationship. I swore I wouldn't make that mistake again.

So even though all I want to do is tell her to run away from this, I can't.

Instead, I take a deep breath. "Noon. Luncheon in the garden. Got it. I'll see you there."

I hang up and drop the phone onto the counter. Memories of Alec and Celine and tears, so many tears, run through my head in one jumbled mess.

It's only when my eyes stray to the mass of paper towels at my left elbow that I remember why I came into the bathroom in the first place. I glance over, almost as an afterthought. I'm jolted back into my body when I notice what's in the window of the stick.

Two thick and definitive blue lines.

"P-pregnant," I stutter. "Oh my god. *I'm pregnant.*"

This jumbled mess just got that much bigger.

10

TAYLOR

Walking back into my home is weird in a way I can't really put into words. The creak of the third front step, the smell of must and Mom's lavender cleaning solution seeped into the floorboards—it's like pressing on a bruise I didn't know I had.

"Mom!" I call out as I let myself in. "Dad!"

"Upstairs, honey."

I take the stairs two at a time and find my mother in the master bedroom. She's lying in the armchair that faces the window, her legs kicked up on the footstool that Dad hand-carved for her on their twentieth wedding anniversary.

"Hi, Tay," she croons weakly, pulling her yellow shawl tighter around her shoulders as she sits up. The chair swallows her whole. She looks like a child in a fairytale who stole into the giant's house and cozied herself up in his furniture.

I give her a quick peck on the cheek and then I place her legs on my lap so I can sit on the footstool. When I look up again,

Mom is beaming. "Celine said she already told you the wonderful news."

"Yeah, she did," I reply cautiously. I want to gauge her reaction before I tread any further. "What do you think?"

"I think—well, it's certainly fast."

"Too fast, you might even say."

"Honey," Mom says in that *pump-the-brakes* tone she uses when Dad tries to push new therapies on her. "I'm not sure this is the kind of situation that requires our opinions. Certainly not our permission."

"I'm not saying that."

"I've never seen Celine like this," she wistfully sighs. "She was so… full."

"She's pregnant?!" I balk. "She didn't say—"

"No, no, no," Mom laughs. "Full as in happy. Full of life."

"Great," I mutter darkly. "Not sure that's something we can cure. At least a pregnancy can be fixed."

"Taylor Marie Theron!"

"Shit," I mutter. "Did I say that out loud?"

Mom leans forward to rap the back of my knuckles in a light scold. But the gesture wears her out and she slumps back into the armchair, wheezing quietly. "I was worried about this, too," she admits as her gaze flits out the window to the bright day beyond. "I mean, this is Celine. She's always been so cautious about everything. But when I saw them together today—"

"Wait. Pause. Back up. You met him?"

"Of course," Mom says. "They came by for a cup of coffee. She wanted to introduce him to us."

"Why wasn't I invited?" I ask, my face falling. Honestly, Mom's the only one I don't mind baring my soul to. She's the one person I know won't judge me over anything.

Even if I happen to deserve it.

"Oh, honey, don't take it personally. It was an impromptu visit," she reassures me, patting my hand. "That being said, you have no one but yourself to blame. You'd have met him if you still lived here."

"Pulling out the guilt card, huh? I'm shocked, Mrs. Theron. Simply shocked."

She laughs, the same musical laugh it's always been. "You're twenty years old; of course you want your own space. I don't fault you for that."

"Dad does."

She sighs, but the smile remains on her face. That's what I love about my mother. Even after everything she's been through, all the doctors, the chemo, the false hope, the painful years—even after all that, she hasn't lost her smile.

"Your father is getting older," she says. "I think he just worries about who's going to take care of you girls once he's gone."

"He's not going anywhere anytime soon. The stubborn ones never do."

The two of us giggle together. "Still," she sighs when the laughter fades, "he's always been a traditionalist. The night we were married, he told me that he was going to take care of me. That I didn't need to work if I didn't want to."

"I'm sure you took that one lying down," I tease.

"Why, I would never," she jokes back. "But once I got pregnant with your sister, I realized that I wanted to be your mother more than I wanted a career."

"You big softie." I tickle the bottom of her bare foot.

She chuckles and waves me off of her. "I worked for three years before I had Celine, though, and he never touched a penny of the money I earned. He told me that his money was ours, and my money was mine."

I do a double take. "I didn't know that."

"There's a lot of things about your father you girls don't know," she chides. "Before he was your father, he was this gorgeous, mysterious, capable man. I couldn't believe that he'd even look my way."

"Hush, Mom. You're beautiful."

She shrugs. "Yes, yes, butter me up. I didn't believe that until he told it to me, though. It took meeting your father to teach me what love—*real* love—was all about."

Hearing her talk reminds me of the old days. *B.C.: Before Cancer.* She and Dad used to hold hands when we walked to the park together. He'd bring her a cup of coffee every morning so that she could drink it in bed. When she fell asleep on the couch halfway through a movie, he'd pick her up and carry her to their room, making sure to skip the noisy floorboards so he didn't wake her up.

"Sometimes, I forget," I murmur.

"Sometimes, I forget, too," she says, taking my hand. "It used to be just Archie and Fiona. Then it was Archie, Fiona, and our girls. Now, you girls are moving into your own lives, so it's back to Archie and Fiona again—and Cancer. We're never really alone anymore."

"You just forgot your love language somewhere along the way, " I say, cupping her cold-to-the-touch ankle in my palms. "It happens."

She shakes her head, and I take a moment to mourn for the beautiful blonde locks that used to fall down her back like corn silk. There were days—B.C. days, of course—when people would look at Mom and wonder if she was my older sister or my mother. Old age seemed uninterested in her.

But the last few years brought what she was owed and then some. Wrinkles came fast, the hair went faster, and gravity pressed her spine into the shape of a question mark.

"We didn't forget our love language, sweetheart. It just changed. Even through the worst of it, your dad's still here, taking care of me. That's our love language."

She pats the empty space beside her, inviting me in. Sighing, I squeeze myself into the armchair with her. She wraps her too-frail arms around me and I rest my head against her bony shoulder.

"Used to be that all three of us could fit into this chair," she chuckles longingly.

"I remember. You used to read us a story every night before bed. You and Dad would take turns doing the voices."

"Celine always wanted stories with princesses and fairies. You wanted the ones with a little more action to them."

"So what you're saying is, I was the more interesting one?"

She nudges me in the ribs and winks. "I know it seems like you and Celine are light years apart sometimes. But the truth is, your deepest nature is the same."

I frown. My whole life, people have told us how different my sister and I are. *You leap before you look. You shoot first, then forget to ask questions. But Celine is an old soul. A wise soul. Cautious, not reckless. Careful, not rash.*

"How do you figure that?"

"You both love with your whole hearts. You're both loyal, kind, and passionate. And you care for each other—that's another thing you have in common."

Again, my mind flashes back to that moment two and a half months ago. The reason that those two little blue lines appeared at all today. To a storm on the horizon and a dark-eyed dream standing in front of a car that kept growling like it was alive.

What do you want? he'd asked. *What do* you *want?*

I told him. And then I let him give it to me.

Celine would never have acted so impulsively. She certainly wouldn't have slept with a stranger without a condom.

Although now, she's engaged to a man she barely knows, so maybe Mom's right. Maybe we aren't so different after all.

"I'm worried that she might be making a mistake here," I admit. "She's already engaged to this guy and she only met him two months ago. She's twenty-two, Mom! Why does she need to get married now?"

"Because she loves him, dear."

"So you're okay with this? Really and truly?"

Mom sighs again, and her soft blue eyes flatline. "I will always worry about you girls no matter what. But I learned a long time ago that you can't force certain decisions on anyone, least of all your children. I raised you and Celine to be strong, independent women, and that's what you are. And now that you're both adults, it means I have to trust you both."

"Trust, huh? Sounds terrifying."

"It is. It's also wonderful." She smiles and touches my cheek. "You should try it sometime."

11

TAYLOR

Whenever Mom is really tired, she starts drooping, like a wilted flower that needs reviving.

It still comes as a shock, even after two long years of her sickness. I think I've frozen her in my mind at a particular point in time. A time when she could kick around the ball with us in the backyard. When she could drive us to Lake Michigan for the day. When she could stay up with us all night telling ghost stories and eating homemade s'mores around our fake fireplace, a.k.a. the stove, saying, *Okay, just* one *more* again and again until we were all so full of sugar that our stomachs hurt.

It's cruelly ironic that every time I see her wilt, I also see the woman she used to be.

B.C.

"Come on, Mom," I say gently, rousing her as I clamber out of the armchair. "Let's get you to bed."

"No, darling. I'll sleep when you leave."

"You can't kick me out that fast," I tease her. "Why don't you take a quick nap and I'll wake you up when it's time for dinner?"

Her eyes light up. "You'll stay for dinner?"

"I'll do you one better and I'll cook it, too."

"Okay, well, you know where we keep the takeout menus."

I suppress a bubble of laughter. "I resent that. At least I don't burn toast like Dad does." I frown. "Where is Dad, by the way?"

"He decided to take a walk right after your sister left with her fiancé. Said he could use the fresh air."

I raise my brows as I coax Mom out of the chair and into bed. She barely makes a dent in her mattress anymore. If I run my fingers over its surface, I can feel where twenty years of sleeping in the same spot wore a groove into it. Now, though, she isn't anywhere close to filling it out.

"I wouldn't read too much into it," she says. "I think he's just processing. In his own way, just like the rest of us are."

"What does he think about *Il-ar-i-on*?" I ask, doing my best not to roll my eyes as I drag out the unfamiliar syllables of his name.

"Be nice, Tay."

"I'm always nice."

Mom shoots me an appraising look that might be insulting if it wasn't so on the nose. "If you want to know what your father thinks of Ilarion, you can ask him yourself."

I sigh. "Do I have to?"

"If you're staying for dinner, you can't avoid talking to him." She grabs my hand just as I'm about to straighten up. "Honey… go easy on your father, okay? I know he's not blameless in this. I know you have every right to be mad, but…but…"

"I know," I say gently as her sleepy lips fail to shape the words the way she wants them to go. "I will. Don't worry, okay? Just sleep."

I drop a kiss on her forehead and run my hand over her bald scalp. It had taken a while to get used to seeing her without hair. She's still beautiful. But there is no avoiding the fact that she is sick.

Celine and I had offered to buy her a wig. She flat-out refused and then barely said two words to us the rest of the day, she was so insulted. "I'll wear my own hair or none at all," she'd informed us sharply. "There's no sense in lying to the world."

I turn at the door to tell her I love her—for that, and for so many other reasons, too—but she's already sleeping. I linger in the threshold and watch her for a moment.

"Mom," I whisper into the soft rasp of her snores, "I just wanted to let you know that I'm…I'm pregnant."

Saying it out loud is as surreal as it is terrifying.

I'm pregnant, and I have no idea what to do about it.

There was a time not too long ago when I would have sprinted straight to my mom and told her everything. I'd have put my head in her lap and cried until the reality of my situation stopped terrifying me so much.

But that was B.C.

And we don't live in those days anymore.

12

TAYLOR

I'm in the kitchen draining rice when I hear Dad come home.

He appears at the doorway. Like Mom, he doesn't fill up the spaces he used to. Once upon a time—B.C., of course, but before he started looking so terrified all the time, too—he'd loom in any doorway he stood. I thought he was the biggest man alive. Now, his shoulders don't even take up half of it.

He clears his throat awkwardly. "Didn't know you were stopping in today."

I put the rice on the stove to cook and turn to him. "I'm cooking dinner."

"Should I go find the takeout menus?"

I roll my eyes. "Very funny. Mom beat you to that joke already, though."

He takes a seat at the circular kitchen table. It came with the house, as the old story goes. Dad wanted to throw it away— "or burn it," he always interjects at that part of the telling, "whichever happened faster"—but Mom insisted we keep it because it was yellow and had pink daisies and purple butterflies painted along the legs.

She's always had a thing about yellow. The whole house has little pops of it sprinkled through. "Like we live in a sunflower patch," she tells anyone who asks. "It's a dark world sometimes. I think it could use some brightening."

"Want something to drink?" I ask, glancing toward Dad. "Iced tea?"

"No, thanks."

"Hot tea?"

"No, thanks."

"Bourbon, then?"

Dad glances at me as though he likes that idea a little too much. He starts to shake his head, but before he can, I nod. "Bourbon it is."

I grab a glass from the china cabinet in the hallway and pour him some bourbon. He almost never drinks before eight o'clock, but judging by the look on his face, I don't think he's going to object tonight.

I hand him the glass and take the other open seat. The silence stretches and folds in on itself. The cuckoo clock on the wall ticks. Dad's heel bounces on the tile. I rap my nails on the tabletop again and again.

I'm keenly aware of the fact that he and I haven't had a proper conversation since I moved out. It's lurking between us, this ugly, unspoken thing, like some rotten stuff we're both pretending not to smell.

He takes a sip of his bourbon and sighs, but he makes no attempt to talk to me. I sit there for a full five minutes waiting for him to say something. When he doesn't, I check on the rice, grab a couple of ice cubes from the freezer and a mallet from the drawer, and head back to my chair.

I place the ice cubes on the table and smash them with the mallet.

"Goodness!" Dad splutters, gawking at me in shock.

"There. Now that I've broken the ice, we can talk," I say with a straight face.

He stares at me for a moment, and then his face cracks. The two of us burst out laughing. "That… that was… Good God, that was terrible," he wheezes, still choking on his cackles and dabbing tears from the corners of his eyes.

"The worst," I agree. "Some guy at a bar used that line on me last year."

"Please tell me you didn't go out with him."

"I let him buy me a drink. I thought it was creative at the time."

Dad just shakes his head and wipes the last of the tears from his eyes. Then he sighs deeply and his shoulders sag and, just like that, he's the same sad old man he was when he walked in again.

"You deserve a man who doesn't need to use a pick-up line at all," he murmurs. "You deserve the best. You and your sister both."

I frown as I watch him. He's got a few new wrinkles along his forehead. It seems like all of us do, me included. "I take it Ilarion didn't impress you? Mom seemed to like him."

His mouth ripples with tension. "He just… doesn't suit her."

"Mom thinks we should just trust Celine."

Dad stays quiet for so long that I wonder if he's going to go back to avoiding me mid-conversation. He runs a finger around the rim of his glass, again and again. "I know. She already told me to keep my big bazoo shut about this whole thing. *'She's your daughter, Archie. Be supportive.'*"

"You don't have to keep your big whatever shut about anything with me, Dad. Tell me what you really think."

He glances up at me warily before sighing again. "She's too young. She hasn't really lived yet. And she's rushing into this relationship. What's wrong with taking your time, getting to know each other over a few years, maybe even living together first?"

"She says she's in love."

"*Love*," Dad grunts, as though the word personally offends him. "What do you girls know about love? You're babies."

I frown, and just like that, there's distance between us again. "That's exactly the problem, Dad. You still think of us as babies. Celine's a grown woman, and so am I. We know our own minds, and I think you need to give us credit for that."

"It's not that I—"

"This relationship might seem impulsive to us," I continue as my head spins with images of the night I got pregnant. "But that doesn't mean it's not right for her. If she doesn't regret it, who are we to tell her she should?"

Dad lifts his gaze to mine. Celine inherited Mom's eyes, and I got Dad's. Those stubborn, green, almond-shaped eyes. It's always struck me as strange, how someone who frustrates me so endlessly and efficiently can be the source of all the things I'm most proud of in myself.

"You're a lot like your mother, you know," he says softly.

I chuckle. "I was just thinking that I was a lot like you."

"No." He shakes his head. "You're better than me. Braver. Stronger."

I frown, wondering what's brought on this dark mood of his. It can't be just about Celine and her surprise engagement. It has to be something else.

"Dad?"

"I never did apologize to you properly," he says gruffly. "I've handled things badly. I've been handling everything badly lately."

I get up and drape my arms around his shoulders from behind. "Don't worry about it, Dad," I say. "We all have bad days."

"I've had bad *years*, kiddo," he whispers, tensing under my arms. "And I'm afraid they're catching up to me."

Of course. Mom's condition is getting to him, too. It must be hard to see her fade in and out, day after day, with no real hope on the horizon.

"We'll get through this," I assure him. "She beat the cancer once before. She'll do it again."

He sighs, and his whole body feels like it's resting on that one heavy breath. "There are some things that can't be beaten, Taylor."

I'm about to ask him what he means, but then I note the smell of burning rice and rush to the stovetop.

"Oh, shit!" I groan, scraping up clusters of charred-to-a-crisp rice. With a sigh of defeat, I turn to him. "Where did you say those takeout menus were again?"

13

TAYLOR

The nervous tension in the car is palpable.

Apparently, this Ilarion—I still can't say his name without exaggerating it in a posh accent—lives clear across town in a neighborhood known as "The Valley." Which means we've been driving for almost half an hour and we're still twenty minutes away.

The further we drive, the cleaner the streets become. It's like we're closing in on hallowed ground. I almost expect to see a sign that reads *"No Poor People From This Point On."*

"I should have worn something different," Mom chimes from the passenger's seat.

She's wearing her favorite blue cocktail dress, a yellow silk bandana on her head, and a pair of thick wedge heels that she hasn't pulled out of the closet in years. She tripped twice on her way to the car.

I blame the nerves more than the heels.

"You look beautiful, Fi," Dad hums immediately, offering her his palm. She slips her fingers through his and takes a deep, steadying breath.

"Seriously, Mom, you look hot as hell."

"Taylor Marie."

"What? You do."

"Can we perhaps keep the swearing to a minimum when we get there? To pretend, for just one afternoon, that we are a family of culture?"

"What?" I tease. "Rich people don't swear?"

I expect Dad to chuckle or pipe in with a quick quip or a word of comfort, but he does neither. He just stares ahead at the road with a deadpan expression on his face. Like a pirate's victim about to walk the plank.

"I want to make a good impression," Mom says firmly. "I should have worn the red dress. This one is too big on me."

"It's not like Cee gave us much time to shop for alternatives," I mutter, pulling down the hemline of my strapless black mini. It's both tight and short, and completely inappropriate for an engagement lunch.

Excuse me—*luncheon.*

But the way I see it, I won't be able to fit into this dress in a few months. And God knows my partying days are going to be dead and gone once the baby comes, so I figure, there's no time like the present, right?

Not that Mom sees it that way. She throws me a disapproving look over her shoulder. She's unaware of my airtight logic or the ticking time bomb in my belly, but I'm in no hurry to tell anyone about my… *situation*… just yet.

For one, I want Celine to have her moment in the spotlight.

And two—I'm a coward.

"We could have gone shopping this morning," Mom persists. "If only someone had answered their phone before half past ten in the morning."

"I overslept," I mumble quickly. "And my phone was on silent."

The second part at least is not a lie. My phone was indeed on silent. But I hadn't been lying in bed like a loaf—I'd been flat on my back on an examination table with ultrasound gel smeared on my belly.

"Is the father coming?" the doctor had asked me.

I answered with the only thing I could say: "There is no father."

She'd given me a sympathetic smile and proceeded to confirm what I already knew: in seven-and-a-half months, I would be a mother.

Which felt extremely anti-climactic, somehow. You expect the big moments in your life to come equipped with a built-in soundtrack. Sound effects, at the very least. *You're going to be a mother. BOOM—confetti, laser beams, a line of dancers doing the can-can.*

But no. It's just you and the doctor, staring at an amorphous gray blob on the screen. And all those big feelings you expect to feel don't actually come.

At least not until the doctor looks at you and asks what you plan to do.

"What do you mean?" I'd asked.

"Taylor, you're clearly very young. You're here alone. It doesn't look like you were trying to get pregnant. I'm asking if you plan on keeping the baby."

And then it hits you. You don't actually have to have a baby if you really don't want to. Which begs the question—do I want this baby?

And the surprising answer is… *yes*. Yes, I do.

So after I cried on the doctor's shoulder for a good ten minutes, after I'd sufficiently embarrassed myself, I'd picked myself up, driven myself home, and gotten myself ready for my sister's engagement party.

"We're here!" Mom gasps suddenly, shocking me out of my thoughts. "We're here. Zakharov House—that's what Celine said it was called."

You know a family is wealthy when they name their properties after themselves. I lean forward, sticking my face between my parents' seats. "What should we call our house?" I ask. "The Theron Thatch? Overgrown Garden Cottage? The Yellow Villa doesn't rhyme unless you say it kind of weird, but—"

Mom glances at me. "Please behave."

I give her a bright grin. "Cross my heart."

"And you," she says, turning to Dad, "are to be *nice*. I want this to go smoothly. It's important to Celine and that makes it important to me, too."

"Mom, we all love Cee," I chime in. "Even if I hate the guy, I'm gonna pretend otherwise."

She sighs. "Couldn't you just like him right off the bat?"

I loft a brow. "Seems unreasonable to me."

"Me, too," Dad mutters under his breath.

For once, he and I are on the same page.

14

TAYLOR

We're saved another lecture when the gates part before we've even reached them.

I'm having a hard time containing my natural inclination to project vibes of "IDGAF." It's like we've entered a whole other world.

The property is nothing short of sprawling. A band of ancient trees, at least an acre thick, separates the road from the home. A paved driveway unfurls like a red carpet up to the marble front staircase of the house—although the word "house" feels woefully inadequate to describe the huge, ornate palace that rises from the earth at the top of the hill.

Dad slows down unconsciously as we approach. It feels like the kind of place you can't just run up to. You need to take your time, be respectful, soak it all in.

A stone fountain dots the middle of the circular courtyard. Water sprays from it in a graceful arc, shooting high in the air before coming down around the head of the statue. Water lilies bob on the surface of the pool.

When we come to a stop, my door is pulled open. I look up to see a wiry older gentleman in a suit.

"Good afternoon, ma'am. Welcome to Zakharov House."

What I mean to say is, *Thank you*. What actually comes out is, "Hot damn."

"Taylor!" Mom snaps as she's helped out of the car by another valet. This one is a little shorter and a lot younger. He gives me a cheesy smile that's not in the least bit professional, and I find myself pulling down the hem of my skirt.

Mom wobbles around the front of the car. I take one elbow, Dad takes the other, and the three of us begin to mount the stairs.

The double doors at the top have been thrown open. It isn't until we reach the landing that I can see through them and into the belly of the house beyond.

"This is batshit," I breathe. The foyer stretches on forever before it reaches an indoor koi pond. Flashes of silver and orange nip at the surface before disappearing again.

I'm not sure Mom even hears me. She's too busy admiring the crystal chandelier hanging over our heads. "You've got to hand it to him: he's got exquisite taste."

"Or his interior designer does, anyway," I mumble.

Beyond the koi pond is a perfectly manicured lawn that seems to stretch on for miles. The perimeter is ringed with flowering hedges bursting in every color known to man. Reds, blues, and, like *Il-ar-i-on* somehow knew Mom loved them, one yellow bloom after another after the next.

At the far side of the garden, I see a cluster of people standing together and talking. A dark-haired head rises from the crowd, looming over the others in a way that draws my eye, but it's too far away for me to tell who anyone is.

"Mr. and Mrs. Theron. Miss Theron." I turn toward a tall gentleman in a perfectly tailored three-piece suit. "I'm Semyon, the housekeeper. I'm delighted to welcome you all to Zakharov House."

"I'm Taylor. The bride-to-be's sister. Nice to meet you, Semyon."

"Of course." He gives me a thin, knowing smile. "Your sister is in the east gardens, ma'am. Please allow me to escort you there."

I nudge Mom forward and the two of us follow Semyon down a broad corridor drowning in sunlight. I'm aware of Dad lurking just behind us, but I'm too distracted by this house to concentrate on how he's handling all the wealth and splendor.

"Did you say 'east' gardens, Semyon?" I ask as we parade through the house. "Meaning there are south, west, and north gardens, too?"

"The manor faces south, Miss Theron," he explains. "So the gardens extend only to the east, west, and north."

"Oh, boy. And here I was, so close to being impressed."

He chuckles, but only briefly, as if it's outside of his job description and he wasn't expecting someone like me to ever turn up at a place like this.

That makes two of us.

"Here we are," he finally says as we reach the end of the hallway. He gestures toward a pair of open glass doors, beyond which the eastern gardens beckon. "I will leave you all to enjoy the party. If there is anything you need, please do not hesitate to ask."

My mother and I thank him with smiles, but Dad just grunts and follows as we all troop into the garden. Tall hedges guide us around the edge and spit us out onto the open lawn we saw when we first arrived.

I thought this house itself was the most intimidating thing I'd have to face today.

But then I take one look at the other guests, and I realize how wrong I was.

The men and women mill around between tables, chit-chatting with the kind of nonchalance that only endless money can buy while clutching champagne in crystal champagne flutes. Pinkies out when they sip, of course.

They're dressed in sharp suits and gorgeous summer dresses too ethereal to be real. And here I am, standing on the periphery of this alien world, in a dress that's gone from sexy to slutty in mere seconds of comparison.

And then Celine emerges from around a rose bush, and for a split second, I don't recognize her. My simple, doesn't-wear-makeup, barefoot-on-the-weekends older sister has been transformed into a glamazon in five-inch heels.

She's wrapped in an emerald green slip dress that glows like it's bejeweled. Her hair is blown out into the most voluminous golden waves and it looks at least a foot longer than it did when I saw her last. Diamonds gleam on each wrist, around her throat, and of course, on her finger, which sports a rock the size of an asteroid set in a platinum gold band.

"You're finally here!" She rushes over to us, though it's a graceful sort of rushing, like a ballerina dashing across the stage.

"Darling," Mom murmurs, every bit as awed as I am by this new woman standing in front of us. "You look gorgeous. That dress is just… wow!"

"Ilarion picked it out himself." She laughs as she gives us a twirl and curtsy. "Oh, I'm so glad you guys are here. Tay!" She gives me a quick hug, and then her eyes travel down my body and her face falls. "Really? Your clubbing dress?"

"I didn't realize I was being invited to a literal castle to mingle with high society," I mumble under my breath. I glance up at her and grin as best as I can. "This is some place, Cee."

"Isn't it?" She beams with pride as she looks around. I follow her gaze to see tables draped with white clothes, more crystalware everywhere, and sunflowers woven into the backs of each seat. Waiters in white tuxedos float from group to group with hors d'oeuvres on silver platters.

I follow her gaze, trying to see if I can guess which of these men who managed to capture my skittish sister's heart in mere months.

"So I feel a little left out being the only one in the family who hasn't met your fiancé yet."

"Oh, of course!" Celine frowns as she searches for him and comes up empty. "Odd. He was just here… Hm, maybe he went to check on lunch. I'll—Oh, wait, there he is. Ilarion!"

She's talking to someone over my shoulder, so I turn around expectantly. But the moment I do, I freeze. I can feel the blood draining from my face. I can feel my stomach churning with nausea. And for the first time in weeks, it has nothing to do with the pregnancy.

I take one look at those misty blue eyes rimmed with hazel, and all I can think is—

Not again.

15

TAYLOR

This.

Cannot.

Be.

Happening.

Surely, he's going to lock eyes on me at any moment and recognize me from that night. Surely, he's going to pale just as I have and the whole jig will be up.

How would that go, exactly?

"Do you guys know each other?"

"Sure do, sis! I just happened to bang your fiancé before I knew he was your fiancé and now, I'm pregnant and there's a ten in ten chance it's his baby. But you know, I'm super excited about your engagement. I hope the two of you will be oh-so happy together."

Oh, God. Oh, God. Ohhhh, God.

Diamond Devil 95

I'm dangerously close to hyperventilating. But thankfully, no one is looking at me. At least, none of my family is looking at me. Their eyes are focused on Ilarion. And his eyes are focused on…

"You must be Celine's baby sister," he says, extending his hand out in my direction. "It's a pleasure to finally meet you."

I stare at his hand for a moment. Because—*what?!* I mean, he has to know who I am. Right? I know I clean up pretty nice, but there's no way I look *that* different from how I looked the night we met.

"I… Uh, yeah. Yup, pleasure," I say, stumbling over my words like a complete moron.

Now, everyone *is* looking at me. Mom looks horrified, Celine looks amused, and Dad looks… well, kinda out of it, if I'm being honest.

Ilarion—I can't bring myself to say his name with the same joking cadence I used before; now, it's just *Ilarion,* with doom and gloom and thunder crashing in the background—releases my hand after one shake and wraps his arm around Celine's waist. She looks up at him as though she can't believe what she's seeing.

Same here, Cee.

"Would you excuse us for just a moment?" she asks. "I want to introduce Ilarion to some of my friends. They're dying to meet him."

"Of course, darling. Go ahead," Mom says.

The two of them walk back into the garden crowd, and I'm left questioning my sanity. Is it actually, truly, humanly possible that my future brother-in-law is the same man I slept with the other night? It can't be. I mean, if it had been, he would have had some sort of reaction, right?

And that's when I see it.

He's clear across the garden, being introduced to a couple of Celine's college friends. I can see only his profile.

Then he turns, his eyes lock on me, and I know I'm not imagining things.

He recognizes me.

He's just pretending not to.

16

TAYLOR

I turn to my mother. "I handled that badly, didn't I?"

Mom chuckles. "I can't blame you. He's a very handsome man."

I feel as though I'm about to throw up my breakfast. "Oh, God, Mom! He's Celine's fiancé!" I'm reminding myself of that fact way more than I'm reminding her. "I'm not—I wasn't—*ugh.*"

"I wasn't suggesting you were doing anything of the sort, sweetheart. I was just—"

"Does he even seem like Celine's type?" I blurt out before I can stop myself. "She doesn't usually go for men who are so… put-together. She likes the shy, awkward guys."

Mom looks at me with raised eyebrows. "Honey, are you sure you're okay?"

"Should you really be asking *me* that question? I mean, Dad's the one who's acting super weird."

Throwing shade in Dad's direction is a little uncalled for, but I don't want anyone looking at me too closely right this second. It works, though. Mom glances at Dad, and seems to notice for the first time the expression on his face.

"Archie—"

"I agree with Taylor," he says suddenly, looking at us with wild eyes. "He doesn't seem like he's Celine's type."

Mom glares at the both of us. "Honestly, I can't believe the two of you. I thought I made myself perfectly clear: this is not our call; it's Celine's. She's an adult and we need to trust that she knows what she's doing. Now, I want both of you to get out there and mingle. Smile, make friends, and most important of all, don't embarrass Celine!"

Sometimes, I forget that Mom has a fierce side to her. The cancer keeps it under lock and key more often than not. But when it breaks out, it's best to do as she says.

Dad nods in defeat. I raise my hands in surrender. "I'm off to mingle and make merry."

"Don't say anything to Celine," Mom warns.

That's a promise I'm more than willing to make. But right now, all I want is a little quiet. Somewhere I can freak the hell out without anyone watching me.

I retreat into the house and find a quiet nook to hide out in. I would have preferred a bathroom, but I'm not about to snoop all over the house until I find one. I just need a second to breathe and put my game face on.

I sink to a seat on a chair drenched in sunlight. Closing my eyes, I let the beam warm my face and I let out a long, rattling sigh.

This can't be real. There's just no way this can possibly be real. Fate or God or whoever's at the wheel isn't that cruel. Not unless I racked up a bunch of bad karma by, like, clubbing baby seals for a living in a former life.

And I guess that's possible, but it still feels cruel and unusual. I'm pregnant—by a stranger—who it turns out is actually not a stranger, but rather my sister's fiancé—the sister who already thinks I'm a backstabbing bitch, and not without good reason.

Confirmed: God hates me.

And as if to double down on that point, a voice shatters whatever semblance of calm I've managed to find here in my hiding place.

"Tay?"

I glance up and see Bradley Martingale standing at the entrance of the corridor, decked out in a blue suit and an open collar shirt. He's taken pains to look good today, and I gotta hand it to him: he does look good.

I mean, not Ilarion-good. But if we start judging all men by that standard, no one will ever procreate again.

I force a smile and give him a weird, half-assed nod. "Bradley. It's been a while."

"I'll say. Used to be that I couldn't take two steps into Crawley Library without running into you."

"Pretty sure that's what happens when you stalk someone."

He smirks. "I forgot what a smart little mouth you have. You know, that's half your charm."

I frown, really wishing this conversation would end soon. "Only half?" I ask. "I was hoping for three-fourths at least."

He takes three quick little steps towards me and suddenly, I find myself backed up against the corridor wall. He's actually got his hand up by my face, and he's leaning in with his whole body.

"You look really sexy in that dress."

Oh, hell *no.*

Bradley and I were classmates—*are*, I guess, although ever since those two blue lines appeared in my life, I'm not sure I'll ever make it back to school. A friend of mine brought him to a study group one day, and he's stuck to me like white on rice ever since.

It was kinda sweet, at first. Then it was neutral. Then it spoiled rotten and it hasn't looked back. He'd show up everywhere I went: library, gym—you name it, he was there. He'd corner me at parties and he had a knack for finding the darkest, quietest, most isolated spot in the whole place to do it.

You looked beautiful in class today, he'd murmur with beer on his breath. *The guys at this school don't deserve a girl like you.*

When I finally and firmly told him to leave me alone, I thought that'd be the end of it. Then he showed up at a lunch with my sister. *Look who I ran into!* he said brightly. *Such a lucky coincidence.*

I shudder. The memories alone are enough to make my skin crawl. The man himself does that and then some.

I duck out from underneath Bradley's arm. "Thanks. I really should be getting back to the party."

"The party will wait for you; don't worry. I'd rather just catch up for a bit first."

"Bradley," I say with forced patience, "this is my sister's engagement party. I can't be M.I.A. for too long."

"Celine won't care," he says dismissively. "She's only got eyes for that new boy toy of hers. And as for me… I've only got eyes for you."

I want to gag. But that'll have to wait, because what I'm realizing with growing horror is that this is the quietest, most isolated space of any party that Bradley has managed to corner me into yet. His timing couldn't be worse.

I must've clubbed a lot of baby seals in that former life of mine.

"I'm sorry, Bradley, but I'm not interested. Now, if you'll excuse me, I'd like to get back to the part—"

"No!" he roars. He reaches out and snares my wrist in a too-tight grip. Then he blinks and his tone recedes back to that sweet, wheedling whine he thinks will make my clothes fall off. "I mean, why? Come on now. Just stay with me here and we can have a little party of our own."

His hand doesn't leave my forearm, though. And he's squeezing hard. I wince. "You're hurting me. Please let go."

"I'm not doing a damn thing you haven't put on the table already," he growls. He drops his drink and it hits the ground. The glass cracks with a dull thump, amber liquid soaking into the rug at our feet.

"E-excuse me?" I stutter. "What—"

"With your fucking jokes and your fucking clothes and your fucking goddamned *teasing*," he snarls in my face. He hedges closer and closer until his hips meet mine and my back meets the wall behind me. "I mean, look at you now. Dressed up like a fucking whore. I can practically see your pussy from here. I can *smell* it."

My tongue is dry and I can't find any words to fight back with. It occurs to me again, just like it did the day I met Ilarion, that ugly things should happen on ugly days. But I'm about to get raped by a creep, and yet the sky outside is sunny and cheerful.

"I'm done asking. I'm done begging. It's time for me to *take* what you keep holding right out of my reach."

"Bradley," I whisper, "please don't—"

"You must not have heard her. She said *no*."

A massive shadow falls across both of us. It blots out the sun, and the scent that comes with it—whiskey, leather, musk—takes my breath away. Bradley and I both turn at the same time.

As Ilarion steps into the mouth of the hallway.

His eyes are dark. One hand holds a glass of champagne. The other is a white-knuckled fist at his side. As I watch, the muscles in his forearm twitch with rage.

"Taylor and I were just talking," Bradley says.

"And now, you're finished."

His face screws up like he tasted something sour. "Who are you to tell me when I'm done talking?"

"I'm the man who will hurt you very, very badly if you try to argue otherwise. Say goodbye and walk away, my friend. Before things take a turn for the worse."

Bradley lasts one more quivering, fear-filled second before he lets go of me. I gasp and crumble forward when his fingers release my forearm. The skin where he held me burns.

He takes a final look at me, then purses his lips and storms away, leaving his spilled glass behind.

For the length of one breath, I'm grateful that I was saved.

Then I remember who did the saving, and I realize that this might have been the worst of all possible outcomes.

Out of the frying pan and into the fire.

"If you're expecting a thank you, you can think again." My words come out raspy but fierce. "I can take care of myself."

To my surprise, he nods. "Oh, I know. I heard most of that conversation. Do you want some champagne?"

"That's not high on my list of priorities right now, thanks," I gasp, still gathering myself. Mostly, I just can't believe that that's his opening question. We're alone together for the first time since…well, *you know*, and he's asking me if I want a freaking drink.

"Very well then. If you'll excuse me, I should be re-joining the—"

"Stop!" I cry out, dangerously close to tears. "Just stop for a second."

He pauses and glances down at me with a detached expression. "Yes?"

I stare into those hazel-rimmed eyes, and I feel something inside me shiver to life. "Don't do that," I say. "Don't act like you don't know me."

He pivots back to face me slowly. The icy distance fades away just long enough for me to see the recognition there. "What would you have me do about it?"

It's a fair question. Fair enough to make me question my own reaction. Shouldn't I be playing along with this? Isn't that the best-case scenario considering the circumstances? The very, very fucked-up circumstances?

"Did you know?" I blurt out.

"Did I know who you were that night?" he asks. "Fuck no. I met Celine two weeks after you and I…ran into each other."

"Did you almost run her over, too?"

A vein twitches in his jaw. "Celine isn't in the habit of running chaotically around the world like a chicken with its head cut off. So no, it's safe to say I did not."

I grit my teeth, but it's mostly to fight back the tears. The pregnancy hormones have chosen a hell of a time to upregulate my emotions. "What is it then? Are you in the habit of trolling suburban neighborhoods, hunting for your next prospect?"

Great—now, my hands are shaking. Of course he notices.

"You need to get a grip," he growls, taking a step closer. "Your sister doesn't need to know what happened between us. I can keep my mouth shut. Can you?"

I shouldn't say it. I really shouldn't. Things will be so much easier if I keep the last crucial kernel of information to myself. No good can come of telling him I'm pregnant.

Good. It's decided. I'm not gonna tell him.

"Great. And what should I tell my sister in seven and a half months when I give birth to a baby who looks just like you?"

Whoops.

17

ILARION

She's lying.

She has to be.

There's no way she can be pregnant.

Except that I didn't wear a condom that night. And I came inside her. And it hadn't occurred to me until right now that both those things had been a colossally stupid fucking mistake.

But the more I stare at those deep emerald eyes, the harder it gets to cling to the hope that maybe she isn't telling the truth. She doesn't look like a woman who's trying to get back at me.

She looks like a woman who's *terrified of what's happening.*

"Are you sure?" I ask, keeping the storm in my head off my face.

She takes a step back as though my composure is proof that I'm some sort of psychopath. Hell, she might be right.

"Yes, I'm sure," she bites out. "I went to a doctor this morning and she confirmed it."

"How far along are you?"

Her eyes narrow into angry slits. "You know exactly how far along I am."

"Does anyone know?"

Her forehead creases. "Are you asking if my sister knows that I'm pregnant with your baby?" she asks. "The answer is no. I never told anyone about that night. It wasn't one of my finest moments."

It's a shame she feels that way. It was one of mine.

"You've asked me a lot of questions, so I think I deserve to ask one of my own," she adds.

I grimace. Out in the garden, I hear the distinctive clink of crystal as someone calls for attention to begin the toasts. Everything is happening too fucking fast. I need the world to freeze in place so I can figure out what the hell I'm going to do about this unforeseen development.

"You said that you met Celine after me?"

She thinks I'm lying about that? If I'd known who she was when I almost ran over her that night, it would have saved us both all this damn drama. "That's right."

"How long after?"

Her posture is all righteous indignation, but the question comes out sounding meek and vulnerable. She seems to realize the same thing almost as soon as she says it, because she shifts her weight back on her strappy black heels and crosses her arms over her chest in an attempt to overcompensate.

It does me no favors. Her dress is so tight in all the right places.

Completely wrong for this occasion. Completely wrong for me. Completely tempting nonetheless.

"Not long after," I say vaguely.

"I want a number. Specifics."

"Why?" I ask in exasperation. "What does this have to do with anything?"

"I just need to know, okay?" She glances around to check if we've been noticed. "Tell me."

"Two weeks, give or take. Does that satisfy you, princess?"

She bites her lip and pivots to the side so that I can only see her profile. She looks like she's trying to work through a math problem in her head.

"I've got another question," she blurts, twisting around so that we're face to face again. "Why are you marrying my sister?"

That one catches me off-guard. I'm not sure if it's meant to be a sideways declaration of her feelings or if she's trying to suss out my motives. Either way, the answer isn't easy.

That is, the *true* answer isn't easy.

Not that I'm about to give her the truth.

"I love your sister."

She stares at my blank face with scrutiny. "You love my sister," she repeats. "What do you love about her?"

"Pardon?"

"I'm sorry—I just find it hard to believe that you can go from meeting her, to loving her, and then proposing to her in a matter of weeks. Especially considering you slept with me the week before."

"What did you think?" I drawl. "That you had ruined other women for me?"

She flushes scarlet. "No, that's not—shit, I just don't want my sister marrying some rich, pompous playboy who's going to stop caring about her the moment he finagles a ring on her finger."

"And you've jumped to that conclusion because…?"

"Because you don't strike me as the kind of man who makes hasty decisions." She blushes and clarifies, "Well, mostly not hasty. Not when it comes to romance, at least. Which means you have an ulterior motive in marrying Celine, and it's not love."

I didn't expect that. Sherlock Holmes in a little black dress. It's inconvenient that I know exactly what that body looks and feels like as it comes undone beneath my touch.

Not exactly the image you need in your head when you're kissing your future wife.

"What other reason could I have for marrying her?"

Taylor's resolve fractures with uncertainty. It doesn't take Sherlock Holmes to discover that she's working off nothing but vague, airy suspicions. I can deal with that. Or I could have—if it weren't for the fact that she's apparently carrying my child.

"The baby," I say, making her flinch. "Are you keeping it?"

She jerks her face up to mine. "Of course you'd ask that. God, all men are the same. Well, fuck you—I'm not doing that. I decided this morning that I'm keeping the baby."

The assumption rankles me. It would have made this easier, of course—but I'm not the man she thinks I am. I'm not the beast she's painting me out to be.

At least, not entirely.

"If you're keeping the baby, then there are things that need to be figured out," I rumble.

"No need. I've already figured it all out," she replies immediately. "You disappear from all our lives, I raise this baby on my own, and my sister gets to meet someone who actually loves her and actually *wants* to marry her."

I nearly laugh before I realize just how unblinkingly serious she is. "That's your plan?"

"Sure is. And it's a good one."

"It's also a fantasy. I'm not breaking up with Celine, and I'm certainly not going to allow you to raise this baby on your own."

She stops short, her face coloring with shock. "Y-you… Wait, what?"

"What is it, Taylor?" I ask, annoyed with how sweet and forbidden her name tastes on my lips. "Does that not fit in with your assessment of my character?"

"Y-you can't be in this child's life," she says as the color on her cheeks spreads to her chest. "That's not possible."

"Why not?"

"Because of Celine!" she spits at me.

I shrug. "Celine might be upset at first, but she'll understand. I didn't know her when you and I met. What she won't understand is why you're trying to convince me to end things with her."

I'm dangerously close to hitting a nerve. If she keeps fighting, I'm done pulling my punches.

Taylor takes a deep breath. I watch as her chest rises and falls, her breasts straining at the thin fabric. It wouldn't take much at all to rip that off of her. I could do it with one hand. Then she'd be bare and flushed beneath me, wet and willing and ready, and I could do what I've been dreaming of doing again for ten endless fucking weeks.

"You don't know me very well, Ilarion," she hisses. "Because if you did, you'd know that I love my sister more than anyone else in the world. Celine is the best person out there. But she doesn't know that the rest of the world isn't as pure as she is. She chooses to believe the best in people, she trusts without reason, and she gives strangers the benefit of the doubt even when they don't deserve it. I want her to be happy. And she's not going to be happy with a man who doesn't love her."

"You're making a lot of assumptions, Taylor."

She shakes her head. "I don't think I am. What I'm doing is trying to protect Celine."

"Mm. And how did you justify what happened with Alec Miller?"

She flushes again. White-hot hurt blooms across her collarbone

It's obvious to anyone watching that I hit a nerve, and a painful one at that. But I've got the entire Zakharov Bratva resting on the razor's edge of this moment. I'm not about to back down now simply to save this little bleeding heart.

"That…that was not the same thing…"

I hedge closer, pressing her back against the wall. "Do you think Celine will see it that way?"

Tears bead up in the corners of her eyes. They aren't because of me, though. They're because of Celine. Because the only way I'd know about Alec Miller is if Celine told me about him. If the hurt that Taylor caused her sister was still fresh and vibrant in Celine's heart.

It is. She put it there. She has only herself to blame.

"Trust me, Taylor—"

"'Trust you'?" she scoffs, shaking out of her shock. "Trusting you is the last fucking thing I'd ever do. I'd rather—"

BAM.

Her words are drowned out by what is indisputably a gunshot. Taylor freezes, the words dying on her tongue. "What the—"

More gunshots break through the civilized chatter coming from the garden.

That's when we hear the screams.

"TAKE COVER!"

"What the hell is going on?" Taylor gasps.

"Get behind me," I order her as I pull out my gun. "The Bellasios are here."

18

ILARION

She doesn't budge. Her eyes are fixed on my gun, and she's backing away from me as though *I'm* the bad guy.

"Don't be ridiculous," I snarl at her without looking. "I'm not going to hurt you."

"How am I supposed to know that?"

"For one, you're carrying my baby."

I snare her arm and reel her in toward me. She's not expecting that. She stumbles forward and her face hits my chest. She tries to push me off immediately. "If you don't let me go right now, I'm gonna scream."

"I've got news for you, *tigrionok*: no one will notice."

Another gunshot. This one's close. Too close. A twitching body falls across the hallway, blocking our path. Taylor screams and suddenly, she doesn't seem so keen to leave my side after all.

"Oh, God—my mom is out there. And Dad. And Celine!"

Celine. I almost forgot about her. I should be at her side right now. There's no doubt in my mind why the Bellasios have chosen this day to attack.

And here I am—protecting the wrong sister.

Of course, this is the sister who is carrying my baby, so I suppose it's justified. I tell myself that's the only reason I'm hanging back, making sure Taylor is safe first before I join the fray.

I'm doing this for the baby.

Not for the little tigress who's lived in my dreams since the moment I almost smeared her across my bumper.

"Ilarion—my family!"

"I'll make sure they're okay," I assure her. "Just stay behind me and do as I say."

"Why the hell are there guns here?" she asks, unraveling with her terror. "Who are they? No, scratch that—who the hell are *you*?"

All good questions. All legitimate questions. But I'm not in the right frame of mind to answer them. I grab my phone when I feel it vibrating in my pants pocket.

"Dima, where are you? Yeah, got it… No, I'm in the east corridor… I've got cargo. Come grab her so I can deal with this shit."

The moment I hang up, Taylor fixes me with an offended glare. "'Cargo?'"

"You have other things to be concerned with than my word choice, princess. Keep your head down."

I peek my head around the corner. Through the open door, I spy at least three Bellasio *mudaks* within range. One of them spots me, but before he can aim, I shoot twice.

The first misses. The second buries itself in his forehead.

I hear a strangled cry behind me, but I don't have time to coddle Taylor through her first sight of bloodshed. I snipe the two other Italians in quick succession, then I grab her hand and drag her out of the corridor.

"Y-you…killed them," she gasps, straining against my hold.

"They deserved to die."

My peripheral vision catches another asshole coming our way. I whirl around, shoving Taylor behind me before I unleash another two rounds. The Bellasio thug drops to the floor like a dead fly. I kick his body out of the way and assess our options.

West leads back out to the gardens, where the people are. Where Celine is.

South is through the kitchens, the quickest route to safety.

South it is, then.

"What are you doing?" Taylor cries out when I start pulling her toward the kitchen.

"What does it look like I'm doing?" I growl. "I'm getting you the fuck out of here."

"I'm not leaving!" she protests. "My family's here."

I'm as amazed at her stupidity as I am impressed by her loyalty. Regardless, I'm not about to let her waltz through open fire just so she can prove she's not a coward.

Before I can tell her to stop being an idiot, she screams. "Watch out!"

I turn, but it's too late. I'm knocked off-center by the idiot who's decided to tackle me to the ground. The gun flies out of my hand and goes skittering down the hallway.

I roll away and jump upright on my feet. "That was a stupid move," I snarl at the Bellasio thug. He blinks back at me dumbly. This has not gone how he envisioned.

I slug him in the stomach first, and while he's reeling from the hit, I throw a hard right hand to his face. His orbital socket shatters under my knuckles and he lets out an ungodly scream that quickly snuffs itself out. He'll wake up in one or two hours with a broken nose and a fuck-ton of regret.

Or, more likely, one of my men will kill him before he gets that chance.

When I glance up, I see that Taylor is back to looking horrified. Three more gunshots sound in quick succession. She winces at each one of them.

Then her eyes flit over my shoulder. I turn to see what she's seeing, just in time for Mila to appear from the garden. Her cream dress has ripped up the side, exposing a length of thigh nearly as inappropriate as Taylor's.

"Dima said you have cargo?" she asks me.

I gesture to Taylor. "Get her out of here."

I can see the question in Mila's eyes. *Why am I so concerned with* this *sister?*

Before I can answer, Taylor rips herself free from my side and runs past us.

"Taylor!" I yell. But she doesn't slow or stop. She makes a beeline for the garden, bumping a surprised Mila off-balance on her way.

Snarling, I take off in pursuit.

I swallow up the distance between us in five long strides. Then I pluck her off her feet and throw her over my shoulder. She writhes like she's being electrocuted and pounds useless fists into my back.

"Foolish fucking girl," I mutter under my breath as I charge back in search of cover.

She's not even pretending to listen to me, though. "Mom!" Taylor screams in panic at the mass of bodies in the distance. "Mom!"

It's chaos beyond the upended garden tables. Bodies are strewn across the grass, some in black masks and tactical gear, others in bloodstained gowns.

Fiona Theron sticks out in the midst of the chaos, her bandana like a scrap of starlight. She stands, silent and stationary, her eyes wide with disbelief as she looks down at a limp body in the grass.

There's a smear of blood across her face. She's not even ducking for cover.

"Mom!" Taylor screams yet again. "*Move!*"

Fiona looks up toward the both of us. Even from here, I can see trauma in her eyes. The woman has stared death in the face, but there's a difference between the death that steals you from your hospital room in the middle of the night and the kind that comes at you screaming from the barrel of a gun.

"Let me go!" Taylor screams. "I have to get to her. I have to save—"

Somehow, the ensuing gunshot feels louder than the rest.

We watch helplessly as it finds its home in Taylor's mother's chest.

Fiona's eyes roll. Her legs buckle. Just as she crumbles to her knees on the grass, we see red blood blossom, soaking the front of her sky-blue dress into a gruesome navy.

"*NO!*" Taylor in a gut-wrenching scream that vibrates through my body. "*Mom!* Mom…"

She tries to wrest herself free from my grip again, but when I tighten my hold on her, she goes slack, like she can't summon up enough strength to fight me anymore.

"Give her to me," Mila says, appearing at my side with two of my men. "I'll get her out of here."

I catch sight of Dima in the distance, but I can't see Celine or her father. Where are they? How many have died? *How could I have let this happen?*

"Ilarion!" Mila shouts, forcing me to look over. "Let go of her."

I only realize then that I'm still gripping Taylor tightly. It takes more effort than it should to release her. One of my men comes forward and I pass her off reluctantly.

"Be careful with her," I growl. "She is not to be harmed."

The soldier nods grimly, then hoists a sobbing Taylor over his shoulder and follows Mila out the back entrance of the gardens.

I cross the lawn to where Dima is standing in the midst of the madness. He's sweating and bloody but unharmed.

"Where's Celine?" I rasp.

He drags his eyes up to mine. It looks like it costs him years of his life to do so. "I'm sorry, brother," Dima croaks, the sweat and blood mingling into a red paste on his forehead. "They have her. The old man, too. They're gone."

19

TAYLOR

I can't breathe. There's an ache in my chest that feels like it's going to bore a hole through me if I don't stop.

If *they* don't stop.

I have no idea where we are, but it looks and feels like a tunnel. The walls are dark, the ceiling is low, and there are no windows anywhere in sight.

Which means I can't hear anything but my own screaming. If there's still gunfire outside, we're completely cut off from it. It's just the echoes of my own terror and my own frantic, stampeding heart.

"Let me down!" I wail, slamming my fists against the grim-faced man's concrete back. "Let me down!"

I have no idea how, but I manage to hit him between the legs. I'm flailing around like a madwoman, and I guess my foot must have made contact with his balls, because the next thing I know, he's dropped me unceremoniously to the ground.

I don't give him time to recover; I just twist in the opposite direction and attempt to run back to the garden. I get about two steps before I'm met with the mouth of a gun.

That halts me in my tracks.

I freeze, staring past the gun to its owner. It's the gorgeous, dark-haired woman who reminds me of Ilarion. Probably because they're both toting around guns like it's part of their outfit.

"You're gonna have to start listening, honey," she says, her tone anything but sweet. "Or my finger just might slip."

Something inside me feels like it's snapped in two. I thought I lived in one kind of world, the kind of world where I went to college and took Mom to chemo and got in spats with my dad that could be resolved at the kitchen table.

Now, though, I've realized there's an alternate world. One where engagement parties end in gunfire, and my sister is engaged to a man who carries around guns and says things like, *The Bellasios are here.* A world in which my mother is dying or dead and I'm being dragged away in the opposite direction.

The woman has a gun to my face, so my instinct should be to do whatever she asks of me without questioning it. But I don't cower and I don't back down. I just stand my ground and look her in the eye.

"My mother just got shot."

"I know." This time, I detect a hint of sympathy under that icy tone. "But going back is only going to get you shot right along with her. And my brother isn't the sort to tolerate insubordination."

"You're his sister?"

"Mila Zakharov. Pleasure to meet you. Now, on you go."

"I'm not moving."

She cocks her gun. "Then I'm afraid I'm going to have to start shooting."

"Go right ahead." I grit my teeth. "I won't just abandon my mother. I won't just let my family die."

Maybe Ilarion is right about me: my sense of self-preservation is sadly lacking. There's a fine line between bravery and stupidity, and right now, I'm doing cartwheels back and forth across it.

Mila regards me with reluctant interest. Then, reaching some conclusion she doesn't seem inclined to share with me, she drops her hand. I can't help but sigh with relief. As tough as I sounded just now, I felt anything but that.

But then she looks over my shoulder and nods at the man behind me. For a split second, I think she's telling him to let me go.

Then his hands clamp around my arms, and I realize I've lost.

"No!" I cry out. "No, you can't do this."

Mila shakes her head and holsters her gun. "When you're confronted by a stronger enemy, the smartest thing to do is just be quiet and accept your fate. I learned that the hard way. I advise you not to follow in my footsteps."

"Then you gave up too fast," I snap. But my words don't have quite the impact considering I'm being hauled off like—what did Ilarion call me? oh, yeah—*cargo*.

Mila smiles darkly. "There may be some truth to that."

There's a cryptic, haunted quality to her words. But I suggest she take that shit to a psychiatrist, because I'm not the one who's going to help her unpack her emotional baggage. My mom is out there somewhere, bleeding and alone. I picture blood soaking the edge of her yellow bandana and I want to die.

"Where are you taking me?" I rasp.

"Somewhere safe."

"Excuse me if I don't feel safe with you people."

Mila doesn't respond to that. She nods once again, and a second later, light hits my peripheral vision. When we emerge on the other side, I realize we've wound our way outside the Zakharov House property. A secret passageway—that's the only way to describe it.

What kind of people have secret passageways in their home?

What kind of people would need one?

"Who are you people?" I ask as I'm set back down on my feet.

"People you don't want to mess with," Mila answers without bothering to look at me.

"Someone clearly does."

She shrugs, as though I've just mentioned an inconsequential detail, as opposed to, y'know, *a giant fucking gunfight at a freaking engagement party*. "Some people need to learn the hard way," she sighs. "Now—get in the car."

I turn when I hear a mechanical growl. Off to the side is an anonymous black sedan, engine humming, another burly brute standing at the passenger door waiting to usher me in.

I cross my arms and stand my ground. "I'm not going anywhere until I know that my family is safe."

She rolls her eyes in exasperation. "What makes you think I'm going to give you a choice?"

"For God's sake!" I scream, ready to tear my hair out by the roots. "Have some humanity!"

"*Humanity*," Mila repeats neutrally, as though the word is alien to her. "What humanity? Humanity left this world a long time ago, little girl. If you stick around long enough, you'll come to realize that, too. Now, get the fuck in the car before I make you."

She doesn't reach for her gun, but she doesn't have to. I can see the determination in her eyes, the certainty that she will do exactly what she's threatening.

I don't want to be the person who crosses her.

So I do what she advised me to do back in the tunnel: I accept my fate.

I get into the car and she joins me in the rear. As we roll away from the property, I stare out the windows. They're tinted so dark that all the color in the world is reduced to shades of gray, but that feels somehow fitting. There's not a trace of yellow to be seen anywhere. I wring my hands together, praying to God that Mom is okay.

Even as I know she isn't.

20

TAYLOR

"Ow!" I gasp, keeling forward at a sudden stab of pain and grabbing my stomach.

"What's wrong?" Mila asks.

"I…I can't breathe…"

She scoots closer to me and cups the back of my neck. Her hands are cool and dry. "Put your head between your legs." She gently pushes me down into position. "And breathe deeply."

"I…I… What if she's dead?" I gasp, trying to suck in air between my words. "She can't be dead… If she's dead, how can she beat the cancer…? Oh, God, something hurts…"

"Take deep breaths," Mila instructs from just above me. She barks something at the driver in what I'm fairly sure is Russian. We pick up speed. The engine whines and growls beneath us.

I can breathe better hunched over like this, but it's not doing a thing for my panic. Every time I close my eyes, I see Mom's face. The shock, the horror, the numbness. It's how she looked when the doctor told her she had cancer. When I found her at the kitchen table with the phone in her hand humming a dull dial tone, the call long since ended but the news of her sickness still fresh and terrifying.

And the rest of my family… I haven't even seen what happened to Dad and Celine. Who knows where they are? If they're okay? If they found a tunnel like I did, or if the bullets found them first?

The more I think, the more I spiral. I see Mom lying on the grass, blood spilling out of her as the life drains from her.

And what did I do?

I ran.

Is that the last image she'll be left with? The fleeting sight of her own daughter fleeing in the opposite direction after witnessing her get shot?

"Taylor!" Mila yells.

I jerk upright, wild with panic. "We have to go back."

"You're bleeding."

"W-what?"

I look down at my torso, the same place Mom had been shot, expecting to see blood there. Is it possible that I was hit as well and just didn't notice? It would explain why I have this pain in my side.

"I think you just got your period," she says wearily, as though I've just sprung an irritating inconvenience on her.

I slide down the seat and realize that I've smeared blood on the black cushion. "Oh, God," I gasp, realizing what might be happening, as another jolt of pain lances down my side. "This can't be happening…"

"What do you mean?" Mila asks. She glances towards the driver. "For fuck's sake, Anton, step on it, will you? Taylor, is there something I should know?"

I should be telling my own family about this. Not this violent, random stranger who threatened me at gunpoint. But the words slip off my tongue, fueled by fear and the growing realization that I *do* want this baby. More than I thought I did.

And that, if I don't speak the truth now, it might be too late.

"I-I'm pregnant," I gasp, clinging to the edges of my seat. "And I think…I think I might be miscarrying."

I close my eyes and lie back against the seat. I spent so much time worrying about this pregnancy that I hadn't stopped to consider everything else that came with it. I've been worrying about the consequences, the reactions—so it's ironic that it takes something like this to make me think of the *baby* at the end of all of it.

"How far along are you?" It's a thoughtful question, but I know she's not asking to be sweet. She's like Ilarion in that sense: gathering info, cold, calculating, always assessing the angles and weighing the odds. I'm just a variable in her equations. My baby is, too.

"Ten weeks," I whisper.

Her eyes meet mine, rife with suspicion. I can practically hear the gears whirring in her head. *Please don't ask me*, I think to myself. I don't have the strength to lie today.

She nods crisply. "We have a doctor on staff. He'll meet us at the Diamond."

"The what?"

"It's another one of the Zakharov family properties," she says. "You'll get the help you need there."

I want to scream, but I don't have the strength to do any more of that. Doesn't she get it? The only thing I really need is to know that my family is okay. The only thing I need is to get out of this fucked-up world as soon as I can.

And take my family with me.

21

TAYLOR

As it turns out, the Diamond is just like Zakharov House, but miniaturized. The same lush wilderness swaddling it from the rest of the world, the same ornate sandstone blocks rising into gargoyles and spires and flanged spikes on the walls. The only difference is the huge diamond shape laid into the tile floors in the foyer. Very subtle.

Not that I'm in the mood to appreciate architecture. I'd rather be in hell, if it meant that I was assured of my family's safety. Surely, *surely*, Celine couldn't have known about all this. She couldn't have known that her fiancé was some kind of crime boss.

I mean, the likelihood that a man as young as Ilarion Zakharov could have amassed so much wealth without doing something illegal is slim to none, and slim just left town. But like I said before, my sister chooses to believe the best in everyone.

Even when she shouldn't.

The car comes to a stop, but I don't move to get out. I feel like I'm floating inside the confines of my own body. My limbs are dead and numb and my mouth tastes like ash. The blood smeared on the insides of my thighs has cooled to a scab.

It's not until Mila pulls open my door that I'm forced back into my body.

"Come on," she says, a bit gentler than she's said anything else to date. "Let's get you inside."

"I don't want to come inside."

She sighs audibly, then bends down so that she's at eye level with me. "If you're miscarrying, Taylor, you need a doctor."

"Then drive me to a hospital so I can see one."

"We have a doctor right here."

"I'm not letting your morally corrupt voodoo mob doctor poke and prod me and then pronounce me ready for euthanasia," I snap, ignoring the pain in my stomach that accompanies my rising temper.

Mila arches one skeptical eyebrow. "So you're okay with losing the baby then?" I flinch, and she nods. "That's what I thought. Dr. Baranov delivered both Ilarion and me. He's a family doctor, not a—what was your word choice?—a 'morally corrupt voodoo mob doctor.' And considering everything I just went through to get you out of that disaster, letting him kill you is not high on my list. Same goes for your child. So unless you decide you don't want this baby, I'd suggest you get your ass out here and follow me."

Geez. And I thought *I* was blunt.

I get out of the car reluctantly, and almost immediately, my head spins. "Shit," I gasp, keeling forward.

Mila lunges forward to grab me before I faceplant in the gravel. I'm impressed at how sturdy she is. Not that she's small or anything; I just didn't expect to feel biceps flexing in those slender arms as she takes some of my weight.

"Okay, dial it back," she croons. "Let's go nice and slow."

She tucks an arm around my waist, loops one of mine over her shoulders, and together, we shuffle up the drive, up the stairs, and through the front doors.

She leads me past a wall of stormy ocean paintings and into a room that overlooks an enclosed part of the garden. There's a bed in the center of the room, a writing desk by the window, and an intricately carved wardrobe that looks like it'll lead me to Narnia.

"Lie down," Mila instructs me. "Dr. Baranov should be here any moment."

She helps me onto my back. Every motion brings a fresh wave of pain, but I grit my teeth and bear it. I won't cry out. I won't beg for help.

Mom would want me to be strong.

I'm not on the bed five seconds before I ask the same question I asked earlier: "Who are you people?"

Her frown sharpens. She's got a lot of her brother in her features. Her eyes are the same shape, but where his irises are a misty blue, hers are such a dark chocolate brown, they're almost black. She also shares his square jaw and thick eyebrows, though her high cheekbones and full lips are uniquely her own.

She's unconventionally beautiful. Still, though, there's a kind of pent-up violence inherent in her posture. Even when she's at ease, it feels like she's poised for attack.

"Who do you think we are?" Her head tilts to one side as she waits for me to answer. It's just short of patronizing.

I roll my eyes before wincing at the sharp jolt of pain that skitters along my spine. "I hate people who answer questions with a question."

"And I hate people who ask questions they already know the answers to," she snaps back.

We glare at one another, eyes narrowed and jaws tightened. It would be a lot more impressive if I weren't lying on a bed, soiling the sheets with blood.

"Okay," I say at last, conceding the high ground. "We've established how we feel about each other. Now, how about you answer my question?"

"You've met my brother?"

"Unfortunately."

Her lips don't so much as twitch, but her eyes shimmer like she's laughing. "He's the *pakhan* of the Zakharov Bratva."

"*Pakhan*? B-Bratva?" I stutter over the unfamiliar words. "Sounds… Russian."

"Ding-ding-ding," Mila says, touching a finger to her nose.

"Sounds a little sus, too."

"Nothing gets past you, does it, angel?"

"Shit." I close my eyes and try to breathe through my shock. It's not difficult to piece things together. I'm surrounded by the Russian mob, away from my family, who may or may not be dead, and all because… oh, *double shit.*

"Does my sister know?"

Before she can answer—if she was ever going to answer—the door opens and the doctor walks in. I suddenly believe Mila's story about him delivering both her and her brother, because this man looks older than time itself. His nose hairs have lived longer than I have.

His gray hair is shorn close to the scalp, and he has the tired grace of a war veteran. He places his black leather medical bag on the floor and looks at me through his round, rimmed glasses.

"Hello, my dear. What's your name?"

He talks to me as though we've just been introduced at a garden party. Presumably one that wasn't overrun by psychopaths wielding guns. "Taylor."

"Taylor," he repeats with a kindly smile that puts me at ease. "My name is Dr. Baranov. Would you mind answering a few questions for me?"

I nod, in part because he does seem genuine and competent, and also because I can sense Mila lurking right next to me, and I don't doubt that she'd love to pull out her gun and convince me to talk to Dr. Baranov if I was entertaining any notions of doing otherwise.

He gives me another warm smile. "Wonderful. How far along are you, Taylor?"

"Ten weeks. I went for a check-up this morning, actually."

"Excellent, excellent. Do you mind if I examine you, Taylor? You'll feel mild discomfort, but no pain."

I nod again mutely.

"Mila," Dr. Baranov says as he tugs on a pair of black latex gloves, "would you mind giving Taylor and me some privacy?"

Mila doesn't look very happy about it, but she slips out of the room without argument. The moment the door snaps shut, I sigh. "Well, that's a relief. Tell me, Doc, did she come out of her mother's womb scowling?"

He chuckles as he begins to poke and prod at my stomach. "No, that was her brother. Mila came out with tears in her eyes. It was almost like she was made for suffering."

I shudder as I regard the old man with new curiosity. "That's… bleak."

"Life is indeed bleak at times, in this house more than most," he agrees solemnly. "The fact that you're here at all proves that."

I have no idea if he's referring to me being here with the Zakharovs, or me being here miscarrying. Honestly, it's a toss-up, and I don't feel like asking him to clarify.

"Can I ask you a question and will you promise to be honest?"

"As honest as I can be." He rummages through his bag for some complex-looking medical device and begins gliding it around the surface of my stomach.

"That's a shady response."

He chuckles again. I like that; it makes me feel more at ease. It makes me feel like things can't be so bad as long as that sound exists in the world.

"Yes, I suppose it is. I can only promise that I will do my best."

"That's not much better, but I'll take it. Are you a mob doctor?"

He doesn't so much as lift an eyebrow. "I'm whatever I need to be to serve the Zakharov family."

"I'll take that as a yes."

He smiles and peers at me over the top of his glasses. "Where'd they find you, little truth-teller?"

"They didn't," I rasp. "They found my sister. I'm just… a casualty." The truth of that statement hits deeper than I intended.

The doctor shakes his head. "No, I think not. You're no casualty."

"What makes you so sure?"

"A casualty would never have made it past the door."

"Are you trying to tell me I'm special?" I snort. "Because I gotta tell you, Doc, I just saw my mother get shot. I have no idea where my sister and father are. I have no idea if any of them are dead or alive. I have no trust in any of the people here, and—no offense, because you truly do seem lovely— that includes you. And on top of all of that, I'm miscarrying. Which I should want, but the fact is, I don't."

The tears are sliding down my face by the time I'm done speaking, but I'm too wrecked to care. Dr. Baranov rests his liver-spotted hand over mine and gives me a smile that makes me feel guilty about telling him I don't trust him.

"You're dealing with many burdens," he says. "But miscarrying isn't one of them."

"W-what?"

"The fetus is intact, Taylor," he informs me, helping me to sit upright. "I heard a heartbeat and it was strong as an ox. You're still pregnant, and from what I heard, it sounds like you're going to stay that way."

I watch as he puts his tools away. He performed an entire examination on me, and I was too busy talking to notice.

"B-but…I was bleeding."

"A result of the trauma you just experienced, most assuredly. It was triggered by stress," he explains. "Bleeding can sometimes occur during even the most relaxed of pregnancies. It's what's known as a 'breakthrough period.' Even given what you've suffered through today, it's nothing a little rest won't cure."

I collapse back against the pillow and stare up at the ceiling for a moment. "I didn't lose the baby," I whisper. "I didn't lose my baby."

I didn't lose *our* baby.

I take a deep breath and it's a relief to realize that they're coming a little easier. Then the door bursts open…

And Ilarion storms in.

His eyes land on me and it's as good as if he'd zapped me with a cattle prod. I shove myself upright on my elbows while my heart rampages in my chest. His hair is mussed, his shirt sweaty, his knuckles bruised at his sides. But of all the signs of war painted all over him, it's his gaze that scares me the most.

He looks like he could kill without blinking.

"Grisha? Is the baby—"

"Healthy, happy, and perfectly safe," Dr. Baranov tells him before he can even finish his sentence.

He nods once, curt and detached. It's almost enough to convince me he doesn't give a damn one way or the other. But there's no way he'd storm into a room and demand to know the outcome if he didn't care about the outcome, right?

Right?

It crosses my mind that having Ilarion care about this pregnancy is an inconvenience I'd rather avoid. Especially considering I don't intend for him to be a part of this child's life. That's a sentiment I'm clinging to for all of us—including and *especially* my sister.

If she's alive, that is.

"Thank you, Grisha. Please give us a moment."

"Of course, sir," the doctor says, collecting his bag and making for the door. When he steps out, I spy Mila lurking in the hallway.

The upside is that he shuts the door behind him, keeping her at bay.

Downside, I'm left alone with Ilarion.

And I have a feeling that being alone with this man—under any circumstances—is trouble.

22

ILARION

"My mother," Taylor pleads, her eyes wide and searching. "If she's dead…just tell me."

I admire that she comes right out and says it. Most people are too afraid to even name their fear. Not her, though.

She stands in the middle of the road and lets it barrel toward her.

I open my mouth to give her the answer she wants, but I pause when I sense her starting to unravel in the seconds before I speak.

"You need to take a breath," I growl instead.

She swings her legs off the bed and struggles to her feet. She's shaky at first, but her fists stay knotted tight, her jaw held firm, and when she raises her gaze to meet mine, it doesn't waver.

"I know I'm just a random, insignificant cog in your wheel—"

"Wrong," I interrupt. "A cog implies that you serve a purpose, and you do not." It's a cruel thing to say. But it's not far from the truth. *She* does not serve a purpose in everything I have going on.

The infuriating part is knowing she could have. That she *should*.

But I fucked up. I fucked up by overlooking some very important details. I have only myself to blame for the mess that's come spewing onto my doorstep.

She ventures closer to me. Her dress is torn in half a dozen places, but she doesn't even seem to register the state she's in. The fact that she's half-naked, blood dripping down her thighs, doesn't seem to faze her at all.

I expected her to vent and rage at me. To spit in my face and call me a monster. But what she does instead surprises me.

She makes a threat.

"I'm going to tell you something now, *Il-ar-i-on*. From this day forward, for the rest of my life, my purpose will be to personally expose your entire operation and put you behind bars for all the criminal shit you're clearly used to getting away with. I will turn over every rock and comb through every scrap of evidence you've ever left behind—unless you tell me exactly where the *fuck* my family is."

The balls on this woman. No one—no woman, man, or beast alive—has made that kind of threat about me, much less to my face.

And yet here she is—half my size, half my weight, and none of my resources… and she's *threatening* me.

Remarkable.

"Your mother is alive," I tell her.

She lets out a relieved gasp. Half broken sob, half delirious laughter. Fat tears slip down her flushed cheeks. "Oh, thank God," she cries. "You're sure? You're sure she's alive? Where is she? I need to see her."

"She's unconscious at the moment."

"Just tell me where to go," she says. "I don't want an escort."

"I don't care what you want," I growl. "You're not going anywhere without my permission."

"And who are you to tell me where I can and can't go?" She storms up toward me, close enough that I can smell her. Vanilla and hazelnut. Enough to make my head swim and my dick stiffen.

"Assuming you've told me the truth, I'm the father of your child," I remind her. "And considering that wherever you go, my baby goes, I do have a right to tell you where you can and can't go."

"Or what?" she asks, her feet brushing against my toes. "You'll sick your big, bad minions on me? You'll pull out your guns? Threaten me with violence?"

"Don't tempt me."

She laughs viciously. "I'm pregnant with your baby. You can't touch me."

Oh ye of little faith, I think to myself. *There are a million ways to break you that don't involve a single touch.*

But my hands stay by my side. There's something about her single-minded determination that I relate to. She is from a different world, but she's someone who would die for her family. In fact, I'm starting to get the impression that she may just be someone who would kill *for* her family.

I know *exactly* what that feels like.

"Your mother is at Northwestern Hospital," I tell her quietly.

She nods. "Fantastic. Thanks for sharing." She starts to step around me, but when I intercept her, her frown furrows deeper. "You must not have such good listening skills. I thought we just established that you have no right to tell me what to do."

"Did we now?"

Her chest rises and falls. Desperation fills her eyes. "Ilarion," she says, her voice cracking with the weight of her fear. "Please."

I hate this. I'd much rather have her fight me, claws out and nostrils flared. This fragility is so much harder to deal with.

"Look at you, Taylor," I point out. "You're in no fit state to be seen in public."

She glances down at her ripped dress, as though she's only just realized what she's been through and the price she's paid for it. "Crap," she mutters under her breath. "There must be something here I can borrow…?"

I gesture towards the pocket door on the other side of the bed. "Go clean yourself up and I'll find something for you to wear."

She wavers in place, skeptical of my sudden generosity. Like she's waiting for the other shoe to drop. "Y-you're not going to lock me in there, are you?"

I almost smile. "No, Taylor. I'm not gonna lock you in there."

But goddamn, I wish I could bring myself to do it. It would make everything so much simpler.

23

ILARION

She nods once and heads into the bathroom. There's blood plastered on the backs of her legs. I find myself watching her until she disappears through the door.

Then I leave the room—only to find Mila waiting for me just outside the door.

"What—?"

"You knocked up the wrong sister?" She gapes at me in disbelief. "How the ever-loving fuck did *that* happen?"

I shrug her off. "I don't have time for this. Get me something that Taylor can wear."

Mila doesn't move. I grit my teeth. I know that bulldog set in her face—she wants answers and she wants them *now*.

But she knows as well as I do that this is not the right setting. The tension ripples through her jaw before she relents. "There's a robe in the bathroom she can wear."

"She's not here for a spa treatment," I growl. "Something she can wear outside. We're going to be taking a little field trip."

Mila raises her eyebrows incredulously. "Do you really think that's a good idea?"

"Of course not. But she wants to see her mother."

"And?" Mila asks. "You can't say no to her, is that it?"

I rake a weary hand through my hair. "It doesn't look like Fiona Theron is going to make it to sunrise," I tell her. "She might as well see her daughter before she goes."

The last of Mila's tenacity fades away. "Fuck. Does she know?"

"No. Not yet."

She nods. "I have some clothes here. I'll get her something."

She disappears upstairs. As soon as I step back into the bedroom, I hear the shower turn off. I'm checking Dima's messages on my phone when the bathroom door swings open and Taylor's head pops out.

"What's the ETA on those clothes?" She's half-hidden by the door, but I can see a bare shoulder and the edge of a white terry cloth towel wrapped around her torso. Her hair hangs down in dark, wet ringlets.

A series of memories flash through my head rapid-fire.

Her hair plastered to her throat by the rain.

The taste of her lips.

The vibration of her moans.

I shake my head and drag myself forcibly back to the present. "Mila will bring them down momentarily."

Her face screws up. "I'm borrowing Mila's clothes?"

"Unless you'd rather dress in one of the maid's spare uniforms, that's your only option."

"Honestly, that might be better."

"The two of you got off to a great start, I see."

"If you say anything about a cat fight, I'm gonna fling something at you. My sister and I used to—" Then something passes over her face, and all the wind in her sails disappears. "Celine. I haven't even... Fuck, I'm the worst person on earth. Are she and Dad with Mom?" She seems to forget the fact that she's still in a towel. She steps out of the bathroom in her bare feet, but she stops when she sees the dark expression on my face. "T-they're not, are they?"

Of all the times to lie, now is it. So why can't I?

"No."

"Then—"

"They're not dead," I tell her quickly. "So don't start freaking out."

"Then don't tell me shit that makes me freak out!" she counters. "Where are my dad and sister?"

"The Bellasios have them."

"'The Bellasios have them,'" she repeats. "Am I supposed to know what that means?"

"If you were paying any attention at all today, then you should."

She takes a deep breath. "Do they have something to do with the fact that you're a mob boss?"

"Bratva don," I growl. Technically, the term is *"pakhan"*, but I'm in no mood to split hairs.

"From where I'm standing, it's the same damn thing. So who are the Bellasios to you?"

"An enemy mafia whose leader has been obsessed with taking down the Zakharov Bratva for as long as I've been in charge."

"Why?"

"Why?" I ask incredulously. "For more power. Why else?"

"Jesus," she mutters. "Men." She shakes her head to clear the thoughts and looks up at me again. "You have to get them back."

"Great point," I retort, rolling my eyes. "Let me just go ask nicely."

"Have you tried that?"

I glare at her. "Did you really think I would let my enemies take off with my fiancé and not do anything about it? For fuck's sake, trust that I'm capable."

"Ha!" she guffaws at full volume. "Trust? Trust *you*? My sister trusted you, and look where that landed her! No, thanks. I'd rather trust in the people I know I can count on."

"Which is who? That Bradley fuck who tried pawing at you when no one was looking?"

"My father. My mother. My sister," she rattles off without breaking eye contact. "That's it. All the people you put directly in harm's way." Before I can respond, she keeps going. "I had a bad feeling about this relationship from the moment she mentioned you to me. She didn't even tell me your name, but I knew there was something off about this whole thing. Celine's a pacifist at heart. She's also the most moral person I know. If she knew about any of what you do—"

"What makes you think she doesn't?"

She scoffs, waving a hand in my face. "There's no way Celine would have agreed to date you, much less marry you, if she knew you were some big, bad villain."

I raise an eyebrow. "Are you so sure?"

Her lip trembles as her confidence comes crumbling down. I saunter toward her, backing her up until she bumps into the doorjamb.

"Maybe you don't know your sister as well as you think you do, Taylor. She did know. She knew everything—because I told her. I told her exactly who I was… and she agreed to marry me anyway."

24

TAYLOR

I wish I could say he was lying.

But in reality, I'm not so sure. It just *feels* so much like a lie. I know my sister, and Celine can't have been okay with the fact that Ilarion is who he is. I watched him kill people with my own eyes. There's no denying the truth of it. The raw, cold, brutal, hideously ugly truth of it. Of *him.*

There's always the chance that he's sold her some weird, Disneyfied version of his life as a Bratva boss, but I can't see Celine buying that. She's naive, she's kind, she was born wearing rose-colored glasses—but she isn't stupid.

"Celine would have told me if that were true," I rasp. I hate how unsure I sound.

He laughs cruelly. "She didn't even tell you my full name. What makes you think she would have told you anything else?"

How does he know that, too? What *doesn't* he know?

That's when it finally sinks in. The only reason he could possibly know as much as he does is if Celine told him.

Which means she trusted him.

"You know what? We can have this conversation later, when Celine can join it," I snap. "But for right now, I'd still like to see my mother."

Ilarion doesn't miss a beat. He looks past me and gestures for whoever is standing at the door to come in. I turn and see that Mila is there with a bunch of clothes draped over her arms. She's probably been listening in for some time.

Great. Now, I'm humiliating myself in front of the whole damn family.

Mila silently hands me the pile of clothes. I force out a reluctant, "Thank you."

"Try not to bleed on my clothes," she says, utterly deadpan, before spinning on her heel and heading back out.

I slink into the bathroom and swap out the damp towel for the jeans and t-shirt. They're snug, because Mila is a twig, but they work.

Enjoy this now. Everything will be too small in a few short months.

When I'm dressed, I step back out into the bedroom, where Ilarion is waiting for me. I try to avoid his gaze as I follow him out of the room and through the house, but that's about as easy as avoiding an oncoming truck. He's watching me like I'm going to run at any moment.

I'm not.

Well, not exactly.

"I, um…lost my phone in the chaos," I tell him. "If you could call me a taxi—"

"There's no need," he interrupts as we step onto the driveway, where a shiny black car is waiting. "I will drive you."

I don't like that idea at all. "There's no need for that."

"Let me put it to you this way," he corrects. "If I don't take you, you're not going."

It's a miracle how that imperious, slice-through-anything certainty in his voice that was such a turn-on the night we met can be so utterly, impossibly infuriating now.

"You're serious?"

"Take a wild guess."

The instinct to push back is there, but I'm too desperate to waste any more time. My mom needs me more than I need to scrap and claw for my dignity.

"Fine," I snap. "You wanna play the chauffeur? Go right ahead."

I get into the passenger's seat and slam the door. He doesn't say anything as he walks around the front of the car, gets into the driver's seat, and turns the engine on.

I hate that he always seems to come out ahead of me. No matter how hard I try, it feels like I'm always lagging behind. And as much as I hate to admit it, it feels like a part of that is Celine's doing.

She wouldn't have done it intentionally, of course. She was sharing parts of her life with a man she trusted. My problem is with how fast she chose to trust him.

I mean, I'm her sister, for crying out loud. She's known me a hell of a lot longer than she's known him. Doesn't that count for a little more loyalty? A little more diplomacy, at the very least?

"How exactly do you plan on getting my sister and father back?" I ask, mostly because staying silent is like hurling lighter fluid on the blaze of my terrified thoughts.

"We have to locate them first. Once we know where they've been taken, I'll go in with a team."

"Will they be in danger?" I ask anxiously. "The Bellasios… They won't hurt them, will they?"

He shrugs without bothering to look over. "I can't speak to that."

I stare at him in shock. "Are you serious?"

"Let me save you some time and assure you that I am always serious. I can't promise you something I can't control, Taylor. The likelihood is that Celine and your father will be safe. They were taken alive for a reason. I don't think Benedict will kill them, but hurting them…? That's different."

I can only gawk at him for a long time, trying and failing to figure out how a human being could possibly be so cold.

"What?" he asks eventually.

"She's your *fiancée*," I whisper, just in case he forgot. "And you're acting as though she means nothing to you."

"You want me to fall to pieces?" he asks in that same detached tone. "Would that make you feel better?"

"Actually, yes." This man makes me want to simultaneously scream and roll my eyes so far back I can see my brain. At least one of us has one. "It would reassure me that you haven't just proposed to my sister for some nefarious, manipulative, bullshit reason. And since it's pretty clear that she has actual feelings for you, I'm hoping that's not the case."

"Tell me more about what you're hoping for," he says sarcastically. "I'll pretend I'm fucking Santa Claus and deliver all your dreams to your doorstep."

What I'm hoping for. Great question. Isn't that what he asked me the night we met? *What do you want?* I knew then what I wanted: him. So how do I answer it now? As the car hums and chews up the road, I think about it with the same kind of breathlessness I thought about it back then. And when the answer surfaces, I know in my heart that it's true.

I want two things. Two things that are in direct contradiction to one another, actually.

I want to keep the baby in my belly.

And I want my sister to be happy with the man who got me pregnant.

"Can I ask you a question?" I ask softly. I can dispense with bickering for the sake of five minutes of honest conversation.

"Go ahead."

"What made you propose to Celine as fast as you did?"

I'm pretty sure I see his knuckles tighten on the wheel. But then again, I could be just imagining it. When he speaks, there's nothing to suggest he has anything to hide.

"She was a breath of fresh air," he tells me. "She was so open and honest and…sweet. It was hard not to like her."

"That's a nice answer." It really is. It's also vague as hell. "But it sounds like you read it off a Hallmark card. It's hardly indicative of a whirlwind romance that's wild, and passionate, and fiery, and…and all-consuming."

He raises his eyebrows in a silent question.

"Well, it would have to be, wouldn't it?" I press. "To have inspired a proposal in such a short span of time, I mean."

"The kind of love you're describing sounds painful."

"'The kind of love'?" I repeat, shaking my head. "That's the only love there is, Ilarion. Real love is painful. It's messy and chaotic and gut-wrenching. If it doesn't hurt, you're doing it wrong."

We stop at a red light and he glances over at me with an expression that's half curiosity and half pity.

"What?"

"I just realized how young you are."

I narrow my eyes. "Screw you."

He turns the corner hard the moment the light turns red. "You want to know why I'm not falling to pieces, *tigrionok*? Because I can't afford to." A vein in his jaw ticks as he takes a moment to chew on whatever thoughts are rolling through his mind. "I am the *pakhan*. Everyone—and I mean *everyone*—relies on me. If I don't keep myself together, it all falls apart. If you see me unraveling, that's when you should start panicking. Because that means it's over."

"Are you trying to scare me?"

"I'm not trying to do anything," he murmurs. "But if you are scared, then maybe you're smarter than I realized after all."

I turn my face away from him and gaze out my window. "It's not about being smart," I tell him quietly. "It's about the fact that I've seen scarier."

That gets his attention.

"The first time Mom was diagnosed with cancer, that was the first time I experienced pure, unadulterated fear. The kind that sinks into your soul so deep that you have nightmares every night until you've processed it. Cancer scared me. Losing my family—that scares me, too. Everything else? I can deal with."

"Cancer can be fought," he suggests quietly.

I snort. If he was a different person, I might have thought he was trying to comfort me. I know better, though.

Comfort. He doesn't know the meaning of the word.

"Cancer fights, but it doesn't fight fair. *You* can fight, and make decisions, and decide to show mercy or not. You know who to aim at and who to avoid. Cancer doesn't know or care whether the victims are young or old or rich or poor. It doesn't even care if you're Bratva."

Ilarion's lips are pursed. He doesn't glance my way, but somehow, I just know he's looking at me. "That doesn't mean you give up. That doesn't mean you stop fighting."

I shake my head. "At what cost? My mother has been fighting her cancer for years now. It's ripped at her from every side, taking bites out of her until what's left of her is unrecognizable. I worry sometimes we won't even have a body to bury."

His nod is slow. Now, he does glance at me. "Worse than a bullet to the head."

I hear the hint of sympathy in his voice. I'm not sure I'm ready to receive it. Not right now. Not while we're driving to see my mother who is now dealing with both cancer and bullets.

"We were all different people B.C. And now… Well, this is the part they don't tell you about. It's not easy looking after someone who's sick. It takes its toll on you, too, no matter how much you love them."

"What did it take from you?" he asks gently.

"It took my mom. It took my dad, too, in a way. It took my adolescence and my innocence all at once." I replay my answer back in my head and cringe. "I sound like a selfish bitch, don't I?"

"You sound like someone who refuses to lie to themselves. That's admirable."

I glance at him from the corner of my eyes. I'm over here pouring my heart and soul out on the dashboard, and yet there's not one crack in that steely armor of his. "My mother's dying, Ilarion." I sigh heavily. "And I find myself getting resentful because I can't live a normal life. Because I have to miss parties to take her to chemo. *Parties.* Fucking stupid, meaningless parties. If that's not selfish, I don't know what is."

"You're human," he says. "You're allowed."

"I'm a human second. I'm my mother's daughter first."

The ghost of a smile dances along the corners of his lips. It brings back a vivid memory from the night we met. Those full, sure lips traversing the plane of my shoulder…down to my breasts…the scrape of his beard against my thighs…

Stop!

"Is that it, then?" Ilarion asks. "Your entire identity revolves around other people?"

"Doesn't everyone's?"

"No," he says softly. "Not everyone's." His eyes are darker now, and I wonder if he's thinking about things he'd rather forget, just like I am. "Not everyone has people in their life worth sacrificing so much for. You're lucky in that regard."

I raise my brow. "Who are you talking about?" The air has the charged feeling it gets when someone is holding a memory in their head that still hurts them. When fresh air reaches somewhere it hasn't reached in a long, long time.

Then his eyes flicker to me, and that steel armor clanks right back into place. "What makes you think that I'm talking about anyone?"

I sigh. I should've expected him to retreat.

Ilarion isn't just some heartless, hardened mob boss. There's a soul somewhere underneath all that iron. There are wounds buried deep down that he's trying to hide from me. He absolutely doesn't want me—or anyone—to see it…but I do.

Which makes me actually care what he thinks about me.

That's the last thing I can afford to do.

25

TAYLOR

Two giant men stand just outside my mother's hospital room like bouncers at a club. Some of the hospital staff eye the men warily as they inch by. Others pretend they can't see them at all.

"They work for me," Ilarion explains when he sees me looking. "I wasn't about to leave your mother alone in a hospital room without any security."

I don't say anything, but I appreciate the gesture. I'd assumed he'd just dumped her by the entrance of the hospital and driven off. I would've been pleasantly surprised if he'd even had the car come to a complete stop before kicking her to the curb. This is…above and beyond my admittedly-low expectations.

We're walking up when the door opens and a nurse walks out. Like every good nurse I've ever met, she's a weary older woman with a weathered face that keeps her emotions tucked out of sight.

"Are you Celine Theron?" she asks.

My breath catches and, for some reason, I turn to Ilarion. "This is Taylor," he fills in, because apparently, I've turned into a moron who can't even speak for herself.

"Ah! Taylor," the nurse says with a soft smile of recognition. "Your mother's been asking for you. For both her girls."

Her girls. That's how she used to refer to Celine and me all the time. We were Fiona's Girls. Celine used to joke about having a ready-made band name if we ever became famous.

"She's awake?"

The nurse nods, but the smile on her face wavers in a way I don't like. The forced-calm veneer of someone managing a crisis. "She's awake. But she's…weak."

"She has cancer."

"Yes, we were given a full report of her condition when she was admitted," the nurse tells me. "Mr. Zakharov passed along her medical details."

I glance at Ilarion in surprise. "Oh. Uh, okay. Well…"

"Why don't you sit down, Ms. Theron? I'll have her doctor come and—"

"I don't need to sit down," I say politely but firmly. "I want you to tell me what's happening."

She glances over my shoulder at Ilarion. I slide over to intercept her gaze. "With all due respect…" I read her nametag and finish, "Madison. With all due respect, Madison, he may have been the one to admit her, but I'm her daughter. If there's anyone here you should be sharing information with, it's me."

Madison pauses, then gives me a sympathetic nod. "Your mother's condition isn't likely to improve, Ms. Theron. We've got her hooked up to some machinery right now, but it's the only reason she's still breathing."

My body chills rapidly. "B-but… She's been asking for us. For me. For me and Celine. Isn't that what you said?"

"She can still talk, but it tires her out."

I swallow and nod. "Okay. Thank you."

She moves aside to let me pass. But I don't move. I can't. I'm frozen in place, terrified of what's awaiting me in that room. I can't see either one of them, but I sense the glance that Ilarion and the nurse exchange over my head.

Then I feel his breath tickle my ear. "Taylor," he says, gentler than I ever would have thought he'd be capable of, "do you need me to come in with you?"

No. That's my gut instinct. And it's the right one, I think.

But for some reason, simple as it is, I can't make my mouth form the word. Nor can I bring myself to ask him for help. Not this kind of help, anyway. The only person who should be leaning on him that way is Celine.

His fiancée.

A few seconds tick past, filled only with the murmured beeping and groaning of the hospital around us. He takes my silence for what it is: terror.

"Come on," he says, his hand gently pressing to the small of my back. "One step at a time."

I draw in a deep breath as he coaxes me through the door.

The room beyond is much larger than I expected. Cancer makes you intimately familiar with hospitals. You learn the cadence of the machine beeps, the tang of disinfectant, the way the nurses' shoes squeak on the tile. You start to have a sense for the space and shape of a room and for what the temperature of the air tells you about the people trapped inside of it.

I was ready for this one to feel like death.

But to my surprise, it doesn't. Sun pours in through the floor-to-ceiling windows and it fills the space all the way up to ceilings that are a touch higher than I'm used to.

It doesn't feel like death. Not yet, at least.

There's a sliver of hope left.

I force my eyes to the sickly woman lying on the bed. It's hard to reconcile her with the mother who raised me. She isn't wearing any yellow, for starters, and it just looks so wrong.

She hasn't spotted me yet. Her eyes are closed and her face is tilted to the side as though she fell asleep praying. She looks so—

I whirl back around abruptly and smash into Ilarion's chest. Forehead pressed against him, I shake my head. "I can't do this. I can't say goodbye to her."

"Then don't," he says. "Just say hello."

He grazes the bottom of my chin with two fingers and tils my face up. Our gazes meet. The blue of his eyes is calm today. An ocean at rest. Just mellow enough to put me at ease, to make me feel like maybe—just maybe—everything will turn out alright.

Even if it's a lie, it's one I desperately need.

"I'll be right here," he murmurs.

And, God help me, I believe him.

I pivot around and inch slowly up to Mom's bedside. I slip my fingers through hers, tender as I can, and her eyes blink open. When she groans softly and squints up at me, though, her gaze is blank. For a moment, I wonder if she even recognizes me.

Then I see that familiar surge of love, and my heart shatters all over again.

"Oh…honey…"

There's so much relief in her voice that the dam I've been building to pen back my tears crumbles and they all pour loose. I bend down and hover over her chest as I sob. Big, loud, full-body-wracking, ugly-girl sobs, the kind that hurt as they come. Mom pats my head with whisper-soft touches, and lets me cry it all out.

When I finally lift my head, I feel both relieved and ashamed. "I'm so sorry," I mumble. "You're the one in the hospital, and I'm the one crying."

She makes an attempt to wipe the tears from my face, but her hand trembles from the effort. I take that hand and hold it to my chest as I perch on the bed beside her.

"I know this is a stupid question and I honestly kinda hate myself for asking it, but…how are you?"

"Been better," she croaks. Her mouth twitches in a smile that she's too weak to see all the way through. "Celine? Archie?"

I lie immediately and without an ounce of guilt. "Don't you worry about them, Mom. They're fine."

Mom frowns. "I saw…Celine. They…t-took her."

I stiffen, but this is no time for heartbreaking truths. Mom needs hope. Healing and hope. I won't be the one to steal that from her. "Ilarion went and got her back," I reassure her. "Dad, too. They're both safe at one of his houses. They told me to send you their love."

She coughs. It's so faint I could almost start crying all over again. "Thank you for lying to me," Mom whispers. "But I'd really rather have the truth."

I gnaw my lip. They don't prepare you for this kind of thing in school. You learn calculus, you learn that the mitochondria is the powerhouse of the cell, but who teaches you whether or not to lie to your dying mother?

"Ilarion is going to get them both back," I promise her. "They'll be here at your bedside soon enough." She cringes, and I reach out to stroke a loose bang from her forehead. "Are you in pain?"

"I've been in pain for a long time, honey. I'm just tired now. You fight and fight and fight and then… Oh my. There are days I just want to stop."

My stomach drops. "You can't talk like that, Mom," I insist. I've never heard her say anything of the sort. She's always been so stoic about her illness. "You're just weak and—"

"I am *tired*," she interrupts. "I just want to rest now."

I squeeze her hand tight. "Think about Dad," I beg her. "Think about Celine. They need you."

"No," she says. Her voice trembles and breaks. "No, they don't. I'm the one who's needed the three of you all these years. And I hate how much that's cost all of you."

"Cost? What cost? We love you, Mom. We all love you so much."

"Oh, honey, don't you think I know that? But I don't want any of you to spend your lives playing Nurse for a sick old woman. I want you to live."

"I *am* living!"

"Are you?" she asks. Even in such a weakened state, she manages to squint at me in that *I-see-you-for-who-you-really-are* way that only a mother can do. "Last I checked, you were majoring in a field you hated, in a college you chose purely because it was close to home."

"I wanted to do that for *you*."

"Exactly," Mom says with a nod. "But you shouldn't be doing anything for me. You should be doing things for yourself. You and Celine both."

I'm a mess, full stop. Tears, blubbering, the works. My heart has never ached so much in all the rest of my life put together. "I still need you, Mom."

"No," she tells me. "You haven't needed me for a very long time." She closes her eyes and a solitary tear slips down her cheek. "And Celine…everyone underestimates her. But she's stronger than they give her credit for. When I couldn't be your mother, she stepped up for both of us."

"Mom, please," I beg her again. "Stop talking like this is the end. You're not dying today."

The protests lodge in my throat. I furiously shake my head. I can't accept this. I *won't* accept her surrender. "Mom, no—"

But my words die on my lips when she folds her thin fingers over mine. "Sweetheart, when I got shot, I remember lying in the grass, looking up at the sky. I wasn't in any pain. In fact, I stopped feeling pain altogether. All I felt was *relief.*"

I want to say something to change her mind. But my mother—my sunflower-loving, dance-in-the-kitchen-while-she-cooks, can't-drive-to-save-her-life mother—has never been one to listen when other people tell her no.

And I can't find the words anyway. They're all caught in my throat, all the things I didn't say enough. *I love you* and *I miss you already* and *thank you for sharing a part of yourself with me.* But my voice won't work and any air I manage to draw into my lungs burns away in an instant like useless fumes.

Then I feel a presence at my shoulder, and suddenly, I can breathe again. It's a big presence. Powerful. It smells like whiskey and leather and summer rain.

Ilarion's hand rests heavy on the back of my neck. "Fiona, you have nothing to worry about," he tells her in a quiet rumble. "I will make sure your daughters are safe and comfortable for the rest of their lives."

"I want both those things for them, Ilarion," she whispers. "But above all, I want them to be *happy.*"

I glance at Ilarion. A war is playing out on his face. The promise she's trying to extract from him is not something he can give her. Because there's no way he can make us both happy.

It's one or the other. Celine or me.

And if it were up to me, I'd take Celine's happiness over mine any day.

26

TAYLOR

"Stop it!" I cry, breaking up the quiet moment. "Both of you, just stop it!"

"Taylor, honey—"

"No!" I leap to my feet. "You are not dying, Mom. Not ever! And *you*," I growl, glaring at Ilarion. "How dare you come in here and act as though letting her give up is a gift that she's owed?"

"Look at her, Taylor." There's actual sympathy in his eyes, but I don't want to see it. Not at all.

"She's my *mother*," I hiss. "She's *our* mother. Do you think Celine will thank you for encouraging her to throw in the towel?"

"Sweetheart," Mom says, "come here."

I watch as her hand falters and falls back onto the thin hospital sheets. Sobs are clotting up in my chest and the urge to scream is overwhelming. Then I look back up at Ilarion.

His face isn't emotionless, but it's like I'm seeing that emotion through a thick wall of ice.

I need some of that in my life. Everything feels too hot and spiky and *real*. He looks like he could stare Death in the face without blinking.

My mother's eyes look more like mine than his. They're liquid with fear. Not fear of death, but fear for what—and who—she's leaving behind.

A wave of guilt crashes over me. I drop back onto her bed and clutch her hand. "I'm sorry, Mom."

"You have nothing to feel sorry about," she whispers. Every breath, every word is an effort, and I'm clinging to each one like it's about to become the last. "You've been the best daughter. I couldn't have asked for better girls." She kisses my hand and then drops it. "Ilarion, I'd like to…" She stops short for a moment, wincing. "I want to talk to you."

He steps up to her bedside. "I'm here."

There's something calming about his presence here. Ask me two hours ago, and I would've said he's the last person on Earth I'd want with me in a moment like this. But now… Now, my world is spinning out of control, and he's gravity itself.

He's stable.

He's solid.

He isn't going anywhere.

"Celine will never admit it, but I've let her down more times than I can count." Mom's confession surprises me. "She was just such a strong, independent child that it felt like she didn't need me. The truth is...I suppose I didn't know how to mother her." Mom closes her eyes for a moment. "Even when she was a little girl, *she* used to make *me* breakfast in the morning. She'd pour me a glass of juice and toast bread and bring it to me while I was nursing Taylor. That's who she is, Ilarion. She doesn't love easily, but when she loves, she loves hard."

"She's never felt neglected by you, Fiona," Ilarion reassures her.

Something inside of me constricts. He knows so much about our family. He knows more about Celine than I thought possible.

"Then she's done a good job of hiding it from you." Mom attempts a small laugh. It comes out more like a series of wincing gasps. "But I know she feels like Taylor is the favorite daughter. She would never say so to me, or to her father, because she's generous, in soul and in spirit. I may not have done as much as I should have for Celine, but I still know my daughter." She winces again, and I can tell it's taking a lot of effort to keep talking. "Promise me you'll look after her, Ilarion. She deserves to be happy. She deserves to have someone take care of her for a change."

He kneels down and takes her hand in his. I used to think the sight of her fragile fingers next to mine was jarring. It's almost horrifying to see just how skeletal she is compared to him.

The whole thing is wrong on so many different levels. I'm watching something that doesn't quite fit together the way it should.

It has nothing to do with them, though.

It's *me*.

I'm the problem.

Because every time I look at Ilarion, I'm not seeing my sister's fiancé; I'm seeing the father of my child. And when I see him talk to my mother, I feel this strange sense of warmth that should belong to Celine, not me.

"I know you're a dangerous man, Ilarion. But…" She coughs and starts again. "But I realized this morning that I don't care if you're a dangerous man—as long as you're not dangerous to her."

"You have nothing to worry about on that front."

Mom sighs. Her body unclenches slowly as she fades into her bed. "Okay then," she says, as though she's signing off for the night.

I'm terrified she's signing off forever.

"Mom." I pick up her hand again. "*Mom.* Listen to me, please?"

She turns her face toward mine and offers up a dreamy smile. It's a smile that's already somewhere else, some place I can't reach. So instead of doing everything I want to do—begging and pleading for her to stay with me—I just do the only thing left for me to do.

I lean in and hug her.

She hugs me back as best as she can. As frail as her arms are now, they still remind me of my childhood. We'd moved houses three times, changed cars six. We'd lost grandparents and pets and neighbors we loved. But those arms—those were always constant.

I can't lose them now. Not when they're wrapped around me and the baby inside me.

"Go home," Mom whispers in my ear. "Get some rest."

"Come," Ilarion murmurs to me when I linger a moment too long. "She needs to rest, too."

Reluctantly, I tear myself away from her and rise. She's asleep before the hug even breaks. Eyes closed peacefully, her breath a mere trickle through her parted lips.

He presses his hand to the small of my back and steers me towards the door. The soles of my shoes scrape the clean white tile on my way out, leaving a few faint scuff marks in my wake. I don't even manage a backward glance at Mom. I'm too far inside my own head, fighting a battle against a relentless rush of dread.

It's a battle I cannot win.

27

TAYLOR

The moment I'm in the corridor, I double over and brace my elbows on my knees. Tears sting hot in my eyes and my stomach burns. "Oh, God…"

"Taylor."

He's right. He's only said my name but I hear the whole damn speech contained in those two syllables. *You can't lose your shit right now. Pull yourself together. Get back up and keep going. Accept it and move on.*

You want me to fall to pieces? That's what he asked me on the way here. It was obvious what he thought—that falling to pieces serves nobody. You can't help anyone else hold themselves together if you yourself are scattered to the wind.

So—for my mother, for my sister, for my father—I take a deep breath and stand up tall.

I round on Ilarion. "You have to do whatever it takes to get them back!" I demand. "You saw Mom in there. It's going to take all three of us to rally around her, get her to stop this insane—"

"Is it so insane?" he asks abruptly.

I stare at him like he's suddenly sprouted three heads. "Excuse me?"

"You're being selfish." He shrugs. My mother is literally dying on the other side of the door, and he's *shrugging*.

"I'm being selfish?" I ask. "*I'm* being selfish?!"

Of course he nods. Of course he doubles down. He's not the kind of man to take back his words. He's certainly not the kind of man to throw them around loosely, either. I'd suspected as much the night we met, and it struck me as an attractive trait at the time. But now…

Now, I want to slap them out of his fucking mouth.

"You clearly don't know the first goddamn thing about family."

His eyes narrow and those dusky blue irises grow darker. "I know far more than you do," he hisses, boxing me in so close that I can count each and every last one of those thick lashes. "I know that you don't force someone you love to suffer simply because you're bad at goodbyes."

My hand twitches with the urge to hit something. Him, preferably. But I have a feeling I'd just hurt myself in the process, so I keep it fisted at my side.

"Listen, motherfucker: you may be engaged to my sister, *for now*. But that does not make you part of this family."

"No?" He puts a hand to my midsection to push me back against the wall. I feel his palm, flat and huge, against my stomach. "And what about the baby you're carrying? How does that factor me into the family?"

"It makes you the sperm donor. Nothing more. A mysterious sperm donor with no name. There's no reason you need to be a part of my baby's life at all."

"If you think I'm the kind of man who's going to walk away from my own child, then you're fucking dreaming."

"I'm doing the exact opposite of dreaming, actually." I'm furious at how shaky my voice is. "Ever since I met you, my life has been one gigantic nightmare. Why does it come as such a shock that I want to wake the hell up?"

"You—"

Whatever he's about to tell me is drowned out in a siren call that has the nurses looking panicked. They start darting around, pressing buttons, grabbing equipment that I don't recognize. Then they form a stampede heading…

In *our* direction.

"W-what's going on?" I stammer. One of the nurses brushes past me to charge into Mom's room. The moment she disappears through the door, I feel the blood drain from my face. "No…"

I'm about to burst into the room when Ilarion grabs me from behind. His arms are steel. Every bit as immovable as the man himself.

"Ilarion! Let me go!"

"Let *her* go, Taylor." His voice is low in my ear. Every bit as soft as his grip is firm. He keeps my back pinned to his chest, and no matter how hard I thrash, I don't get even an inch freer. "It's time."

"*No!*" I cry, straining against his weight. "Mom! *Mom!* Please, Ilarion!"

To my shock, he actually releases me. I fly forward and hit the door so hard that my palms throb from the impact. But by the time I get inside the room, the commotion has died down. It's eerily quiet in here. Three nurses stand helplessly around my mother's bed, and none of them seem to have any idea what to do.

"W-what are you doing?" I yell. "Help her! Fix it!"

I feel a breeze on the backs of my legs as the door opens. I assume it's Ilarion, but instead, a tall doctor in a white coat steps through. I spin on my heels to beg him for help. "Doctor, please…my mother…"

He walks over to her bed and looks down at my mother. She might as well be sleeping. That dreamy smile is still on her lips.

He sighs. It's the only sound in the room. Then he turns to me with a mask of professional sympathy. All he says is, "I'm sorry."

"I don't understand," I sob as I reach out to the wall for support. "I was… I was *just* in here!. She was awake, she was breathing—"

The doctor picks a chart up off the foot of the bed and frowns. I don't really hear much of what he's saying, or how the nurses respond. My heartbeat is drumming too loud in my ears for me to give them all my attention. But I hear enough.

"Pulled out the IV…"

"…Forcibly…"

"…Difficulty breathing…"

"…Suicidal…"

The doctor looks at me. Says something that's vaguely an apology. Instead of reaching for paddles or syringes or anything that could possibly bring her back, the nurses reach for the sheets and carefully draw them over her face.

I'm about to scream at them to do whatever it takes to bring her back to me. To stop this nonsense and do their jobs.

Then I catch sight of Ilarion by the door.

That's the sight that makes it all real. Him standing there, framed by the rectangular trim, tall and huge and so grim-faced. When I see that, I know I'm not dreaming. I'm not having a nightmare, either.

This is real.

I can't breathe. The doctor's condolences are drowned out in my own despair. I just want to close my eyes and sleep forever. When my knees buckle, I expect pain to follow immediately after.

But someone catches me. I know who without having to look.

And despite everything…

It feels good to be caught.

28

ILARION

Taylor falls asleep before we even arrive back at the Diamond. I carry her up to the master bedroom and lay her down on the bed. Her dirty blonde hair fans around her face, but she never stirs, not even when I slip off her shoes and pull a cover sheet over her goosebump-riddled skin.

When was the last time I put someone to bed like this?

The memory forms clear as day. It was years ago now, and I was on the cusp of becoming *pakhan*. Mila hadn't been nearly as deathly still as Taylor is now, though. She'd tossed and turned, her sleep as fractured and broken as the nightmare that was her waking life. I'll never forget the smear of blood at the corner of her mouth. The busted lip. The fingerprints practically tattooed across her throat.

"What are you doing?"

Speak of the devil. I turn towards the door and find Mila standing there, watching me watch Taylor.

"She fell asleep in the car," I explain gruffly, glancing away.

"That's not what I meant." She strides into the room and stops at my side. "I mean, what the hell do you think you're doing marrying one sister and romancing the other?"

"Mila—"

"No, don't 'Mila' me. You use that tone any time you know you're wrong but you're still trying to outrank me. You may be the *pakhan*, but you're still my brother."

"So you insist on reminding me."

"Only because you refuse to listen," she snaps. "The baby's yours, isn't it?"

Denying it would be meaningless at this point, and I don't have the energy to go through a whole song and dance. "Yes."

"For God's sake," Mila breathes. "How could you—"

"You think this was planned?" When I hear how loud I sound, I wince and drop my voice lower. Even though she's out cold, I don't want to risk waking Taylor from her much-needed sleep. "You think I *chose* this?"

Mila arches a brow. "You expect me to believe that this is a coincidence?"

I grit my teeth and lean against the bedpost. "I met Taylor first. Nearly ran over her in Evanston. Celine and I didn't meet until two weeks later."

"You met her *in Evanston*?" Mila asks. "And that didn't tip you off?"

"How the hell was I supposed to know? There's a hundred thousand people jammed into that town. And it's not like the two of them look alike."

Mila scoffs. "Oh, sure, and it's not like you had plenty of time to do your research, either. Gather intel. *Verify relations.*"

Taylor stirs a bit in her sleep. Incensed, I grab Mila's elbow and drag her out of the room. She shakes me off when we're on the other side of the door, her nose scrunched in disdain.

"Where's Dima?" I ask her.

"Oh, no, you don't," she snaps. "We were in the middle of a conversation."

"Which I'd rather not have."

"Tough—we need to have it. If for no other reason than to figure out damage control for this *huge fucking oversight.*"

"I can handle it myself."

"Can you?" she scoffs. "Because from where I'm standing, this whole thing is a ticking time bomb about to explode in your face."

"Celine, I can handle," I growl. "Taylor…I'll find a way to handle."

Mila holds a hand up, dangerously close to pressing against my face. "I'm still trying to wrap my brain around how you missed this. Didn't you check the family before you even went?"

Not well enough. I grind my molars together. I know I rushed through what should have been a much more thorough reconnaissance. I just cannot afford to openly admit it.

"…Yes."

I know she can smell the bullshit. "And didn't Celine mention having a sister? Even casually?"

"She did," I admit. "Often. But the woman I almost hit with my car didn't give me her name."

"You turned a narrowly avoided traffic fatality into a one-night-stand? Even for you, Ilarion, that's scraping the bottom of the barrel." She tries to hide the derisive laugh behind her hand.

I want to throttle her laugh away. Not because it's irritating—but because it's irritatingly well-deserved.

I nearly committed vehicular manslaughter, and my first inclination was to fuck a baby into the unsuspecting pedestrian.

Yet another thing I absolutely cannot afford to openly admit in front of the Bratva. These are the people who depend on me to make wise decisions and always act with a carefully thought-out strategic plan. The people who trust me to lead with my brain and not my dick. The people who would riot if they knew what I've done.

"Mila—"

"Wow," she breathes before I can deliver my mea culpa. "That must have been one hot night. Gives a whole new meaning to the word 'plowed.'"

I glare at her. "It wasn't meant to happen at all. It was…a lapse in judgment on my part."

She guffaws. "Ya think? It's kind of amazing, actually. You kept yourself off the shelf for so long, and when you do finally jump into the dating pool—you catch your fiancée's sister? When they say there's more than one fish in the sea, I don't think they mean that there's only two of them."

"I'm glad you're finding all this so amusing. I don't. It was—"

"Yeah, a lapse in judgment—you said that already. I know what it was. You know what else it was? *Stupid.* It was so fucking stupid, Ilarion. And your plan, which apparently you're still sticking to, is insane."

"Which is exactly why it's going to work. The Bellasios aren't going to see this coming."

"Maybe not. But neither will your woman. Excuse me—wom*en*," Mila points out. "At some point, Celine is going to figure it out. She's no dummy."

"She's in love with me," I say, unable to keep the regret from my tone. "I can convince her of anything."

Mila flashes me a sarcastic smile. "Charming. Love that plan. And what about *her*?" She glances at the bedroom door. "Something tells me this one's not going to be nearly so easy to emotionally manipulate."

"Like I said—I'll figure it out."

Just as soon as my sister is done psychoanalyzing my every move.

Mila crosses her arms and smolders. I find myself wondering how I missed her transition from giggling little girl who used to follow me around like a puppy to this spitfire woman constantly questioning me. Constantly challenging me to be a better leader.

I love her for it—but my God, it's a pain in my fucking ass.

"There's going to be a baby in a few months, Ilarion."

"I understand how pregnancies work."

She rolls her eyes and sighs. "I suppose none of this really matters until we get Celine back. *If* we do."

"There's no *if*. We will get Celine back," I snap. "That part is imperative."

She shrugs. "But still. If we don't…at least we have a spare." She jerks her chin in the direction of Taylor's room. Her eyes are hooded with darkness, her features foiled together with detached professionalism.

Is that new, or was that always there?

She had been such a lively little girl. Her laugh came easy and her smile was constant. Somewhere around her fourteenth birthday, she lost that smile, and it never quite came back.

Even after I'd delivered her the head of her monster.

It just goes to show—killing your demons doesn't really end the torment. Real monsters leave behind damage. You can slay the beast a million times over—but the scars they inflict last forever.

29

ILARION

"Come," I say, leading Mila to my office.

It's bright in here. I had them rip out the curtains when I first made this place my home away from home. I hate dark spaces. Always have. Mila does, too. It's the reason she still sleeps with a light on.

Makes it easier to spot when there's a monster coming.

I take a seat on the brown leather sofa. Mila bypasses the seating area and goes right to the bar. She doesn't have to ask what I'm drinking—she just pours two vodkas and brings them back over.

I toy with it for a long, quiet spell, dragging my finger in slow circles through the condensation. She finishes most of her drink before I've even taken a sip of mine.

"Heard anything from Dima yet?" I ask when she sets the glass down.

"Still undercover," she explains. "I got a text from him a few hours ago, but nothing since. Said he's got a lead. He's following it as we speak."

I nod. "I'll need you to keep an eye on Taylor for me."

Mila sighs. "I thought you might. What do you want me to extract?"

"I don't want you to extract anything," I tell her. "I just need you to look after her."

She frowns. "Look after her?"

"She lost her mother tonight."

"Oh." Her voice falls flat.

Mother. As far as Mila is concerned, it's a dirty word.

"We're going to have to help her bury Fiona, and I don't think Celine or Archie are going to be around to support her through the process."

"So *I* have to?" She snorts. "Ilarion, you know I'm not good with that type of thing. You're setting me up for failure here."

"It might help you. You know, to have a woman your own age to spend some time with."

She narrows her eyes. "Are you trying to set me up with the mother of your child?"

"I'm trying to keep her here. It's not safe for her out in the wild with the Bellasios running rampant. If it was just her, that would be one thing. But she's carrying my baby."

"Ah, I see," Mila muses shrewdly. "You want me to do it so that *you* don't have to."

I bristle and say nothing. She's got me there and she knows it. No point adding kindling to her fire.

"She's really made an impact on you, hasn't she?"

I bristle. "She's pregnant. My interest in her ends there."

"You haven't been with a woman in months, dear brother," she says with a playful smirk. "What was it about this particular specimen that caught your interest?"

"You don't know a damn thing about who I've been with."

"Dima talks," she answers dismissively. "Like an old fishwife, actually."

"That fucking—"

She raises her hands. "Oh, calm down. We were just worried about you."

"You were worried I wasn't getting laid?"

"Well, Dima was worried about that. I was just worried that you were fixating too much on Benedict Bellasio. I don't actually give two shits about your sex life."

"The two of you need to get lives of your own."

She rolls her eyes. "You didn't answer my question."

"I didn't hear any questions in there."

"What about Taylor caught your interest?"

I don't expect a dozen different answers to float up to my lips the moment the question leaves Mila's.

Her warm eyes. Her luscious lips. How her moan sounds in a sweat-slicked car when the rain is pounding on the roof overhead...

But even as I rattle off the list in my head, I realize it had more to do with the way she'd fought back. The way she'd matched me, stride for stride, without any fear. The way she tempered that strength with enough vulnerability to make me understand what was fueling all her rage.

The way she'd opened up and let me in. The way she'd made me feel like a man. Not a mob boss. Not a killer.

Just a man.

"Well?" Mila presses. "I'm all ears."

"Nothing. Nothing about her interested me," I growl. "I was just horny."

30

TAYLOR

It's an ocean of flowers in front of me. Pastel pinks and eye-burning oranges and whites in cream, ivory, and eggshell. The color cacophony is making my head swim.

"Do you want to go carnations or gladioli?"

I blink at Mila, wondering why she's here at all. She clearly doesn't want to be. Not that she's said anything to that effect. It's just this distant look in her eyes that gives me the impression she'd rather be anywhere else than here.

I don't blame her; I don't want to be here, either.

The display window has *Chapman's Floral Boutique* printed in elegant gold script across the glass. I've passed this place before, more than once. Three years ago, I walked in to buy Mom flowers for her forty-sixth birthday. They were so expensive that I walked right back out, with only a single red rose in hand because it was all I could afford on my college-student budget.

I'd filled a champagne flute with water and stuck the rose in there. Celine and I put it on the side of her breakfast tray, and I vowed that I'd go back to Chapman's one day and buy Mom a proper bouquet of flowers when I could afford it.

Now, here I am.

Too little, too late.

"Taylor?" When I don't turn around, Mila steps in front of me, forcing herself into my eyeline. "I need you to make some decisions here. What kinds of flowers do you want on your mother's funeral wreath?"

I cringe and shake my head. "I don't care," I whisper. "You choose."

"She's not my mother."

"Well, maybe if she had been, you'd have been a fuck-ton nicer," I snap viciously before I twist around and walk to the opposite end of the store.

I stop in front of a trough filled with orchids. They're gorgeous. Whisper-soft and ethereal. But as beautiful as they are, my eye goes to the yellow sunflowers sitting next to them in a rough cement vase.

A tear slips down my cheek. *It's a dark world sometimes. I think it could use some brightening.* Mom's words, not mine. As always, I hated them whenever I heard them. As always, she was right.

"Here."

I look down and realize that Mila is offering me a tissue. I take it gingerly and wipe away my tears. I'm so wrecked right now that I don't even care that I'm crying in front of her. I don't give a damn who sees me sobbing. Her or her brother or the whole damn world—let them all watch.

Let them all know I loved her.

"I'm sorry," Mila says in the awkward, curt voice of someone unused to apologizing. "I… I'm not good with this kind of thing."

"Death?" I mumble. I hold back the urge to arch a brow. I've seen just how much death she should be "good with."

"No," she says. "Not death, per se. Just the sensitivity that should come with it. I've buried two parents now, and I didn't cry at either one of their funerals. I didn't even go to my mother's."

"Why not?"

She shrugs. "I was only nine when she died. I guess I was more interested in playing with my dolls. I didn't really process that it was a permanent sort of thing, anyway." She scowls when she sees my jaw drop. "You don't need to feel sorry for me. She wasn't really cut out to be a mother."

"Still, it can't have been easy."

She lifts her eyes to mine, and for just a second, I glimpse a flash of her inner trauma. Scars seen from a distance, but ugly and twisted enough to trigger a moment of sympathy pain.

"I had Ilarion," she says softly. "He made things easy for me."

It's the first thing she's said that makes her feel *human*. It's also the first time I realize that her love for Ilarion goes far deeper than I realized. It's just hidden behind a veneer of aloof disinterest.

"I wish Celine were here with me," I admit. We finally have some common ground and I'm going to take advantage. "Sometimes, I don't realize how much she supports me, until she's not around to do it."

"Maybe that's a good thing," Mila suggests. "Relying on other people is a good way to get—to be disappointed."

To get hurt. Those were the words she'd just avoided saying. And it begs the question: how many people have hurt her?

Enough to have broken the naive little girl who used to play with dolls, clearly.

Mila clears her throat, an obvious ploy to change the subject. "Do you really want me to choose the flowers?"

"I…" I trail off as I continue staring at the sunflowers. They're pretty, but altogether too happy a flower for a funeral. "You're right. I should be the one to choose them."

And then I burst into tears.

It's a pattern I've been dealing with over the last twenty-four hours: I'm fine, I'm handling it all, and then I'm not. It's just worse right now because I'm in public.

A few heads swivel in my direction, but I can't stop the shaking sobs from pouring out. The dam is broken, and I have enough experience to know that trying to stop the tears will only make them come harder.

"*Blyat'*," I hear Mila mutter under her breath as she steers me to a secluded corner of the store.

She sits me down in a cushioned chair beside a large clay pot filled with lilies. "Everyone here probably thinks I'm crazy," I mumble once I've exhausted Mila's tissue supply.

"Oh, fuck them." She rolls her eyes, pulling up a chair next to me. "Caring about what other people think is a waste of time."

I glance at her sidelong. The question has been on the tip of my tongue this whole time, but now it feels more appropriate to ask. "Mila, why are you here?"

"You'd prefer to be alone?"

"No, I mean, why did you come out with me today? You don't even like me."

"I don't like anyone," she says, like it's a self-evident fact. In a way, it is. "So don't take that personally. And as for why I came with you today…" She sighs. "No one should have to be alone in their grief."

"Is that code for 'my brother made me'?" I guess with a pained laugh.

She smiles. "Both things can be true at the same time."

I gnaw at the inside of my cheek and pick the beds of my nails simultaneously. All my nervous habits coming to play at once. "Your brother knows what he's doing, right?"

She nods with understanding of the question behind the question. "You're worried he won't be able to rescue your sister."

"And my dad," I remind her. "I want them both back."

She nods again, her expression falling back into impassivity. "If anyone can get them back, it's Ilarion." She says it like she believes it. That makes me believe it, too.

Somewhat.

I run a hand over my face. "I've been going over that day over and over again in my head," I whisper hoarsely. "Why would they take Celine? She doesn't have anything to do with whatever dispute they have with Ilarion."

"Yes, but the Bellasios got wind of their engagement. They see Celine as a bargaining chip they can use to control Ilarion," she explains.

I hate that it makes so much sense.

"What about my dad?"

Her expression remains hard to read, but I get the feeling she's trying not to upset me further. "I don't know, Taylor," she hedges after a long, hesitant pause. "Maybe they took him as insurance. I can't claim to know what Benedict Bellasio's plan is."

I shake my head. "Celine can't have known about all this. The Bellasios, the feud, any of it. She would never have gotten involved with Ilarion if she'd known."

Mila raises an eyebrow. "Or maybe you don't know your sister as well as you think you do."

"You know, I'm getting really sick of people telling me that," I snap, jumping to my feet. "Maybe you guys are the ones who don't know us."

"Okay." Mila follows me with her calculating gaze. "You think you know your sister so well? Tell me: how will she react to your pregnancy?"

My hands flutters to my stomach automatically. "I… That…" I take a deep breath. "As far as I'm concerned, Celine doesn't have to know who the father of this baby is. But she'll be happy for me nonetheless."

I feel like an asshole for even thinking it, but that's the only path forward that I can see.

Mila nods. "There's things you don't tell your sister. Well, maybe the same is true for her, too. You can know a person your entire life and still not really *know* them."

"Who hurt you?" The question flies out of my mouth before my brain can even register it.

I expect her to avoid answering, but she meets my eyes levelly. "My mother was the first. My father was the second and the last. The only person who has ever had my back is Ilarion. Which is how I know he'll get your sister back. Whatever my brother does, he does for the family. For his Bratva. And he doesn't let emotion get in the way of what he knows he must do." She sighs and rises to her feet. "Now, I know it's hard, but you've got to pick the flowers for your mother's funeral. We can't linger here forever."

Something nags at my brain as I follow Mila to the front of the store. *He doesn't let emotion get in the way of what he knows he must do.* Mila might think that's a positive characteristic.

But it scares the shit out of me.

"Well?" Mila says when we're faced with the florist. "What's it going to be?"

"I want yellow," I tell the lady behind the counter. "Yellow sunflowers. As many as you have."

"Yellow?" The florist looks at me, a bit uncertain. "Are you sure, ma'am? People usually go with white for funerals."

Given how I feel right now, I'd be picking out rotting black flowers if I could find them. But this is not about me or what I want. This is about what my mother would have wanted.

And she wanted to go.

The least I can do is make her last moments above ground a little bit brighter.

31

ILARION

I'm in the gym pushing through the burn of a bench press when Dima finds me.

He's dressed in a scruffy black hoodie and ripped jean shorts that end just above his knees. "What the hell are you wearing?" I scoff, looking at his clothes with distaste as I rack the weights.

"Kiss my ass, man. I was undercover."

"As what? A douche-y high school jock with a room temperature IQ?"

Dima rolls his dark eyes and sits on the bench across from me. "Do you want to know what I found out or not?"

"Fine."

He pushes up his sleeves and cracks his knuckles as he launches into his report. "My intel suggests that they're being held in separate locations. I've got a lead that's close to cracking. I just have to find the right incentive to make him talk."

"Fists usually work."

"You'll catch more flies with honey than with vinegar," Dima says, running his hand over his fresh crew cut.

"I had a *vor* who used to say that. He's dead now."

Dima picks at a fraying thread on the bench. "Don't worry; I'll use my fists if I have to. The guy's weak. He's on the verge of singing like the fat lady, and when he does, I'll be able to deliver you both Celine and Archie."

"If it comes to a choice—"

"Don't worry." He very obviously resists rolling his eyes again. "I know which one to choose."

"Good." I load a hundred more pounds onto the bar and get in position for another set. My arms are trembling and burning, but I know better than anyone that pain is a hungry bitch. If you give into it, it only asks for more and more, until you have nothing left to give and nothing to show for your effort.

You ignore pain. You never feed it.

Lust is exactly the same.

Dima watches me with a sour expression. "You don't need to show off, you know. We get it. You're strong." He sighs and scratches at the back of his head. "How are things here, by the way?"

I tense and sit up, abandoning the weights altogether. "Mila's helping Taylor plan her mother's funeral."

He winces. "Fuck. Fiona's dead?"

"I forget how much you miss when you go undercover," I muse. "She died yesterday. Punctured her carotid after extracting a promise from me on her deathbed."

"Christ," Dima curses, his eyes going wide. "What was the promise?"

"That I'd take care of her daughter."

"Yeah? Which one?" I narrow my eyes and he gives me an apologetic smile. "Come on, brother, I've seen the way you look at Taylor."

That rankles, because I do not look at her in any specific way. In fact, I take pains to avoid looking at her altogether.

"Tell me: how do I 'look at her'?" I drawl.

"Like a man who hates the fact that he can't *stop* looking at her," he says with a shrug. "I saw the two of you in the corridor talking during the engagement party."

"So?" I say. "It was small talk."

"Brother," Dima chides, "it didn't look like small talk. It looked like a full-blown argument between two…"

"Two what?"

"Well…two lovers," he explains. "And, just a heads up, I wasn't the only one who noticed you. Celine was watching when I walked up to her. I tried to talk to her, get her attention off you, but she was definitely…*distracted*."

"Who was distracted?" Mila asks, walking in. She stops short when she catches sight of Dima. "Dima!" she cries, flying to him and throwing herself into his arms.

He catches her in a bear hug and presses a kiss to her cheek. "You been keeping busy while I was away?"

"I guess," she says, releasing him and sitting down on the bench next to him. "Boss man stuck me with the boring job. I think this is the first time in my life I've had to pretend like I cared about flowers. It went about as expected."

"I heard about the funeral," Dima says, turning to me. "When's it gonna be?"

"Tomorrow," I reply. "Arrangements have been made."

"You're going to do it without Celine?" Dima asks. He sounds as incredulous as he looks.

"That was Taylor's decision." I lift my hands up in self-defense. "Apparently, Fiona wanted to be buried as soon as possible after her death. I told her we could keep her on ice, wait it out. She refused. Vocally."

I watch Mila, waiting for her to supply more information on their day together, but she remains tight-lipped about the outing.

"What did you find out?" she asks, bumping shoulders with Dima.

"Nothing yet, but I should have something soon."

Mila shakes her head. "This is why you should have sent me undercover. Celine would have been here for the funeral."

Dima scoffs. "Please, you think you're better than me?"

"Without a doubt," Mila says, her smile cracking a little easier now that Dima is back. "By the way, what the hell are you wearing? You look like you belong in a *Say No to Drugs* commercial."

"Geez," Dima mutters, scowling. "The Zakharov siblings and their exacting fashion standards. Will this make you both happy?" He stands up and pulls the hoodie over his head.

He's wearing a white ribbed-cotton tank top that shows off his muscled arms, and the hoodie momentarily catches the hem and drags it up over his stomach. I catch Mila taking a long look before she pointedly turns away. It's not the first time I've seen her check him out, but I figure if "that" hasn't happened all this time, it never will.

The scars on my sister's heart might just be too much to overcome.

"Now, you look like a street rat," Mila mutters, though her cheeks are flushed.

"There's no making you happy, is there?"

"Some people aren't meant to be happy." Only part of her tone sounds sarcastic. "Anyway—what were you two talking about before I walked in?"

"Nothing," I blurt.

Dima looks at me with raised brows.

"Aw, come on, you can't leave me out of the loop," Mila whines. "Dima? Wanna rat?"

"Never mind," he mumbles and looks away, his version of waving her off. He's better at reading the room than my sister. Between the two of them, he's usually the one to know when to let things go.

"Does this have something to do with the baby?"

Dima looks startled. "What baby?"

Mila stares at him in shock, then at me. "You haven't told him?"

"Told me what?" Dima presses. "There's a baby I don't know about? Whose? Where? What species?"

"Mine," I growl, suddenly remembering why I prefer to be alone most days. "Taylor is pregnant."

Dima does nothing but blink at me for a long moment. "I'm sorry—did you just say that Taylor is pregnant? Taylor, as in, Celine's sister?"

"That's the one," Mila says, looking like she's enjoying herself a little too much. "Talk about sister wives, huh?"

"You are not funny," I snarl at her, before looking at Dima. "I was going to tell you. I'm still processing it myself."

"*Fuuuuck*," Dima groans. "This is…big."

"That's what I keep saying. It also screws up the whole plan." Mila rolls her eyes and sighs.

"It doesn't screw up anything," I spit. "It's a wrench in the works, that's all. I'm going to handle it."

"How?" Dima arches a very skeptical brow. "Celine seems like a top-notch gal and all, very laid-back, but there's no way she's going to be okay with you having a baby with her sister."

"Hell, if I were Celine, I'd stab you in the heart," Mila teases, flashing me a wolfish grin.

I grit my teeth. "My first priority is getting Celine back. The rest, I will deal with after."

"Or, hear me out now," Dima suggests. "You could marry Taylor instead of Celine."

"Fucking hell," I grumble, getting to my feet. I've always been an angry pacer, and right now, I'm on the cusp of being furious. It has nothing to do with Dima or Mila, though. This is about all the control I've managed to lose in a matter of days. "Not a goddamn chance."

"Why not?" Dima insists. "You need a wife. The fact that they're sisters is actually pretty convenient. You have your leverage, *and* you have your heir. It's perfect."

Mila sighs and shakes her head. "Except for the fact that Taylor would never agree to it."

"Does she need to?" Dima asks innocently.

"Even if she was open to it, I'm not," I insist. Something tugs inside my chest when I say it, but I very quickly and pointedly ignore it.

"What are you trying to prove, big brother?" Mila asks shrewdly.

I glare at her until she lowers her gaze. "Celine is teachable. Taylor is not. I need a wife who can do the job, and Taylor is too opinionated and combative. Celine, on the other hand… She'll be easy to mold."

Mila twists with disgust. But I don't give a damn about her propriety.

I need to marry Celine because she's a means to an end. Taylor, on the other hand? She could be the start of something I never asked for in the first place.

Disaster.

32

TAYLOR

"Are you okay?"

I turn my back on the tall man who spoke. I've seen him by Ilarion's side fairly often. I return to my hyperventilating, hoping he'll get the hint and leave.

Instead, I see his shadow grow bigger as he moves closer to me.

It took some time to find this little corner of the church. It's partly hidden by tall columns and tucked away behind the looming arrangement of sunflowers I ordered from Chapman's on Ilarion's credit card. It smelled like Mom back here, just a fleeting whiff of it, and it felt like the perfect place to panic and cry and melt down out of sight.

I don't appreciate him invading my oasis.

Not that I have the energy—or the oxygen—to tell him to fuck off.

"Breathe from your diaphragm," he instructs me. I hate how gentle and reassuring his voice sounds. "Try to slow your thoughts."

I glare at him from my hunched position. "If…if I could…do that…I would…be able to…to *breathe*."

He smiles placidly. He's handsome. Not in the dark, broody, confronting way that Ilarion is, but more of a boyish charm. Non-threatening. Approachable. I have a feeling the faded crew cut was a way of giving those pretty features some grit, but I'm not sure it has the desired effect.

"Here," he says, offering me something in his hand. "Have one."

"I don't do drugs," I inform him, disregarding the little bag in his palm.

"Your loss," he says. "But incidentally, they're not drugs. Not the harmful kind, anyway."

I straighten slowly and take another glance at his palm. On closer inspection, they appear to be… "Are those toffees?"

He nods. "*Iriski*. They make them special at this little coffee shop in Kazan. It's toffee with a chocolate center. You have to work to get to the chocolate, but lemme tell you, it's so worth it."

I eye him suspiciously. "It's not spiked or anything, is it?"

He recoils in horror. "Do I look like the kind of guy who'd do a thing like that?"

"No. Sorry." I reach out and take one of the toffees from his bag.

"Not everyone gets offered an *iriski* from my personal stash, so consider yourself lucky." He takes one for himself and pops it into his mouth.

"You'll excuse me if I don't consider myself lucky today."

He meets my gaze and gives me a sympathetic smile. "Hey, I get it. You loved your mother. You don't want to have to say goodbye. But you know that cheesy saying?"

"Which one?"

"Um, something about hard goodbyes and people you love."

"I'm lucky to have someone who makes saying goodbye so hard."

He snaps his fingers, pleased. "That's the ticket. Walt Whitman, I think. Or maybe Gandhi. Can't recall."

"It's from *Winnie the Pooh*."

"Is it? Well, I'll be damned. That doesn't sound quite as sophisticated. You sure it wasn't Gandhi?"

A corner of my mouth wants to twitch up in a smile, but the rest of me is still heavy with grief. "Yeah. Mom used to read us *Winnie the Pooh* tales when Celine and I were little girls. We had a whole collection. It's still in the attic somewhere. She never threw anything away."

"You know what my mom used to read me when I was a boy?" he asks. He pauses for dramatic effect before delivering his punchline: "The riot act."

I roll my eyes as I bite back a snotty laugh. "I'm sure that was the story that never ended."

He snorts. "You don't know the half of it. She wouldn't just read me the riot act, either. She had a cane that she named

Horace, and she liked to say that 'Horace was gonna come visit me' if I didn't behave. Mind you, her definition of 'behaving' changed daily. Some days, it meant I couldn't track dirt into the house. Other days, I didn't tighten the cap on the milk carton to her liking. Horace hurt the same either way."

"Is this your way of reminding me that I'm lucky to have had my sweet, loving mother who read me storybooks before bed?"

"Phew, glad you got that. I was worried I was too subtle."

Finally, I can't help it—I smile. But it's grudging. "What was your name again?"

"Dima."

"Dima," I repeat, finally unwrapping the toffee and popping it into my mouth. The caramel hits my taste buds like a boost of pure adrenaline, and I feel my body rally around the rush of sugar. "Did Mila send you over here?"

"No, why would she?"

"Because she's tired of babysitting me."

"Neither one of us are babysitting you," he says in a tone that's naturally—and, given his line of work, strangely—compassionate. "We're just…looking out for you."

"Why?"

That takes him back. "Because you're important." He says it like I'm supposed to already know.

I suck on the caramel and peek around Dima's shoulder. The service will start soon. I can see people filing through the doors. I'd informed our extended family only this morning in the hopes that most of them might not make it. We've got a whole mess of aunts, uncles, and cousins in Denver who won't make the journey. But I notice Uncle Peter and Aunt Monica waltz into the church in their best mourning attire.

I ought to go out there and greet them. But it's so much easier standing here, sucking on a toffee behind a wall of sunflowers, talking to a violent yet weirdly thoughtful stranger about storybooks and dead mothers.

It's like the world I've always known has already been left behind.

And I'll never, ever get it back.

I turn my attention back to Dima. "'I'm important'? What you really mean to say is that my baby is important. Am I right?"

He just smiles. "I like you, Taylor," he says simply. "You've got that no-nonsense *je ne sais quoi* that I've always appreciated in a woman."

"Then you should hook up with Mila," I half-joke. "That woman is the epitome of no-nonsense. Probably because of that giant stick she has up her ass."

He snorts with laughter, which draws Mila's attention. She's standing across the pews, speaking to some guy in a full suit and dark shades. A member of the security detail, no doubt.

Dima irons out his grin and pretends like he wasn't just laughing at a funeral. "Funny—she says the same thing about you."

"I just lost my entire family in the span of a few hours. What's her excuse?"

"Oh, she has a few tragic excuses of her own," he says cryptically.

I want to ask about what he means, but she glances our way again and I decide to tuck that question away for later. I glance toward the other side of the church to see if I can spot her brother, but I'm pretty sure if he was here, I'd have seen him by now. Ilarion's not the type of man who can go very long without being noticed.

"Neither one of you have to be here, you know."

"I know. I—" He groans as his lashes flutter like he's orgasming. "Oh, yeah…Finally hit that chocolate. Got there yet?"

I shake my head. "Not yet." I fidget in place for a minute before I work up the courage to look at Dima again. "Can I ask you a question?"

"That's one."

I roll my eyes. "Can I ask you another question?"

"That's another one."

"Oh, for God's sake—I'm trying to ask who you are."

"Who am I?" he parrots.

"Yeah, like…" I wave a hand around. "In all this. Who are you to Ilarion?"

"His right hand man, of course," he answers. "And the token eye candy, obviously. I'm sure you guessed that part, though."

"So you've known him a long time?"

"Since we were nineteen." He scrunches his face in thought. "So…nine years now. Shit. I'm old."

I ignore his joking. The man is constitutionally incapable of being serious. "And do you believe he loves my sister?"

I'm watching close enough that I don't miss the way he stiffens when I pose the question. From across the church, Mila is firing questioning glances our way like she can sense us wandering into dangerous territory, but Dima doesn't notice.

"I mean, he asked her to marry him. I think love is implied."

"You would think," I agree dourly. "But something Mila said the other day got me thinking. She believes that her brother doesn't do anything without a reason. She also believes that he doesn't let emotion get in the way of his decisions."

Dima doesn't say anything. I think he's starting to realize just how thin the ice beneath our feet is.

"A man like that would never marry impulsively. And an engagement after only two months… Seems out of character for him, wouldn't you say?"

Dima shrugs. "If you believe *Winnie the Pooh,* love is the kind of thing that makes you do things out of character," he says. "And Ilarion doesn't like to be predictable."

I shake my head. I know a runaround when I hear it. "Do you think I'm an idiot, Dima?" I ask. It's blunt, maybe even a little rude.

But so is trying to sidestep the obvious.

He arches his brow, but there's an amused smile underneath his surprise. "No, Taylor. Less and less so with every passing second."

I nod. "Good. I understand why you're willing to lie for Ilarion. I appreciate loyalty. You're protecting your family.

Just remember—that's exactly what I'm doing for mine."

I take a deep breath and prepare myself to face the music. Can't hide forever, as they say. "Thank you for the *iriski*," I say, before walking out of my hiding spot.

I reluctantly make my way toward the small group of Theron relations gathered around the casket holding my mother. It's a closed casket, but that hasn't stopped people from approaching for their final regards.

"Darling!" Aunt Monica says, spotting me first as I walk up to them. She grabs me and pulls me into her soft, expansive body. "Darling, we had no idea the cancer had progressed so far."

I nod, hating the lie I forced myself to tell. "It was very sudden."

"Where's Celine?" Uncle Peter asks. "And your father?"

And there it is—the question I've been dreading since I picked the damn flowers. Which, now that I see them here in the chapel, are entirely too yellow.

"Celine's with Archie."

I startle when I feel a warm hand press to my side. Ilarion steps into our loose circle as though he belongs there. As though he's *always* belonged there. My aunt and uncle look at him with wide eyes laced with shock.

I can't exactly blame them. The man has a way of eating up the atmosphere in a room. It gets harder to breathe, harder to move, harder to do anything but gawk.

"Sorry to interrupt. We haven't met yet," Ilarion says, taking my aunt's hand first, then my uncle's. "I'm Ilarion, Celine's fiancé."

"Oh!" Aunt Monica breathes, her eyes trailing over Ilarion in amazement. "Fiona did mention the engagement to me when we last spoke. I think… Wasn't it the day of the engagement when she called me? Oh, how awful for Celine, to have lost dear Fiona so soon before she could see you wed."

"You said Celine's with Archie," Uncle Peter grumbles impatiently, dispensing with the polite condolences. "Where are they?"

"Fiona's death was sudden," Ilarion explains. Probably the only time I'll actually be grateful for his interruption. "Archie…didn't take it well."

Scratch that. He should have consulted with me before grabbing the reins and making shit up.

"So Celine's at a private clinic with him, trying to soothe him through this very difficult day. I'm here representing Celine. And of course, to support Taylor." He nods at me, tacking me on like an afterthought.

Uncle Peter clears his throat gruffly. "Right. Of course. I'm sorry, Taylor. This can't be easy for you."

"No," I say, glaring at Ilarion. "It's not. I—"

"If you'll excuse me," Ilarion says abruptly. "I need to go speak to the priest before the service starts. It was nice to meet you both. I just wish it had been under happier circumstances."

He turns and walks away, taking that all-consuming presence with him.

The most shocking part of all?

I'm actually disappointed to see him go.

33

TAYLOR

A strange sense of numbness engulfs me when I watch the casket being lowered into the ground.

I stop feeling much of anything. I concentrate on the lingering sweetness of *iriski* in my mouth and Ilarion's rich scent in my nostrils.

Not that he's standing anywhere near me.

He's taken up a post on the opposite side of the yawning chasm in the earth. It feels strategic, deliberate—though I can't decide if the point is to make me look at him or to make me feel all alone. Either way, it's working.

Mila and Dima flank me on either side. It might have been touching, if it weren't for the fact that I know they were ordered to do it.

They aren't here to comfort me.

They're here to watch me.

The moment the casket settles into the deep soil, I turn and walk away. I can feel them all gawking, but to my surprise, no one stops me.

I find a spot under a weeping willow surrounded by concentric rings of weathered gravestones. I sit on the soft bed of grass and read the closest inscription.

Maya Crane. Beloved wife to Thomas Crane. Devoted mother to Daisy and Henry Crane.

She was forty-two when she died. Even younger than Mom.

It strikes me how odd it is that we make cemeteries beautiful. It can't be for the dead that we tend the grass and water the flowers, right? I mean, they're obviously not around to appreciate it. It has to be for us, then. For the living. The ones left behind.

I wonder what stole Maya from her family. An accident? An illness? Fate? In the wrong place at the wrong engagement party?

I laugh bitterly under my breath. My mom hasn't been in the ground for more than two minutes and I'm already making sick jokes. Maybe I *am* fucked up in the head.

I glance up and notice Ilarion watching me from a distance. He turns away when I catch his gaze. Again, I feel the sting I felt when he brushed past me at the gravesite and kept walking clear to the other side.

I'm not sure why I expected him to stand next to me. I shouldn't expect a damn thing from him.

If he's here for any reason at all, it's for Celine. Not me.

I need to keep reminding myself of that. To keep pressing on that emotional bruise until finally—hopefully—it stops hurting.

"Taylor, honey?"

I look up and squint. "Aunt Marianne? Oh my god!"

I'm struggling to my feet when she stops me. "Don't bother. I'll get down there with you," she says with a wave of her fingers, lowering herself heavily onto the grass next to me.

She clutches my hand the moment she's seated and takes a deep breath. "I'm sorry I missed the service. I got on a plane the moment I got your message, but—"

"It's okay." I feel like a bitch for hoping that no one would show up. That was me being incredibly selfish. "I'm sorry it was so last-minute."

"Terrible things never have good timing, do they?" She knocks her shoulder gently against mine.

I gulp. She has no idea.

"I can't believe you flew across the country to be here at the drop of a hat."

She sighs and grief lines consume her face. "I really shouldn't say this, but she's dead now, so I'll say whatever the fuck I want: Fiona was always my favorite sister."

I almost snort at the sudden and unexpected curse word coming from my otherwise graceful aunt. Instead, I give her a warm smile. "I know. And I really shouldn't say this, but you were hers."

She pats my hand as a tear slips down her cheek. "Monica's not all bad, you know. She's just fussy. Too serious about everything. But your momma, she knew how to have fun even when life was shitty. And life was really shitty for her the last few years."

My own eyes sting with fresh tears. I thought I was out of those by now, but I guess not. I'm not sure if I'm crying because Aunt Marianne knows exactly how much these last few years have hurt, or because, when I close my eyes, her perfume smells just like Mom's used to.

She keeps patting my hand. It's like she's trying to remind me that I'm not alone. "So," she says, "is that Celine's man?"

I glance in the direction she's looking and spot Ilarion talking to a few of Mom's cousins. We were never very close to any of them, but they live in the state, so they couldn't avoid coming.

"That's him," I say reluctantly.

"She told me he was good-looking, but I really didn't expect... well, *that*."

"Mom told you?"

"No, Celine did," Aunt Marianne says. "We speak every week or so. And your mom and I talk—talked, rather—pretty much every day. Which is why I knew something was wrong before I even got your message."

I blink and two fat tears slip down my cheeks. I wipe them away hastily and concentrate on the way Aunt Marianne's hand keeps me anchored to reality.

"What else did she tell you?" I ask. "About Ilarion, I mean."

"Lots of things," Marianne admits. "But mostly, she was worried that you might not understand."

"Understand what?"

"Why she wanted to marry him. Why she was rushing into marriage."

I do a surprised double-take. "She told you that?"

Marianne nods. "I think that's when I realized that she really was in love with him. She knew that you wouldn't like it, that your father would hate it, and she did it anyway. It was the first time she made a decision for herself, regardless of how it made anyone else feel. I think that realization is what brought Fiona around, too."

I'm listening closely, but what I'm hearing is the words between the words. *Celine told me...* Told everyone but me, it seems. That's a hurt I wasn't ready for.

"I…" I trail off when my eyes land on Ilarion. He's talking to Dima now, but his eyes flicker to me every so often, almost like he knows that we're talking about him. "What if…?"

"What if what?" Marianne asks.

I tear my eyes away from Ilarion and look at her. Her features are similar to Mom's, but where Mom was slight of frame, Marianne is bigger, rounder, built for hugs. She's graying at the temples and her hair is thinning out, and it reminds me that nothing in life is constant. Nothing is guaranteed.

I have a freeze frame of her in my mind from about ten years ago. Marianne and Mom, both sprawled out across the lawn on a picnic blanket, laughing about their terrible childhood dog while Celine and I kicked a ball around next to them.

They both seemed so young. I'd had the feeling that they would go on forever. I *needed* them to go on forever. Because a world without my beautiful mother, a world without my fearless aunt—it just wasn't a safe one. I wasn't sure I wanted to be a part of it if they weren't.

Now that the choice is being forced upon me, I'm still not sure what I want.

"Honey?"

"Sorry," I mumble, realizing that I've dazed off yet again.

"Something's bothering you about him?"

There's so much I could tell her that would make her understand where I'm coming from. But there's no reason to drag her into something that she won't be able to fix. And this is well beyond the power of even an Aunt Marianne hug to remedy.

"I just... I'm worried for Celine. I don't want her to make a mistake. I don't want her to get hurt."

Aunt Marianne pats my hand again. "There's two ways to look at it, if you want this silly old lady's input," she remarks. "The first is that you could be wrong and Celine might actually know what's best for herself in this situation."

I sigh. "And the second?"

"That you might be right, and Celine is making a mistake. In which case, it's a mistake she's going to have to make and learn from. There's no forcing anyone to see the light, darling. Especially not when it comes to love."

"But—"

"Do you remember Ronny?"

I raise my eyebrows. I haven't heard that name in years. "Your ex-husband?"

She nods. "That's the devil. I was thirty-seven when I met him, and I guess I was worried that if I didn't get married at that point, I never would. So I married him."

"I remember. Celine and I were the flower girls."

She smiles fondly at the memory. "What you probably don't know is that both Monica and Fiona told me not to do it. They practically demanded it. Your mother was this close to locking me in a closet until the wedding date passed."

"Really?" This is news to me.

"Monica thought he was flaky, and your mother thought he wasn't good enough for me. They both tried to talk me out of it. But I told them that I'd prove them wrong. Turned out, they were both right. I ended up a forty-year-old divorcee with nothing to show for my marriage but an empty bank account and three years' worth of faked orgasms." She laughs heartily, that big, fill-the-whole-room, from-the-toes-up laugh she does as well as everyone on Earth aside from my own mother. "But, I also have no regrets, because I recognized that I wouldn't have listened to anyone at that point. The only way I'd have known it was a mistake was by making the damn mistake. It was my life, and it was my right."

I exhale tiredly, my eyes veering towards Ilarion once again. I desperately want to tell my aunt about the baby, but I know I won't be able to take it back once I do.

So I sit there miserably, arms linked with the last living remnant of my mother's laugh, drinking in her nostalgic scent and deciding that maybe sunflowers were the right choice after all.

"I'm scared, Aunt Marianne."

"I know," she says, more tears sliding down her cheeks. "I haven't lived in a world without your mother for fifty-odd years. That scares me, too."

"She wanted to die." I force out the words. Part of me hopes she doesn't catch their full meaning. Part of me hopes she does, just so I don't have to bear this alone.

Marianne sighs. "I know that, too. But the same principle applies here, too, honey: her life, her choice."

"She can't take this one back, though."

"No," Marianne agrees, wrapping an arm around my shoulder and pulling me into her warmth. "But for what it's worth…I don't think she would want to."

34

ILARION

I have Dima and Mila drive Taylor back to the Diamond after the funeral.

Then I spend the next twenty-four hours throwing myself into new leads, new strategies, and new revenge plots that will leave the Bellasio mafia decimated.

They're all beautiful goals, but they succeed in keeping me distracted for only a short time. Dima's back undercover, so I don't have a sounding board until he returns. And Mila disappeared shortly after we got back from the funeral, so it's not like I can get her to do my dirty work.

Which, in this case, would be checking in on Taylor.

I sigh and make my way towards Taylor's bedroom. Technically, it's *my* bedroom. But since I made the mistake of putting her there, I've been sleeping in one of the guest bedrooms downstairs.

It feels good to slip into the familiar space. My collection of antique weapons hangs on the far corner of the room, and the sunlight streaming through the window lights them up.

Now that I think about it, housing Taylor in a room with free access to weapons might not have been the best idea. Not that any of the displayed weapons are in battle-ready condition, but they can still do some damage with the right amount of force.

But the moment I walk into the room, I realize that Taylor's not in a fighting mood.

She's sprawled out on the bed, her arms hiding her face as she sobs into the sheets. I should announce myself, considering she has no idea that I'm here at all, but I can't for the life of me think of what to say.

I move closer, watching the way her sobs shudder through her body. The last time I saw someone cry like that, I'd asked them a question that changed the course of both our lives.

I won't make that mistake again.

"Taylor?"

She jerks upright, her tears waterfalling down her cheeks. "What are you doing here?" she stammers, glancing toward the door.

"I came to check on you."

"Oh, you care about me now?" She laughs bitterly. "That's news."

"I care about the health of the baby."

Liar.

Well, maybe not entirely a lie. Just certainly not the whole truth.

She falls back against a pillow and hastily wipes her eyes clean. "Don't be. The baby's fine. Mission accomplished. You can go now."

I should do exactly that. I've fulfilled my duty by checking on her. But for some reason, I move closer to her bed instead. "I am sorry, by the way. About Fiona."

That takes her by surprise. "I… Thank you," she says, appearing to think better of whatever jab she was about to make at my expense. "The funeral was… It was really beautiful. How much do we owe you? I can't pay you back immediately, but I'll make sure we figure something out."

"That's not necessary. I don't want to be paid back."

She narrows her eyes at me. "I don't want your charity."

"It's not charity. I did it for Celine."

She cringes. Or maybe she shivers; I'm not sure which. She doesn't look comfortable either way. A stray tear slips down her cheek but she's quick to wipe it away.

"Right. Have you heard anything?" she asks. "About Celine? Dad?"

"We're close to locating them."

She shakes her head. "They should have been there today." Her whole body slumps when she sighs. She looks so delicate and drained, and it bothers me more than I'm allowing myself to admit. "They should have been there to bury her with me."

"I know."

"I had to lie to everyone, you know," she blurts, suddenly glaring at me. "With some people, it was easy. But I had to look my Aunt Marianne in the eye and tell her the lie you made up to explain their absence."

"It was a necessary lie." I feel like I'm scolding a child. It would be easier if she wasn't acting like one. Exhausted or not, grieving or not, I expect her to at least see the sense in the strategy. "There's no sense involving more people in this. It only puts them in danger."

"Don't lecture me; I know why I had to do it. That doesn't mean I had to like it."

I replace my urge to roll my eyes with a heavy sigh. "If you understand, then why are we debating it?"

She eyes me warily, reminding me of exactly why I can't just swap out the two sisters. Taylor would never be able to assimilate into my world. Celine, on the other hand, will fit into whatever box I choose to lock her in.

I take a tissue from the bedside table and hand it to her. She takes it reluctantly, but instead of dabbing at her eyes, she toys with one corner of it until the threads start to fray.

"Mila mentioned that you lost your mother young," she says suddenly. "Do you remember it?"

I wonder what exactly Mila has told her. I'm surprised that she's said anything at all. She despises talking about our parents. "Yes, I remember it." I nod once. The memories deserve nothing more.

"So you know what I'm feeling right now?"

"If it's relief, then yes."

"*Relief?*" She gapes at me. "*That's* what you felt when your mother died?"

"She was miserable for so long," I admit, realizing even as I say it that no amount of explanation can properly convey what I felt when her internal war finally came to its inevitable conclusion. What I experienced just before that happened can't be explained in a simple story, either. "She was depressed, among other things. It was easier watching her die than it was watching her live."

I expect to be faced with disgust and judgment. After all, how could I expect someone like Taylor, someone who actually loves her parents, to understand what I felt about mine?

But instead of judgment, I watch as she furrows her brow.. "I suppose that makes sense."

She might just be the first person who's ever said that to me.

"Does it?"

She glances at me, her expression distant but thoughtful. "You recognized something in Mom, didn't you?" she asks. "Something that you saw in your own mother."

I feel my legs bend at the knees, and somehow, against my better judgment, I find myself sitting on the edge of her bed. She doesn't flinch away from me. She just watches me with a weary sense of curiosity.

"Fiona was ready to go, Taylor. She's been ready for some time now. I think the bullet gave her permission to say something she'd been waiting many months to say."

Her bottom lip starts to tremble. "It's weird—I keep digging up all these old memories that I didn't even realize I had. It's almost like…human nature's way of trying to distract me from the fact that there won't be any new memories." She trips over the last few words, her face dropping into her palm. "Fuck me. I can't seem to stop crying."

"Then cry," I tell her. "Cry until you run out of tears."

"You should probably leave then," she says. "I doubt you want to see me ugly cry."

"Too late for that."

She snorts through her tears. "Asshole."

I laugh for just a moment before I catch myself and kill it dead. Truth be told, I should get the fuck out of here immediately. Alarm bells are going off at the back of my head.

But they're easier to ignore in the face of those tear-stained hazel eyes.

"Tell me about her," I murmur.

"Mom." She sighs, smiling through her grief. "Where to start? I have so many things to choose from."

"Tell me the first one that pops into your head."

She starts talking immediately, as though the reservoir of memories stored in her head has just been waiting for an excuse to erupt. "When I was about eight, I got pneumonia. It was pretty bad, and I had to be hospitalized for a week. After I was released, I was so weak that I had to stay on bed rest, mostly. So Mom decided that she would start a wall mural for me." She smiles a bit wider. "She'd bring in new paint cans every morning, and by nightfall, there was a new story sprawled across one part of my wall. She used to sing when she painted. Badly, but it made me laugh. She used to make up stories, too. Some of them even got up there on the mural.

I came to love those bed-ridden days. After Dad went off to work and Celine went off to school, it was just Mom and me—making up stories she could paint, singing out of tune together, living off junk food and laughter." Her eyes connect with mine. "I have this…feeling," she says, her voice suddenly soft as her face falls. "This feeling like there's nothing holding me together anymore. That if I fall—there'll be nothing left to catch me."

Words leap out of my throat before I can consider just how fucking stupid they are.

"I'll catch you, *tigrionok*."

Fuck. Did I just say that—to my future sister-in-law?

Her eyes waver, but she doesn't look away. She doesn't look like she wants to. Her breath tickles the end of my nose. Hazelnuts and vanilla. She's close enough for me to trace every contour in her lips.

As I watch, they part, ever so slightly. The tiny sliver of blackness between her lips is the edge of a cliff that I absolutely, positively, under no circumstances can allow myself to fall over.

So when I do exactly that—when my lips graze hers—I'm not even sure who to blame. If she pulled me over the edge or if I made the plunge myself. I'm not sure it even matters.

Not when I realize that I would burn the whole world to ash for the sake of a single kiss.

35

ILARION

She's the one who pulls away.

Her eyes are still swimming with tears, but now, I suspect there's a different reason for them. "What are you doing?" she croaks, her voice strangled with guilt.

I get to my feet, parsing her expression with the precision of a coroner's blade. Instinct is telling me that the kiss was both our faults. She's vulnerable. And I…

I want to say that it was about nothing but her lips, but I can feel the truth becoming more and more obvious in my head.

There was something about this woman that drew me from the second I first saw her. It was *her*. Strength and vulnerability in one. She fought in one moment and fell to pieces in the next. Fierce and fiercely loyal at the same time.

The fact that she's beautiful strikes me as a mere afterthought. Icing on the cake, as they say.

Desperation boils in her eyes. Her own guilt screams, *Blame him; it's his fault, all of this.* And if I were a better man, I would let her.

But if I were a better man, this whole situation would be a thousand times less fucked-up.

"Nothing you didn't ask for," I snarl in answer to her question.

She cringes, but doesn't stay hunkered in her recoil. There it is again—that balance. "You are engaged to my *sister*."

"A fact that you're just as aware of."

She sucks in her breath. "This is not about me!" She gets up and circles me with eyes blazing, my little *tigrionok* on the prowl. "I knew—I *knew*—from the beginning that your feelings for her weren't real."

"Kissing me was just a way for you to prove your suspicions then?"

"I… that's not—you're a cheater!" she cries. She's desperately clawing for an excuse and we both know it. "I don't know why you're marrying Cee, but I know it's not for the right reasons."

Her instincts are sharper than she could ever comprehend. But the future of my Bratva depends on gaslighting her into submission. Like I said—a better man wouldn't have to do the things I'm doing.

But I've been sinning for so long that I don't know any other way to live.

"And what are *your* reasons, Taylor?" I ask. "You claim to love your sister. You claim to want to protect her. So why do I still feel the way you kissed me back?"

Her eyes widen. "I didn't—"

"Maybe it's because you want what your sister has," I growl, cutting her off. "Maybe it's because you've always wanted what Celine had. She was right about you."

That makes her stop in her tracks. Her whole frame trembles. She doesn't want to give voice to her question, but I know she won't be able to stop herself.

In fact, I'm counting on it.

"W-what are you talking about?"

"You think Celine hasn't told me things?" I muse. "I know more about you than you realize, Taylor Marie Theron. And I know that even though you like to play the innocent, you're nothing but a conniving bitch trying to steal your sister's man." I meet her horrified gaze and drop the final bombshell. *"Again."*

Something dies in her. For a moment, I wonder if I've gone too far. If I've broken her irreparably. I turn to leave right after I see the first fresh tear fall.

It's bad enough seeing her cry.

It's worse knowing that I'm the one who created her tears.

36

ILARION

I end up pacing outside her corridor for far too long before I abandon the second floor for the gardens. I'm not in the right clothes for it, but I start jogging around the pathways. I keep going until I've burned off all the extra adrenaline poisoning my veins.

I don't know what she does to me. I sure as fuck don't understand it. But whatever it is, in her presence, I become a weak man incapable of sheathing his lesser impulses. I become a man too deaf to listen to his better judgment.

I've spent months thinking up the perfect plan, and I'll be damned if I burn it all to the ground for a woman. Any woman.

Even her.

When my lungs are double-clutching in agony, I end the run and go back to the house. I find Mila at my office door about to knock.

"I thought you were in there," she explains. She scrunches up her nose when she takes note of sweat-stained shirt. "Why are you all gross?"

"I went for a run."

"In those clothes?"

"Why are you here, Mila?" I don't have the time or patience for any more games. "Has Dima cracked our lead?"

"Not that I'm aware of," she says. "But security just informed me of an issue at the entrance."

I tense immediately. "The Bellasios?"

"The Bellasios, you can handle. This problem…I'm not so sure."

She's enjoying herself a little too much. I'm in no mood for it. "Cut the shit and tell me what you're here to tell me."

She suppresses an amused smile. "Taylor's at the front gate, and she has a bag packed."

"The fuck…" I clench a fist just so I don't start ripping my hair out. "Get security to put her back in her room."

"You're not going down there?" Before I can answer, understanding dawns on her at the same time the stone in my gut sinks lower. "Ahh. Something happened between the two of you."

"Nothing happened. She's just stubborn and arrogant."

"Hm. Reminds me of someone I know."

I narrow my eyes. "Go and check in with Dima. I'll handle this."

"Good luck."

I head straight for the security gate at the bottom of the driveway. As I approach, I see Taylor facing five of my men with her back to me and a packed bag at her feet. They've formed a loose semi-circle around her, fidgeting uncomfortably in place while they itch for guns they know far better than to use.

Taylor doesn't notice me coming. "…This is abduction! I hope you realize that!" she shrieks. "I can have you all arrested!"

"You can try."

She spins around, her face flaring up with renewed fury. "*You*. Stay away from me."

I stop a few yards short to give her the space she wants. "Get back in the house, Taylor."

"In your fucking dreams."

I glance over her head at my men. "At ease, gentleman. You're excused. I'll take it from here."

The men leave without bothering to hide their relief, and I turn to Taylor impatiently. "I understand why you want to leave. And believe me, I'm counting down the days until that will happen. But it's not today."

"I have an apartment I need to get back to."

"It'll keep."

She grinds her teeth together. "I don't know why I stayed here as long as I have. Chalk it up to shock. I was reeling from what happened to Celine and Dad. And then…Mom." She takes a deep breath. "I should have left that same day. You have no right to keep me here."

"Don't make this unpleasant," I warn, taking a step forward. She moves back, keeping the same distance between us. A fucked-up tango between two people who don't belong anywhere near each other. But who are stuck together nonetheless.

"Are you trying to tell me that I'm a prisoner here?"

"I'm trying to tell you that it's not safe for you out there."

"What do you care?"

"I care because you're carrying my baby, and that is my concern. For as long as you're pregnant, that makes *you* my concern as well."

She looks around in frustration, her shoulders dropping. She's tired, that much is obvious, but it's not in her nature to admit defeat.

Another thing that we have in common.

"No one knows I'm pregnant."

"It's only a matter of time."

"No it's not," she argues. "But it will be if I stay with you."

She has a point there, but it's not one that I'm willing to entertain. The idea of watching her stroll out from under my protection feels unnatural somehow. Like losing a limb. I tell myself it's about the fact that she'll be walking out with my baby, but I'm not so sure that's the whole reason.

I just can't afford to examine any other possibilities.

"The Bellasios managed to not only find out about my engagement to your sister in record time; they also attacked my private home in order to abduct her. I'm not taking chances."

She shakes her head in disgust and resignation. "So what's the plan then?"

"The plan is to get your sister back. I'm working on—"

"No," she interrupts, "I mean the long-term plan. What happens after you get my sister back? Because I know one thing for sure: you cannot marry Celine *and* have a baby with me."

I'm starting to realize the same thing. But the stubborn asshole in me refuses to accept that it has to be one or the other.

"What are you really asking me, *tigrionok?*" I murmur. "Are you asking me to leave your sister for you?"

Anger flashes across her eyes. "Fuck you, you egotistical bastard. Are you already forgetting the promise you made to my mother? Because I certainly haven't."

"I remember."

"Good," she hisses. "So I'd much rather keep this secret than make my sister unhappy."

Every muscle in my body tightens. I know for sure that whatever she says next, I'm not going to like. "What are you suggesting?"

"I was convinced that the only move going forward was to get my sister to leave you," she admits. "But I was convinced that she didn't know who you really are. I was so sure that what she felt for you was infatuation, not love."

I wait patiently. Dread coils low in my gut.

"But talking to my aunt, I realized that Celine doesn't do infatuation. She doesn't fall often, but when she does, she falls hard. So if she agreed to marry you, it's because she really does love you." She meets my gaze. I watch in real time as the fires in her eyes cool into dense sadness. "Don't get me wrong—I still think she's making a mistake. But it's her life, and her mistake to make. So I'm not going to ask her to leave you. I'm not going to get in the way of your marriage. And that means this baby has to be mine, and mine alone."

I stride towards her, covering the last of the distance between us. This time, she doesn't back away from me. She holds her ground and stares up at me with those astonishing hazel eyes.

"You're asking me to abandon my child. To pretend that I'm not the father. To bury my fucking head in the sand."

My voice quivers with pent-up fury at the mere suggestion.

The worst part? *She's right.*

She's right and I fucking know it. Even as every bone in my body is screaming to pour lighter fluid on the plan I've painstakingly put together over the last few months, to cast it all aside and grab the infuriating woman in front of me to finish what we started on the bed earlier tonight…

I know deep in my marrow that I can't.

"That's what I'm asking you," she agrees. "Are you still going to marry Celine?"

I close my eyes and say the only thing I can say: "Yes."

She nods. "Then I can only be your sister-in-law, and this baby can only be your niece or nephew. Not your child. Certainly not your heir."

Everything she's saying makes sense. Too much sense. Which is exactly why I don't address it. I snatch her bag off the ground, and then I grab her arm.

"Ow!"

I ignore that just like I'm ignoring all the reasons I shouldn't be doing this as I drag her up the driveway and back into the house.

"Stop!" she cries out. "Let go of me!" She slips out of my grasp and whirls around to face me, hair mussed into a furious mane around her head. "I can walk up by myself. I know the way."

"You're here for as long as I say you are," I snarl as I get right up in her face. "You got that?"

She meets my eyes for only a fleeting second. I see so many things written on her face.

Fear.

Disgust.

And worst of all…

Hope.

Then she nods. "Fine." She takes her bag and disappears into the house.

I can feel myself rapidly losing control of this situation, but at least she agreed to stay. For the time being, she's under my roof.

As long as she's close, I can handle the rest.

37

TAYLOR

It's been twenty-four hours since I left my room.

I've spent some of that time sleeping, some of it reading, but most of it staring at the antique weapons lining the opposite the bed. There's a giant two-handed saber that I'm particularly taken with. It's got a hundred years' worth of nicks and grime on it, but the edge on the blade seems pretty sharp still. I don't know much about weapons, but I could do some damage with it. How hard could it be? Aim the pointy end at the person you don't like and swing it, right?

Celine would be horrified with me. She doesn't even like movies with too much gore in them. I stepped on a butterfly by accident once when we were little and she cried for a week.

Which makes it all the more darkly comedic that she's marrying a man like Ilarion. A man who hangs bloodstained battle axes on his walls and inspires otherwise innocent people like me to daydream about committing violence against that smug smirk of his.

When the door opens, I'm not at all surprised to see Mila in place of her brother. I'm guessing he's in no rush to talk to me since our "negotiations" at the gates.

Fine by me.

I swing my legs down from where I had them propped on the back of the couch and glance at her with disinterest. "Tell me, Mila: do you ever resent having to follow your brother's orders like a trained lackey?"

She shrugs. "I am a lackey. Just not a very well-trained one." Then she falls onto the opposite end of the sofa, kicks off her shoes, and pulls her feet up. "You haven't been eating."

I roll my eyes. "Being kidnapped can really mess with your appetite."

"You're being protected, not imprisoned."

"That's a nice spin. You and your brother should really consider going into politics."

"Just because you don't agree with it doesn't mean it's not true. You're carrying the heir to the Zakharov empire. That's no small thing."

The way she says it has goosebumps traveling along my arms. "Stop," I say, holding up a hand. "My baby is no heir to anything, okay? This is *my* baby.. And since Ilarion and Celine insist on marrying each other, whatever children *they* have together will be the heirs. Leave me and mine all the way out of it."

I expect my tone to piss Mila off—hell, part of me was hoping for it—but instead, she leans back and regards me with curiosity. "What made you decide to keep the baby?"

I'm wary she's pressing for information. "My decision had nothing to do with Ilarion."

Mila lofts a brow. "I wasn't implying it did."

They keep saying I'm not a prisoner or a caged animal, but I sure feel like one or the other. I'm acting like it, too. My first conversation after a day in self-imposed solitary confinement and I'm ready to lash out at anyone who wanders too close.

"I'm twenty," I finally say. "Having a baby never crossed my mind. It wasn't even something I thought about wanting in the future. But then I saw those lines on the test, and I saw this little nugget in my belly when I went to the doctor's, and…" I look up to find that Mila is watching me closely. "And…I don't know. It's hard to explain. But I just felt this strange, instinctive need to protect this little alien. I knew I couldn't bear to get rid of it, and if I couldn't do that… keeping it was the only option."

She takes all that in with a solemn nod. "Do you think you'll be a good mother?" It's not a snotty question or a rude one. Just a curious one.

"I have no idea," I admit. "But I do have a good example to follow. My mother was…" I choke up, but manage to hold down the sob. "She was the best."

"Yeah, I got that at the funeral. Watching you cry over her grave…I felt the love you felt for her."

When I glance at Mila, I start to realize that maybe her curiosity has to do with the fact that for perhaps the first time in her life, she's seeing a different kind of family dynamic. From what little they've shared, it seems like the

Zakharov siblings experienced a vastly different childhood with their own parents.

"Do you remember your mother at all?" I'm careful with how I ask because there's no telling how she might react. Whenever the subject has come up before, however tangentially, she freezes and walls up.

Today, though, she just shrugs. "Some things," she says. "Mostly that she had no interest in being a mother at all. She had Ilarion and I because she was required to provide heirs. We were just a part of the bargain she struck with our father."

Her voice hitches strangely on "father," but I don't want to interrupt her.

"I was older than I'd like to admit before I realized that my nanny wasn't actually my mother. That she had no relation to me at all, and that she was actually paid to look after me. That was a bucket of ice water, let me tell you." She glances at me through her long lashes. "I think it's admirable that you want to protect your baby, and he isn't even born yet. I think that alone makes you a good mother."

A beat of uncomfortable silence follows. I can't help but wonder, *When did she start to respect me?* I don't want to get ahead of myself, but there's no denying that that's what the soft glow in her eyes is: respect.

I'm beginning to doubt I'll ever understand these people.

"So…is there a reason you've decided to be your brother's lackey? Not judging or anything. I'm just curious."

Mila scoffs. "Bullshit. You are judging. And I can't exactly blame you. I'd be judging you if the roles were reversed."

"So why do it?"

She sighs, and as she does, her posture folds in on itself. Like she's trying to keep something embarrassing cupped in her arms so I can't see it. "Honestly?"

"If you can manage it."

She throws me a glare, but there's humor behind it. "Because he's my hero." I raise my eyebrows and she chuckles. "I know—it sounds ridiculous, doesn't it?"

"No," I say softly. "Not if you mean it."

"I didn't have parents growing up," she explains. "Not real ones. But I had Ilarion. And he was the best big brother anyone could ever hope to have. He would kill for me. Literally."

I shudder. "Yeah, that's the part I have trouble with."

"It doesn't take as long to get used to as you would think."

"That's not what I want for my child," I tell her. "Or for myself."

"Well, then you chose the wrong man to sleep with."

I run my hand through my hair, catching a few painful knots in the process. I really need to drag a brush through it at some point. It's one thing to isolate myself up here; it's another thing to let myself go entirely. Just because I feel like a caged animal doesn't mean I have to look like one.

"Does your brother love my sister?" I ask bluntly. I'm very aware that I sound like a broken record by this point. But no one has ever given me a straight answer.

At least not one that's believable.

Mila's expression doesn't change, but I suspect that's because she's trying very hard not to give anything away. "What's the answer you're hoping to hear?"

I bristle. "That's not fair." And not the direction I want this conversation to turn, either. This is about Ilarion and Celine, not about me.

She winces and holds up her hands. "Sorry. In case you haven't noticed, my default setting is 'bitch.'"

I can't help but smile. As annoying as it was being at odds with her, turns out it's equally annoying to find that I like her. I don't want to like anything about Ilarion or his world or the people who've chosen to join him in it.

"You love your brother, right?" I say. "Well, I feel the same way about my sister. And I happen to believe that his feelings for her aren't pure."

"Nothing in life is pure, Taylor," Mila says. It's the first time I've ever heard her voice crack quite like that. A crack that reveals a glimpse of something beneath it. Pain. Heartbreak. *Damage.* "Even if you find something that comes close, it's only a matter of time before it's tainted."

I shake my head. "That's not true."

"Yes, it is. The most we can come to expect from life is to survive it. My brother proposed; your sister accepted. That's all there is to it. We just need to get out of the way."

I just nod miserably. Some lines can't be crossed. I've asked Mila to speak against her brother and I have to accept that she will never do it. "Okay, I get it. You have his back."

"No matter what," she confirms.

"And I've got my sister's." I sigh. "Which is why she can never know about this baby, Mila." My hand trembles over my stomach. "You need to convince Ilarion that this is the only way forward. He can't claim this baby as his."

Mila looks wary. "You're asking for a lot, Taylor."

"I'm asking for what's necessary. It's the only way forward. Ilarion wants to marry Celine; well, she's not going to marry him if she knows I'm carrying his baby."

Mila mumbles something and gets to her feet. I think she's about to walk out on my request, but she turns to me with a sympathetic smile. "You've been cooped up in this room for long enough. Come on."

"Where are we going?"

"Outside. A walk in the gardens will do us both some good. Unless, of course, you'd rather stay in here and get even pastier than you already are."

I roll my eyes, but join her. "So I need a tan. Fine. But why will it do *you* good? Something going on?"

"Oh, you're a regular super sleuth, aren't you?" She rolls her eyes. "There's no particular reason, honestly. Not anymore. I just got into the habit of walking the grounds when I was younger. I guess it was an attempt to outrun my demons."

I frown. "Do you have a lot of those?"

"I did," she replies. "But my dad is dead now. So there's one less than there used to be."

38

TAYLOR

It's hard not to gawk. The gardens at the Diamond are an endless labyrinth of lush hedges and ancient trees. Around one corner is a water-lined grotto; around another is a grid of statues watching over the night.

Mila catches me looking around slack-jawed. I hear her chuckle softly under her breath. "It's a lot, I know. I forget that sometimes. It's hard to remember that not everyone grows up with—"

"Fairytale castles on every coast?"

She laughs again. It's funny how much her face changes when she smiles. Mostly, it makes me realize how little she does it. "Right. People think that that's enough reason to be happy, but I haven't met a single property that's made me feel as good as a person can."

I glance at her sidelong. "Who's your special person?"

Mila rolls her eyes. "There is no special person. It was a general statement."

"Sure. And I'm a monkey's uncle."

She gives me the finger as she pretends to scratch her nose. "Come on, wiseass," she mutters, gesturing to a huge tree that looks out over the rest of the property from a perch at the top of a gentle hill. She sits down against its trunk and pats the grass at her side.

"What's your dad like?" she blurts once I settle in. "Are you close with him?"

"More so when I was a kid," I admit. "As Celine and I got older…things changed."

"What kind of things?"

"I don't know. I mean, I used to think that Mom's cancer pushed him over the edge. Made him paranoid and scared of his own shadow. But honestly, it started before she was diagnosed. He started seeing, like, capital-D *danger* everywhere. He stopped letting Cee and me have sleepovers; he used to insist on dropping and picking us up from school because he didn't want us taking the bus. If he could've implanted tracking chips in our skulls, he wouldn't have even hesitated."

"Sounds like a lot."

"To say the least. Things got worse after Mom was diagnosed. It's like he thought the world was out to get him."

"But you still love him?"

"Of course I do. He's my dad. And as annoying as it is to have him hover over us all the time, Celine and I both know he does it because he loves us. He wants to keep us safe, like any other father."

Mila snorts. "Not all fathers are like yours, Taylor. Not all mothers, either."

I tilt my head to look at her in the gloom. She's got Ilarion's chiseled profile, though slightly blurred, feminized at the harshest edges. "You said your dad was your demon."

It's not really a question, and I don't really expect an answer. It's more of a game. Me wondering which topic is going to be the one that shuts her down. Talking to these people is like walking on eggshells—if the eggs all had bombs inside.

"I don't think he was capable of being anything else. Not all Bratva *pakhans* are like Ilarion."

"Meaning…?"

"Meaning Ilarion isn't cruel without cause. He's not sadistic or power-hungry. He meets violence with violence, but always within reason. And if you're not violent, neither is he."

"Is there ever a reason to be violent?"

Mila meets my gaze. "Only someone who was raised in a happy home with two loving and protective parents would say something like that."

It's meant as a rebuke, and it has the intended effect. I clam up and look out over the spread of the garden below us. City lights twinkle in the distance. The warm night breeze tickles my nose.

Next to me, Mila looses a weary sigh. "I really am sorry about your mother," she says. "Sometimes, it's hard to remember that other people love their parents. It's sort of a foreign concept for me."

I guess, in a way, I can sympathize with that. I can certainly appreciate the thoughtful apology. "Thank you for helping me out with the funeral."

She shrugs. "I was ordered to."

I resist rolling my eyes. *Way to ruin the moment.* She takes after Ilarion in that department, too. "You act like you follow your brother's orders, but I have a feeling you don't do anything you don't want to do."

She smiles shyly. "Okay, I'll give you that."

"You know I'm right, don't you?" She's in a good mood, so I'm going to risk it by veering into forbidden territory. "About convincing Ilarion to let me claim my baby belongs to some other random guy. Anyone but him."

She purses her lips in distaste. I admire her loyalty to him; it runs deep. But even though I respect it, I'm not above trying to whittle it down if it means I can spare Celine some pain.

Because my loyalty runs deep, too.

Her face swivels in my direction, and her eyes are thoughtful. "You're really okay with letting your sister marry the father of your child?"

"Things didn't exactly happen in chronological order." I try to muster a joke to lighten the weight in my chest, but it works only a little bit. "I mean, she loves him. At least, that's what everyone keeps telling me."

"Who's 'everyone'?"

"My mother, my aunt," I admit. "Celine told me, too, but not in so many words. In fact, she was pretty tight-lipped about Ilarion, right up until their engagement party."

"That seems unusual, especially for sisters who seem so close."

"We are close," I assure her. "But it's also…complicated."

"See what I mean?" Mila crows. "Nothing is pure."

I start playing with the rocks at my fingertips. The soil is packed tight around the base of the tree, but there's still tiny little creepers growing out of the earth. Little shoots of life finding their way to the surface against the odds. "Celine's one of those reserved people. She keeps her feelings close to the chest. I guess I just assumed if she felt strongly about something, she would tell us…or at least tell me."

"Ah." Mila shares a knowing nod. "This is about a boy."

I wince. It sounds so trivial when she says it like that. In my heart, it feels like anything but. "I wish it were something better. Something more important." I meet her eyes. "His name was Alec. He and his parents lived in the house across from ours when we first moved to Evanston. He was the only kid on the block who was in our age range. You kinda just gravitate toward each other when it's like that."

The memories start to flood my mind. Memories I've kept buried since it all happened almost a decade ago.

Even at thirteen, you could tell that Alec Miller was born to break hearts. Blond hair, blue eyes, the kind of smile that made smart girls do stupid things.

Not that I noticed, of course. I was eleven. I mostly liked the fact that he was always up for a scooter race with me on the weekends.

"You both fell for him," Mila deduces.

I nod sadly. "There was a point when I suspected that Cee might have a crush on Alec. But every time I asked her, she flatly denied it. She told me that they were friends and that's all it was."

"And you believed her?"

I sigh. "She and Alec spent a lot of time together. I'd come home from swim practice, and Celine would be over at the Millers' house, hanging out with Alec in his room. They were the same age, they had more in common… It made sense. I felt left out sometimes, but I kinda expected that friendship to, you know…*evolve*."

"It didn't?"

I shake my head. "Celine turned fifteen, then sixteen, then seventeen. She brought her first boyfriend home and introduced him to Mom and Dad. Alec brought a girlfriend of his own home a few weeks later. I figured that was that."

I glance at Mila, wondering if this whole story is as foreign to her as her life feels to me.

"Then, just before my sixteenth birthday, Alec broke up with his girlfriend. Cee had been single for a few months at that point, and one day, I caught her looking at him. I asked her again if there was something there, and again, she denied it."

"So you felt free to date Alec," Mila surmises.

"He kissed me on my sixteenth birthday. I didn't expect it. I really, truly didn't. I mean, he was two years older and when you're in high school, that kind of age difference seems big. I figured he just saw me as Celine's tomboy little sister. I guess not, though. Anyway, we kept it a secret for a while. We didn't want our parents to know because we assumed they'd be weird about it. Turned out, Celine was the one who was weird about it."

"What did she do when she found out?"

I shudder and close my eyes. I can still see her face like it's seared on the backs of my eyelids. Tears. Red cheeks. Hair wild, and the way her voice trembled before it cracked entirely…

"It was the first time I felt like Celine might never speak to me again." I open my eyes and look at Mila, who hasn't moved. "I broke up with him. He stopped talking to me, and eventually moved out of state for college."

"And Celine?"

"Celine took some time, but she eventually started looking at me like I was her sister again," I say. "But she never stopped treating me like I was plotting to steal everything she had."

Mila nods. "So that's why she didn't tell you about Ilarion."

"She's never going to believe me if I tell her I met him before she did. Hell, I don't even believe me, and I was *there*," I groan, feeling my heart sink at the thought of seeing her cheeks go that red again. "I can't hurt her like that. Not for a second time."

She breathes softly in the night. "What the fuck were you supposed to do?"

I shake my head. "I was supposed to have my sister's back. I should've—

"No, Taylor. Stop paying the price for her mistakes. You've got your own life to account for." Her gaze flickers down to my stomach.

I snort. "Right. Trust me—*my* feelings won't ever get in the way again." Mila raises her eyebrows and I realize what I've just inadvertently revealed. "Not that—I don't mean—I don't have feelings for Ilarion."

Fuck. Why didn't I just keep my big mouth shut? Nothing sounds guiltier than an admission of innocence.

"Mila!"

We jerk upright as Dima appears on the path. He waves, and Mila springs to her feet. "When did you get back?" she exclaims.

He doesn't return her enthusiasm. "A couple of minutes ago. We need you in the den."

My shoulders tense. "Don't you worry," Dima tells me when he sees me on edge. "We've got the situation under control."

Mila turns to me. "Why don't you head back up to your room and rest, Taylor? I'll catch up with you later."

I nod. "Okay." I know when I'm being dismissed.

She reaches out and her fingers touch my shoulder. "Thanks for sharing all that with me," she says.

"About that… Can we keep it between us?"

Mila nods. "I'll take it to my grave."

I watch her walk up the path until she and Dima melt into the mass of shadows at the mouth of the gardens.

When I'm sure they can't see me anymore, I follow.

39

ILARION

"…do you mean, 'it went wrong'?" Mila asks, walking her and Dima's conversation into the den.

I'm standing there with my back to the window, staring at the bloody piece of paper on my desk. I can't bring myself to look away from it. Not even when Mila and Dima walk in and close the door.

"I mean that the lead I was chasing is dead."

"So Benedict knew he was close to cracking."

I glance up just in time to see Dima shake his head. "It wasn't Benedict who pulled the trigger," he says, his gait filled with barely-contained adrenaline. "The guy did it on his own."

"Come again?"

"Shot himself in the neck while I was standing a foot away," Dima explains. "I really thought he was going to tell me everything. I was so sure he was ready to crack."

"Fuck," Mila spits. She turns to me as though I'll have all the answers. "So…what's next?"

I gesture wordlessly to the note on my desk.

"What's that?" she asks.

"I found it on the body. In the pocket of his pants." I take the note and hand it to my sister.

She wrinkles her nose as she takes it and examines it carefully. Over her shoulder, Dima is frowning. "This is blood… Why does the writing look so familiar…?"

"Wait." Dima peers at the note. "Those are coordinates. It's a location."

I nod. "Correct."

"Fuck," he mutters under his breath. "He actually coughed something up. Didn't see that coming. I don't get it, though. Why didn't he just give me the note?"

"I have a feeling he didn't know about it," I speculate. "Just a hunch, but something tells me that note was slipped into his pocket without his knowledge."

"That's a big jump to make."

"But we're not dealing with a normal mole. This one is smart."

"Okay," Mila says, her game face on. "We have a location. But *whose* location?"

"Has to be Celine's," I say confidently.

"Okay, so we have her location." Dima paces back and forth. "Can we assume this note means that the old man is dead?"

"It's blood," Mila points out. "Not a body. He could still be alive."

"We're not assuming anything," I say firmly.

"We have to assume some things," she retorts. "Especially if we're going to bust in and get Celine back. *Assuming* that's who these coordinates are for." She stops short when she sees the look on my face. "You think this might be a trap?"

"It's possible." I'm running through all possible scenarios in my head and yes, a trap lying in wait for us is definitely at the top of the list. I'm picturing kicking down a door and swallowing a bullet for my troubles.

Mila and Dima exchange a look. He clears his throat. "What are you thinking?"

I glance out the window for a moment, a dozen different possibilities rattling around in my head. I don't have long to dwell on any of them. The location I've been given could be legitimate, which means it could also change at any moment. There's no guarantee that Benedict will keep a precious commodity like Celine in the same place for long.

"If that note was forged by Benedict, then we're walking straight into a trap," I muse out loud.

"The alternative is ignoring the note altogether," Dima suggests.

"No," I growl. "Ignoring it is not an option."

"But if Benedict did forge—"

"Even if he did, ignoring it implies weakness. As far as the underworld is concerned, Celine is my fiancée. If I don't make a show of trying to get her back, my strength will be called into question. I can't lead a Bratva if my reputation starts to suffer."

"So we have to go in." Dima folds his arms as he leans against the wall. The look on his face tells me he's got his own list of scenarios swirling around—and none of them are any better than mine. "But be prepared for the worst."

"Wait!" Mila holds up a hand as she takes her turn to pace around the room. "Let's take a moment here. There has to be another way. Something we aren't thinking of."

"Like what?" Dima asks. "Short of sending in someone undercover? That kind of mission takes years of prep. We don't have that luxury."

Both of them glance at me with uncertainty. I wonder if they can sense that something's off. It's strange that chaos makes me calm. I'm never quite as clear-minded as when there's a plan of action to piece together and a thousand obstacles to maneuver around.

Usually.

But this time, it's different.

This time, it's personal.

"We don't need to plant someone," Mila says. She pauses, then sighs. "Send me in."

Dima snorts with laughter. When my sister turns her glare on him, his mouth drops open with incredulity. "You're not serious."

"Why wouldn't I be?" she demands.

"Because it's ludicrous!" he growls. "Tell her, Ilarion. Tell her she's fuckin' crazy."

"He's right," I agree. "There's no way I'm sending you in."

"Why? Because I'm a woman? Or because I'm your sister?"

"Either. Both." I offer a not-so-apologetic shrug. "But mostly the second."

"Fuck you."

I ignore that. "We go in, guns blazing," I decide, turning to Dima. "We have to be prepared for a full-scale attack. It might all be for nothing. Celine might not even be there, but—"

Mila steps up to me before I can finish, pushing herself into my face. "I can get in undetected," she hisses. "I can scope out the place, see if I can get a read on where Celine is being held. If she's not on the property, I get out before you risk yourself and your men on a wild goose chase."

I stare down at her, reminded of how stubborn she is and always has been. The fire and brimstone was there even as a little girl. She used to follow me to the shooting range when she was barely old enough to hold a pistol level. I told her no once and she snuck into the back of my car to hitch a ride there.

If she was a boy, our father might have been proud. As it stood, he beat her so badly that she couldn't sit for a month.

Now, I go back and forth. She's not wrong; it would be very easy for her to sneak in, assess the situation, and leave without getting caught. But I don't know if catering to her pride is the best thing for her. Ultimately, it's the same question I always ask and never quite manage to answer: did her childhood mold her…or break her?

"I'm not risking your life to sate your pride, Mila."

"Right, of course not," she says bitterly. "Because *your* pride is the only thing that matters, isn't that right? Your pride, Dima's pride… Father's pride. A man's pride is worth so much more than a woman's."

"Don't make this about something it's not."

She scoffs bitterly. "Don't deny it's anything but."

"This isn't a question of your ability." I grimace and rub my temples. "My job is to protect you."

"Maybe I don't want to be protected!"

"Unfortunately, I'm not giving you the choice."

"I'm not Taylor!" she snaps, gnashing her teeth. "I was born into this world, same as you. I can handle myself in it. I'm not some scared wallflower that you need to pamper."

My sister is a smart woman. She's also an observant one. And she knows exactly what she's doing. Taylor has fast become a trigger for me, and if Mila wants shit to go *boom,* all she needs to do is squeeze.

I'd be quietly amused if I wasn't busy being fucking furious.

I grab Mila's hand and haul her around to pin her against the nearest wall. It's a wordless reminder that I know her triggers, too.

"Let me go," she snarls, even as fear flits across her eyes while I loom over her.

"I will when you start listening. You're not going into Bellasio territory on your own. Is that clear?"

Tension flares. Peaks. Then subsides. Gritting her teeth, Mila snatches her wrist from underneath my fingers, leaving faint nail marks on her smooth skin. "*Da, Pakhan* Zakharov."

I stare into her eyes for another long moment before I'm satisfied that I've made my point. Only then do I let her go.

She rips herself free and stomps away to the other side of the room.

"I could go," Dima suggests with a casual shrug from behind me.

Mila laughs humorlessly. "Fuck you both." She's eyeing the door like she wants nothing more than to be rid of us. She doesn't leave the room, though. Her pride won't let her.

"No." I turn to Dima. "You'd be recognized. No—this is an all-or-nothing situation. No half-measures. Whether I choose to believe the authenticity of that note or not, we have to commit to a course of action." I nod toward the door. "Go get the men ready. Make sure they know this isn't just a rescue mission; we're making a statement."

"Got it, boss."

Dima slinks toward the door while Mila turns to me, resentment still burning in her eyes. "I hate that you still see me as a victim."

I sigh. *Here we go.* "I don't—"

"Don't lie to me," she hisses. "I see the way you look at me sometimes. Like I'm the same girl you found crying on her bed all those years ago."

"Mila—"

"If you remember, I fought back. I stood up to him. *I* did that."

"I remember."

I'll always fucking remember. It was the worst day of my life. Of both our lives.

"Then stop treating me like I'm not as much a part of this Bratva as Dima is."

"I'm not trying to exclude you, Mila."

"Good. Because I'm coming with you." She squares her shoulders. "I'm not playing babysitter to your baby mama."

I've seen that look on her face before, and I decide to pick my battles by letting her pick her own. "Fine."

She raises her eyebrows. "Fine?"

I nod. "You can have your own team."

She gives me a tentative smile. They're rare and fleeting these days. Like snowflakes that dissolve as soon as they hit the ground. "I won't let you down."

"You've never let me down, Mila," I tell her as she's moving toward the door. "You are not the one I'm underestimating. You are not the one I'm disappointed in."

Her scowl softens. "It's all behind us now, Ilarion."

But it's not. I know it's not. I'm pretty sure she knows, too.

This is only just beginning.

40

TAYLOR

My heartbeat is physically painful as it thrums against my chest. It hurts even when I swallow.

"Get a hold of yourself, Taylor!" I hiss under my breath.

But now that the panic has taken hold, it's not as easy to push off. I've spent the last few minutes in the broom closet opposite the den where Ilarion, Dima, and Mira were just arguing.

I had to take cover when Dima left the room, which means I have no idea what they've decided. Is Mila going with them? Is Ilarion serious about getting Celine back? Who wrote the note with the location?

There's only one thing I know for certain anymore, and that's that I do not trust Ilarion. All my worst instincts about him turned out to be accurate.

I need to make a show of strength.

And in order to do that, I have to get Celine back.

As far as the world is concerned, she's my woman.

'As far as the world is concerned'? Screw that! What about Celine? What about where *she's* concerned?

As much as my sister may keep from me, there are some things she just would not do. And marrying a man who's using her as a prop rather than a person is at the top of that list.

I hear someone leave again and I press my ear to the closet door. The footsteps are lighter than Dima's, which means they're probably Mila's.

Then I hear a second pair of footsteps, this one heavier. Has to be Ilarion.

"Mila?"

I freeze, waiting anxiously.

"Yes?" she responds.

"Where's Taylor?"

The sound of my name sends goosebumps rushing over my skin.

"I just left her in the garden. Pretty sure she went up to her bedroom."

"Check on her before we leave. Don't give anything away."

Mila doesn't respond, so I'm assuming she nodded. I wait until the footsteps recede, then I risk opening the door and peeking out. The corridor is clear, but there are windows on one side further down the corridor that could give me away if I'm not careful.

I sneak out of the broom closet and inch my way past closed doors, staying hunched low so no one sees me through the window panes. I make it to the foyer, but I still need to get to my room before Mila does.

A few men are gathering in the courtyard, but none of them are looking toward the house. I steer myself in the direction of the gardens and re-route from there. I bump into two maids on my way up to the room, but I'm pretty sure no one saw where I came from and they wouldn't think anything of it if they did.

By the time I get upstairs, I realize that Mila has beaten me there. She's standing in the center of the space, looking around in bewilderment when I walk in. I swallow hard and wipe my expression clean. I don't have a firm plan yet, but there's one beginning to take shape. And I can't afford to screw it up before I've got momentum.

"Hey," I say, trying my best to sound casual. "What are you doing up here?"

Mila turns to me. Her face is carefully devoid of emotion. "Just…checking on you. I thought you'd already be up here."

I shrug and meander over to the window seat. "I decided to walk around the gardens a little more. It was nice being outside."

Mila nods, but her eyes stay narrowed suspiciously. "Did you see the rose bushes on the west side?"

"I didn't go that far. Just down by the walkway with all the baby's breath on the sides. It's really pretty down there." I know the game she's playing, and I can play it just as well. "So what did Dima want?"

She doesn't give anything away. She doesn't even flinch. Even her shoulders are relaxed. "Just following a lead about your sister. He thinks he might have some new information that could be helpful."

"Have you found her?" I feign anxiety and hope.

"No, not yet. But we will. It might take a few days, though."

"And what about Dad?"

"We're doing our best, Taylor. Just sit tight, okay? Sometimes, these things take longer than we expect." Then she turns to the door. "I'm stepping out for a bit, but I'll see you tomorrow."

"I'm sure you will," I say with a harsh laugh. "It's not like I can go anywhere."

She leaves, and I watch as the door clicks shut. I count to fifty, then slip back outside into the broad hallway. It's open enough that it wouldn't be hard to spot me from the staircase, but I inch closer anyway. I'm counting on the fact that everyone's going to be too focused on the mission to pay attention to anything else.

I manage to get all the way downstairs before I hear voices approaching. I glance around and hide behind the first door I find. Turns out to be a bar of sorts—leatherbound stools, a luxuriously long counter, shelves upon shelves of opaque glass bottles, and everything an insanely wealthy crime boss could want in his personal liquor stash.

I keep the door ajar so I can see what's happening on the outside. Through the crack, I catch sight of Dima. He's changed clothes into tight-fitting, all-black tactical gear. Two holsters hang from his hips, a pistol handle oiled and gleaming in each of them.

Ilarion joins him a moment later. They exchange what look like small walkie-talkies. Static crackles as they test the channels. The two men exchange a few muttered words and then stomp outside to the driveway.

Seconds later, Mila skirts past my line of vision. She stops at the entrance and looks back over her shoulder. "Disen?" she says to someone I can't see.

"We're just loading up the last of the Hummers," says a man with a raspy voice and a thick mop of dirty blond hair. "We should be able to leave in three."

The panic is making me miss things, so I bite down on my tongue until the pain washes out all the extra noise. I have to do this. Fear be damned.

"Tell Ilarion and Dima to move out," Mila orders. "We'll catch up to them on the road."

I push the door open a little bit more and watch as Disen goes outside. Mila is polishing her gun against the leg of her jeans. When she's done, she reaches around back and pushes it into a holster positioned over her rear.

Perfect.

The hard part is going to be sneaking up on her before she notices.

She leans against the threshold of the doorway. When her back is all I can see, I decide it's now or never. And if one of her men or one of the maids decide to make an appearance in the next ten seconds, I'm screwed.

But for once, I choose not to think about all the things that could go wrong. I choose to focus on things going my way for a change.

I tell myself I can do this, and the more I repeat it, the easier it is to believe. There's a thin line between confidence and delusion.

The commotion of tires and clacking guns outside masks my footsteps and labored breathing as I inch closer.

And closer.

And closer.

Mila is three steps away, then two, then one. Then she's within reach. I take a big inhale…

Then I make my move.

41

TAYLOR

By the time Mila has whipped around, I'm aiming her own gun directly in her face. She's surprised, but even now, she isn't afraid. I'll have to ask her how she does that—once this is all over, of course.

"What are you doing, Taylor?" she asks calmly.

"Holding you at g-gunpoint."

"I can see that," she chuckles with a nod. "What I don't know is why."

"You really think I'm going to leave it up to your brother to get my father and sister back?" I scoff. "I don't think so."

It's insulting how relaxed she looks right now. Her hands aren't even up in the air like I expected them to be. It's making me wonder if she sees something I don't know about.

"Ilarion is—"

"Ilarion is using my sister!" I yell, earning myself some attention from the men outside in the courtyard. A few of them pull out their guns, but I ignore that and focus instead on Mila. "I heard everything! I know that whatever Ilarion's reasons for marrying Celine are, and it sure as hell is not because he cares about her."

Mila nods again with understanding spreading across her face. "You didn't stay in the garden."

"I appreciated our little heart-to-heart, I really did, but screw you if you think you can manipulate me with that shit. Contrary to what you believe, I'm not some pathetic little wallflower who needs to be saved."

Her eyes widen when she realizes just how much of their conversation I overheard. Then she drops her gaze to the gun in my hands."

"You're going to hurt yourself, Taylor," she says quietly. "Put the gun down."

"Let me say it again: screw you."

Her men have slowly surrounded us. Ten of them, armed to the teeth, fanned out in a ragged semi-circle. They're looking back and forth between Mila and me, ready to make their move as soon as she gives the word.

It doesn't matter. I'm not about to lower my gun.

"I'm coming with you."

Mila raises her brow. "No, you're not."

"Yes, I am. I have no faith that any of you are going to do everything you can to bring back Celine or Dad. So I'm coming with you to make sure you do."

Mila glances over to her men. "You realize that you're severely outnumbered, right? Hell, even if you weren't, I could disarm you in seconds."

I don't hesitate. I cock the gun, point at a spot close to Mila's feet, and fire. The gunshot is louder than I expect, and the recoil stings my hand. I barely manage to hold onto the weapon.

Still, it has the desired effect. The men step back, and Mila moves back as well, shock and disbelief clouding her face. "Y-you…just shot at me."

"That was a warning shot," I inform her. The tremble in my arm is gone; both of us realize I can and absolutely will follow through on my threat. And as inexperienced as I am, it's hard to miss from point-blank range. "I told you—I'm not messing around. Your men may be able to disarm me, but I'll do some damage before that happens."

She stares at me as though she's seeing me clearly for the first time. Then she raises one arm. "Stand down." When no one listens, she scowls. "Do it."

The men lower their guns but no one takes their eyes off me. Mila looks at me and smirks. "My brother will kill me for letting you tag along."

"You're not 'letting me' do anything. I'm forcing you to."

"Somehow, I don't think he will agree." She laughs. "I will say this, though—you only missed by a few inches, so you're already a better shot than Dima." She toes the hole in the floor, then looks up at me with a bemused twinkle in her eyes. "You sure this is what you want?"

I nod and swallow, though my mouth is dry as sandpaper. "Positive."

"Okay then." Mila turns to face her men. "We've got one more person on board, gentlemen, and she's precious cargo. You don't need to know why. All you need to know is that no one gets near her. Is that understood? If someone touches so much as a hair on her head, you kill the motherfucker. If someone blinks too aggressively at her, you kill the motherfucker. Or else, it's all our lives at stake. The *pakhan* will make sure of it."

Satisfied that her message has been received, she turns back to me.

"Well?" she asks. "Are you coming or not?"

42

ILARION

"Well?" Dima asks, passing the binoculars to me.

"It's not a trap," I say confidently. "The letter's legit."

"How can you be sure?"

"Look at the security around the place." I point out each of the squadrons we can see. "Thirty men in the front and only twenty out in the back. If they'd been anticipating an attack, there would be three times as many on duty."

Thanks to the thick forest just outside the Bellasio estate's boundaries, we're able to hide out in here and scope out the place without fear of being seen. Of course, we sent a scout in half an hour ahead of us to make sure the forest was clear first. Now that we've established a base, it's easy to anticipate how the attack will pan out.

"Boss," Petro says, approaching us from behind one of our armored trucks, "a vehicle just left the property."

I look back at the high rust-red walls of the property, searching for any signs about what might be happening. "Who was in it?"

"Gregor Bellasio."

Ah. Not Celine, but Benedict's younger sibling. "Didn't know that little shit was in the country."

"Neither did I," Dima admits. "But I've heard he's working closely with Benedict now."

"Figures the only one Benedict can trust is his brother," I grumble, turning my binoculars toward the windows on the third story of the ugly building. "Put two of our guys on Gregor."

"Is two enough?" Dima asks. "He's probably traveling with more men than that."

"The fact that he left the property at all suggests that they're not expecting any trouble," I reason. "I just want to keep a tab on him. We're not about to engage him openly."

Dima nods, then glances at his phone again. He frowns when his notifications are empty. "Where is Mila? It's not like her to be late. She can't have left more than a few minutes after we did."

"I told her to take a position at the other side of the property. She'll let us know if there are any developments. So far, she's only confirmed what we already know: they're not expecting this. We—"

Before I can finish, my phone vibrates in my side pocket. "Speak of the devil. There she is." I glance at the screen and read her text. "She's noticing movement on the third floor.

About five guards patrolling the level. She thinks Celine is being held in a room in the south quadrant."

Dima lights up. "Then what are we waiting for?"

I jump out of the armored Hummer and turn toward my men. "On my signal, we drive through those gates and take the whole place by storm. Dima, you're with me. Petro and Goga, I'll need you to flank us when we're inside. We have to get up to the third floor. And as for prisoners…we don't need any. If a Bellasio fucker comes at you, kill him where he stands."

Adrenaline and bloodlust churn in the men's eyes. There's nothing like the furor of battle to rally the soldiers together. I can feel the excitement build as I get into the vehicle and raise my fist in the air out of the window.

When I drop it, a dozen engines roar to life.

The Bellasio alarm blares just before we plow through the gates and open fire on every man who comes running at us. The fleet of vehicles takes hits, dents, and scratches as a hail of bullets tries to cut us down, but it's pitifully easy to crash through their barriers and bulldoze the poor bastards who chose the wrong brotherhood. In the blink of an eye, two dozen Bellasio goons are dead.

The house's façade is made out of large glass windows flanking an ugly iron door. Dima takes one look at me and smirks. "Are you thinking what I'm thinking?"

I nod. "Smash it."

Dima whistles and then steps on the gas. We shoot forward like a bat out of hell, and when we come up on the windows, we don't stop.

The crash of shattering glass is deafening, an auditory "fuck you" to the bastards who believed they could attack me in my own home and get away with it. It sounds like the sky breaking wide open.

The Hummer comes to a stop with tires smoking in the welcome hall. Shattered glass is strewn everywhere when Dima and I jump down out of the vehicle. It crunches under our boots as we make our way over to the gold elevator in the far corner.

Dima, Petro, Goga, and I climb in and ride up three floors. "Get ready," I tell my men as we near our destination.

Predictably, Bellasio men are waiting for us the moment the doors whoosh open. We stick to the sides of the elevator and take out several of the men before forcing the firefight out of the enclosed space.

I can smell shock and fear on the Bellasio minions as I force my way through the corridor toward the unmarked doors lining the adjoining hall.

My fiancée is bound to be behind one of them. While my men cover me, I kick down each door, searching for her. I hear another round of gunshots go off.

"Fuck!" someone cries out. Definitely one of mine. Either Petro or Goga.

"Go, Ilarion!" Dima yells. "We'll fend them off. Mila's team just joined the fold."

I shoot off two more bullets, saving Dima from a blind attack over his shoulder, and then I race down the hall. I find her behind the third door that I kick down.

"Celine!"

She's cowering beneath a four-poster bed with her hands over her ears. The moment she sees me, her eyes fill with tears of relief. "Ilarion," she sobs, stumbling out from her position behind the bed. "Oh, thank God! Thank God!"

She runs right at me, and before I know it, she's got her arms wrapped around my neck and she's clinging on for dear life. "I knew you'd come," she gasps. "I knew you'd come for me."

"Take a breath," I say, gently peeling her hands off and placing them back by her sides. "Are you okay? Are you hurt?"

She shakes her head. "No, I'm not hurt."

I take a step back. She's wearing a soft cotton dress that's too big for her—not her style, but it's clearly new. No visible damage on her skin. No blood. Judging by her overall appearance, she's been treated well.

I take a quick scan around the room. The windows have been sealed, but they offer a pleasant view through the drawn curtains. There's a bronze tray by the bedside with an empty salad plate.

So she hasn't been starved, either.

"What's going on out there?" Celine asks as another round of gunshots blasts through the air.

I keep her near me as I stride over to the window. My men are busy fending off a fresh wave of Bellasio grunts pouring in from somewhere unseen. I can't spy either Dima or Mila, but I'm willing to bet both are securing the grounds to make sure we can get Celine out.

"Stay here," I order. I start to make for the door.

"No!" Celine cries out. She pulls into my side, tucking herself under my arm. "Please don't leave me."

Her strawberry blonde hair smells of lemon and lilac. It feels wrong…like my nose is searching for hazelnuts and vanilla. Her eyes are curious when they skim over my face. She's probably wondering why I don't look happier to see her.

It's a fair question.

"Celine, listen to me," I say urgently. "My priority is getting you out safely. We don't have time to lose."

I pull myself out of her arms and go to the other side of the room. The distance helps. I push aside the nagging doubt that threatens to undo everything I've worked toward in the last few months. I focus only on the next few minutes, as I pull the door open and take a look down the hall.

There's nothing on the right, but when I turn to the left, I catch the eyes of two Bellasio guards who've managed to sneak their way up here.

They rush toward me. I duck back into the room and pull out both my guns. "Celine, take cover. Now!"

She pales visibly and drops down to the floor. But she's still out in the open. There's nothing between her and them but me.

"Fucking hell," I growl. "The bed! Get behind it."

She's trying to crawl over to the bed when the door bursts open. I hit the first *mudak* right between the eyes, but the second avoids a similar fate by using his dead companion as a shield.

He twists to the side and sends three bullets my way in quick succession. I avoid all three shots and lunge towards the panicked soldier, grabbing him around the waist and forcing him to the floor. I can feel the ground shudder as I straddle the asshole and punch him in the face before he can unleash another round.

I get in three more hits before his eyes roll back and he loses consciousness. Then I grab his gun and use it to shoot him under the chin. Blood sprays and he stops moving.

"Celine," I call as I get back to my feet, "you okay?"

All I get in answer is a frightened little squeak. I look over to the bed and find her peering at me around one of the legs. "I... I can't leave th-this room... Th-they'll c-c-come for me..."

I walk over to her and peer down at the terrified woman who I've chosen to be a part of my world. "Celine," I say, trying to be as gentle as I can, "you have nothing to worry about. I'm with you now."

A tear escapes down her cheek. "Did you get Benedict?" she asks.

"You don't need to worry about him. He's far away."

She frowns. "W-what?"

"Our intel says he's not in the country."

Her frown turns into open horror. "Yes, he is. He came to see me a few minutes before the shooting started."

Oh, fuck.

I'm about to grab my gun when I feel the shadow descend.

"Make another move and I'll blow your brains out, Zakharov."

I freeze, seeing only his outline in my peripheral vision.

"Good. Now—turn around slowly."

I keep my hands where he can see them as I pivot toward the door.

Benedict Bellasio is standing there, dressed in dark tailored pants and a long-sleeved shirt. His light blue eyes are trained on me with the mocking hunger of a predator.

"Benedict," I say darkly.

He gives me a wry smirk. "Pleasure to see you, Ilarion."

43

ILARION

The first time I met Benedict Bellasio, I was seventeen.

It was my father's turn to host the dons' council meeting that year. It was also the first time that the Bellasios would be in attendance. Andrea Bellasio brought along his only son and I watched hidden from the staircase as the two of them bickered.

"Why can't I come in with you?" Benedict whined. "I'm twenty years old!"

"This meeting is for the men, not the boys. Keep arguing and I will have to make an example of you. One day, you will lead my soldiers, and they're not going to have respect for you as their don if they've seen him get disciplined by his father."

Benedict scowled and glanced around for bystanders. Even then, he had this furtiveness about him that anyone with half a brain immediately mistrusted. I wouldn't have trusted him to watch water boil for me.

"They need to see me as an equal," he protested. "They need to respect me *now*, if I'm going to be their don later."

Andrea grabbed him by the collar of his shirt and yanked him forward. "You are *not* an equal," he spat in his son's face. "You want their respect? Earn it. And that starts with submitting to me. Don't make me correct you again. Those who see it will never forget."

He shoved Benedict away and strode into the meeting room. That's when Benedict turned to the side and spotted me. I still remember how his face twisted into a horrified grimace.

I was the witness to his humiliation.

Thirteen years later, it's clear from the look on his face that he still hasn't forgiven me for what I overheard.

"I could shoot you right now, you know," he remarks, inching into the room and closing the door behind him.

"No!" Celine screams. "Please, Benedict—don't!"

I glance at her in surprise, noting the way she uses his first name. There's a familiarity there that I wasn't expecting. "Celine, dear," Benedict says, shaking his head, "I have enjoyed our time together. But not enough to convince me to spare this *stronzo*."

"Spare me?" I ask. "That implies you have the upper hand, my friend."

He scowls at me. "I'm the one holding the gun."

"Better men's bullets haven't stopped me before. What makes you think yours will?"

He narrows his eyes. "You've always thought you were better than me."

That's what it comes down to for Benedict at the end of the day: respect and humiliation. Betters and lessers. His world is a game of chutes and ladders, a squirming pile of rats vying for top position so they can shit downhill on everyone beneath them.

Which is why he can't just put a bullet in my head and be done with it.

He needs me to *know* that he's won.

"Does the better man lose his own fiancée the day of his engagement?" he continues, sauntering closer with the gun held loosely in his pale, unscarred hands. "What kind of man *allows* his woman to be kidnapped?"

A gasp escapes Celine's lips, but I don't chance a glance in her direction. I keep my eyes on Benedict. He's smiling now, smirking from ear to ear. His canines are sharp and gleaming in the light.

"Does it matter?" I ask. "I'm here, I've got her back, and at the end of all of this, there will be a wedding."

Benedict laughs. "You're a fool if you believe that."

"The fool is whoever makes the same mistake over and over again. You underestimated me once before, didn't you? And here you are, doing it again."

The smile withers on his face. His eyes are beady and bulging in their sockets. "Death is too kind for you," he hisses.

"Do it, then," I growl. "Pull the fucking trigger."

"No!" Celine cries, scrambling up to her feet. She places herself right in front of me. "Please, Benedict—don't kill him."

Oh, for God's sake. What is it with these Theron women? She's as much of a fool as her sister is. I go to move her out of my way, but as soon as my hand finds her hip, Benedict's voice lashes out in a shrill shriek.

"NO! Don't move! I will slaughter you both."

The two of us freeze at the same time. Through my hand on her waist, I can feel the terror coursing in Celine's body. But she stands her ground, right in front of me.

She's like her sister in that regard, too.

Stubborn to a fault.

"How touching," Benedict drawls, with an expression that says it's anything but. "She really is a prize, Ilarion. Where did you find her?"

The cloying sweetness in his tone puts me on edge for a moment. If he decides to call my bluff, this entire dance is done. I'm saved from answering when Benedict launches into a speech, spurred by his love for his own voice.

"Pretty, smart, interesting…hopelessly loyal," he drones.

"Is there a point you're trying to make?" I ask, rolling my eyes.

"Tell me, which quality would you consider the most important in a woman?" Benedict asks. "Because if you were to ask me, I would suggest that loyalty stands above the rest. And yet…she certainly enjoyed my company."

Celine stiffens. "What are you—"

"She was more than happy to talk to me, listen to me. To do whatever I asked of her."

"Ilarion, don't listen to him. None of it is true."

"None of it?" He arches a brow. "I wouldn't go quite that far, *fiore mio.*"

She hesitates, her eyes darting back and forth between the two of us. "I mean, we did talk. We had conversations. All I did was listen."

"Is that *all* you did, Celine?" She tries to turn to face me, but Benedict roars, "Don't move! I won't warn you again!" Then he switches his gaze to me, the hate burning deep in those listless eyes. "I fucked her countless times, on that very bed. Your own wife-to-be, moaning like a whore not two feet from where you're standing right now."

"It's not true!" Celine wails. "I swear, Ilarion. It's not true!"

"Of course she'd lie to you about it," Benedict spits. "Of course she'd tell you it didn't happen. Just look at her. Does she look like a woman who's been held captive?"

She ignores him this time and whips around to face me. "Ilarion, I promise you, it's not true. He did treat me well. But I was still a prisoner. I couldn't leave or take calls. He would come and talk to me every day and I…I listened, but—"

"Enough." I hold up my hand.

She immediately falls silent. Her eyes churn with fear. She's not scared for her life, though.

No, she's scared of losing *me*.

I can hear the promise I made to her mother echoing in the back of my head. I swore that oath in good faith, and I'm not about to renege on it now. Not just because I've discovered I'm more human than I once believed.

Tears cascade down her cheeks as Celine waits for me to say something. I have one eye on Benedict, who's still smiling maniacally, convinced that he's managed to drive a wedge between us.

He'll be very disappointed in just a moment.

"I believe you, Celine," I tell her.

Her face twists with relief at the same time that Benedict's face flushes with anger. "You're lying."

I shake my head and look him in the eye. "Do I look like I'm lying?" I laugh. "You know why I asked Celine to marry me? Because I knew that I could trust her."

His eyes glow like tiny embers. His sweaty hand grips and re-grips the gun again and again, like all his problems will be solved if he just holds it right.

"You want to believe it," he growls. "That's why—"

"No." I shake my head. "I believe Celine. In any case, I can rest easy knowing that after a woman has been with me, she's not about to settle for anything less. And you, Benedict Bellasio, are far less."

His teeth grind together. "You motherfucker—"

He jabs his gun at me just as Celine lunges toward him to stay between us. I'm lunging along right after her, roaring, ready to drag her to the ground and blanket myself on top of, when all of the sudden—

BANG!

The gunshot rings through the air.

Celine falls against my chest, a horrified gasp caught in her throat. I look up, expecting to see the smoking tip of Benedict's gun, the last thing I'll see before he ends my life.

But it's not there.

His hand is empty. His weapon is on the floor.

He's not the one who fired the shot.

He's not even standing anymore. He's sprawled on the floor, groaning incoherently, while blood wells between the fingers clasped to the meat of his shoulder. And above him, standing framed in the doorway with her jaw wide open and a pistol clutched inexpertly in both hands…

Taylor.

44

TAYLOR

For a moment, nothing moves. Not space, not time, not the beating of my heart.

I hear my sister's voice. I see her standing in front of Ilarion, like a soldier ready to lay her life on the line. I see a skeletally thin, dark-haired man with his back to me and his gun pointed at Celine.

And I act on instinct.

I have no real idea how to handle a gun, but Mila gave me a quick lesson while we were waiting out in the forest. She hadn't actually expected me to use it. Hell, I never actually expected to use it, but when chaos descended down on us, I couldn't just sit in the armored car and wait for someone to bring me my sister.

So I waited until all the Bratva troops, including Dima and Mila, were otherwise engaged. Then I snuck into the house.

Up until I stepped into that room, everything felt like it was happening at high speed. Gunshots, screams, angry yells and shouted orders and the groans of dying men. I smelled smoke and blood and the taint of death in the air. I passed more bodies than I could count.

But the speed helped. It was like I was fast-forwarding through the experience just to save myself some trauma later. Because who are we kidding—I really can't afford therapy.

And then I caught sight of my sister. I looked at the man who held her at gunpoint.

No one noticed me.

I raised my gun, remembering everything Mila taught me, and fired. I didn't even really aim to kill. I just knew I had to shoot before he did.

I sucked in a sharp breath when the bullet hit his arm. But even though it wasn't a fatal shot, it succeeded in forcing him to drop his gun. That's when I looked at Ilarion.

And *that's* when the high speed slowed to absolute stillness.

Our eyes lock and I see the shock on his face. It's nice to see something I'd never seen before. Then the shock disappears slowly, and it's replaced by Ilarion's default emotion.

Anger.

The three long seconds that follow hold an entire conversation in the pregnant—*no pun intended*—silence. And then the noise filters back into my ears. Life smashes the *Play* button.

"Taylor!" Celine cries.

I blink and lunge towards my sister, but Ilarion steps around her and blocks my path. "What the fuck do you think you're doing here?"

He snatches the gun from my hand, tucks me behind him, and points it at Benedict where he's lying on the ground.

"No!" Benedict says in a strangled cry. "No, you can't kill me."

"And why the fuck not?"

"My b-brother." Spit flies from his mouth as he clutches his arm as though it's about to fall off, though I think I barely even grazed him. "My brother… We have an army…He'll come for you…"

"I'm not scared of your fucking army."

"No!" Celine and I scream at the same time.

"Our father. He still has Dad!" I say.

Benedict lets out a bubble of bloody laughter. "Exactly… I…I have their father. And if I die…he joins me."

Ilarion glances between the two of us, his eyes murky with conflict. Footsteps thunder on the stairs as we wait for him to make his decision.

"Ilarion," I gasp, grabbing his arm and forcing him to look at me. "Please—he's our father."

A heartbeat later, with Ilarion's gun still hanging in the balance, Dima appears at the threshold of the door, several men clustered close at his back. He scans the room and catches sight of Benedict. "Ah—see you caught vermin. Glad I got here in time to witness the bug get squashed."

Ilarion's jaw twitches wildly, but I know when the hardness settles into those misty blue eyes that he's made his choice.

"Not today," he tells Dima. "Gag and bind him. We're taking him with us."

45

TAYLOR

"W-what?" Dima stammers, gawking at Ilarion in bewilderment. His gaze swings to me and he does a double-take. "Taylor?!"

I give him a wink. The adrenaline crash is making me giddy, like I'm high or dreaming. "Hi, Dima. You don't happen to have an *iriski* in your pocket, do you?"

He just continues to stare at me with his mouth hanging open.

"Dima!" Ilarion barks, pulling him out of his state of shock.

"Right," Dima mumbles. "Right. Talk later. The situation is contained downstairs, by the way. Every Bellasio man on site is dead."

He shakes his head and turns to oversee the men as they bind and gag Benedict. Ilarion waits until they drag him out of the room before he turns to me. "What the *fuck*, Taylor?"

He wants me to cower and crumble in the face of his anger. But I won't. I'm riding this high of having the upper hand for as long as I can.

God only knows when I'll get another chance.

"I told you before: I'm not some shrinking violet. I can take care of myself. More importantly, I can take care of my family."

"It's not your responsibility to—"

"She's my sister," I interrupt furiously. "Of course it's my responsibility."

"Like fuck it is," he growls, stepping forward. He's so close to me now that if he leans in just a fraction of an inch more, the tips of our noses will touch. "Who brought you?"

"No one brought me. I stole Mila's gun and shot her in the foot. Sort of. Then I stole her Hummer and made her drive me here."

"Do you really expect me to believe that?" he asks coldly. "On second thought, never mind. Foolish. Fucking foolish. Why the hell did you think you belonged here?"

I gesture incredulously at the trail of blood on the carpet. "Are you blind? *That's* why! I just saved you! *Both* of you!

Ilarion runs a frustrated hand through his hair. "You're out of your mind."

"That's a weird way to say, *Thank you.*"

He splutters with rage. "Thank y—? No. *No.* Get the fuck downstairs. Now!"

He grabs my hand and twists me towards the door, and I swipe my nails at his face. We're about to thrash into our own battle when we both hear a scream that stops in our tracks.

"Stop it! Both of you!"

Guilt and shame flood through me when I realize that I've completely forgotten about Celine's presence. I yank my arm from Ilarion's grasp and turn to face my sister.

She's looking between the two of us with an expression that's one part shock, two parts disbelief, and ten parts anger. I can count on one hand the number of times I've seen her cheeks go quite that red.

"You realize that I'm in the room, too, right?" she demands. "I'm the one who was kidnapped!"

"Celine…"

She turns to Ilarion, expecting him to finish his sentence. But for once, he seems at a loss for words.

"Okay. Clearly, I've missed a lot," she whispers, her voice trembling. "And I know this is an intense situation. But I'm here, I'm safe, and everything is okay."

"No, it's not, Cee," I say, grabbing her hand just to remind myself that she's alive and everything is okay. Or rather, that it *will* be okay—once we rescue our father and get our family the fuck away from Ilarion forever. "You can't trust him. He's not who you think he is."

"Tay—"

"Please, listen to me."

"I *am* listening to you," she insists. "You're the one who never listens to me."

I drop her hand. "What?"

"I've told you before: I *chose* Ilarion. I trust Ilarion. And that means that whether you like it or not, you're going to have to accept the fact that I'm with him."

I'm about to say something when she holds up her hand. The same way that Dad used to do when I got mouthy with him. My lips snap shut, and my cheeks burn with embarrassment.

"That's enough. You think I don't know who I'm marrying. I'm marrying Ilarion Zakharov, *pakhan* of the Zakharov Bratva. He told me who he was on our first date, Tay. I knew the risks going into our engagement and I chose to accept them."

"He doesn't really l—"

"STOP!" Celine screams so loudly that I take an instinctive step back. "Just…stop." She takes a deep breath. "I love you for wanting to protect me, but you don't have to do that. I don't need your protection. I need you to trust me. To trust that I know what I'm doing." She meets my gaze and holds it. "Can you do that for me? Please?"

When she asks like that…what choice do I have? I don't so much as glance in Ilarion's direction as I nod silently to my sister.

She smiles and floats forward to hug me. "Thank you," she whispers in my ear. "I know this isn't easy for you, but it'll all work out. You'll see."

And Ilarion called *me* delusional.

I release Celine, and she turns to her fiancé. "Ilarion," she murmurs. "I…oh my God! You're bleeding!"

His eyes flicker to mine for the briefest of moments before they divert back to Celine. "It's nothing. Just a scratch."

"Let me see it," Celine insists, taking his arm tenderly.

I turn and walk out of that room as fast as I can. I don't stop until I reach the truck that we arrived in. Mila is standing by the open passenger door, one leg on the runner, the other on the forest floor.

"Dima filled me in," she says, watching me with incredulous respect. "*You* shot Benedict Bellasio?"

"Yeah. But I missed. Mostly."

She stares at me for another long moment. Then she bursts into laughter. "You're full of surprises, Taylor Theron. I can't wait to see what you do next."

Yeah, I think miserably. *Me neither.*

46

ILARION

"I'm fine," I snarl. "You don't need to keep fucking petting me."

Celine freezes, her hands hovering inches away from my skin.

I curse inwardly as I attempt to act like a normal human being to my fiancée. "Fuck. Forget it. I'm just—"

"On edge," she fills in. "I know. It's okay."

I look up to see her eyes filling with tears. "Celine, I believe you, okay?" I say. "I don't have faith in a word that fuck said to us."

She smiles self-consciously, but shakes her head. "No, that's not what… I mean, I'm glad that you believe me, of course."

"There's something else on your mind?"

She nods, her hand still fluttering like a wounded bird over my arm. "You and Taylor seem really…"

I find myself holding my breath, waiting to see what will follow. Suspicions? Accusations? Instincts? Either way, I'm tempted to just answer with the truth.

Not that I know what the fuck the truth *is* at this point.

"Really pissed at each other," she concludes. "Did something happen?"

"Lots of things happened, Celine," I tell her with a grimace. "You and your father were abducted, for one. In case you forgot."

"Right." She looks down and shuffles her feet on the carpet. "That must have been hard on Mom and Taylor."

A lightning bolt of unease strikes me out of nowhere. Oh, fuck.

She doesn't know about her mother.

I should tell her immediately, but as I open my mouth to do it, I change my mind. Why not give her a few more hours of blissful ignorance? She's been through a lot. And when the time does come, why should I be the one to tell her?

"You will get Dad back, won't you?" she presses. "They're not going to hurt him, especially now that you have Benedict?"

"Gregor isn't really known for reining in his worst instincts," I murmur. It's only when I see the look of horror on Celine's face that I realize I'm saying too much. "He's not going to risk his brother's life, though. Don't worry."

She sighs. "All I do is worry."

It's hard to look at her and see a person. I see those tears and I can imagine what it feels like to be the one crying them, but at the same time, she's not a person to me. I can't afford to let her be that.

She is a pawn. She is part of a plan. She is Taylor's sister.

All good reasons to keep my distance.

"Let's get you home," I tell her wearily. "Mila and Taylor will be waiting for us."

"Taylor's living with you?"

I make a mental note to have a meeting with my dear sister once I confirm she is not, in fact, limping on one foot. We need to coordinate lies. "Taylor has been living at the Diamond until Zakharov House is rebuilt. I didn't think it would be safe for her to go back to her apartment."

Celine smiles shyly. "I'm glad. Tay can be stubborn sometimes. I'm happy you managed to convince her to stay where it's safe."

I snort as I guide her to the exit. "I didn't convince her to do anything. I didn't really ask, to be honest."

Celine frowns. "I'm beginning to realize why she seems to hate you so much."

I bite back another sigh. *If only that were true.*

47

ILARION

When we get back downstairs, I see that Dima has loaded the restrained Benedict into the back of one of the armored trucks. He's surrounded on all sides by thousands of pounds' worth of loyal Zakharov soldiers.

"Don't let him out of your sight," I order Dima.

"No chance of that," he assures me. "Where are we taking him?"

"Zakharov House. We can keep him confined to the cellars until I decide on the next move. We'll drive with you until the interstate and split up there."

The rest of the truck caravan is waiting, engines purring, for us to board and depart. At the lead vehicle, Mila and Taylor stand shoulder by shoulder.

I do a double-take when I see them. Taylor is dressed much like my sister, in dark jeans and a dark tank top that shows off her toned arms. Blood, grime, and sweat mingle on her tanned skin and capture the light until it looks like she's glowing. But what catches my eye the most is the resolute set of her jaw, the fire in her eyes, the grace in her stance.

She doesn't look like a fish out of water. Not the way that Celine does.

She looks like…

Like she belongs.

I tear my gaze from Taylor and focus on my sister instead. Mila gives me a guilty smile and starts sauntering towards me. "Celine," I say. "Why don't you get in? I'll only be a minute."

She doesn't question me; she just nods and gets into the backseat of one of the cars. I shut the door and turn to Mila, whose feet look relatively intact.

"This explanation better be good," I snarl.

She doesn't have to ask to know what I'm talking about. "She had me at gunpoint. What was I supposed to do?" She's not nearly as contrite as I expected her to be.

"Is that a joke? You could have disarmed her in seconds. Not to mention the fact that you had her outnumbered ten to one."

Mila shrugs. "She was tougher than I expected." She glances over to where Dima is silently taunting Benedict. "And a far better shot."

"You don't have a hole in your foot, so I'm guessing her aim's not all that good." I keep my voice low, well aware of the fact that Taylor is watching us from afar. "You are so predictable."

"What's that supposed to mean?"

"It means that she got to you, didn't she?"

Mila raises her eyebrows. "You're telling me she didn't impress you, too?"

I glare down. "Careful, *moya sestra*."

"I'm just saying—"

"Well, don't. I have to get both of them home immediately. We have Benedict, but Gregor isn't exactly a wilting daisy. He could be back any moment with reinforcements."

"I'm going, I'm going," she grumbles, backing up toward her contingent with her hands held up in surrender. She glances at Taylor and hitches a thumb in my direction. Taylor takes one look at me and shakes her head. Then she climbs into the same Hummer as Mila.

Grinding my teeth together, I get into the back seat with Celine and punch the roof of the vehicle. As soon as I do, we start to pull out.

I keep my eyes on the window, but I can feel Celine watching me. "You're upset about something," she says abruptly as we leave the burning trees of the broken Bellasio property behind us.

I force myself to turn to her with as patient a smile as I can muster. "No, I'm not."

She frowns. "I know we haven't known each other all that long, Ilarion, but I can still tell when something's not right with you." When I don't say anything, she sighs. "You deserve to know what happened while I was with Benedict."

"I already told you—"

"He offered me a deal," she explains, rushing through the words as though she's scared she won't have the courage to say them if she holds out any longer. "He told me that he would marry me if I agreed to end my engagement with you."

My blood had just begun to settle after the firefight, but at those words, it starts to churn all over again. "He did *what?*"

She nods. "He didn't bring it up right away. He would come to see me every couple of hours and he would talk to me."

"About what?"

She shrugs. "His childhood, his family, his interests. It was almost like he wanted me to get to know him. To see that he wasn't so bad. Then, around the third day…that was when he offered me the deal. He told me that the marriage would come with safety for my entire family, with property and wealth and travel. Whatever my heart desired. He also told me that he wouldn't hurt Mom."

"And you said…?"

Her eyes freeze on me for a moment. She passes right through shock and veers quickly into hurt. "You're not… You're really asking me that?"

"Celine—"

"I love you, Ilarion," she snaps. "Do you really think I'm so fickle that I would throw you away for whatever some crazed mafioso promised me?"

"He was dangling your father's safety in front of you, Celine. All I'm trying to say is that I wouldn't have blamed you for considering your options."

She eyes me angrily. "Yeah, well, maybe that would have been enough to convince you, but it wasn't enough to convince me. I wasn't about to trust a man who threatened to kill my loved ones if I didn't sign away my life to him."

"So you said no."

"Of course I said no. I'm not gonna lie; I was terrified. I thought he would…would quit asking and just *make* me at one point. But he just told me that one day I would regret my decision. Then he left."

"Did he touch you?" I swear I will stop the entire caravan and beat the fucker within an inch of his life if he laid a finger on her.

She shakes her head. "No. I think he just wanted me to believe that he would. That he could. I told him that if he forced himself on me, that would just prove how weak of a man he was."

I feel a reluctant bloom of pride. "Smart girl."

"And," she adds, "I knew you would come for me."

I turn my face out the window so she can't see me grimace. As forest fades into the highway, I think about the way she yelled at Taylor to back off. She's only known me for a matter of months and she was ready to go to battle for me. Against her own sister.

The more I talk to her, the longer I'm in her presence, the more I realize something that I can't quite escape from: this is a woman who deserves to know the truth.

The problem is, *I can't give her what she's asking.*

"You shouldn't have started something with your sister over me."

"You're going to be my husband," she says firmly. "Taylor needs to respect that. I understand that this has been hell for her, too. She's gotten caught up in the chaos of it all. But she still doesn't have the right to tell me what to do with my life. No one does."

"What about your father?" I suggest gently. "Considering everything that has happened, he might agree with Taylor."

"It doesn't matter," she answers. "It won't change my decision. I know what I want, Ilarion. I want *you*. Maybe that's selfish considering everything I've put my family through, but…I can't stop wanting you."

Fuck me. I'd known from the moment I met Celine that I could never love her.

But I never foresaw this.

Suddenly, the fact that Taylor is pregnant with my baby seems too big a secret to keep from this innocent, open-hearted woman. It feels like a betrayal considering how much she's willing to sacrifice for me.

"What's wrong?" she asks, reaching out and cupping my face with her palm.

The fact that I want to duck out of her reach only cements my decision. I have to tell her. "Listen Celine…there's something I need to tell you."

She frowns, unease and fear seeping back into her eyes. "Okay…"

"I—"

The explosion that sounds right then is like the world tearing itself in two. My eardrums nearly burst. Every thought, every memory, every sensation I've ever experienced condenses down to one tightly knotted fear in my chest. And that fear has a name.

Taylor.

48

ILARION

We skid to a stop with an ear-splitting screech of the tires. Celine is too terrified to even scream. I shove her down into the wheel well, then grab her face and force her to look at me.

"Stay here. Do you understand that? *Stay here.*"

I don't wait to see if she's following orders. I leap out of the car, my boots hitting the gravel hard. "What the fuck was that?" I ask Ivan, my driver, as he climbs out with me and cocks his gun.

"Not sure, *pakhan*. Looks like someone is trying to block our path."

I look to the front of the caravan. All the other trucks have come to a halt like us, strewn at awkward angles around the road. Smoke is billowing in every direction. I can't see farther than ten or twenty yards ahead.

"It has to be Gregor. Get back in the car and stay there with Celine. Lock the doors. Don't open them for anyone but me."

I don't wait to see if he understands, either. I just unholster my weapon and charge toward the source of the explosion.

Dima and Mila fall into step along the way. I glance at my sister as we all run with guns in hand. "Is—"

"Taylor is fine," she reassures me. "She tried following me out, but I managed to lock her inside."

"Good. Keep her there while I find out whatever the fuck is going on. If she makes a fuss, threaten her with violence."

Mila snorts. "Like that's ever worked before."

But she does as I say, falling back to make sure the little *tigrionok* stays where she belongs.

"I don't think it's a good idea that you go," Dima says as I resume my jog toward the front of the line. He grabs my shoulder to make me grind to a stop. "Let me check first."

"Like hell I will." I shoulder-check him out of my way. He sighs, but I hear his stride pick up as he follows me.

My car was the sixth in line. Benedict was two cars ahead of me. I approach his and pop the trunk to reveal the Bellasio don tied up like a Thanksgiving turkey, with half a dozen Bratva guns trained on his face. Few sights make me more pleased.

Though I do see a glint of excitement lurking behind the venomous glare in his eyes. He thinks he smells a rescue in the air.

"It's not happening today, motherfucker," I growl. Then I slam the trunk on his moronic smirk.

I stride the last bit of the way to the first car in the procession and immediately see the problem. A massive tree has fallen across the path, kicking up dirt that I mistook for smoke. It's three of me in diameter, far too big to cut to pieces without specialized equipment. Driving around isn't an option, either—it's densely thicketed woods on either side.

My men milling around the scene of the accident have already reached the same conclusion: the only way out is to retrace our route and go back the way we came from.

"Fuck," I mutter, looking back over my shoulder. This isn't right. Something is missing from this equation. "I heard an explosion."

"Over here, sir," Stepan says from a few steps off the road. I can see him through the looming trees, squatting down and examining something on the ground.

"What is it?" I ask, inching closer.

"This wasn't a freak act of nature." He points at the charred black remains of earth where someone had detonated an explosion large enough to take down the monstrous tree.

"Motherfuckers," I growl.

Dima straightens up immediately. "This has Gregor's fingerprints all over it," he says. "Ilarion, we need to take cover. There's an attack coming."

I turn back toward the vehicles where the women are. Armored vehicles can only hold off so much. We're still entirely too exposed for my liking, and strung out along the road.

Easy pickings.

I grab hold of Dima. For once, I let him see just how panicked I am. "Protect her at all costs," I growl, my eyes darting around the forests, looking for signs of the hail of death that's surely on its way. "Over everyone. Do you hear me?"

"Brother..." Dima says gently, forcing my gaze to him. "Protect *who* at all costs? Which one?"

Not so long ago, the world was in the palm of my hand. I had the perfect plan, all outcomes laid out so neatly before me. I was the fucking puppet master.

Now, it's a disaster. All because of a tiger cub who ran across the road without looking and stood crying in the rain when I asked her what she wanted from her life.

How the fuck did it all go so wrong?

"Taylor," I say without hesitation. "Protect Taylor."

Dima nods solemnly. "With my life."

"Men!" I yell.

The ones closest to me gather around, while the others climb on top of their vehicles so that they can hear and see me. "The Bellasios think they can corner us here and take us out." My grin is wolfish but it does not meet my eyes. "We're about to show them just how stupid they are."

I'm answered with a hearty war cry that sends the blood pumping harder in my veins. "We hold our ground for the next ten minutes while our scouts check the area. Then, we turn around and find another route home."

They stamp their approval of the plan. Satisfied, I walk towards...

I stop short when I realize I'm not sure which car I'm stopping to check on first.

Taylor's?

Or Celine's?

49

ILARION

I stand there marooned in no-man's-land for far too long, knowing that despite the tinted windows, both women can see me from where they sit. I glance up. My sister is staring at me from where she's leaning against one of the other trucks.

"Bit off more than you can chew, huh?" she says with a knowing smirk.

"This doesn't mean anything," I say firmly. "Taylor just happens to be the mother of my child."

Mila nods. "And she also happens to be just ballsy enough to have caught your interest and kept it. Let's see, how many women have done that in the past?" She pretends to take a moment to think about it. "Oh, right—none."

"The die has been cast, Mila." But, with a clench of my jaw, I make my way to Celine's car.

When I open the door, she's sitting with her hands together, staring out the windshield, nervous tension splayed across her face. "Ilarion!" she gasps the moment she sets eyes on me. "What's going on?"

My plan had been to tell her the truth, prepare her for an imminent attack. But the moment I see the naked panic on her face, I know I can't do it. It will break her, and she's already so fragile.

"Nothing I can't handle," I tell her confidently. "Just sit tight, okay?"

"We're not heading out yet?"

"Not just yet. There's an obstruction blocking the road, so we may have to turn back."

It's obvious that she suspects something is going on, but she doesn't ask. Instead, she bites her tongue and leans back against her seat. "Okay. I'll wait here."

I believe her, too. She really will sit where she's told and keep her head down. She won't charge where she shouldn't be. She won't steal a gun and shoot a hole in my sister's foot and risk everything for the ones she loves. She will never, ever bite back.

Maybe that's the problem.

I close the door and step over to Taylor's vehicle. I've just thrown open the car door when a foot flies out and nearly hits me in the chest. "Shit!" I grunt as Taylor lets out a startled scream. She's grabbing the seat for dear life, having very nearly fallen right out of it. "What the hell do you think you're doing?"

Behind me, Mila tries to stifle her laughter.

Taylor looks flushed, but she quickly straightens up. "I, um… I was trying to kick down the door." I narrow my eyes at her and she throws her hands up in frustration. "Well, Mila locked me in!"

"With good reason," Mila shoots back. "You would've done something stupid if I hadn't. You did something stupid anyway, actually."

Taylor huffs. "I deserve to know what's going on."

I sigh and pinch the bridge of my nose. There is no question about one thing: this sister is the far bigger headache. "What's going on is that Gregor Bellasio set off an explosion that took down a huge tree. Our way home is blocked."

"Can we just turn back?" she asks.

"Thanks, genius. I hadn't thought of that."

She rolls her eyes. "I suppose you're anticipating an attack?" she says, her voice rippling with a thread of anxiety. But again, unlike her sister, it seems to prepare rather than cripple her.

"Yes. We need to make sure we're not caught off-guard before we turn these vehicles around."

I stop short when I hear something. A distant rumble. Thunder? Earthquake? An...engine?

An engine.

"*TAKE COVER!*" someone screams from a few feet away.

As soon as he says it, a huge truck explodes out of the forest —and crashes right into the Jeep that Celine is inside.

The truck spins the Jeep sideways, throwing it several feet before it flips into its side. It does one, two, three somersaults before it plows into the trees on the far side of the road.

Metal crunches. Glass shatters. "No," I hear Taylor gasp. Then she starts to scream. "*NO! CELINE!*"

She jumps out of the Hummer, but I catch her around her waist before she even hits the ground. "No," I growl, even as Bellasio thugs rush out of the truck. "Get back inside!"

"Celine!" she continues screaming, completely ignoring me. "Let me go! That's my sister!"

I want to tell her that I'll take care of it. That I won't let anyone get hurt. But I don't have time for words. So I hurl her back into her truck and slam the door on her furious screams. Mila and Dima are already returning fire at the Bellasio reinforcements.

It's fucking madness all over again. I have to shoot my way through the onslaught to get to Celine's upturned car.

But it's like battling locusts. They're everywhere, dozens upon dozens of them. Each one individually is crushed with ease, but as a whole, there's just too fucking many.

"Secure the prisoner!" I yell, but my voice is lost in the chaos of screams and gunshots.

I vault onto the hood of one of the trucks and scale up onto the roof. I stand there, looking down at the entire scene unfolding.

I don't know where to go first. Benedict, Celine, Taylor, Mila, Dima—I have too many weak points. Too many vulnerabilities to exploit.

Once again, I have to ask myself, *How did everything go so wrong?*

"Ilarion!" Dima screams from the ground next to me. "What the hell are you doing? You're too visible up there!"

A second later, a bullet scythes past my head, narrowly missing. I feel the sting of air pressure as it whips past me. I can't even locate the shooter; there's too much going on.

"Cover me!" I bellow to Dima. I pick out three, four, five Bellasio men, and each of them die by my gun.

But with the small group of soldiers closing in on Celine, I'm forced to make a split-second decision.

Save her?

Or keep Benedict?

Taylor's face flashes through my mind just before I jump down and sprint towards Celine.

I slam my gun handle-first into the face of a stray Bellasio thug as I fight my way to the car. Two are trying to break down the door from the top to get in. I shoot one in the back of the head and the other one between the eyes.

"Celine!" I call.

No answer.

It takes a few minutes to get the tortured metal of the door to rip free. My muscles are straining as I pull, pull, before finally it gives way. I bend low into the smoky darkness of the car.

For a moment, I don't see her. *Am I too late?*

But then—there.

She's slumped against the opposite window, eyes closed, face pale, blood smeared across the glass and leaking from her scalp.

I crawl in, scoop her limp frame up, and drag her out. Her head lolls lifelessly against my shoulder as I free her.

"Fuck," Mila hisses, materializing from the mayhem with a gun in each hand. "Is she alive?"

I press my fingers to her neck. "She's got a pulse."

I look up past Mila and realize something: it's suddenly quieter. The Bellasio men have gone back the way they came, disappearing into the forest. My men, the ones who survived, are slumped against the cars or ducked down in defensive positions. Everywhere I look, dust swirls and wounded Bratva men grimace with pain.

And in my arms, Celine still hasn't moved.

A silhouette draws closer through the gloom and smoke. It takes shape—Dima. He's got blood and sweat and his hair matted to his forehead. I see before he even approaches that he's coming with bad news.

"He's gone, isn't he?" I ask through gritted teeth.

Dima nods heavily. "I'm sorry, brother. The Bellasios got him back."

50

TAYLOR

I cradle my sister's head in my hands as we speed through the streets.

I buried my mother only days ago. I don't have the strength to bury my sister right next to her. So I cling to Celine like I'm the only thing keeping her above dark water. I talk to her in the hope that some small part of her can hear me.

"It's going to be alright," I whisper again and again until my throat is hoarse from smoke and tears. "Everything's going to be alright."

Dima, Mila, and Ilarion are all in the same Hummer with us. None of them look at me as I continue my steady stream of pointless affirmations. None of them say anything. Like they've already written her off.

Not me.

I'm not giving up.

When the truck finally stops, the door is opened for me. Dima looks at me with the kind of aching sympathy I never want to see again in my life.

"Give her to me, Taylor," he says gently. "I'll be careful."

I can trust him, can't I? He's got a kind smile and a pocketful of sweet toffees he's willing to share. He would never almost run me over with his car. He would never show me what freedom tastes like, then rip it away, along with everything else I've ever loved.

I'm aware that my logic is severely flawed, but I don't have the mental bandwidth to pick it apart right now. *He has toffees. He must be kind.* That has to be enough.

So I help him scoop Celine from the seat. He takes her as tenderly as he can. When my arms are free, I stagger out of the Hummer and look around for the first time.

As Mila steps to my side, I turn to her in horror. "This isn't a hospital," I exclaim. "This is the Diamond!"

"Don't worry," she reassures me. "We have a doctor upstairs waiting for her. He has all the medical equipment he needs to—"

"She needs a *real* doctor!" I cry. "And a *real* hospital!"

"She's in good hands here," Ilarion interrupts, stepping in front of his sister before she can answer.

"Good hands?" I repeat furiously. "*Whose* good hands? *Yours?*"

Ilarion grits his teeth. "Mila, go inside and talk to Dr. Baranov. Stay with Celine and let me know what needs to be done."

Mila nods and slips away from my anger. That's fine with me; she's not the object of it. "Why the hell aren't we at an actual fucking hospital?" I demand of the man I'm blaming for all of this.

"Because that will raise too many unnecessary questions. We don't need the police getting involved."

"Oh, so you're going to compromise my sister's life because you don't want to deal with the inconvenience of a bunch of cops asking some *very* good questions?"

"Nothing is being compromised, Taylor. Dr. Baranov knows what he's doing."

"I want her taken to a hospital!"

"You just want her far away from me," he grits out. "Which is understandable, but inadvisable. She will get the best treatment possible right here."

I stare up at him, at his beautiful, terrifying face stained with the blood and sweat of battle. It's a stark contrast to how calm he is, how calm he *always* is. Even in the face of chaos, his breath is steady and level.

I can't even explain how much I fucking hate it.

It's yet another reminder that both Celine and I are just pawns in this game. The pain is personal. And that cuts deeper than it should.

Maybe it's because this is the first moment of quiet I've had in hours, but I can feel the exhaustion taking my body hostage. I'm not sure what's keeping me on my feet, but it feels treacherous, as though the strings holding me upright are going to snap at any moment.

"You need to rest," he says, reaching for me.

"Don't!" I cringe away from his hands. "Don't touch me."

But even as I say it, I wobble forward and nearly crash to the earth. The only reason I don't is because Ilarion grabs me, his arms caging me against him, forcing me to surrender to the fact that I'm too weak to fight him off.

"Taylor," he whispers in a voice so soft that I'm wondering if I imagined it.

I look up and find myself caught by those cloudy blue eyes. I get lost in them for a moment. I lose myself to relief that I'm okay. Relief that *he's* okay. Relief that at the very least—we can be here, together.

I hate how good it feels to be caught in his arms. I hate how good it feels to have someone strong to lean into.

But his strength is not mine to benefit from. His comfort is not mine to take. It belongs to my sister. And she's lying on a fake hospital bed somewhere upstairs, unconscious and bleeding from the head.

I shake my head and push myself off him. "You should be with Celine right now," I remind him. "Not me."

He doesn't miss the bite in my tone, the thinly veiled accusation. "I need to make sure you and the baby are alright, too." It's a reminder that his concern is not for me alone.

I shouldn't care.

I don't.

I can't.

"I'm fine."

"I'll let Dr. Baranov be the judge of that. Come with me." His expression hardens when I stay put. "If you don't come willingly, I'll be forced to carry you. I don't think either of us want that."

I grit my teeth and nod. Satisfied, he turns and leads us into the house and up to the second floor. I've never been up here. The floor is wide and open, except for one annex sealed off from the space. The subtle printed wallpaper bears the geometric pattern of mountaintops crowding into the sky.

Through the windows of the annex, I spy what I have to admit is a stunningly well-equipped hospital room.

I can just make out Dr. Baranov through the glass. He's not alone. It looks like there are two nurses with him, maybe more. Machines beep and chime and chug along like breathing animals in the background.

Mila is standing off to one corner, biting her nails like I used to do as a kid. Seeing it draws the instinct to my fingertips and it takes all of my willpower to stop myself from falling off the wagon.

She drops her hand from her mouth when she sees us. The moment I take a look at her, the tunnel vision abandons me completely. It's like my ears popping after a plane ride.

I can hear. I can see. I can think.

"She's stable," Mila says when she sees me looking. "For now." But that's all she offers, even though her clenched jaw and gray pallor suggests there's a lot more left unsaid.

I frown. "What aren't you telling me?"

She glances past me at her brother, whose presence I can feel looming behind my shoulder like a shadow I never wanted or asked for. "That's not for me to say. Dr. Baranov will be out here in a moment. I'm sure he'll explain everything."

"If she's dead, Mila, just tell me."

"She's not dead." Again, she doesn't elaborate. "I'll give you two some space."

She turns and leaves. The moment I hear the door shut, I turn to Ilarion. "She's wrong to trust you," I hiss, letting out the words I've been holding in since Celine yelled at me to stop.

"She made it very clear how she feels."

"Except that she's wrong!" I cry. "She doesn't have all the facts. But I do." He tenses, and it's obvious enough that I catch it. "That's right. I overheard you talking to Mila and Dima earlier, before you left on your little rescue mission. I heard you admit that Celine is merely a chess piece on your board. You don't actually love her. You never did."

He just stares coolly down at me, face giving nothing away. I hate that so much. I want to push and punch and shove him until that godawful mask cracks and shows that there's a real person in there.

I know there is. I've seen it with my own two eyes.

But now, when my sister and I both need him more than ever, he's chiseled from stone. Unblinking. Unyielding in the worst way possible.

"Well?" I press. "Don't you have anything to say?"

"No." He meets my gaze, and there isn't a hint of apology in him. "You've made your mind up about me. Nothing I say is going to change it. So I'm not going to waste my time or my breath defending myself."

I glare at him. "Don't you feel bad? Isn't there a single part of you that feels guilty for putting her in this position?"

He looks away from me. I wonder what he's trying to hide. The fact that he doesn't feel anything? Or maybe the truth is that he feels too much?

I laugh darkly against his silence. "I suppose this is a more convenient outcome for you, isn't it?"

"Taylor—"

"Don't," I snap, hating how hearing him say my name makes my insides feel weird and gooey. Or maybe I just hate what that says about me. "I need to know why you asked Celine to marry you. Because it sure as hell wasn't for love."

"You want the truth?" he asks.

"No," I drawl sarcastically, "I want you to keep lying to me."

"Fine." He clenches and unclenches his fist at his side, the only sign that he's anything other than perfectly at ease. "I asked Celine to marry me because I needed a woman to carry my name and my heirs. Your sister is beautiful and intelligent. She also happens to be compliant. She will do what I say, when I say it. That appealed to me."

I recoil. "You married her because…you thought she'd be a doormat?"

"Because I knew she wouldn't be a problem. To put it crudely."

"It's not just crude; it's terrible. Terrible and…shallow. And insanely selfish."

He shrugs. "Perhaps you're right about that."

I shake my head. "But you're still going to go through with the wedding?"

"Unless she has changed her mind, then yes."

"And if she chooses differently when she wakes up?"

He raises his brows. "Then I will let her walk away. I'm not about to force Celine—or anyone—to marry me."

He leaves the last part unspoken: *Because I won't have to.*

His confidence infuriates me—because I know he's right. When Celine yelled at me back on Benedict Bellasio's property, I saw the determination in her eyes. I knew what it meant.

"Have you told her what you just told me?"

Ilarion rolls his eyes. "What do you think?"

"Fine. Then when she wakes up, I'll tell her myself."

He nods. "Do what you must."

I gawk at him, open-mouthed and wavering. "You don't deserve her."

"I won't argue with that. But it won't stop me from doing what I must, too."

51

ILARION

I'm accustomed to always winning. I know what it feels like, even when I tell myself it's necessary for survival. There's pride attached to the feeling, and a deep-seated sense of satisfaction that few other things can rival.

I suppose, logically, I know that Taylor isn't wrong. I do have the upper hand here—and we both know I'm going to win this argument.

So why doesn't it feel that way?

All I can do is stand here, staring back at her with my face wiped clean of any real emotion and give her cold, robotic answers that do nothing but make her despise me more.

Normally, I wouldn't give a damn. But today, there's a gnawing in my gut that tells me I *do* care. I care what this firestorm of a woman thinks of me.

And not just because she's carrying my baby.

No matter how many times I throw that fact between us like a smokescreen.

I walk to the corner of the room and pour her a glass of water from the pitcher. She looks at me incredulously when I offer it to her.

"Drink," I tell her. "It's not poisoned. You watched me fill it."

"I'm not thirsty."

"Yes, you are."

She hesitates for a moment and then she takes the glass of water. Her first sip is tentative. She finishes it with her second.

"Fine," she mumbles as she wipes her wet lips with the back of her hand. "Maybe I was a little thirsty."

"Battle does that to you."

She glances at me through her long lashes. "You seem used to it."

"This war with the Bellasios has been brewing for a long time."

Her brow ripples with curiosity, but she refrains from asking anything else. Instead, she mutters, "I can't believe Celine's okay with all this."

"Give her more credit. She's tougher than you think." But even as I say that, a whole new gnawing in my gut joins the first. I've now seen both sisters in the heat of battle, under intense stress and life-threatening situations…and one handles it far better than the other.

One is fit for this life.

One is barely clinging onto it.

"Being opposed to violence doesn't make you weak," she says. "It makes you moral."

"And there's no way an angel like Celine could possibly love a demon like me?"

"Your words. Not mine."

I smile. "Do you want more water?"

"No," she says, before tacking on a grudging "thank you" at the end.

I set the glass down on a nearby end table. "I can understand your concern for your sister. And you're right: I don't love her." Her eyes grow wide, but she doesn't interrupt me. "But the truth is, I don't think I'm capable of loving anyone."

"It's human nature to love," she says, looking as though she's surprised even herself with that statement.

"Maybe so, but it's not in my nature."

"You're saying you're not human?"

"If that makes it easier for you to digest, then call me whatever you like," I say with a shrug. "The point I'm trying to make is that just because I can't love Celine doesn't mean I won't treat her well. She will be taken care of. Pampered and protected."

"Like she is now?" Taylor scoffs, jerking her head toward the medical annex that Dr. Baranov still hasn't emerged from. "Very impressive. Just do me a favor and don't ever try to 'pamper' me, please."

I bite back a smile. Nothing about this is funny. The fiancée I can't force myself to love is dying one room over. The tiger cub I can't let myself have is spitting fire in my face. I'm at war with an enemy who just slipped through my fingers like sand and I'm bleeding from half a dozen cuts and everything I spent too fucking long crafting is falling apart right in front of me.

And yet the little *tigrionok* bares her fangs, and it makes me smile.

I don't have any goddamn clue what that might mean.

"You're not the pacifist you claim your sister is," I observe.

"I don't take attacks lying down, if that's what you're asking."

"You and I have that in common."

"Probably the one and only thing we have in common," she retorts. "Because the fact is that I do love Celine. And I can't just sit idly by and—"

"I thought you were going to trust your sister?" I say. "Her life, her mistake. Right?"

Her gaze falters and drops to the floor between us. When she speaks, it's a raspy whisper. "That's assuming she still has a life to throw away."

As if on cue, Dr. Baranov walks out of the adjoining room, his face kept carefully blank.

"Is she okay?" Taylor clamors as soon as she sees him, her eyes darting toward her sister's room. "Is she awake?"

Dr. Baranov focuses on Taylor. He lets loose a weary sigh, and my heart double-clutches in my chest. "Your sister suffered major trauma to the head. She's stable for the moment, but it appears…"

"Yes?"

"It appears she's slipped into a coma."

Taylor gasps, her body rocking with a sob that doesn't come out. "C-coma… Are you sure?"

"There's still a reasonable chance that she'll come out of it. We'll have to monitor her closely over the next few days and hopefully—"

Taylor doesn't wait to find out what follows "hopefully." "So you have no idea when or if she'll ever wake up?"

"The next seventy-two hours are crucial," Dr. Baranov gently explains. "If she wakes up within that time frame, then the rehabilitation process will be simpler."

"And if she doesn't?"

Baranov's eyes flit to mine. "Then recovery will be more difficult. She might need to be re-taught certain things. Walking, talking, and reading, for example."

Taylor swallows. "That's fine. We can help—"

"But…"

Her head snaps back up to Dr. Baranov. "But what?"

"The likelihood of her waking up after seventy-two hours is…slim."

She sucks in her breath, and I can feel her teetering towards me. Is it instinct? Is it purely coincidental? I don't wait to find out. I gently grab her arm and twine my fingers through hers.

She doesn't push me away. Her eyes stay trained on Dr. Baranov. "How slim is 'slim'?"

His perfectly orchestrated mask cracks just enough to let her see just how much hope he has for Celine's recovery: vanishingly little.

He doesn't say a word, but I can feel Taylor collapse in on herself. "No…" She whispers it so softly. So heartbreakingly hopeless.

She takes a shaky breath and her legs give out underneath her. I grab her before she can even falter, plucking her up into my arms. She's weightless and limp. Her head lolls against my chest like a newborn fawn.

"Let me check her," Dr. Baranov says to me with concern. "The stress can't be good for the baby."

"No…" she mumbles weakly. "Please, no…"

The faint hint of hazelnuts and vanilla lingers in my nostrils as I give the doctor a nod. "Tomorrow. For now, keep an eye on Celine," I tell him. "Make sure someone is with her around the clock."

I turn and leave the medical bay, carrying Taylor with me. I take the last flight of stairs up to the third floor and settle her onto the bed. Her eyes flutter open when I place her on the soft duvet cover, but they're glassy and unfocused.

Her clothes are raggedy and covered in the grease and grime of battle. The speckles of blood make me wince, but I quickly see none of it's hers. She's okay.

She's okay.

"I'm going to have one of the maids come up and help you change," I murmur.

She doesn't respond. Doesn't even acknowledge that she's heard me.

Sighing, I straighten up and turn to go, when Taylor's hand jerks forward and grabs my wrist. "I don't need to change. Just…stay with me. For a little bit."

It's the first time I've seen her this vulnerable. No, that's not exactly true. The first time I saw her vulnerable was the night I almost ran her over. That ended in disaster, which is why I'm more than a little reluctant to agree to her request now.

She meets my gaze. "Please?"

Fuck.

"Okay." I sigh. "I'll stay. Don't move."

I leave her on the bed and dip into the bathroom. I splash some cold water on my face, then I do the same with the white hand towels hanging next to the bath sheets.

I walk them back to the room, sit down on the edge of the bed, and gently rub them over Taylor's skin. She lets a sighing little gasp escape past her lips. As the towels come away dirty and stained, one after the next, the last of the tension in her body eases until she's melted into the blankets.

Her voice, when she finally speaks, takes me by surprise. "Celine used to give me massages when I got sick as a kid."

I let my hand come to rest against her hip. The blankets are between us, bunched up and tucked around Taylor's frame, but I still relish the heat of her body where it seeps through.

"I had bronchitis all the time. All the other kids in the neighborhood used to go swimming in the public pool, but I couldn't. I'd try, I'd want to hold my breath and play with them, but it gave me these crazy asthma attacks. Celine could've gone with them. She could breathe; she could swim.

But she didn't. She'd stay with me and rub medicine into my chest until I could finally inhale again."

Taylor cracks open an eye to look at me. I'm holding my breath—partly out of some kind of bizarre sympathy for the air-starved little girl she once was, and partly because I see where she's going with this and I already know it can't possibly end without more heartache.

"She was always so selfless. There weren't very many things she asked for. It was enough for her to be of service. To be there for me…for all of us. Do you know what she did with her very first paycheck? She spent a whole summer scooping ice cream, and as soon as she had money, she took the family to dinner."

"Taylor—"

"It should have been me," she concludes, a sob escaping her lips. "It should have been me."

"She is going to be okay."

"You don't know that. And you have no right to promise me that."

"I think you need to rest now." I'm barely resisting the urge to touch her face. It feels alien and uncomfortable to sit here with my hands so close to her but not close enough.

"It should have been me," she says again. "It should have been me. It should have been—"

"Stop!" I snarl. " Stop, Taylor."

Her eyes meet mine, lit from within by a fever only she can feel. "Why? Am I wrong?"

Don't answer that, I tell myself. *Don't you dare answer that, because if you do, then the last pillar holding up this disastrous fucking house of cards will tumble and everything will come crashing down.*

I take a deep breath and prepare to lie…

And then the truth comes out instead.

"Because I need you alive," I hear myself say. "I need you with me."

Taylor blinks at me as though she's sure she heard me wrong. Something starts to surface in her eyes—hope, perhaps. It has to be hope. I know that glow, that trust, that daring to believe that a better world is possible.

I saw it in my car while rain poured around us and Taylor came so beautifully on top of me.

That hope needs to die.

"I'm sorry," she says softly. "I shouldn't have asked you to stay."

I drop my hand, letting the dirty towels fall to the floor. Then I get up and walk out of the room. I try to leave the regret behind, too, but I don't have much luck.

It follows me wherever I go.

52

TAYLOR

Who would have guessed that twenty-four hours could go by so slowly?

I watch every passing minute with hope and dread. Hope that Celine will wake up. Dread that another minute will waste away without any update, bringing us that much closer to the three-day cliff where all my dreams will die.

I stay in my room unless I'm visiting Celine. The first time I go, I stay an hour. I try to talk to her, but nothing I think of saying seems right. Nothing I'd come back from a coma for if I were the one in the hospital bed.

The second visit, I whisper a few clumsy words. It ends up feeling more like a eulogy than an apology. I slip out again, tears burning tracks down my face.

The nurses keep telling me to rest. I know they're right, and it's not like I haven't tried. But every time I close my eyes, I think about the fact that Celine can't open hers. I think about the fact that our mother will never open hers again. And then

I remember that Dad is still in the hands of the psychopath who killed our mother and abducted Celine.

It's too much. I'm sinking under the weight of it all.

The only time I feel a spark of something like energy is when I hear Ilarion's footsteps down the hall. He comes to check on me as faithfully as I go to check on Celine.

And every single time, I rush into bed and pretend to be asleep. He'll walk in, hover over my bed just long enough to make sure I'm still breathing, and then he leaves again.

I try not to read too much into it. I also fight the urge to ask him if he sits with Celine this often.

I'm perched on the window seat, staring unblinkingly into the gardens outside, when I hear footsteps again. Same old song and dance—I race into bed, pull the covers up over my chin, and let my breathing settle into the soft rhythms of a fake sleep.

The door groans softly as it opens. I barely hear Ilarion as he circles the bed and his shadow falls across my face. His scent is off, though. The dark muskiness that I've come to expect has been replaced with nutmeg and merlot.

"Cut the shit, girl. You're not fooling anyone." My eyes fly open and I sit upright to see Mila standing over my bed with her arms crossed. "Mhmm. That's what I thought."

Sighing, I draw my legs into my chest. "Are the Zakharov siblings on suicide watch or something? There's really no need for all the random check-ups."

Mila looks mildly interested at that tidbit. "Ilarion's been checking up on you?"

Dammit.

"Uh…no?"

She rolls her eyes at my terrible lie and nudges my legs away so that she can sit down. It's weird how she feels so familiar now. Like a sister I never knew I had.

"I hear you've been visiting Celine like clockwork. I've come to tell you that you're going to drive yourself crazy."

"What if I'm already there?"

"Doubtful," Mila scoffs. "You're a tough cookie. It's gonna take more than that to break you."

Her certainty startles me, mostly because I feel none of it. "How do you know that when I don't even know it?"

"Intuition. It's never let me down." She smiles as her eyes dance over to the food tray on my nightstand. A transparent cloche hovers over the still-uneaten sandwich on the plate beneath. "You need to eat, Taylor."

"I'm not hungry."

"I'm not concerned about *you*," she says fiercely. "I'm concerned about the baby in your belly." I flinch as though she's used a dirty word. Those eagle eyes of hers miss nothing. "Forgot that you were pregnant, hm?"

I shoot her a glare. "Of course not. I just…I don't like being reminded."

"I got news for you: seeing your belly grow is going to be reminder enough."

I inch away from Mila, desperate for some space. Sometimes, I feel like she's stealing away my oxygen just to hoard it all for herself. I feel that way about her brother, too.

"Have you checked on Celine?" I ask. "Are there any updates from Dr. Baranov?"

"Not since you last checked in yourself," she says. "Celine's still being fed through a drip. She's still getting oxygen from machines. And yet she's still alive."

I close my eyes. "It feels like déjà vu. First, Mom; now, Cee."

"Enough doom and gloom. You're neither a doctor nor a fortune teller. Now, eat the sandwich." I shake my head and she sighs. "Don't be stubborn, Taylor."

"I don't deserve to eat."

"Why do you say that?"

"Because when Dr. Baranov told me that Celine might never wake up…" I choke on a sob, and I have to wait until it passes to continue speaking. "I…I had this thought, this horrible little thought, that Celine not waking up meant I would never have to tell her that I'm pregnant with her fiancé's baby."

Mila just looks at me, her expression devoid of judgment. "It's an understandable thought to have."

"No, it's not," I snap. "It's inexcusable. It's…it's despicable. I accused Ilarion of wanting the wrong thing for selfish reasons, and here I am, guilty of the exact same sin."

"A stray thought does not define you, Taylor. We all have instincts. Some of them are bad. That doesn't make *you* bad."

I lift my gaze to hers. She really is trying to comfort me now, and that's a far cry from where we started. "You're being kind."

"Trust me—no one has ever accused me of that."

"Then what would you call it?"

"I'd call it being strong," she says simply. "You go through enough shit and you learn not to blink too much, if you get what I'm saying. You just keep on going."

"If that's the only way to do it, I'd rather not."

"You say that, but you're already stronger than you realize. A coward would never have hijacked the rescue mission and invited herself along for the ride. I mean, goddamn—you shot *the* Benedict Bellasio. Not many seasoned *vors* can claim that."

"I got lucky. I was just running on adrenaline and fear."

"Well, what the hell do you think the rest of us run on?" She snorts. "Superhuman strength and heroic conviction?"

She's chuckling, but my face feels weighted down, like I'll never laugh or smile again. "I'm not really strong or brave, Mila. I'm just pretending to be."

She scoots closer and palms my hand. "My point is, what's the difference?" she asks. "The strongest of us have the deepest scars. I was twelve years old when I was first raped by a man three times my age and size. I thought it would break me; it almost did. But I survived it. And here I am, ready to fight another day. Sometimes, life kicks you between the legs, Taylor. You just gotta get back up and keep going."

I blink stupidly for way too long. All I can conjure up is a weak, pathetic, "I'm sorry."

"Why?" she asks. "You didn't molest me."

"Ilarion didn't know?"

"He didn't know until I told him, and that wasn't until years after it started happening. Of course, he tried to save me. He was always trying to save me back then. Still is."

"Save you from what?"

"Myself, mostly. I was this close to saying, 'Fuck it all,' and jumping off the top of the house," she says with a bitter laugh. "Those were bad days. But now…I'm fine. Mostly fine. The only bad days left are the ones where I remember how long it's been since I let anyone else that close. You start to wonder if it'll ever happen. But who needs it, right?"

My eyes go wide. "You mean…you've never…?"

"No," she says with a firm shake of her head. "I haven't been able to. The idea of another man, any man, touching me like that…It makes me feel…" She shudders and I lean in instinctively to put my hand on her leg.

She flinches, but she doesn't move away.

"I hear you," I murmur. "It's okay."

Mila sighs and fiddles with her bracelet. "I don't talk about this with many people. In fact, I don't talk about this with anyone at all."

"I'm honored."

"Don't be," she says. "It's just a testament to how broken you are that I'm bringing up my own shit."

I smirk. Classic Zakharov—lash out to keep the attention off of yourself. "Still, I appreciate it."

She sighs and relaxes. I watch how the tension in her shoulders eases just enough to let me see past the armor she's built over the years to protect herself. Like a wild beast finally rolling over to show you the thorn in its paw.

"Maybe you just haven't met the right man yet," I suggest. "Maybe that's why the thought of being with—"

"No," she interrupts.

"No?"

"I've met the right man; I just can't bring my walls down long enough to let him in. And since I can't give myself to him fully, it would be selfish to get involved with him in the first place."

I loft a brow. "Maybe you should let *him* make that decision."

She shakes her head. "I'd much rather be alone. It's simpler that way. I have only myself to worry about. That kind of independence is…freeing."

"It does sound that way, doesn't it?" I muse. "But it seems to me that loving freely is more important than living independently."

Mila glances at me. Her eyes are murky with half-formed things. There's doubt there, and a certain hungry restlessness that she's not able to feed.

Surviving is one thing.

Living, though? That is another thing altogether.

She focuses on me and smiles conspiratorially. "Look at you, being all optimistic in the face of grief. Maybe you're not so broken after all."

I shake my head and scowl at her. "You're just as much of an ass as your brother, you know that?"

She laughs and the sound breathes new life into me. "Why, thank you. It's one of our best qualities."

53

ILARION

"What do you smell?" I ask.

"Piss," Dima answers, wrinkling his nose. "And shit."

"Not that, *mudak*," I say impatiently. "Sulphur. Do you not smell that? It's everywhere. Sticking to the walls, under the floorboards…"

I walk around the now-empty warehouse. By the tracks dragged through the dust and that groaning of the structure, I'd guess that it was vacated recently—and in a hurry. "Benedict's been using this as a storeroom. He and that little shit of a brother of his are bringing out the big guns. Literally."

Huge windows loom on either side of the large space, but they've been boarded up. Only little fingers of light creep in, stretching to touch the dusty expanse of the floor.

I see four dots marked in a square. Footprints. A scrap of rope. "He was scared," I mutter under my breath. "I think he was keeping the old man here."

Dima meets my gaze when I glance up. "The fact that he's keeping Archie alive means something."

"It could mean any number of things." I leave it at that, vague as it is. I refuse to give voice to the doubts that are already starting to perforate through my resolve.

"He knows that Archie is your future father-in-law."

"And for now, that's the only thing we're sure he knows," I fire back. "There's no point jumping to conclusions before we have all the information. We're playing poker here, Dima. Neither one of us wants to show our hand."

"Based on the letter we got—"

"There's too many unknown variables." I shake my head. "For now, the plan is simple. We find Archie; we get him back."

Dima strokes his chin, his eyes wary and watchful. "Have you thought about what it would mean if Benedict took Archie out?" he asks. "It would be simpler."

I stiffen. Not because he's wrong—but because I've had the exact same thought too many times to count.

I've never given a damn about lives lost in the struggle before. That's just the nature of my business, of my world. But this one sits unpleasantly. The thought of digging a grave for Archie right next to Fiona's makes my stomach churn nastily.

A few of my men come around through the back entrance. Sergei leads the pack. "We combed through the entire property, *pakhan*. They didn't leave anything behind."

I nod. "Start the engines. We can head back soon."

I glance up at the misshapen roof as Sergei herds the soldiers back outside towards our two vehicles. Bullet holes puncture the ceiling here and there. As I watch, I see a rat squirm its way through one and out into the night above.

Dima moves to my side, radiating broodiness. His silence is starting to grate at my nerves. "What is it?" I snap.

"If we get the old man back…that might be a problem in its own right."

"You think I haven't already thought about that myself?"

Dima clamps his mouth shut, but it doesn't take a genius to realize he isn't satisfied. Muttering under his breath, he digs into his pockets and pulls out an *iriski*. He tosses the wrapper onto the floor and pops the candy into his mouth.

"You still carry those things around with you?" I ask.

"Yeah. Reminds me of home."

I roll my eyes. "You were born in California."

"Yes, but the motherland is ingrained deep."

I couldn't agree less. For Dima, the home of our ancestors has life. Mysticism. History. For me, it's a frozen tundra that gave birth to the man who gave birth to me. Of all its sins, that one is by far the worst.

Maybe that's why I rejected so much of my heritage. Because it was the easiest way to piss off my father.

I exhale sharply. "I know Archie will be a problem. But there's no point planning ahead when the road is unpredictable."

"In other words, you're procrastinating," Dima says, swirling the toffee in his mouth. "He'll have to be dealt with, Ilarion. There are a few *vors* who know."

"I'll deal with them," I say. "My priority right now is T—Celine."

Dima gives me one of those piercing gazes that says *you aren't fooling me*. "You're always a second away from saying Taylor's name," he muses. "One day, you just might slip."

I scowl and glance away from him. "That won't happen."

"Because you won't slip?" he asks. "Or because you've decided to take my advice and swap the two sisters out?"

"You clearly don't know much about women, do you?" I growl. "And even less about these two. Neither one will go for it, and I'm not about to make the suggestion."

"Because you're worried she'll say no?"

He's skating on thin ice right now, but he pushes through anyway. It's the reason he's lasted this long at my side. It's also the reason I'm never more than a few seconds away from smacking him upside the head.

"I know she'll say no. That's not the point. I'm not about to exchange a tamed mare for an unbroken filly."

"Even if you have real feelings for the latter?" he asks.

"She's nothing more than the woman who's pregnant with my baby."

"Right. You know, you never did tell me what led to that night in the first place. You claimed it was coincidental—"

"Because it was."

"...But there was something about this woman that forced you to break your dry spell." I glare at him and he just smiles unapologetically at me. "Yeah, I was keeping track. You hadn't gotten laid in ages before Taylor came along. And as for Celine, we both know—"

"What do you want me to say?" I interrupt. "That harps started to play? That there was a magical connection? A rush of chemistry? Fireworks in the background?"

"Oh, really? Sounds magical."

"Fuck you," I grumble. "I was horny; she was willing. That's all there was to it." I turn away before he can spot some telltale sign on my face. It's easier to keep the mask on when you're with people who don't know you that well. It's why I try to avoid Mila as much as possible these days.

"Benedict's pride is wounded right now," I remark, changing the topic back to more relevant matters. "He's going to want to strike back hard. He's going to want to erase the image of his hands in cuffs with a ball gag in his mouth."

Dima squats down to the floor and picks up a stray bullet casing lodged between the boards. He toys with it before tossing it aside and rising again. "There's one thing I'm trying to figure out."

"Just one?"

"Two, actually. This, and 'Why are you such an asshole all the time'?" He rolls his eyes. "No, my question is, *What is Benedict's end goal?* All these years, things have been simmering. He's wanted to be the one on top, but both of you have power, property, and influence. It's an abundance of riches and he owns half of it. Does it matter that you own the other half?"

I think about the day that Benedict and I met. People assume that if the circumstances had been different, we might have been friends. But I knew from the moment I laid eyes on the snot-nosed Bellasio boy that it would never happen.

Benedict was a grade-A narcissist with no concept of loyalty. He expected it, he demanded it, but he wasn't accustomed to giving it. Which was why he came to blows with his father so often.

Not that I could fault him with that. I came to blows with my father often, too. But then, he was a fucking monster.

"It matters," I say. "It's not enough for him to succeed. He needs to see me fail, too."

Dima shakes his head. "Because you beat him in a fight once upon a time when you were kids?"

"No," I say. "Because I humiliated him in front of his men and mine. And Benedict Bellasio never forgives a slight."

"Time to humiliate the fucker once more, don't you think?" Dima asks with a sly smile.

I nod. "Soon enough. For now, a meeting will have to suffice."

"A meeting?" Dima asks incredulously. "With Benedict? After everything he tried?"

"I need a jumping-off point before this goes further. And we need to determine how much of a player the old man will be going forward. For that, I need him alive."

Dima whistles low. "I smell a shitstorm brewing."

54

TAYLOR

I freeze when I catch sight of his broad shoulders.

He ignores the chair at Celine's bedside. He's just standing beside her, looking down at her pale, lifeless face with the frown of a man facing a river he doesn't know how to cross. I'm not sure if I'm the right person to judge—scratch that; I *know* I'm not—but I still can't see any real love there.

It strikes me again, not for the first time, how it's cruel to the point of heartbreak for a person like Celine—who has so much love to give—to tie herself to a man who has none to offer in return.

The nurse notices me standing in the doorway and gestures for me to enter, but I shake my head and try to back out of the room before Ilarion sees me.

I've got one foot in the hallway, so close to a clean escape, when he lifts his gaze and spots me. His frown somehow morphs without actually moving. The storm in his eyes worsens.

I have two options. I can hold my ground, do the mature thing, and just talk to the man. Say what I need to say and be done with it.

Or…I can turn tail and run.

In the face of the emotional upheaval I've dealt with in the last few days, I take the coward's route. I slam my palms against the swing door of the hospital room and nearly run headlong into Dr. Baranov.

"Taylor!" he says in surprise.

"Sorry, Doctor," I mutter, maneuvering around him with my head down. As soon as I have a clear lane, I take off running down the corridor toward the staircase.

I hear Dr. Baranov cry out a second time when he's almost hit in the face by the door as Ilarion bursts through and nearly mows him down. I don't wait; I start moving faster.

It's juvenile. I'm in his house; I can't exactly outrun him forever.

But do I stop?

No.

Hell no.

Not until I'm in the south gardens. This stretch of the property is riddled with little alcoves, small clusters of shrubs and statues where I can hide. And hiding is exactly what I intend to do.

Right now, the thought of speaking to Ilarion, of looking him in the eye and pretending…

It's more than I can take.

"Taylor?"

Fuck. I crouch down and find a spot under one of the lilac bushes. It's smaller than I anticipated, and I have to cram my body into the space. Thorns prickle at my skin. My legs come up to my chin and I try not to breathe when I feel him draw closer.

"This isn't a game, Taylor."

I bite my tongue and say nothing. At least not until his legs appear in front of my hiding spot. Then he squats down and I find myself staring at those hypnotic blue eyes.

"Don't be a child."

I grind my teeth together and extricate myself from under the bushes. "A smarter man would take the damn hint."

"I'm plenty smart. I'm just not very patient."

"Well, at least you're aware of your failings."

I pat down the soft cotton dress that I'm wearing in search of my composure. It's nowhere to be found, though. I peek at my little nook under the lilacs, but no luck there, either.

So with an exhausted sigh, I straighten up and give him a glare. I'm telling myself that avoiding Ilarion is just a matter of simple dislike. "What do you want?"

"I wanted to see how you were doing."

I narrow my eyes and start counting off my fingers. "Well, let's see. My father is currently a missing person, but we can't get the police involved. My sister is in a coma that she may never wake up from. And my mother died a few days ago and I'm the only one in my family who knows she's gone. Oh, and yeah—I'm also pregnant with my future brother-in-law's baby!"

I suck in a breath at the end, but it doesn't make me feel any better. I try again, but that doesn't work, either. Every breath I take in feels like it's stealing oxygen from my lungs, not giving me any. My head starts to pound and collapse in on itself and my chest is deflating and *fuck, fuck, fuck,* I'm gasping and twitching and the world is blackening around the edges and—

"Breathe."

Before I can stop him, Ilarion wraps his arms around me. My back presses against his chest and I feel his lips at my ear. "Breathe," he rasps again. His palms flatten against my abdomen, huge and hot.

And all of a sudden, I can breathe.

The moment that first gust of air rushes into my lungs, the rest comes easier. I feel myself relaxing. The pressure soothing. The pain disappearing.

Is this what I needed all this time? Did I need to be held?

Or did I just need to be held by *him*?

"L-let me go, Ilarion," I mumble, but there's not an ounce of fight in my body.

He must feel that, because he doesn't release me. He doesn't even loosen his grip. He just holds me as though our lives depend on it.

Hot, confused tears sting at the corners of my eyes. Over the distant treeline, the sun is setting. Something about that catches in my head. *The sun is setting... The sun is setting...*

Oh, fuck. The sun is setting.

On the third day.

Seventy-two hours have passed.

55

TAYLOR

"Oh, God," I whisper. I might have fallen to the ground if Ilarion weren't holding me up. "T-three days… It's been three days."

"Shh," he murmurs in my ear with an easy confidence that just has me unraveling even faster. "It's going to be okay."

"No, it's not!" I stammer through my tears. "Nothing's going to be okay. I've lost my mom and my sister in the same damn week. And I've probably lost my dad, too."

He doesn't say anything to that. The silence only makes it worse.

When he finally releases me, he does it gently. I feel the cold tickle of air nipping at my exposed skin. It feels like invisible snakes taking bites at me from every angle. I feel vulnerable on a skin-deep level, a soul-deep level. More vulnerable than I've ever felt in my whole cursed life.

I keep my gaze trained on the gravel footpath beneath me. I still can't look him in the eye. If I do, I'm scared he'll see all the betrayal I've been carrying around in my head these last few days.

"You should be up there with her," I remind him.

"Why?" he asks in that blunt way that always feels like whiplash even when I'm expecting it. "She doesn't know I'm there. I don't believe in empty gestures."

I sigh. "What do you believe in, Ilarion?"

"Before you? Very little. But lately…more than I once did."

I asked the question, but now, I'm scared to push this conversation further. He's not touching me anymore, and I hate that my body misses that. Even the distance between us now feels offensive to me.

He's not yours…

And yet he doesn't feel like Celine's anymore, either.

"She deserved so much better than this," I whisper. "She could have been so much more."

"There's still a chance—"

"Ilarion," I plead, my voice cracking darkly against the shimmering afternoon glow, "please just say the things you really mean, instead of what you think will make me feel better. I'd rather have cold reality than false hope right now."

"People always say that. They rarely mean it."

I square my shoulders and look him in the eye. "Well, I mean it. Do you really believe she's going to wake up from this?"

His eyes flicker over my face, quick and cold. "No," he says shortly. "I don't."

I know I asked for it, and I don't regret doing that. I'm just not expecting my reaction. Those invisible snakes are slithering over me now. Cold and scaly and devastating. I don't think I've ever felt so alone before.

All the people who made up my childhood are gone. I won't get to speak to Celine or Mom ever again. I'm quickly losing hope that I'll ever see my father in this life. It's all so cruel, so inhumanely cruel, a nightmare I'm screaming and screaming through but I can't find a way to wake up from.

That's the only explanation I can come up with for how deeply terrible everything is—this isn't real.

I *must* be having a nightmare.

"None of them even knew about my pregnancy." A single tear glides down my cheek. I feel Ilarion's warmth as he inches closer to me. I hate that it makes me feel better. "I know Mom would have been thrilled. Dad would have come around the moment he saw the baby. And Celine…" I glance up at him, wondering if I should give voice to certain thoughts, or just leave them floating around in my head.

"Tell me," he says.

His lips are shaped like a bow. The one feature on his face that gives some levity and warmth to what is otherwise as cold and alien as a mountain ridge.

"If I'd told her the truth from the start, she would have hated me at first…but I think she would have come around. She was always quick to forgive." I shake my head as my voice wobbles and breaks. "God, I'm horrible."

"Why do you do that?" It's almost a growl. Twilight crashes over us, blurring the world into mottled shades of black and indigo.

"Do what?"

He meets my gaze and holds it. "Punish yourself for being human."

I frown, wondering just how much of my thoughts are written across my face, and just how much of them he can read. He's not supposed to be able to read anything at all. He doesn't actually know me, one vulnerable night in his car notwithstanding. At least, that's what I've been telling myself since I arrived at his home. Thus far, it's been a comfortable belief to cling to.

Until he says things that make me feel like he's ripping my chest open and running his fingertips over the scarred grooves of my soul.

"It's okay to admit you want things that you shouldn't want," he continues. His hand lifts to my cheek, and he uses the backs of his knuckles to brush away my tears.

He's dangerously close. So close that his scent is crowding out every reasonable thought in my head. So close that my sense of self-preservation has taken flight.

"Ilarion…"

His lips hover mere inches from mine. I've been fighting to maintain that distance, but God help me, I'm getting so weak now. How many hits can a person take and stay standing? I'm weak enough to need something to hold me up. To keep me on my feet. To keep me moving forward.

My lips part as if they have a mind of their own. "No…no… I have to…"

I don't finish my barely intelligible sentence—I just turn and trip my way away from him.

"Taylor!" he calls after me, but I run away from the sound of his voice. I had the right idea earlier. Nothing good can come of us being near each other.

Celine is still lying up there in that hospital bed. She may not be fully alive, but she's not dead, either. And yet here I am, staring at her fiancé's lips, imagining a different future than the one that exists.

It isn't right. It isn't—

I cry out as my foot catches a loose stone and my ankle twists. It's not enough to be truly painful, but it's enough to take me down. I hit the earth hard, and when I do, I stay down. I lie sprawled on the grass, my fingers combing through the blades, as I try to find a way out of the fogginess in my head.

Ilarion's shadow emerges from around the bend. I watch it stretch along the footpath as he approaches. As it consumes everything in its wake: the gravel, the grass, and, eventually, me. It feels appropriate to be swallowed up by it. By him. For his darkness to devour all of me.

"Are you okay?" he rumbles.

"No." When I shake my head, the grass tickles my swollen lip. "No, I'm not even close to okay."

I hear him sigh. His scent intensifies as he bends down and scoops me up in his arms. I'd protest, but what's the use? He wouldn't listen. It wouldn't matter.

He walks me to the huge oak that stands sentinel in the corner of the garden. He sets me down on the far side, where we can't see the house anymore. Where it's just water and grass and the darkening night sky. Over here, it almost feels like we're in a different place altogether. Like we left reality in the gardens at our back.

He settles me against the trunk, then squats down to examine my ankle. "It's a mild sprain. You'll be fine."

"I deserve worse."

He glances at me. "Have you always been this hard on yourself?" His fingers make tender circles around my ankle. As non-invasive as his touch is right now, it still feels like too much. Too intimate, too…comforting. A comfort I don't deserve and can't let myself sink into.

"Please stop," I whisper.

He looks at me, but he doesn't stop touching me. "Stop what?"

"That," I say. "This. All of it. Helping me… Touching me…"

He withdraws his fingers from my calf. But my relief is short-lived when he slides in next to me. Our shoulders knock against one another as he exhales softly. "You feel guilty?"

"Of course. Don't you?"

It's ironic how uncloudy those misty blue eyes are right now. "No," he says.

And then he kisses me.

56

TAYLOR

I don't know what's happening. I can feel him, I'm aware of what he's doing, but I don't really *know*.

Until I smell him.

Then the world blooms into color.

My stomach quivers and my eyes close, and I melt into him. I don't question or struggle. My mind has been wiped blank and everything boils down to a choice that's so stupidly obvious that I don't even know why I'd bother asking it in the first place: *to kiss back or not?*

It's a yes, to say the least. It's a yes from the tips of my toes to the top of my head. From the whisper of my breath to the deepest, darkest parts of me.

And as long as I'm united behind this yes, it feels okay. If I can cling to that yes for a little while longer, I can enjoy it more. I can take a little more before I have to give Ilarion Zakharov back to where he truly belongs.

His tongue tangles with mine as his lips move, soft and tender. He has one hand cupped against my cheek, and it's like he's the last thing keeping me upright when the whole damn universe is trying to drag me down into the dirt.

It's everything I need.

Which, in the end, is exactly why I have to push away.

It's not far. Just far enough to break the kiss. I'm not strong enough to do much more than that.

Ilarion looks at me with burning eyes. Everything I'm on fire with is blazing inside of him, too. I don't even have to ask to know that that's true.

"I want you, *tigrionok*." His hand drops to my hip. "I'm so fucking tired of denying it."

How easy it would be to sink into those words. To forget all the reasons to run and cling to the one reason to stay right here.

But I can't.

I push his hand off my hip and shake my head. "Please, I'm begging you… Don't. You have to stop touching me. I…I can't think straight when you touch me."

"Taylor—"

"No!" I gasp, the word bursting out of me like a desperate prayer. "No! It hurts too much."

He stops short. His eyes see everything I'm not saying. "Taylor."

"I'm having your baby. That's all there is between us. That's *all*."

Oh, how I wish that were true. But I don't sound convincing. Not to God, or to Ilarion, or the little sparrow on the tree above us.

Even that bird is judging me. I can feel it. I deserve it.

"The night we met," I continue in a teary rasp, "that was a mistake. I was vulnerable, and—"

"Do you regret it?"

"I...I regret doing that to Celine."

"Nothing was done to Celine," he insists. "You and I met. We had sex. Celine had nothing to do with it. I didn't know her then. She was still a stranger to me. What happened between us was...singular."

I blink, and another tear runs down my cheek. It feels like I've shed a lifetime of tears in the span of days.

And yet I feel like I haven't really been living—until I met him.

He leans in, but I brace my palm against his chest and stop him from moving any closer. "No. I can't—"

"But you want to."

Does he even realize how much he's asking of me? Does he know that it hurts to breathe near him? Much less admit that I want what belongs to my sister?

"You were mine before I was ever hers," he whispers.

I make the mistake of looking up into his eyes. I make the mistake of falling into his words. Of trusting something that I can barely understand.

"I know what you're thinking," he rumbles. "You're thinking you can't do this to Celine. That it's Alec all over again."

I suck in my breath, feeling the muscles of my stomach tighten painfully. "She told you everything?"

There I go again, asking questions I'm not sure I want the answers to.

"Yes—including the fact that she knew you were not to blame for what happened," he confesses. "You asked her about her feelings for Alec and she lied to you. When you got involved with him, it hurt her. But you didn't betray her, Taylor. She knew that."

She knew that. She knew, and she still punished me for something she *knew* I didn't do. She let our parents punish me for something that wasn't my fault.

And she made me carry this guilt ever since.

I'm surprised at how numb I am to the idea that Celine has fallen into the past tense now. Just like Mom.

I shake my head. The future that Ilarion is dangling in front of me is way too tempting to let myself reach for it. I want it too bad to hope.

"What happened back then doesn't matter. You may not have been her fiancé when we met," I say. "But you are now. Celine believes that, and that's what matters."

"Celine's not believing anything anymore." His eyes are bright in the darkening night. "She's gone, Taylor. I think we both know that."

"She's still up there, Ilarion. She's still breathing. I just…I can't stop thinking… I can't stop—"

He places a finger over my lips and my words die against his touch. "You think too much," he murmurs. "It's time to quit."

"Ilarion—"

"Listen to me. I'm going to kiss you until you stop thinking. I'm going to touch you until you stop worrying. I'm going to do whatever it takes to make you forget everything and everyone else inside that pretty, stubborn, messed-up head of yours—until there's no one left but you and me."

"But—"

"No," he growls, grabbing my face and pulling it to his. He doesn't kiss me, though. His lashes flutter against my cheek as he draws his lips from my jaw up to my ear. "For right now, you're mine. And mine alone."

His voice is deep and gravelly, his tone all possession and power. There's so much that he has that I lack. His strength, his constancy… He's so solid and I feel like I'm barely even tethered to the earth anymore. I want so badly to anchor myself to him, just enough to get me through the here and now of all the tides of grief crashing down over me again and again.

"It's selfish…"

"Is it selfish to be honest about what you want?" he demands, his voice silky with resolve. "Because I've been lying to myself since I met you. And it's exhausting."

"Lying to yourself?"

He doesn't so much as blink. "You know this, Taylor. You've known it from the start." He strokes my cheek again. I shudder beneath his touch. "This isn't just about the child we're having together. With or without that baby, we'd still be right here."

"Don't say that."

"I'll say that and more," he snarls.

"Ilarion—"

"You're mine. You were mine from the beginning. In a way that Celine never was, never will be, never can be. You know that, don't you?" He looms closer. His face is all I can see. Pure and terrifying and beautiful. "You know you're mine. And I want to hear you say it."

I close my eyes, but not before another tear breaks loose. "I'm… I'm…"

"Louder."

"I'm yours."

He nods. "Good. Don't you ever forget it."

Then, finally, his lips press to mine. He steals my breath away as though he's going to replace it with his. I fall back against the soft grass and he engulfs me.

He trails kisses down my throat while his fingers undo the buttons of my dress. I gasp and groan softly as my vision of the trees spreading above us blurs into paintbrush strokes of green and black. In the distance, the very last of the sun winks out.

I hiss when Ilarion peels down my shoulder straps and cold air peaks my painfully hard nipples. He's on it in an instant, suckling with his hot mouth while he palms the other breast.

Sliding further down my body, he hikes up my dress until it's bunched up around my hips. I hiss again.

He straightens up just long enough to meet my eyes. The hunger in his face frightens me for a moment.

Mostly because it's a reminder that there's no going back. Not for either of us.

And I don't think I want to.

That frightens me even more.

He pulls my panties down my legs and tosses them aside. He teases a kiss on my left ankle, then works his way up my leg until his tongue passes delicately over my aching center.

His hands are strong and firm on my hips as he parts me with his lips and laps up my desire.

I'm seeing stars. Cheesy as that sounds, there's no other way to describe the explosions of pleasure blinding my vision as he swirls his tongue around and flicks my clit between firm pulls of his soft lips. He laps and sucks and nips until I'm gripping his hair at the roots and shuddering through an orgasm that takes a piece of my soul with it.

When I finally stop writhing, he rises up over me, blocking the sky and trees from view. I cup his face with my hands and pull him down onto me. I kiss him desperately, the way that I've never dared dream I could ever kiss him again.

I wrap my legs around his waist and he gathers me into his arms to pull me up onto his lap. His cock slides inside me as easily and as naturally as if I were made for him. He grips my ass as I ride him, hard and urgent, hungry and needy, forever and ever.

I meet his gaze and he meets mine. Neither one of us can look away. I can see his demons wrestling inside those captivating eyes. He's tried to hide them from me, but I know they're there.

That's what happens when you let someone under your skin. You give them a power over you that can be dangerous and destructive.

It can also be freeing.

His jaw clenches as he pulls me harder on him. The muscles of his arms flex as he holds me down on his cock and grinds, ripping a groan from me. I trace a thumb against his lips and he sucks on the tip, making my inner walls ripple tightly up and down his cock with every pulse of that wicked mouth.

"Fuck…" he growls. Inside of me, I feel him twitch and explode. His fingers dig into my hips almost painfully, but the heat filling me and the orgasm curling my toes erases everything but pure pleasure.

He collapses back onto the grass, pulling me with him. His arm drapes around my back, his hand strokes along my spine, and my head presses over his heart. I close my eyes and listen as the wild pounding gradually slows to a steady throb.

He kept his promise. In this moment, no one else exists.

It's just him and me.

57

ILARION

She lies on my chest for what seems like forever. I'm not mad about it. In fact, I'm doing everything I can do to keep her from moving.

The sky overhead is an ocean of black. Only when the first stars begin to light themselves does Taylor lift her head from my chest and look at me.

She doesn't quite smile, but it's the closest thing to it I've seen on her in a while. When I run my hand down her back, I realize she's covered in goosebumps.

"You're cold."

I wrap my arms around her and roll us onto our sides. The grass is comfortingly soft, but I still wish there was a bed beneath us. And blankets. She deserves both.

"Better?"

She nods meekly. "Yes."

I'm not used to her being this quiet. I tuck a stray lock of her hair back into place. "Are you okay?"

She rests her forehead against my chest for a moment. The heat of her exhale blooms across my skin. "I think so," she says at last. "Just…processing."

"Don't work too hard. You'll give yourself a migraine."

"Things are simpler for you," she sighs. "You don't love Celine the way I do."

I had hoped for more time to pass before we mentioned her name. But Taylor's family takes up every second thought in her head. There is no way we could avoid this for long.

"Maybe not. But I do care about her."

She sighs. "Perversely, that helps. Just a little."

"I—"

"Ilarion!"

Taylor jerks upright and looks around for her clothes in a panic before whoever just yelled my name arrives. "Shit, shit, *shit!*" I pick up her discarded panties and pass them to her as she scrambles clumsily to her feet.

She's just barely rearranged herself to something passable when Dima appears on the curved path encircling the hill upon which the oak tree stands.

"There you…" He trails off when he notices Taylor. "Oh. Uh, sorry to interrupt—"

"You weren't interrupting anything," Taylor blurts a little too emphatically.

"Right. Of course not. I just need to talk to Ilarion about something."

"I'll leave you to it." She charges down the stone path, cheeks flaming. I let her walk a few paces ahead of us before I step to Dima's side.

"Sorry, man," he mutters. "I didn't…um… Was there something—?"

"What's going on?" I ask. I try not to sound impatient; I know it must be important.

But so is holding that beautiful woman in my arms.

"Benedict got back to us about the meeting."

I notice Taylor glancing back over her shoulder at us, but she's too far away to overhear anything. "And? What's it going to be?"

"He's open to it. He sent along a location as well as his terms for negotiation."

"Unreasonable?"

"More like…suspicious," Dima hedges. "He wants to meet you at the Hotel Caravaggio tomorrow at ten. You each bring one man. No weapons."

"Hm. Reasonable."

"Which is exactly why it's suspicious," he underscores. "He could be lying."

"He probably is. But I'm not going to be the one to break a gentleman's agreement."

Dima snorts derisively. "Benedict Bellasio is no gentleman."

I nod, my eyes still fixed on Taylor. She's just entered the aura of light emanating from the house. Lit like that, I can make out her perfect hourglass silhouette through the soft fabric of her dress. It occurs to me that in only a few short weeks, I'll be able to see a gentle swell to her belly.

Despite our romp in the grass being barely minutes-old, that thought stirs up new hunger.

I sigh. "No, but maybe it's time I tried to be one."

Dima's eyes veer from me to Taylor. He swallows audibly. "Good luck with that, brother."

When we reach the house, Taylor is standing on the deck, her bare feet pale against the dark bluestone. Dima slips in ahead of me. I stay behind for a moment.

I give her a curious glance. "You planning on camping out on the patio tonight?"

Her face blushes and her gaze drops. "It's just a…a nice night," she mumbles. "Thought I'd enjoy it for a little while longer."

I nod slowly. "You don't want to go inside, you mean."

Taylor's blush deepens, caught in a lie. "It smells like death in there," she whispers. "At least, it does to me. I'm probably just hallucinating."

I watch how her eyes whirr in their sockets with anxiety, how her hands flex and unflex again and again at her sides. The curve of her neck looks so delicate to me, like a swan's.

"Have you eaten anything today?"

She frowns as she considers it. "I can't remember."

"Come on." I take her elbow, gently but firm enough to erase any argument. "I'll make you something."

Dima is gone when we enter. Taylor perches herself tentatively on a stool at the counter as I go rummage through the pantry and begin to cook.

The chopping is soothing, meditative. I dice onion and press garlic, relaxing into the simple sensations of the work. It feels good to do something so straightforward.

Tomorrow, things will get complicated. I will meet with Benedict. Maybe he has Archie, maybe he doesn't. Maybe he's dead, maybe he's not.

Maybe I'll survive the meeting.

Maybe I won't.

But when I look up to see Taylor watching me, and when I see her smile—that slow, soft, shy smile that says, *I shouldn't be looking at you like this, but I just can't stop...*

When I see that…

…I know that I'd do anything to see it again. And again. And again.

For as long as we both shall live.

58

ILARION

Dima and I have been sitting directly outside the Hotel Caravaggio in my Porsche. It's been thirty minutes since we arrived, and ten minutes since Benedict Bellasio pulled into the circular driveway of the grand Italian-style hotel, climbed out of his ostentatious yellow Ferrari, and sauntered into the lobby with a brooding man close on his heels.

Dima glances at his watch. "Fifteen minutes 'til the meeting."

I nod. "What do you think?"

"I think just because it seems legit, doesn't mean it's going to be," he grumbles. "Also, I don't trust that snake."

"No, nor do I. But I need to know what he wants."

"He wants *everything*," Dima says. "More than his fair share. It's no different than any other time we've run into him. Nothing new and nothing good can come of this meeting."

"Yes, it can." While he has a fair point, I'm determined to make something useful out of this dog-and-pony show. "I might be able to negotiate some sort of exchange for Archie."

"He's never going to give up Archie. That's his only bargaining chip."

I glance at Dima with raised brows. "What's the point in having a bargaining chip if you're not willing to cash it in when needed?"

Dima sighs. He takes out his gun and places it in the glove compartment. "Well, fuck… We're actually doing this." He takes a deep breath. "You shouldn't have made her any promises."

I nod. "I know."

And yet I did.

I'd do it again, too.

"So… Seeing as how we might not get out of this alive, I'm gonna ask you something I would never have otherwise asked."

"I doubt that. But go ahead."

Dima smirks. "Is it love?"

I tense, the breath stuck in my throat. "I…I don't know." But how true is that? There are moments when I feel like I do know.

I'm not sure which answer makes my blood churn more: *Yes, I love her*—or no, I don't…but I've done far too much for her anyway.

"*Fuuuck,*" Dima laughs. "I never thought I'd see the day. It has feelings after all." He pokes me to make it clear which "it" he's referring to.

"Come on." I step out of the car before I have to endure any more of his prying questions or irritating side-eyes.

We step through the gilded doors and over to the concierge. The lobby sits beneath a massive stained glass dome, the walls decorated with a sprawling mural painted in baby blues and delicate pinks. Fat-cheeked cherubs flit between clouds and topless goddesses gossip next to stars.

"I'm here for a meeting with Benedict Bellasio," I inform the pencil-mustached man behind the counter.

"Of course, sir," the man says in a distinctly French accent. "He is waiting for you in the Palazzo Roma Room. Follow me."

Dima and I trail him down the ornate halls. Every flourish is exquisite and extravagant and wildly unnecessary. I'm not in the least surprised that Benedict chose this as our meeting grounds.

He leads us to a bronzed door on the first floor. On either side of the entryway are two alcoves where naked Venus statues stand holding white marble torches.

"Here we are, gentleman," he says with a polite bow.

I give him a terse nod and open the door.

The carpet is a crimson velvet stretching the length of the narrow space. Every wall drips with oil paintings and crystal light fixtures. The curtains at the far end have been drawn close over the arched windows, suffocating all the sunlight.

Benedict sits on a patterned velvet fainting couch. A huge gold chandelier hangs above us, casting a dim amber glow onto his brocade suit and the flashy Patek Philippe watch on his wrist.

"Look at you, Benedict," I remark as Dima shuts the door behind us. "You match the room."

"I thought I'd dress up for the occasion." He chuckles without getting up. His man stands behind the couch like a trained dog in a black suit, eyeing us with the same suspicion we feel.

"Ah, Dima," Bellasio continues. "Nice of you to come. Although I have to admit, I'd have kept my best stooge home. You know…just in case."

"He did," Dima replies. "Mila is probably browsing the pantry as we speak."

Benedict barks out a laugh. "Clever! And wise. No good in losing two Zakharovs. It would be a pity for the whole family to be snuffed out in one go."

I take the wingback chair opposite Benedict. Dima takes the second seat beside me. "Nothing will be getting snuffed out today, Benedict. This is a peaceful meeting. We've made a gentleman's agreement. I know you'd never break that."

Benedict leers at me. "Indeed. How is that beautiful fiancée of yours? Did she survive the crash?"

The casual way he asks about Celine pisses me off. I let him see the anger in my eyes, if only to drive home the connection he believes I have with her. Which isn't a lie, either. Technically.

We're still connected.

Just…not how I'd originally planned.

"As a matter of fact, she did," I say smoothly. "She's doing very well now."

"Ah, I'm relieved to hear that. I like her."

"I'm sure you do," I say, channeling more self-control so the words don't come out from between gritted teeth. "Why else would you have wanted to marry her in my place?"

His smile drops just for a moment. A millisecond, really, but I'm not blinking during this conversation.

"She told you, did she? I just thought she was smart enough to back the right horse."

"I'm not a horse, Benedict," I growl. "I'm a lion."

Benedict leans back while his doorknob of a man stares between Dima and me with a vacant expression on his face. "You know the tragedy about lions? They live in prides. Alone, lazy, and they let the females do all the work." He gestures to his arm where the suit is a bit thicker—no doubt padded by bandages from where Taylor shot him. "So your metaphor suits you perfectly."

"And what does that make you?"

He grins at me, but the smile doesn't reach his eyes. "I know how to win, Ilarion. I run hard, I work hard, and I don't accept loss or defeat. I'm not just the winning horse—I'm a *champion*."

I snort. "I believe your father would've disagreed."

Benedict's fist white-knuckles on the armrest. "My father was a fool. He underestimated me. And he's not the only one to make that mistake. I'll admit, it used to bother me…but not anymore."

I rest my elbows on my knees and lean in. "You agreed to this meeting, so I'm assuming you want to resolve this without any more bloodshed."

Benedict purses his lips. "If you'd like."

I resist the urge to roll my eyes and cut to the chase. "What do you want?"

"Me?" he asks innocently. "I'm not the one who asked to chat."

"Cut the shit, Bellasio. You wouldn't have accepted the meeting unless you wanted a soapbox to stand on and something to win. So tell me, what will it take to get you to fuck off?"

He chuckles darkly. "Let's start with an honest conversation first, shall we?"

Dima and I exchange a glance. "I'm capable of one," I say. "Are you?"

His eyes narrow, but he manages to keep that sickly smile in place. "Archie Theron. You want him back."

"Obviously."

"I'm aware of who he is."

"You want a prize for that?" I ask sarcastically. "As for wanting him back, he's my future father-in-law. It's not really a matter of what *I* want."

"I wonder what your fiancée would think about your generosity of spirit." He picks imaginary lint from his pants and recrosses his legs. "Tell me: Did money change hands *after* the engagement, or before? Did you see her and bargain, or was Archie the pimp?"

I don't look at Dima. If I do, Benedict is going to suspect something. He's going to know that I know. I hide my clenched fist by drumming my fingers on the arm of the chair. "It was a coincidence."

"Probably not for the old man, though. He's more cunning than you realize."

Oh, don't I know it.

"His daughter, though, not so much, right?" I hesitate, and he laughs. "Don't worry. I already know she has no clue what's going on. The woman is pretty, but not very bright."

"I'd say you're projecting, but then again, you're neither bright *nor* pretty, are you?"

His forehead reddens instantaneously. The man is so easy to needle. His every nerve is exposed and raw, waiting for someone who knows how he's wired to drive him to the brink of madness.

"She would have passed you over for me," he snarls. "Another couple of days working my magic and she wouldn't have been able to refuse."

"I wouldn't put it past you to try, fruitless as that may have been." I arch a brow to match my smirk. "You've always wanted what someone else has."

He glowers at me, anger flashing in his eyes. "I saw the look on her face when she saw me," he spits. "She wanted me. The little tart. The *whore.*"

"Celine would never be interested in a worm like you."

He grins wide. "I'm not talking about Celine."

I can't help it. My hands ball into fists. I suck in a breath to calm myself, and he hears it.

Benedict laughs like we just shared some playful secret. "Ah, that's it, isn't it? Broke through that glacial composure of yours and I didn't even have to say her name. Don't like when I talk about your baby sister, do you, *Don* Zakharov?"

"Brother..." Dima warns from where he's seated next to me.

I bite down my anger. "Quit stalling. You didn't agree to this meeting to ask me about my fiancée or my future father-in-law."

"Didn't I?" Benedict coyly asks. "I'm so curious about your chosen family, though, Ilarion. There's so much I'd love to know."

"You've done enough prying for the night. Now, tell me what you want before I walk out of here."

He folds his hands in his lap. Behind him, his mute guard still scans back and forth, back and forth, as robotic as a sprinkler head. "Do you really think you can keep this secret from Celine forever?"

"It's not my call to make."

Benedict nods. "What are you prepared to do to get him back?"

"And there it is. Fucking finally." I sigh with relief. "For the hundredth time—*what do you want?*"

Benedict gives me another wolfish smile. "Your ancestral home in Russia transferred into the Bellasio name. In addition to half of your largest properties on this continent, plus half your businesses and profit sharing on every other enterprise you choose to keep in your name."

I raise my brow. "Is that all?"

"Two more things. You'll stop coming after my men, period. No more raids, no more shoot-first, ask-questions-later nonsense. And…" He pauses, regarding me with actual seriousness now. "I want Mila."

Dima and I both jump to our feet. Now, he's as pissed as I am.

"The fuck you do," he growls. I subtly motion for him to stand down, but I have no problem letting him speak for both of us in that regard.

"That's right," Benedict says with a smile. "Don't worry—I don't want to marry her or anything. Just one night will suffice. Honestly, it's more for her benefit than mine."

"You son of a bitch," I snarl. "This is a fucking game to you."

He spreads his hands wide with that same stupid shrug and that same stupid smile. "You asked. I answered."

"You certainly are a dreamer, Benedict," I say, sauntering one step towards him. He and his bodyguard both tense up in unison as I approach. "We've known each other a long time, and that's never changed."

I extend my hand out to him. He looks dumbfounded by the gesture, but he takes it. I tighten my grip and yank him to his feet hard against me, so that I can snarl into his ear, "Take your demands and stick them up your ass, you pathetic fucking excuse for a man."

Then I shove him away from me. His man stands there looking shocked and uncertain of the next best move. Benedict lands hard on his ass on the fainting couch, his face purpling into something bright and mortified.

I turn my back on the *mudak* and make for the exit.

"You walk out of here, I will kill the old man!" Benedict yells after me.

I throw him a cold glance over my shoulder. "Go right ahead. He's not worth as much to me as you think."

"What are you going to tell your fiancée? Do you really think she'll be so keen to marry you after you sentenced her father to death?"

"Celine will believe whatever I tell her," I say with a roll of my shoulder. It's a half-shrug, half-warmup in case I do, in fact, need to kill him with my bare hands. "Including the fact that you were the one who reneged on your part of the bargain and killed her father before I could do anything about it. Who do you think she'll believe, Benny? The man she loves, or the man who abducted her and then tried to seduce her?"

I've got my hand on the doorknob when I hear the cock of a gun.

All I can think is, *How predictable.*

59

TAYLOR

Mila glances over at the clock hanging above the cavernous two-door refrigerator. "Isn't it time for your visit?"

I shake my head, ignoring the plate of gnocchi that she just shoved in front of me. "I-I can't."

Mila fixes me with that bold, direct stare of hers. "Listen. I know that people put doctors on some kind of pedestal. But the fact is, they're only human. And they're as prone to error as the rest of us."

I blink at her. "I'm sorry—is that supposed to be comforting?"

"In this case, it should be," she says. "I know Dr. Baranov put a three-day timer on Celine's life, but fuck that. Not everyone is the same. Maybe she'll wake up on Day Five and everything will be alright."

Everything will be alright. I don't see how that can possibly be true.

"No. Even if she does wake up, nothing will be 'alright.'"

"Because of your feelings for my brother?" When she catches my jaw dropping, she holds up a hand. "You don't have to say anything; I already know. It's pretty obvious, anyway. The way you look at him. The way he looks at you."

I blush. "I…I'm having his baby. So obviously, there's history. Kind of. It's just a little confusing."

"I would think that having this baby makes it *less* confusing," she offers. "The two of you want to be together. Now, you have the perfect excuse."

The moment she says it, I feel my heart drop. "For that to happen, Cee has to… She would…"

"No, Taylor." Mila sighs, leaning in and putting her hand over mine. "That's not what I meant. Even if Celine wakes up, I think you owe it to her to be honest. Tell her the truth and let whatever happens just happen."

I shake my head. "No. No way."

"Why not?"

"Because I love her," I explain. "She's my sister, my best friend. We have always, always had each other's backs. Why would I stop now?"

"Because you saw him first?"

I pause. I want to have a good, snappy comeback, but I don't.

Mila shrugs. "Look. You've been carrying around this guilt as if you're stealing her man. Technically, she stole yours." I open my mouth to object, but she holds up a hand once again to stop me. "I don't care what the technicalities are or were.

The fact is, you and Ilarion saw something in each other or felt something or whatever romantic bullshit it took to make both of you climb into a backseat and make a baby. *Before* Celine even knew he existed."

I sigh and rub my eyes. "That doesn't change the fact that he asked *her* to marry him. Besides, she deserves to be happy. He can make her happy."

She frowns. "You've changed your tune."

"Because I realized that under all that macho toughness, he's actually a decent man," I admit. "And I believe him when he says he'll take care of her."

Mila shakes her head. "You're really willing to sacrifice your own happiness for Celine's?"

"Yes," I say without missing a beat.

She smiles quietly, then sighs. "Dammit."

"What?"

"I really didn't want to like you."

"I have been told I have a magnetic personality," I joke, tossing my hair playfully. It feels good to experience a small moment of lightheartedness amidst all the darkness I've been going through.

The silence settles and thickens. Both of us look in the corners of the room, wondering if there are maybe some answers hidden there that will solve all of the shit swirling around us.

"Mila…" I chew on the inside of my cheek for a moment. "Can I ask you something? You mentioned earlier that

Benedict has devoted himself to getting Ilarion back. I was wondering…"

"You haven't heard the story?"

"Not sure if you're aware, but your brother's not really the chatty type."

"Didn't think I was, either. But then, here we are, chatting the day away." She pushes my dinner plate closer to me. "I'll make you a deal: you eat and I'll talk. Sound good?"

"Damn," I mutter. "Relentless."

"I'm just looking out for my little niece or nephew."

That makes me feel warm and fuzzy on the inside, and at the same time, incredibly nervous. But I push the worry away and fork a gnocchi. The prongs slide in like a knife through butter. I pop it into my mouth and sigh.

"Okay, I'm eating," I mumble between bites. "I believe you have a story to tell me."

Mila leans against the counter. "When we were kids, our father used to have meetings that included all the most influential men in the state. It was a sort of sizing up of each other, cloaked behind a façade of professional civility. The main players would take turns to host, and one year, it was my father's turn. The Bellasio don decided to bring his son along."

"Benedict?"

"Benedict," Mila confirms darkly. "He was nineteen or twenty at the time. Ilarion was a couple years younger. They were both at a point where they were being included in some things concerning the 'family business,' but not all. I guess

Benedict felt he was old enough to have a seat at the table, and he got pissed when his father shut the door on his face."

"What does Ilarion have to do with it?"

"Ilarion saw the whole thing," she explains. "And from that moment forward, Benedict had to throw his weight around, had to prove he was the alpha." She leans over and steals a gnocchi from my plate. "He started strutting here and there in the courtyard, ordering men around, scrapping with the security, too bullheaded to see that none of the *vors* would engage him because of his last name. So he decided to pick a fight with Ilarion. He suggested they have a sparring match. Nothing too serious. Just a dick-measuring contest, really."

"Ilarion agreed to that?"

"Not at first," she admits, her skin slowly flushing. "Ilarion had a good head on his shoulders. He didn't want to get into it with Benedict, and he said as much. That just pissed Benny off even more. I guess he assumed that Ilarion was looking down on him or something. So, he decided to give Ilarion a reason to fight."

"Oh, no…"

Mila sighs. "Benedict figured the fastest way to piss Ilarion off would be to mess with me."

"He didn't!" I gasp before I can stop myself. "Please tell me he didn't…he didn't…" I can't make myself say the horrible word. "Did he?"

Mila raises her brows. "Oh, fuck no. He didn't get that far. He *did* force a kiss on me, though."

"Shit," I breathe. "How old were you?"

"Thirteen, just about."

My eyes go wide. "Mila…"

She shakes her head. "Don't worry—it wasn't my first kiss. But you have no idea how many times I've wished it was."

That takes me by surprise. "What?"

She seems to collect herself. "Never mind. I shouldn't have said that."

But even that doesn't sit well with me. It's almost like she feels bad for *saying* it, rather than for feeling it. For suffering through it.

Whatever "it" may be.

"Anyway, Benedict had his hand halfway up my skirt when Ilarion heard me shout. He pulled that bastard off me and accepted his 'sparring match' right then and there."

"And he beat Benedict?"

She smiles. "Oh, yes. He beat Benedict stupid, surrounded by both Zakharov and Bellasio men. The cheering pulled the old fogies out of their meeting and our fathers watched Ilarion whoop the absolute shit out of him." She pauses for a second and sighs. "I think it was the first time I've seen our father look so proud."

"What about Benedict's father?"

"Like any mob boss, he mastered the poker face, but even I could see how angry he was at watching his chosen heir get embarrassed in front of everyone who mattered. Once Ilarion let him up, the old don walked up to his son, put his foot on his chest, and spat on him. Then he left with his men. Benedict had to find another way home."

I shiver. "That's awful."

"I know it seems brutal to you. But that's mob life."

"Is it?" I ask. "Seems to me that's just hell."

"Maybe you're right." Mila sighs. "But if this is hell… what happens when we die?"

60

ILARION

The click of Benedict's gun echoes through the room. I release the golden doorknob, sighing at how close I was to getting out of here without any bloodshed.

Then I turn to face the *mudak* I've embarrassed too many times to count already.

He and his stooge are both bristling. Both have guns in their hands trained in our direction.

"A gun, Benny?" I ask. "Really? And after I agreed to your terms, no less."

Benedict narrows his eyes. "Trying to goad me, Ilarion?"

"Trying to *teach* you, my friend. I did once before, but I guess the lesson didn't stick. So here it is a second time: when you strip away all the excess, all the bluster and bravado, a man's word is the only thing he has. Trust, Benedict. Trust can be worth a lot more than you realize."

"How long do you think you can stay on your high horse?" Benedict scoffs. "It's going to buck you off sooner rather than later. In fact—" He checks his watch. "My bet's on 'sooner.'"

I snort. "Of course you're cocky now. You've got two guns on two unarmed men. But then, I suppose that's your best chance of winning."

His expression turns black. "Pissing me off right now isn't your wisest choice, Zakharov."

"Don't you understand, Benedict? I can do and say whatever I want. I'm not scared of you. Never was, if you recall. And I never will be."

His face flushes with anger when I bring up The Incident. He may be the one holding a gun, but the past is the only weapon I need to bring him to his knees.

"It's going to look bad, wouldn't you say?" I muse, meandering in his direction. "Killing me and my man in what was supposed to be a peaceful meeting? It's not as if our respective families don't know what happened fifteen years ago. Hell, who *doesn't* know? Half the city was watching. So do it, fine—but you'll come off looking like a coward. To no one's surprise, of course."

"You'll be dead," he growls. "I can tell the world whatever story I want and they'll have to believe me."

"Have to?" I ask. "No, I don't think so. We both have reputations. My men know who I am. They know I would never dishonor a gentleman's agreement. Not even for you. You, on the other hand…" I move my gaze to his goon. "Your men know damn well that you're a coward."

He cringes and marches closer to me, though he pauses just out of arm's reach. His finger is trembling on the trigger.

Dima sidles up to my side. I know him well enough to guess that he's planning to push me out of the way if he needs to.

But I understand Benedict better than he does. Better than anyone does. He's not going to attack me until he's got the last word in. Until he feels like he's won the argument.

"Look at you," he spits. "The only don I know with a moral compass. Tell me, Ilarion: where was your moral compass when you murdered your father?"

I loft a brow. "It was aiming the gun."

"Ah, yes." He nods. "That's the party line, isn't it? Except I know you would never kill your father. He was your *pakhan*. Loyalty is everything with you Zakharovs. Well, most of you, at least."

I tense up as he keeps talking, but I also take the opportunity to inch towards him. He's so caught up in the melody of his own voice that he barely seems to notice.

"But there's something to be said for a son who usurps the seat of his father. It was yours to take and the old man was making mistakes. It must have been easy for your men to accept."

"Like I said, my men have faith in me."

Benedict nods somberly. "Do they have the same faith in your lovely sister?"

My eyes narrow when he mentions Mila. Dima is similarly tense at my side. "I don't know what you're talking about."

"Don't you?" he taunts. "Because as far as I understand it, you weren't the one who killed your father. *She was.*"

61

ILARION

Fuck him. Fuck this motherfucker to hell. If the circumstances were different, I would leave him to rot in the corner of my darkest prison.

"I don't know who your source is, but they're wrong."

Benedict shakes his head with a haughty chuckle. "No, no, I don't think so. I think my source knows exactly what they're talking about. That little hellcat has a look in her eyes... She's capable of anything. I saw that in her fifteen years ago."

"She was thirteen years old, you pervert," I snarl. "She was a child."

"Said like a protective older brother," he drawls. "One who's willing to look the other way when his sister performs the ultimate act of betrayal. Tell me, would your men be as willing to forgive if they knew Mila was the one who killed their *pakhan*?"

Waves of disbelief and confusion roll off Dima. He wants to ask me; he wants me to tell him it's not true.

But I can't.

"It's a lie," I say simply. "Mila had nothing to do with our father's death. It was all me."

"Ah, big brother to the last. How lucky that sweet little flower is."

"She's a flower with thorns, Benedict. I wouldn't get too close if I were you."

He laughs. "Was it one of the thorns that finished off your father, then?" The gun droops; the bastard is clearly starting to enjoy himself. "Fuck, I would have loved to see it. She must have looked glorious. Was it bloody? Or did she do it clean? Poison, maybe. I could see her loving how it looked to watch the life slowly fade from his eyes."

"You really do love the sound of your own voice, don't you?"

He flashes me his teeth. "On the contrary, people love hearing my voice. I've been known to make women wet without so much as touching them. Your little sister certainly was when I put my fingers up her cunt."

Dima growls low. I don't have to be psychic to know he's mentally cursing me for not letting him bring his gun.

I shake my head and give Dima a subtle signal. Then I lunge toward Benedict, ducking low and shouldering him hard in the gut.

BANG!

The gunshot blasts my hearing and I feel pain sear down the side of my body in one hot stroke. My brain calculates the damage fast. I know I've been shot, but it's not fatal. It's just my arm, which will freeze up in a few minutes, but not before I get maximum use out of it.

I tackle Benedict to the floor and he lands with a loud grunt, fumbling his gun in the process. I punch him in the face, knee him in the gut, and make a grab for the gun.

Another gunshot pierces the air, but this time, Benedict's weapon is not the source. I don't have time to check on Dima. I focus on disarming Benedict, who flings the damned weapon across the floor. It spins violently and disappears underneath one of the patterned sofas.

I smash my fist across Benedict's face. His eyes wobble, but he focuses back on me almost immediately. "*Déjà vu*, huh?" I ask him.

He tries to spit up at me, but I dodge and crack his nose open.

"Ilarion, we have incoming," Dima warns from the door. I glance back over my shoulder. The mute thug is slumped unconscious at his feet, and the *mudak's* weapon is in Dima's hand. "The hotel staff are on their way. Police are en route."

I nod, slap Benedict's face once more for good measure, and then clamber off him. I gesture for the gun in Dima's hand and he hands it over. I cock it and point it directly at Benedict's face. "Where is the old man?"

"*Vaffanculo!*" he snarls.

I don't have to speak Italian to understand he isn't being cooperative.

As much as I want to puncture one hole after the next in his rotten gut until he tells me what I need to know, we don't have time for that right now. The pain in my arm is getting more pronounced and I can smell the faint metallic scent of blood. Benedict is half-drenched in the stuff. I've lost more than I realized.

"I could kill you right now," I point out to Benedict.

"Yes," he snarls. "But then my brother would kill the old man. And what would your pretty little fiancée say about that?"

"She would say that I did all that I could—"

"Bullshit!" he screams. "Bullshit! She'd hate you! And my brother would see to it that she died as painfully as that old *stronzo* she called a father!"

"Ilarion, we have to go if we want to avoid a whole thing." Dima doesn't want to end my fun, I can tell, but he's also not ready to risk getting arrested. Too much is at stake to spend time in a cell.

I kick Benedict in the side, making him roll into a painful, groaning ball. "I'd leave you with a parting gift," I growl, "but it looks like we're even. An arm for an arm. But just to be sure you've learned your lesson…"

I kick him between the legs. He screams like he's been gelded. Dramatic, even by his standards.

Then Dima holds the door open for me and we run like hell.

We sprint down the corridors, passing shocked guests who dart to the sides to avoid us, then through the kitchens and out the back door into the alley behind.

"You should have killed him," Dima sighs. "Why didn't you?"

I shake my hand, splattering wet blood across the asphalt beneath my feet. "Archie."

He shakes his head. "This is not about Archie at all, is it? It's about the girls. Although which one of them, I haven't decided." He raises his eyes to meet mine. "I don't think you have, either."

"Now's not the time," I warn him.

He combs sweaty hair out of his eyes and sighs again. "Is it true?" he asks. "Was it Mila?"

I avoid his gaze. "Now's not the time for that, either."

62

TAYLOR

I've been holding Cee's hand so long, I can't feel my own anymore.

When the door opens, I expect to see Dr. Baranov or one of the nurses, but it's Mila. She's carrying a bottle of lemonade that she offers to me.

"Have some. You need to stay hydrated."

"You don't need to take care of me, Mila."

"Well, you're certainly not taking care of yourself," she retorts. "And anyway, having something to do is a good distraction." Her eyes glance at the watch on her slim wrist.

"Shouldn't they be back by now?"

"It's been a few hours," Mila concedes. "Nothing out of the norm." Somehow, I don't quite believe her. A second later, her forced calm shatters and I see that she's every bit as anxious as I am. "That being said, if they're not back in an hour, I'm gathering the men and we're going in."

"But—"

"They never should have agreed to those stupid fucking terms! My brother might honor his agreements, but Benedict Bellasio is a piece of shit with no honor."

"He has Dima," I offer, trying to say something comforting. It's not easy to do when I need to be comforted every bit as much as she does.

Her lip twists. "That's the problem."

"Oh my god," I blurt without thinking. "You love him."

Mila's head whips up. "Do you want the damn lemonade or not?"

"Mila."

"Fine." She shrugs. "More for me."

"Mila," I say again.

She glares at me. "Dima and I have known each other for years. We train together, we eat together, we practically live together. We're good friends."

"But…"

She grits her teeth, eyes whirling like a cornered animal. I shouldn't have put her on the spot like this. I just don't understand why they aren't together after this long. *Unless...*

I've met the right man. I just can't bring my walls down long enough to let him in. And since I can't give myself to him fully, it would be selfish to get involved with him in the first place.

Mila's words. So crystal clear.

"Does he know?"

"No," she says sharply. "No one does. I mean, Ilarion probably does. Nothing gets past him. But Dima? No. He just thinks we're buddies."

"Good lord, Mila. I always figured you'd go for exactly what you want, no matter what."

"That's because you don't know me. Not really."

"I would like to, though. I'd like to understand."

"Trust me: you're gonna regret saying that."

"Try me."

She shakes her head. "Not today, okay?"

I can see the pain written across her face, and I'm thankful that at the very least, she allows me to see it, if not to do anything about it.

"Okay," I agree. "Another day then."

I turn back to look at my sister. It's so strange to think she might not wake up. She looks like she's having the best sleep of her life. Eyes closed, chest rising and falling, her hair fanned neatly around her face.

Wake up, I beg her silently. *Wake up and make me do the right thing. Because the longer you stay asleep, the easier it is to convince myself that it's okay to succumb to something that's so, so wrong...*

Mila frowns suddenly and cocks her head to the right. "Do you hear that?"

"Hear wh—? Wait."

Thumping. Running footsteps. Then raised voices, tires crunching over gravel, the clatter of panicked men moving in many directions.

Mila and I rush to the window in the far corner of the room and rip the curtains apart. But since we're facing the gardens instead of the front entrance of the house, we can't see anything.

"It must be them," Mila says, an air of panic radiating from her. "I'll go check."

"I'm coming with you," I insist.

We head out of the medical wing together and rush towards the staircase. We've just reached the first floor when I notice a trail of blood dripping on the white marble.

One of the security men zips past me, but before he can get far, I grab his arm and pull him to a stop. "What happened?" I beg. "What's going on?"

He doesn't immediately answer me, but then his gaze veers to Mila. "It's the *pakhan*," he says. "He was shot."

63

TAYLOR

It's my fault.

That's the first thought that pops into my head the moment I register the news. I'm cursed. I'm a bad luck charm. I should come with a warning.

Don't get too close to me, people! If you do, you're likely to get shot or abducted or knocked into a never-ending coma.

"Taylor?"

I jerk to the side at the feel of someone's hand on my shoulder. Mila gazes at me with those searing eyes of hers that remind me, for the first time, of her brother's.

I tremble under her touch. "I…I can't… If he's dead…"

"We don't know that. We don't know anything. We don't —Dima!"

Relief floods her face and she takes off at a run, jumping right into Dima's embrace. He wraps his arms around her, letting out a low grunt when their bodies collide. "Oof! You put on a few?"

"Fucker," she growls, hitting him on the back but clinging to him all the while.

"I'm okay," he says. "Seriously, it's all good."

"And…Ilarion?" I call over, my voice trembling. "H-he was shot?"

"Come on," Dima says. "I'm sure he'll want to see you."

He steers Mila around and leads us to the den. That has to be a good sign, right? If it were serious, then he'd have been brought up to the medical wing. Unless, of course, it's so serious that he couldn't be moved.

My heart is seconds away from flatlining. "Dima…"

But he doesn't hear me. He pushes the door open, and I see that Ilarion is not lying unconscious on the table, bleeding out from a gunshot wound to the chest. Instead, he's sitting up, gritting his teeth while Dr. Baranov stitches up his arm.

He looks up the moment we enter. Our eyes lock. Every internal moral conflict that's been raging inside my head since I was brought to the Diamond fades away.

All that matters is that he's alive.

Which is why I run at him the same way that Mila ran at Dima. Dr. Baranov wisely steps out of the way just before I throw my arms around Ilarion.

"Thank God," I whisper. "Thank God."

He hugs me back with his one good arm, circling my waist and drawing me as close as possible.

I always said he was the anchor tethering me to a world that's trying to buck me off of it. One by one, my lifelines have been snipped.

I've lost everything else. I've lost every*one* else. My father, my mother, my sister.

Ilarion Zakharov is the one person who feels invincible to me. And for a long, horrifying moment, I'd believed that the world was going to rob me of him, too.

"It's okay," he whispers, pressing his lips to the side of my head. "Everything is okay."

I still don't let go of him. I can't. He doesn't seem impatient about that, either. He just holds onto me as Dr. Baranov hovers in the background.

"I hope you gave as good as you got, brother," Mila says from behind me. The relief in her voice is as obvious as my own.

He chuckles. "I did my best."

"Mr. Zakharov, sir, I need to finish stitching you up," Dr. Baranov interjects awkwardly.

That's my cue to release Ilarion and let the doctor do his job. But I can't seem to let him go. I'm probably going to regret this embarrassing display of whatever you'd call this, but for right now, holding onto him is self-preservation.

"It's okay, Doc. Work around her," Ilarion says. He shifts me to his left side so that Dr. Baranov can work on his injured arm.

I press my forehead to Ilarion's neck and shut my eyes. I'm not sure how long the stitches take, but eventually, I hear Dr. Baranov shuffle away and the door clicks shut.

When we're alone, I breathe in Ilarion's musky scent and revel in the fact that he's here at all. That he's breathing. That his heart beats in time with mine, one steady thump at a time.

He's here.

He's mine.

He isn't leaving.

"I'm sorry for being a baby," I whisper after a while. "I can let go now if you want."

The sound of Ilarion's chuckle sends a bolt of excitement zig-zagging through my core. "I like you right here," he reassures me. "But don't worry, *tigrionok*—I won't disappear if you let go."

"You promise?"

"I swear."

With that assurance, I slowly release my hands from around his neck. In my head, I was planning to keep them to myself, but they seem to have a life of their own, so they slip down to his chest instead.

"What happened?"

He shakes his head. "Later."

I don't like that answer, but I'm in no mood to argue. My gaze drifts to the bandage around his right arm. "How bad is that?"

"This? This is practically a bug bite."

I almost smile. "I was so scared, you know. I can't lose anyone else."

"Not even me?"

I shake my head. "Especially not you."

His eyes darken, but it's not the stormy darkness of anger. It's more than that.

Which makes it that much more terrifying.

"Ilarion—"

His lips crush mine, and I gasp. I'm unable to stop myself from returning his fervor, meeting his hungry kisses with my own. I can feel his desire poking me in the stomach, and he lets out a low growl when I rub against him.

He tugs at my shirt with one hand, then works my pants open. I help him, lifting my arms and wiggling my hips to discard my clothes because every layer between us is a layer too many.

His eyes light up as he drinks me in. But it's not until his hand strokes my hair back over my shoulder that something else occurs to me: did he worry, too? Did he worry he'd never make it home?

I kiss him again. Slowly but thoroughly. I need him to feel me. We both need to feel each other—he's home, he's safe, and so am I, and we're both right here.

As long as that's true, everything will be okay.

I'm peeling the shirt off his shoulders when he winces with pain. "Shit!" I yelp, dropping my hands and leaning away from him. "Your wound. I'm sorry."

"Looks like you'll have to be gentle with me," he chuckles, pushing himself off the desk and walking over to the sofa across the room.

He shrugs off the shirt himself, but I undo his belt before he can get to it. I undress him gently, taking my time, marveling at the beautifully sculpted contours of his body.

I want to kiss every single inch of his body.

I want to taste him.

I want to feel him move inside me.

"We shouldn't be doing this," I rasp, even as my hand circles his cock.

He tucks his fingers under my chin and tips my face up to his. "We resisted for long enough," he growls. "There's nothing stopping us anymore."

That's wrong, though. It's so fucking wrong. The thing that's stopping us is upstairs, still living and breathing.

But what if she isn't? What if part of her—the important part, her soul, her life—is gone?

What if it's gone, and it isn't coming back?

A tear rolls down my cheek. "I'm a horri—"

"Stop." His voice is swift but not harsh. "Stop. The only thing that you are is *mine*."

He leans in and kisses the tear from my cheek, and when his lips slant over mine again, he tastes salty. I'm tasting myself, my sorrow, on his tongue, and it feels right.

Like we're sharing the pain, and that makes it easier to bear.

To know I'm not alone.

One by one, everyone I've ever loved has been ripped away from me. But not Ilarion. He won't leave me. He'd never, ever leave me.

He pulls me down on top of him on the couch, so that I'm straddling his hips and that throbbing shaft between his legs is stroking a tease against my wetness. He bends down and sucks a nipple between his lips, biting down gently enough to elicit a gasp and a riptide of pleasure.

His lips and tongue work my sensitive nipple without mercy, each suckle and flick and tug sending more shockwaves straight to my pussy. He reaches between us, dragging his fingertips along my slit and teasing my clit until I whimper for more.

That's when he sinks two fingers inside me.

I gasp and squeal, riding his fingers while he teases my nipple. I'm the one on top, the one who should be in control, and yet Ilarion steals that away so that all I am is a mess in his hands. I'm whimpering and moaning and begging him for more.

"Now," he growls, once my thoughts are mush and my body is a live wire. "Ride me, my little *tigrionok*."

I'm not naïve enough to believe that anything has been sorted out. This feels right for now, but then again, it always does when we come together like this. It's everything in between that complicates matters.

But I don't want to think about that right now.

Now is for giving and taking. For falling apart.

My mouth falls open in a silent cry of pleasure as I push down, taking him inside me. Ilarion grabs my hip again and pulls me the final few inches.

Fuck.

Fuck yes.

I grind and rock my hips back and forth, listening to my body, feeding it after all those torturous weeks of denying it what it really wanted.

I'm in control, and I want to lose it with him.

Our breaths mingle together as I lean forward for balance, wrapping my hands around the back of his neck. He's panting as hard as I am, and with the way my breasts are rubbing against his chest, I can feel his heartbeat pounding as fast as mine.

It crosses my mind that this is the kind of sin that might land me right in hell's lowest circle. But with every labored thrust, every delicious rub against the sweet spot he hits so perfectly inside me, I'm coming to realize something I unconsciously decided a long time ago.

If sinning feels this good, hell might be worth it.

64

ILARION

When it's over, I walk her back to her room. The whole time we're snaking through the house, all I want to do is take her hand.

But it's one thing to fuck her on the couch.

Touching her like *that* is something else entirely.

She's silent as we walk, and the silence is somber. She's thinking about Celine. She's worrying about the consequences of what we've done. We haven't crossed the line once; we've done it twice now.

We can no longer call it a simple mistake.

When we reach her door, she stops and turns around before she's even opened it. "I don't think you should come in," she says abruptly, as though she's been working up the courage to say that the entire walk here.

"Okay."

Her forehead crinkles with anxiety. "We shouldn't have had sex, either."

"Which time?"

The lines in her forehead only deepen. "Oh, God…" she mutters, dropping her face into her hands. I pull her body against mine and she shudders. "I know it sounds stupid, considering what we just did, but we can't actually spend the night together. I know Celine's not waking up, but…it still feels wrong to share a bed."

I nod, loosening my grip on her just enough to tell her that I'm listening. "We won't do anything you're not comfortable with."

She sighs, but it's more of a tired sound than a relieved one. "Thank you."

"I have an idea."

There's nothing I want more than to make her forget about all the imagined consequences she's dreading. Well, that's not true—there's one thing I want more: to do what we just did again and again and again.

The way she rode me…the way she came on top of me…

I'll remember that shit to my dying day.

"Uh-oh," Taylor says. "What idea?"

"Let's go away for a while."

"Pardon?"

"Just for a few nights. Somewhere quiet and remote. Just the two of us."

Her eyes brighten. But something's holding her back. "That sounds nice, but… I don't know. It feels so selfish to leave everything behind and go."

I bring my lips so close to her face that I'm in danger of kissing her all over again. But I hold back, as fucking impossible as that feels. I want her to hear this.

"I don't care," I growl. "I want to be selfish for a little bit, and I want to be selfish with you. Unless you're gonna stand there and tell me that you don't want me?"

"I think what just happened between us is proof that I do want you," she says tentatively. "That's exactly the problem."

"Then let's go. I want to be able to touch you whenever the fuck I please," I croon, backing her into the door. "I want to be able to kiss you, and hold you, and fuck you whenever and wherever and however I damn well want."

My hand traces up her thigh as I speak. Taylor shivers against me and her lips part in a soft, silent exhale. She presses a hand to my chest, but she's not even remotely convincing when she tries to push me away.

I grab her by the wrist. "If you don't want it, then say that. Look me in the eyes and lie to me, Taylor. If you say that, I'll relent. If you don't…"

She chews at her lip for a long time before she finally drags her gaze up to mine. "Okay," she murmurs. "Let's go."

I nod and step away, giving her the space I don't think she actually wants. "Good. I'm glad we settled that. We'll leave in the morning."

"What about my father, Ilarion?" she asks suddenly. "He's still with that lunatic."

"Don't worry," I assure her. "I've already set things in motion to get him back. I've got it under control. Just…trust me."

She hesitates for a moment, as though she's trying to figure out how to tell me that's the last thing she should let herself do. Then she nods. "I do trust you."

I smile. "Good."

"What happened today?" she asks. "The meeting with Benedict?"

"He did what he always does," I say with a shrug of my good shoulder. "He went back on his word."

She brushes her fingers gingerly down my bandaged arm. My cock twitches back to life, and all I want to do is carry her into her room and fuck her on the bed. *My* bed.

"Does that mean you fought him while he was armed? And you weren't?"

I give her as carefree of a smirk as I can, given the circumstances and the hammering pulse in my veins. "Something like that."

Taylor swallows. "Right. Well, I just wanted to say…thank you. For coming back." Then she pushes herself up on her tiptoes, kisses my cheek softly, and retreats into her bedroom. "Goodnight, Ilarion."

"Goodnight, *tigrionok*."

The door swings shut. The lock clicks closed.

I look down at my erection. "Fuck," I mutter. But there's no fixing *this* right now, so I head downstairs in search of Dima and Mila.

I find them out on the porch, next to the pool. They're both fully dressed and soaking wet. Mila shrugs when she catches my judgmental look. "He pushed me in, so I took him down with me."

Dima shoots me a mischievous smile. "I needed to let off some steam after that shitshow of a meeting."

I roll my eyes. "Don't you usually do that by fucking the first unfortunate woman you lay eyes on?"

The moment I say it, Mila stiffens visibly. It's not the first time Dima and I have made comments like that, but it's the first time she seems to notice.

"You okay?" he asks her. "Cold?"

"No," Mila says quickly. "No, just… Yes, actually. I am cold."

"I'd offer you my clothes, but I'm all wet, too," he says, winking at her.

She rolls her eyes. The annoyed expression she wears is quite convincing. But I can see through it now. I learned to read the signs a long time ago.

After it was too late.

The two of them sit up as I take one of the pool chairs facing them. "Did you fill her in?" I ask Dima.

"Yup. Right down to the stupid suit that prick was wearing," he grumbles.

"I hate to say I told you so," Mila says, glaring between the two of us. "But…I told you so."

"Did you say you hate to say it?" Dima asks. "Because I didn't quite get that."

She ignores him and turns to me. "You know Benedict," she points out. "Why on earth would you choose to trust the *mudak?*"

"It wasn't about trusting him. It was about upholding my own reputation."

"So basically, the meeting tonight was completely pointless?" she asks, folding her arms like our mother used to do. Not that I'm about to tell her that. She'd probably rather I spit in her face.

"Oh, no. I wouldn't say that."

Dima and Mila exchange a glance. "What do you mean?" he asks.

"Remember when I grabbed for his gun?"

Dima raises his brow. "To save yourself from getting shot? Again?"

I scoff. "Fuck no. I needed an excuse…" I say, pulling out a tiny black tracker out of my pocket. "To plant one of these on him."

Dima's eyes pop as he looks at the small device I'm holding up. "No fucking way. I can't—You didn't—Did you actually?"

"Of course," I scoff. "Why else would I throw myself at a gun? Now, we have a location, and I'm willing to bet it's the same place that he's holding Archie."

Mila gives me an impressed smile. "I'm sorry I ever doubted you."

"You should be." I gently nudge her with my elbow. "He's not going to suspect this one, which is exactly why I want the two of you to gather up a team and strike while the lead is still hot."

"The…two of us?" Dima repeats, glancing at Mila. "I'm pretty bad at math, but I'm pretty sure you plus me plus Mila makes three. Is there something I don't know?"

"I've decided to take Taylor away for a few days. We're leaving tomorrow morning."

Both of them look surprised, but there's an understanding on Mila's face beneath her shock.

"Are you serious?" Dima asks. "You're going to relinquish control of a mission this big?"

"I trust you two." The pair of them fix me with knowing smiles. I grit my teeth. "She's been through a lot. She needs time away to get her head on straight. And hopefully, by the time we get back, Archie will be on my property, not Benedict's."

Dima nods mockingly at me. "Riiight…"

"And what about Benedict?" Mila asks.

"It's not enough to take out Benedict," I say. "We need to take out his brother, too. Just do what you can, and I'll handle the rest when I get back."

Mila rolls her eyes. "You'll be busy 'handling' something while you're gone, I'm sure," she snorts under her breath.

I laugh. "Don't make me throw you in again."

Mila rises to her feet, and her expression turns solemn. "I'm glad for you, Ilarion," she says. "It's been a while since anything has made you happy."

Happy? Is that what I am? I wouldn't go that far.

But for the first time in my life, I see happiness on the horizon. And happiness has green eyes like emeralds. Happiness has blond hair that soaks up the sun. Happiness has a dimple in its left cheek when it smiles, and a V-shaped crease in its forehead when it frowns, and happiness makes me feel like nothing else matters as long as I have it.

As long as I have *her*.

Mila slips into the house. Dima watches her go, but he pulls his gaze away—somewhat reluctantly, if I had to put a word to it.

"So…you and Taylor, huh?" Dima asks, eyeing me curiously.

"Right now, there's just me. And there's Taylor."

"But after this little getaway of yours…?"

"Celine's still here." I almost wince as I say it—I hear myself echoing Taylor and I don't like it.

"She won't be for long," Dima gently reminds me, but it doesn't really soften the harshness of what he's saying. He seems to realize that, too, because he adds, "I'm just saying: the body's here, but the mind is…well, who knows where?" He sighs and flicks water off the tip of his nose. "Mila's right, though. You deserve to be happy."

He stands and follows after Mila. I sit there for a while after he's gone, watching the sapphire surface of the pool ripple in the moonlight.

Happy. I'd like to be.

But I'm not sure he's right that I deserve it.

65

TAYLOR

I've never been to a cabin in the mountains before. Now that I'm here, I'm just mad I've spent my whole life not knowing that it's like *this.*

There's something about the way the amber sunlight and cerulean sky peeks through the trees, bordered by majestic slopes and snow-capped mountains, that makes me feel *alive*. The cold air burns away everything impure inside of me. I feel like my whole body has been scrubbed clean within and without.

I'm only wearing a cable-knit sweater and jeans, but I welcome the cold. It crowds out all the other emotions I don't need to be feeling right now.

My breath plumes out in soft white fog as I approach the lookout point on the cliff beyond the cabin. "This is insane."

I risk a glance over my shoulder to Ilarion behind me. The sunlight glints off the high planes of his cheekbones. His black sweater fits snugly across his broad chest.

He's as immovable as the mountains beyond him.

"Hungry?" he asks when he sees me looking.

"A little."

He nods. "I'll go inside and get dinner ready."

I linger to soak up the view for one more moment before I follow him inside the cabin. It takes all my willpower not to touch everything we pass. The crown molding is flawless, the timber looks like it's still quivering with life, and the sandstone in the walls soaks up the sun that passes through the windows. It's all perfect—because, of course, Ilarion Zakharov couldn't possibly have anything less than that.

"I'm assuming this isn't an AirBnB," I mutter.

"No," he replies with a chuckle. "This is a family home."

"So you don't bring back girls here to wow them out of their clothes with the view?"

"Dima has been known to sink to those depths from time to time," he admits. "But I made sure the maids disinfected everything thoroughly. As for me? No. Never."

"Forgive me if I don't believe you."

He keeps his back turned to me as he pulls frozen cuts of meat from the deep freeze chest and sets them out on the counter. When he turns around, though, his eyebrow is arched high and skeptical. "If you thought I used this place like a whorehouse, then why did you come?"

"Because, as you might have already realized, I don't always make the best decisions," I drawl.

He laughs again. It's such a musical sound when he's like this. I could sit here and watch forever, just staring, mouth agape, as he glides gracefully around the kitchen and laughs and smiles and wields a chef's knife like it's an extension of himself.

"Go explore, Taylor," he tells me, pointing down the hallway with the blade. "The master bedroom is down at the end there. You'll love the view."

"Is that going to be your room or mine?" I ask. I'm shooting for a light, airy tone. Easy and breezy. Totally chill, a cool girl voice.

But the moment he turns those stormy blue eyes on me, I know I've stepped in it.

"Ours."

I swallow hard. "I'm not sure that's the best idea, Ilarion."

His eyes narrow dangerously. He sets the knife down with a quiet *shhiiiink*. "You don't think that's the best idea," he repeats. He emerges from behind the counter and stalks closer, backing me into the wall.

"No…we—"

"I didn't bring you all the way up here to go fucking bird-watching," he growls. "We're here so that we can be free of the shadows hanging over us. We're here so that I can fuck you as many times as I want, and you can scream as loud as you're able while I do it." He runs a surprisingly gentle finger along the curve of my neck. "And you're not leaving my bed after."

My cheeks flush, and I have a hard time meeting his intense gaze. Some of it is embarrassment, but most of it is arousal. And I'm worried that if I look back at him, he's going to know that.

Something tells me that he knows it regardless.

I try to push him away, but he doesn't so much as flinch. Honestly, the man could be one of the boulders outside for all the good my pushing does.

"Move."

"Why?" A playful smirk tugs the corner of his mouth. "There's nowhere to run."

"I'm assuming the doors in this place lock?"

"I'll just break them the fuck down if you even think of locking me out," he growls, his good hand landing possessively on my hip. "I didn't come up here for the damn conversation, *tigrionok*."

"Right," I snap, angered by his sudden, and very presumptuous, attitude. "You just came up here to fuck me. To *use* me."

"Why did *you* come up here?"

It's my turn to narrow my eyes. He's not off the mark, turning the interrogation on me. I did come up here with him. Willingly. Even after he told me what he wanted from me…

Because I wanted it, too.

I just don't have to *admit* that. Not to him, anyway. Not to myself.

And definitely not to my sister.

"I came up here…" I shift my gaze to one of the windows, hoping to avoid looking at him while I come up with some sort of excuse. "…for the air. Fresh, crisp, cool mountain air."

He snorts. "Bullshit."

I flinch. "I need to think about this, Ilarion." Now, I do dare to look at him, glaring, but a slight stammer edges out the anger in my words. "We can't just…jump into bed with one another and assume there won't be consequences!"

Ilarion presses a warm hand to my stomach. The way he gently rubs, even as I feel the tension in his fingers, makes me want to moan. Moan in frustration…and pleasure.

How does he do this to me so easily?

"Consequences already happened, Taylor."

There he goes again, making valid points I can't argue against. I want to slap him. I want to shove him away.

I want to rip his pants off and ride him until I can't think straight.

Instead of any of those options, I slowly shake my head. "It doesn't matter. It's still wrong."

"I never pegged you for a coward."

I slap his hand away. "Fuck—"

"You? I'm trying to, believe me."

I stop short, trying desperately not to smile. The storm in his eyes has faded. But more lightning is never far away.

"Tell me something," I say, spinning on my heels. "Would you be here with any random woman you happened to knock up?"

I'm trying to hide my insecurities behind a wall of self-righteousness, but it's a thin wall, and a precarious one. Any half-decent wind will take down.

He eyes me carefully as a small, knowing smile plays across his lips. "Ah. Is that what you're worried about?"

"I just…" I sigh and throw my hands up in exasperation. "I'm not interested in being one of your conquests. Okay? I'm not interested in being the convenient choice, either."

"You want to know if you're special?" He shakes his head in disgust. "Fucking hell, Taylor, how can you be so blind?"

That makes me pause. "What?"

He steps into my personal bubble again, his breath tickling my nose. "I was going to end my engagement to Celine in order to be with you."

The air is officially vacuumed from my lungs. I can't breathe. Or hear.

I definitely did not hear *that*.

"Do you really think I could have married her?" He reaches for me, caressing the side of my face with more of that gentleness that seems so alien coming from him. "When all I want is you?"

"Ilarion—"

"Stop thinking," he growls. "I did, and it makes a world of difference. You're mine now, Taylor. Do you understand that?"

I can't get the words out, so instead, I nod. It doesn't dispel the guilt sitting in the pit of my stomach, but I doubt that's going away anytime soon.

"I want to hear you say it," he rasps, tilting my face up to his.

I want to say it. God knows, too well, how much I want to say it. But the words stick to the roof of my mouth, blocked by my thickening tongue.

"No," I croak. "I can't… Not while she's alive."

"She's not waking up, Taylor. We both know that." He's quick to catch the next falling tear with his thumb. "And you're going to have to make a decision about that soon."

"A-about what…?"

"I spoke to Dr. Baranov before we left. He recommends that we take her off life support in a few days if there's still no improvement. But the decision is ultimately yours."

"And if I choose not to?

Ilarion lowers his hand to my shoulder and gives me a comforting squeeze. "Then we keep her as she is, and try to make her body as comfortable as possible for as long as you need to say goodbye."

I flinch as a bolt of lightning zigzags through the sky. Raindrops pepper the roof in a sudden torrent. They sound like the tears in my heart every time I think about Celine.

I take a deep breath and meet his beautiful, somber eyes. My body's tingling for him, despite everything. It feels like a shame to spoil this feeling with regret and guilt.

"Don't you feel bad?" I ask.

"Yes," he admits with a slow nod. "But I've lived with worse things."

The rain is coming down in heavy sheets now, but I can still see the mountains through the kitchen windows. It feels a little on the nose, considering what my life is like at the moment. Sporadic crying with glimpses of happiness, and a large, immovable, impassible mountain of a man looming over me.

"It's easier for you," I say. "She was your fiancée for a few days. She's been my sister my whole life. My best friend. She was—oh, God, I'm already talking about her in the past tense."

"I have a solution for that," Ilarion says gently. "Let's stop talking about her at all."

My eyes go wide. "We can't just forget—"

"Yes, we can," he insists. "Up here, in these mountains, in this cabin, we don't need to talk about anything or anyone that isn't present. It's you and me and that's it. Leave the rest of the world down below us."

"But—"

"Not 'buts,'" he says firmly. "It's you and me, Taylor. No rules. No relationships. No doubts or guilt. No judgment and no consequences. Just…freedom."

I take a deep breath. "You and me."

"That's right, baby," he murmurs, his lips tickling my ear. "Tell me that doesn't sound good."

Fuck, I'd follow this man into the mouth of hell if he whispered in my ear long enough. I look over his shoulder at the rain pelting down on the pine trees, and I want to melt into his arms and never, ever leave.

"It sounds perfect." I close my eyes for a moment and finish the thought in my head. *Forgive me for feeling this way.*

"You have goosebumps," he suddenly remarks, pulling back. "I'll get more firewood."

He moves toward the fireplace. I stare out at the rain. My head doesn't catch up with my feet until I'm standing out on the porch, the rainfall misting on my skin.

"Taylor, what are you doing?" Ilarion calls out after me.

I turn to face him. "No rules, right?" A silly grin spreads across my lips. "Just…freedom."

Then I walk backwards, right into the rain, spreading my arms out and turning my face up to the sky. I hear Ilarion swear, and then the sound of his footsteps as he runs onto the porch.

"What the fuck are you doing?"

I laugh maniacally. "I'm being free!" I say, throwing my hands up in the air as I start dancing. "Come on! Dance with me."

"You'll catch pneumonia. Come back inside."

"I don't care." I pirouette on the spot as my face is drenched with icy raindrops. Clouds shift in the sky above, and I can smell river and earth and bark and hear animals scurrying for shelter. Everything feels fresh and new and alive.

Everything feels like freedom.

And then I spin right into him. He's joined me in the rainstorm, and he wraps his arms around me as I burst into a fit of uncontrollable laughter.

"You're insane," he laughs, half-shocked and half-amused.

I nod, leaning up on my toes. "I know."

He holds me closer, his nose brushing against mine. Ilarion is soaking wet, too. Raindrops catch in each thread of his hair and cling to him the way I would if I were a raindrop that was blessed enough to fall on him.

Maybe that's exactly what happened, that first dark and stormy night. I was a raindrop falling, falling, falling…until I all but landed on Ilarion's car.

I grin at him. "Wanna go insane with me?"

Something flickers in his eyes. Something deep and primal and intense. "Again and again and again," he rumbles.

Then he crushes his lips to mine.

66

ILARION

We're a fucking cliché.

I couldn't care less.

Sex in the rain. Two lovers, so overcome with their feelings for one another that they rip their clothes off and fuck under the open skies.

I thought it was all a bunch of bullshit. I know damn well life is not what the movies make it out to be. They glorify death, too, but I've seen men die, and it's not pretty or heroic. It's gruesome and visceral and it sticks with you for life.

I've wanted a woman, and it didn't end with us running through fields of daisies while the orchestra swelled in the background. It's painful and thorny and it fucks you up forever.

So as the skies break open and happiness has never seemed so close and so far away at the same time, I decide: *fuck it*. Fuck what the movies say should happen next.

This is our story. Hers and mine.

We'll write it however we see fit.

When our lips part, Taylor's face is soaked with raindrops and joy. "The first time you and I met, it was raining," she says with a wistful smile. After all her protests, I'm surprised at her sentimentality. Her smile widens. "Maybe rain is lucky for us."

Something roars to life inside my chest. The fact that she considers herself lucky to have met me… I never realized how much that would mean to me until the words slip through her lips.

"Ilarion," she says before I can kiss her again, "I have a rule of my own while we're at the cabin."

That gives me pause, but her eyes are so bright and hopeful. If she's going to embrace this cabin trip, then I'm sure as hell not going to give her a reason to backpedal.

"Tell me."

"While we're here, we have to be honest with each other," she says. "Always."

Well, fuck me.

I can't promise her that. There's so much I haven't told her. Things that would make her run from me screaming. Things that would make her rue the day she met me at all.

Things that would prove that *none of this was an accident.*

"Okay?" she asks when I don't say anything.

I put my fingers to her swollen lips. She smiles, and I trace the curve of her mouth. "Okay." I agree to it before I say something stupid.

Like the truth.

She grabs me and pulls me in for another kiss. *Goddamn*, she tastes so fucking good.

I barely notice her hands sliding up beneath my sweater, but the cold of her fingers yanks my attention away from her sweet mouth. There's something almost feral in the way she looks at me, and I'd be surprised if I wasn't so fucking turned on.

I want her to look at me like that more often.

Every day for the rest of my life, preferably.

"I shouldn't be encouraging this," I growl, even as my lust yells at me to shut the hell up.

"You're not scared of a little thunder and lightning, are you?" She's working my sweater off me, and I now have a deep hatred for wet wool. It's heavy and impossible to rip apart no matter how fast I want to throw it aside.

"I'm scared that you're going to be electrocuted, or that you'll catch a cold or worse," I explain through gritted teeth. I want her to think I'm irritated and not at all feeling the pain from my wounded arm shooting through my fingertips. The moment she notices I'm in pain, she'll stop. I don't want her to stop.

Fuck, I don't want her to ever stop.

She just ignores me and works my pants open, tugging them down with a naughty smirk I'm ravenous for more of. She brushes her fingertips across my hardness.

"I'll be fine," she says confidently. "You'll protect me."

Her conviction makes me feel invincible. Like I'm the one controlling the storm that's now raging around us.

Taylor steps back and peels off her own sweater, quickly stepping out of her jeans with a sexy wiggle of her hips that takes my cock from hard to throbbing. I watch the rain caress every soft curve of her body and it's now my life's mission to lick each droplet up.

I want to take my time with her, enjoy every single moment like it's my last…

But I need her *now*.

I drag her to me, my hands grabbing her hips for leverage. She gasps when the cool metal of the parked Hummer hits her naked skin. I don't even remember pushing her against it —all I know is I need to be inside her.

She lays herself back on the hood, which makes her spine arch and display her swollen breasts for my hungry gaze. It's been hell and a half pretending not to notice the way her pregnancy has plumped up her curves so perfectly. But now, she's spread for me, begging for me, and I intend to feast on every inch of her.

Once I've sated the beast pulsing between my legs.

I wrap her legs around me and guide myself to her slit. She's so fucking hot as I push inside; it's enough to completely forget about the cold rain pelting my back. I lean over her to block some of it out, to keep her warm and pressed to me as I push harder, thrust deeper.

She takes me so good. So fucking good.

I brace my hands on either side of her head, hypnotized by the way her breasts bounce and sway with every thrust. Her nipples have tightened into perfect nubs begging to be suckled, and it would be rude of me to deny her. So I dip my head and suck a sweet bud into my mouth, coaxing and massaging with my tongue.

Taylor squeezes and pulses on my cock in time with each suckle. *Fuck*, that feels incredible. It makes me go harder, deeper, faster. I want more. I need more. Her moans pitch high and loud as I stop holding back and fuck her the way I've wanted to since the moment I met her.

And just like I'd predicted, she bucks her hips and lets out a loud, long, uninhibited scream.

"Yes," she moans. "Please, please, please…"

I slam my hips against hers. It's the only thunder I can hear, and the only wetness I want or notice is the surge of her warmth bathing my cock as she orgasms around me. I keep going, and she keeps writhing and begging for more. I lift her leg and rest it against my good shoulder as I lean forward, and we both cry out at the insane pleasure the new angle gives us.

Her hand slams down against the hood of the Hummer as she cries out my name. I run a palm over her stomach, marveling at what's growing in there right now. I can't quite tell if it's starting to swell yet, but I know for a fact that once she does start showing, I'm never going to not be hard as a rock. I'm never going to not want her.

I've never felt more deeply possessive of anything in my entire life. All I can think, other than that I need to ruin her for every other man on the planet, is that she's strong enough to take me as I am.

My *tigrionok*. My wild tiger.

Once I've reduced her to a quivering mass of hormones, I pull her closer, grinding my cock inside her as deep as she can take it.

"Sure you don't want to go back inside?" I ask her, testing how far this sense of adventure of hers will go.

She grabs my face with her hands and meets my gaze. "Don't you dare," she warns. "I haven't had nearly enough."

I grin. "Is this what happens when you stop thinking and start living?"

"Apparently," she says softly. Her eyes flicker with excitement as she runs her hand through my drenched hair. "Tell me something. Why did you bring me here?"

The woman certainly doesn't dance around the hard questions. I could give her the conservative answer, the easy lie—but I promised her the truth.

As much of it as I can bear to give her.

"I was trying to correct my first mistake." It's hard to talk normally when I'm still inside of her, still teetering on the edge.

A fresh raindrop strikes her cheek. The rain above us has slowed, as though the sky has tired itself out.

"What mistake?" she asks.

"I chose the wrong sister." But then I shake my head. "No, actually, that's not quite right. I should have made you tell me your name."

The truth doesn't flush out everything that has happened since then. But it's a start. I've been haunted by the would've-could've-should'ves since that damned engagement party, but in reality, they were whispering in my ear from the moment I drove away that first night.

I would have chosen Taylor from the start if I'd known who she was.

I could have done things right and avoided this mess.

I should have turned the car around and pulled her back inside.

Taylor's eyes are heavy with emotion, but she bites her tongue. "You didn't want a marriage based on love," she reminds me.

I nod. "I didn't."

"Why?" she asks boldly. "You know, since we're telling the truth."

I sigh. "I was scared to love my wife…because loving her meant the risk of losing her would cripple me. It would make everything harder."

Those rosebud lips of hers part. I can sense that I've crossed some sort of invisible line that I didn't even know to look for. Somehow, this wild, wonderful, stubborn woman has backed me into a corner.

"You love me?"

And there it is—the one line I drew in the sand myself. So long ago that I forget when it first appeared.

Doesn't she understand that she's asking too much of me?

"Taylor…"

"It's okay," she says, cupping my face. "It's okay. I don't need you to say it. I already know."

I frown, desperate to fuck her into silence so we can avoid burning my heart with her magnifying glass. "How?"

She lightly traces the corner of my eye and smiles. "I can see it in your eyes. And I can feel it in my bones." She looks away for a moment, her eyes growing sad for a fraction of a second. "And I suppose, if nothing else, that comforts me."

"What does?"

"The thought that, if I'm going to hell, at least I'm going there with you."

One last crack of thunder rumbles across the sky. She doesn't flinch and neither do I.

That's the problem with freedom: sometimes, it goes to your head. It makes you feel invincible, even when you're not.

I pull her off the hood of the Hummer and spin her around. My hand presses firmly between her shoulder blades, and she arches her hips back toward me at the same time her breasts mash against the metal.

I sear the image of her like this to memory—the way her fingers curl against the hood as I kick her legs open wider… the way her lips part in a gasp when I push deep inside her… the way she throws her head back and screams my name as I grab her and fuck her without an ounce of control left in me.

Until the only flash of lightning left is the spine-tingling flood of release that shoots through my body as I pour into her.

We haven't waited out the storm.

We've ridden it home.

67

TAYLOR

Ilarion carries me into the cabin because I can barely walk. My legs are limp from spasming so hard for so long. Not to mention the utter fullness keeping me warm and sated from the inside.

We leave a trail of rainwater in our wake, but he doesn't seem to give a damn about the wooden floors as we go through the foyer, down the hall, and into the master bedroom.

Not "his" bedroom.

Ours.

The ceiling is vaulted high, with wooden beams as thick as my waist flowing from wall to wall and meeting in a skylight at the apex. An entire wall is nothing but glass, framing the world beyond like a painting. I feel like we're suspended in the treetops. Floating in the clouds. High above the world splayed out at our feet.

We pass through into the bathroom. Beneath another wall of glass is a claw-footed bathtub the size of a ship.

I'm naked already, so he sets me gently into the tub and opens the faucet. Hot water gushes forth instantly, smoothing away my goosebumps. Steam spirals up off of my bare skin, and I moan with relief.

Ilarion waits until the tub is half-full and then he clambers in himself. He slides in behind me and pulls me into the fork of his legs, my back nestled against his front. We fit so perfectly together.

Only in this cabin. Only for now.

But perfect.

"I don't know why you don't just live here," I say, glancing out at the view. "It's so peaceful."

"It can get boring."

I splash some water on his knee. "Maybe boring is what you need. The Bratva can do without you for a while."

He snorts. "They'd crumble before I even left the house."

"Fine. You could run it from here."

Ilarion nibbles my earlobe playfully. "If you're trying to get me to move up here, then the answer is no. But we could make it our summer home. Winter home, too, if you're feeling daring. We can fuck on bearskin rugs in front of huge fires in the heart. I'll lick cold snow from the inside of your thighs. I'm kinda talking myself into it, actually."

I twist around so I can see his face. The image he's painting is almost enough to make me come again from the words alone. But I'm hung up on one word in particular.

"'We'?"

He shrugs. "Our child will love it here."

It's a backtrack, I get that. Or maybe he's just too self-conscious to admit to seeing a future for the two of us. Either way, I'm not willing to press. Not when this moment feels this good, and the future sounds that tangible.

For right now, being here with him is enough.

He starts shampooing my hair, and I close my eyes as he massages my head and works the knots in my shoulders at the same time. When's the last time a man has taken care of me this way?

Never.

It's only ever been him.

I suppose a small part of me feels that I'm owed this little slice of happiness. After all, I gave Alec up immediately, as soon as Celine told me how she really felt. Why should I be expected to give Ilarion up, too? Especially when what I feel for him is a thousand times stronger than what I felt for Alec.

"You're thinking about things you shouldn't be thinking about," Ilarion gently scolds, breaking through my reverie.

I scowl. "How can you tell?"

"I just can."

He leans down and presses a feathery kiss to my lips. He tastes like mountain rain. Beneath me, his body is hard as stone.

One kiss is good, but two is better. I drape my hand over his neck and pull him closer for another one. The second is as good as the first, so I go for three, and then I just keep him there, swiping my tongue across his soft lips until they part and I can taste more of him.

He grabs me and pulls me to him, tickling me beneath the water. I squeal with laughter and try to get away from him, but he holds me close, silencing my laughter with his tongue in my mouth.

We make out in the tub for ages, until all the bubbles are gone and our fingers are wrinkled from the bathwater. He fucks me again slowly, and the orgasm breaks over me like dawn over the mountains. The sun has almost completely set by the time we come up for air.

My stomach grumbles and, of course, Ilarion catches it. "I promised you dinner. I should've known you wouldn't let me forget."

"It's my fault. I'm the one who changed the plan."

"Get dressed and relax," he orders with a wry smirk. "I'll go cook."

"Need any help?"

He looks at me with an arched brow. "Do you really want to help?"

"Not even a little bit."

Laughing, he hauls himself out of the tub. I admire his sculpted ass while he towels himself dry and pulls on a pair of sweatpants. Bare-chested and sexy as hell,, he leans down and kisses me one more time as I rise to meet his tempting mouth. He takes the opportunity to grab me around my waist and pull me out of the now-cold water, wrapping a fluffy towel around me with another warm kiss.

Then he saunters off to the kitchen, leaving me to pat myself dry and figure out something to wear.

The mirrors in the walk-in closet connecting the bathroom to the master bedroom are almost as big as the windows they're facing. There's no way to hide from my reflection.

I cast a critical eye over my body. It has changed somewhat since the pregnancy…and, to my surprise, I'm not hating it.

My breasts are fuller, and there's a roundness to my belly that's new, too. I turn to the side and examine my stomach. I let my hand run over the almost-imperceptible swell and I imagine our baby inside.

Our baby.

Most women have dreams of this moment. I don't. I suppose it was too unplanned, and I was too young to have longed for it. It just came upon me suddenly and violently and beautifully. Like a devil driving a car too fast down the street when you aren't looking.

I rifle through the suitcase we brought and pull out one of Ilarion's t-shirts. I add a button-down sweater over it, but I leave it undone.

I emerge from the closet and examine the bedroom in the twilight. The bed is a pastiche of varnished wooden panels. Aspen and birch glow white and bands of pine are black where they run in between. Just above it hangs a Coronado wagon wheel chandelier, dripping with lit candles. I run my bare toes through the thick, earthy carpet.

On the far side of the room, I notice a series of staggered floating shelves. They hold books, mostly, but in between are tchotchkes and knickknacks. Antlers, a music box, a chunk of crystal, a snow globe.

The snow globe catches my eye. It's just big enough to fit snug in the palm of my hand. Inside, snowflakes swirl down around a mountain range that matches the one outside the window. At the foot of the mountain is a herd of deer grazing in snow-covered grass.

And in the very heart of the shadows clustered behind them, where the sun can't reach, is a pair of predator's eyes.

I feel my stomach twist suddenly, and I'm filled with a strange sense of foreboding. We can't stay up here forever. I have a feeling that the real world will catch up to us sooner than we want.

As much as I want to stay…our snow globe will eventually shatter.

I put it back on the shelf and go downstairs to join Ilarion.

68

TAYLOR

"As loath as I am to inflate your ego any further, I have to admit: you cook an amazing meal, Mr. Zakharov." I set my fork down with another sigh of contentment, the latest in an evening full of them.

He inclines his head in thanks as he collects my plate and carries the dirty dishes to the sink. "And to think, you haven't even tried the chocolate mousse yet."

"Stop."

"I'm not joking."

"I will literally explode if you make me eat a single bite of dessert, Ilarion. I'm serious."

He winks. "So am I."

My mouth is still zinging with the taste of butter-poached elk and wild rice. "How about we go for a walk before dessert?" I suggest. "I kinda wanna see the mountains at night."

I expect him to tell me it'll be too cold for a walk, but instead, he says with a chuckle, "You might want to put on some pants first."

I glance down at my bare thighs and remember that I'm both naked from the waist down and sinfully wet from how unexpectedly hot it was to watch Ilarion cook. *Those hands—* my goodness. I'd call them panty-droppers, but I hadn't even bothered to put any on.

Once we're both fully dressed, we step out. He doesn't take my hand as we leave the cabin, but I don't mind. It's enough to see it twitching by his side like it's taking everything he has to resist the impulse.

A small footpath leads away from the cabin and into the dark woods. But as dark as it is amongst the trees, the sky is unbelievably bright. The stars are sprawled out above us in brilliant constellations, and the moon is perched full and high, bathing everything it touches in silver.

I breathe in the fresh air. I can't get enough of the stuff. I want to bottle it up and take it with me. "This place is magical."

"It's far away from cities and people and bullshit. That's why."

I laugh. "You may be right about that."

We stop at the edge of the cliff that looks down over the lake. I turn to him, an agenda written all over my face.

"Oh, boy," he says. "Here we go."

I smirk and punch his arm playfully. "Let's play a game."

"Unless it's a sex game, I'm not interested."

"Two truths and a lie," I press. "Come on; it'll be fun. I'll go first." He inclines his head, and I know he's going to play along. I sidle closer to him. "I won a beauty pageant when I was six. I broke my arm when I was eight. I learned to ride a bike when I was fifteen."

"You've never won a single beauty pageant in your life."

I punch him again, harder this time. It's like punching a mountain. "Rude!"

"Well? Am I right?"

"You're right. I wasn't six when I won; I was seven." He raises his eyebrows, and I laugh. "Just kidding. It wasn't me, actually. Celine was the one who won."

I'm not sure if mentioning my sister is breaking cabin rules, but how can I not? She's been such an integral part of my life that there's no way I can avoid mentioning her altogether. Nor do I want to. The only thing sadder than losing her would be forgetting her. She's tied up in everything.

She's part of me.

I'm part of her.

"Why on earth was she entered into a beauty pageant at six?" Ilarion asks incredulously. "I didn't take your mother for that type."

"She wasn't." I shrug. "It was this random little impromptu thing they set up at a carnival. The people organizing the thing were recruiting people in the crowd, and one of them approached Mom. She thought it would be cute to see Celine in one of the big, puffy dresses, so she said okay. We still have the pictures. Dad looks like the wrong end of a donkey, though. He was so pissed that Mom decided to enter her."

"I would be, too," Ilarion says. "If we have a girl—no beauty pageants."

I feel a tingle when he says that. *If we have a girl...*

And just like that, I picture the two of us with a baby girl. A cooing little thing swallowed up in Ilarion's arms. A daddy's girl. An angel.

"Is it my turn?" Ilarion asks.

"Huh? Oh, right. Yeah. Shoot."

"I earned my pilot's license three years ago. I was thrown off a horse when I was sixteen. I watched *Titanic* and shed a tear. Just one."

I clasp my hands together and offer up a prayer to the heavens above. "God, please let it be the *Titanic* one." I glance at him out of the side of my eye. "But even I'm not actually that hopeful. What kind of horse was it?"

"None," he says, straight-faced. "I hate horses. I hate planes, too, actually."

My jaw drops. "You're not—You can't be—No fucking way. There is no fucking way you cried at a movie."

Ilarion chuckles. "Mila forced me. I got surprisingly emotionally invested."

"How long ago was this?"

"Would you judge me if I said that I was a full-grown adult?"

"Yes."

"Then no, I wasn't."

I giggle, and instinctively, I reach out and take his hand. His eyes betray the unfamiliarity of the gesture, but he doesn't let go.

"Again," I say with renewed excitement. "So we can find out what other movies have made you bawl like a little girl. Here are my three. I almost became a child actor. I dropped out of college. I'm a self-taught guitarist."

"If your father hated making your sister a beauty queen, I can't imagine he would've liked you ending up on a casting couch."

"Yeah," I say, suddenly crestfallen. "Not his favorite plan. There was an agent who thought I had some spark, but… yeah. Dad said no."

Ilarion frowns. "I get the feeling that he wasn't really into exposing you two."

I nod in agreement. "He was always an intensely private person. It got worse with age," I explain. "You can give it one more shot, if you want."

"Has to be the guitar one, then."

I smile. "Correct. Dad signed me up for lessons, but I hated the teacher so much that I used to snip the guitar strings when he wasn't looking so the lesson had to end early."

"Why didn't you just tell him no?" he asks. "Why are you so afraid to ask for what you want?"

I stiffen and rub my arms against the suddenly invasive chill. "They're my parents," I offer up weakly. "I felt like I owed it to them."

"Because they fucked once upon a time and produced you?"

"Thanks for that image; it'll haunt me to my grave." I shiver again. "I guess what it comes down to is…I love them so much, I'm willing to do whatever it takes to make them happy."

"At the expense of your own happiness?"

When he says it like that, I feel like a fool. But then, everything always seems simple when you let him tell it. The world in Ilarion's eyes is black and white. You love what you love. You kill what you kill. You take what you want. You leave behind what you don't.

"It seemed worth it at the time," I mutter. I sigh deeply and add, "It feels good though…to admit what you want. You taught me that."

"Now, maybe you should start *doing* what you want," he suggests with a gentle nudge to my side. "It could make a world of difference."

"Either that, or I'll crash and burn."

He pulls me roughly toward him. "No," he growls. "I'll be there to catch you."

I look up at him, his face half-lit by the moon, the other half shrouded in darkness. "That's exactly what I'm afraid of," I whisper. "Believing that."

"Don't be a fool, Taylor. You've made too many decisions for other people your whole life. Time to take what you want."

"I did," I say softly. "I took you. Even though you weren't mine to take."

"This is what I'm trying to tell you, *tigrionok*." His scowl sharpens. "Don't you get it? Don't you see? I was yours from the very beginning."

69

TAYLOR

Has someone ever whispered the key to your heart? Have they ever told you the words you were dying to hear? Murmured them right into your ear while the wind howled through the treetops and the rest of the world felt like it was thousands of miles away?

I was yours from the very beginning.

It's what I've wanted. It's what I've been waiting for. It's what I always hoped life could be.

I press my lips to Ilarion's and kiss him passionately, letting my tongue tangle with his. He pulls back and starts walking.

"Where are you taking me?" I ask in heartbroken confusion.

"Fucking hell, woman," he grumbles, glaring down at me. "I want to fuck you on a bed for once."

Then, before I can protest, he scoops me up. He practically jogs back into the cabin and throws me on the bed. I hit the mattress with a surprised yelp. He's on me almost immediately, pawing and tearing at his clothes and mine until we're both naked.

Then he pulls back once again. His eyes are gleaming and ravenous. The candlelight in the chandelier overhead dances over every nook and cranny, every crag and crevice of his sculpted frame.

"Fuck," he rasps at last. "You are a work of art."

I blush deeply. If I weren't already lying down, my legs might have buckled. What am I supposed to say to that? The answer is nothing. It's just more of his words unlocking every part of me I've ever tried to hide away so it can't be hurt.

But he's coaxing it all out of me. I'm exposing every last inch of myself to him—of my body, of my heart, of my soul.

And he's saying it's beautiful and asking for more.

I reach for his hips and pull him to me. My hands encircle his girth and stroke gently. His moan, a deep, rumbling baritone, sends a shiver straight to my core.

This kind of power is intoxicating.

I lean up and wrap my lips around the tip. When I suck, his hands instantly tangle in my hair. I run my tongue over his cock as I suck harder on him. I take it slow at first, and then deeper the more comfortable I get. He's huge, so it takes considerable effort to relax my jaw and swallow him down more.

But by the way he tugs on my hair and groans, but holds back from rocking into me, I can tell he's willing to wait while I adjust.

And I do, with every pull of my mouth and every downward breath. I figure out very quickly that when I moan, I don't gag, so I moan some more.

I moan a *lot* more, actually, both from my own pleasure and for the way it's driving him wild. Before long, he's all but fucking my throat while he groans and trembles.

But then, suddenly, he grabs me by the roots of my hair and yanks me back. Ilarion gazes into my eyes with this wild hunger that should terrify me.

Instead, it only makes me want more of him. More of his wildness.

"I'm going to come in your mouth if you keep doing that," he warns. "And I can't let that happen. I won't be satisfied until I ruin that beautiful pussy of yours."

He takes my hand and drags me up to my feet. Then he lifts me into his arms again and walks me over to the glass window that overlooks the mountain range. He pushes my back against the cold surface and sheathes himself inside of me.

"F-fuck!" I splutter. I'm soaking wet but I still feel like he's stretching me as far as I could ever possibly go. In the distance, I'm vaguely aware of his phone vibrating on the nightstand, but we both ignore it. Too lost in this to care.

His hand squeezes my ass as he brings me to an impossibly fast orgasm in his arms. My tremors and spasms must be too much for him to withstand, because he buries his face in my neck and floods my inside with his seed.

I can feel the amount of strength it's taking him to hold me up with one bad arm, but he never so much as flinches. Once he's caught his breath, he carries me back to the bed and lays me down on top of it.

"That was… Wow," I breathe, closing my eyes and gazing up at the ceiling.

The peaceful silence is broken again when Ilarion's phone goes off for a second time. His eyes swim with a wary look as he circles the bed and grabs it.

He checks the screen, and just when I think he's about to cut the line, he answers.

"Mila."

He doesn't say anything for a long time. He just listens. Apparently, there's a lot to tell. I keep a close eye on his expression, but I have no idea if it's good news or bad.

"What?"

His voice snaps like a whip. The tension in my body crowds out the pleasure it just experienced. I sit up and grab Ilarion's shirt.

"Are you sure? Did he check—? Yeah. Okay. Yes. Yes. Okay."

He hangs up, but he doesn't immediately look at me.

"Ilarion?"

Only then does he force his eyes to mine.

"Two things," he says quietly. "We've got your father back."

I have no idea why he looks so somber if that's the news he was just given. "Oh my god," I gasp, springing up to my feet with joy. "What's the second thing?"

He looks away from me, out into the dark mountains, just before he answers. "Celine is awake."

70

TAYLOR

Celine is awake.

She's awake.

My sister is awake.

I'm ashamed that my second thought is that my first thought wasn't bad. Does that make sense? Like, I wasn't crushed when those three crazy little words finally processed. It's proof that I'm not a sociopathic monster. I wasn't disappointed she woke up. I wasn't heartbroken. I'm just happy that she's alive.

That lasts for about ten long, blissful seconds.

Then guilt rushes in to ruin the party.

Celine is awake. And instead of being at her bedside like I should have been, I'm shacked up in a mountain oasis with her fiancé.

"Oh, God."

"Taylor. Taylor, listen to me."

Ilarion is whispering my name, but he sounds like he's far away. I'm not even aware I'm retreating from him until the backs of my legs hit the writing table in the corner.

He reaches out to steady me, but I flinch away. All the comfort, all the familiarity, all the stupid fucking *hope* I deluded myself into nurturing since we first stepped foot on this godforsaken mountaintop…it's all disintegrated into ash.

"No." I shake my head. I can't look at him. "Don't touch me."

He drops his hands, but he doesn't step away from me. "Nothing has to change, Taylor." It almost sounds like a plea.

I finally look at him. "What are you talking about? *Everything* has to change! We're only here because Celine wasn't waking up. And now that she has—"

"You can't just pretend like nothing happened." He's just this side of shouting, but I don't blame him.

Because I feel like screaming.

"Watch me," I say instead, shoving past him toward my suitcase. "We have to leave. Now."

"Fucking hell, are you really going to keep making the same mistakes over and over again?" He throws his hands up in the air. "Look at you, with that fucking mask back on—"

"What mask?" I whirl around to face him.

"The pretend-it's-all-good face you wear whenever you're doing something you don't want to be doing. At some point, Taylor, you're going to start hating your family for the choices you felt you had to make for their benefit. Choices no one ever actually asked you to make. Let me be the first to tell you: the fault isn't theirs. It's yours, and yours alone."

His words flay me open, but I shake my head like that'll keep the truth of what he's saying at bay. I turn my focus to throwing clothes haphazardly into my open suitcase. "I'll meet you by the car," is all I say.

I sense his brooding. I sense him radiating that furious thrumming energy of his. Then I sense the breeze of his motion, which has a weird, scary kind of violence of its own.

A few seconds later, the door slams. My hands freeze on my remaining clothes. That ended so fast. So cruelly fast.

Fate ripped away my hope like a flower from the ground.

I drop the blouse in my grasp and turn into the room. My eye catches the snow globe on the shelf again. I find myself drifting toward it. When I pick it up, snow blooms inside the glass like white roses.

I don't make the conscious choice to take it with me; I just float back to my suitcase, wrap it up in the blouse for safekeeping, and stash it away between layers of clothes like it's something I have to hide.

A memory of the last time I'll ever let myself believe.

71

TAYLOR

When I get downstairs, Ilarion is already loading up the vehicle. He's changed, too, in the last few minutes. The air of unyielding confidence is gone from him. He just looks pensive and angry. More like an ocean in a storm than a mountain in the distance.

I walk my bag to the trunk. He takes it from me without a word. The silence is a good thing, though.

If there's silence, there can't be fighting.

I take one last look back at the cabin. Then I climb into the passenger seat and buckle in. I don't look again. There's no point now. It and everything that happened beneath its roof is all behind us.

We drive for hours without a word. The silence is suffocating me, but every time I glance at the map, we still have hours yet to go.

What is Celine thinking? Is she wondering where I am? Is she wondering where Ilarion is? What has she been told? Is she even capable of asking questions?

My only point of happiness is the knowledge that Dad is back, too. He's been found, and he's safe. Which means there's a chance to salvage *something.*

By the time Ilarion finally breaks the silence, I have a plan in mind.

"We have to tell her," he grumbles.

I don't even glance at him. "No, we don't. There's nothing to tell."

"This weekend—"

"Was a mistake," I finish. "It never should have happened. That was my fault. I shouldn't have agreed to come here with you."

"But you did."

"Because I gave up on my own sister, which is a betrayal in itself. For you as well, but especially for me. As long as she was breathing, I should have kept my distance from you. Fuck, I should have kept my distance from you regardless."

"That's your guilt talking."

"Yeah, well, maybe I should have listened to it."

He curses furiously under his breath, and I can practically feel the waves of anger rolling off him. "I thought you were going to listen to yourself for once in your life?"

I shake my head. "It's not worth it."

"Excuse me?"

I whip my glare to his. "You heard me—it's not fucking worth it. I can't and won't hurt my sister! My father's back, and Cee's awake. Neither one of them knows about Mom. Which means I have to tell them, and they have to grieve. And afterwards, well…we're all we've got left, and we need to be there for one another. Of course, you won't understand anything about that."

"About what?" he snaps back. "Family loyalty?"

He slams on the brakes so hard that I almost go through the windshield. I put my hands out and grab the console, but luckily, my seatbelt holds me in place as we come to a dead stop in the middle of the highway. "What the hell?"

"You don't think I know about family loyalty?" he continues. "Why? Because I'm a selfish asshole who only cares about power and victory and money?"

"Ilarion—"

"I'll admit, I've been guilty of a whole hell of a lot of sins in the past. Ignorance chief among them. But when I finally decided to be honest with myself, I knew what I had to do." He's glaring at me, but there's something softer flickering in his eyes. "For my family, *and* for us."

I frown. I want to ask him if he's talking about Mila. I want to ask him if he means what he said back in the cabin: how he was planning on leaving Celine for me.

But I don't ask—because I'm a coward afraid of the answers.

His jaw sets and the vein near his neck pulses as he grinds his teeth. "You sit there and assume that you have the moral high ground because you're willing to sacrifice your happiness for your family? Fuck that. I had to sacrifice my own *father* for my family. And you know what? As difficult as it was…it was fucking worth it."

I have no idea what he's talking about, and I'm even more scared to ask. "What do you mean?"

His glare hardens. "You don't deserve to know."

I flinch back as though he hit me. Deep down inside, he has.

And he knows it, too.

My eyes turn slowly towards the road stretched out ahead of us. We have so much more distance to cover.

"We should keep going. Celine will be waiting."

"She can wait a little longer," he growls. "You can backtrack all you want, *tigrionok*. You can take back everything you said this weekend; you can pretend none of it happened. But I won't."

"You have to!" I yell, suddenly panicked. "Cee can't find out about any of it!"

"So your plan is to lie to her."

"Yes, if that's what it takes!" I nod desperately. "How do you think she'll take it if we go back and tell her we were away at a cabin together, fucking each other's brains out?"

"It's the truth."

"It's a betrayal!"

"It's not if you fucking love me!"

He may as well have shouted, because those words scythe right into my soul and tear me open from the inside out.

I look up, down, anywhere that's away from him. "Please don't." My voice is a broken husk.

"Admit it."

"I can't." I try so hard to swallow back the lump of tears growing in my throat. "Not now."

"Fucking hell, you are a coward."

"And you don't understand how much I've lost already!" I cry. "How can I risk losing more?"

"So you're choosing your sister over me?" He doesn't blink when he asks. His face is stiff with that same stoic calm, but I can still hear the hint of emotion thick in his words.

"I've already lost you," I whisper, a sob escaping my lips.

He turns back to the road. The silence is long and heavy. "You're the one walking away," he mutters. "Just because you pretend it didn't happen doesn't erase the fact that it did. You can tell yourself that you don't love me, but we both know you do. Just like nothing will change the fact that you're mine still, Taylor. You will always be mine."

I open my mouth to argue, but instead, all that comes out is a heart-rending sob.

I scramble out of the car and slam the door. I run a few paces before my legs give out and I'm collapsed on my hands and knees in the dirt while tears turn the world into pixelated diamonds.

It's impossible to blink them away. They just keep coming, and falling, and blinding me.

Get your shit together, I demand of myself. *Mom...help me.*

But I don't feel an instant burst of strength or courage. I don't even feel Mom's presence around me. All I feel is alone, caught between when I want and what I know I have to do.

The question is…*which one is which?*

Hell if I know. So I let out the scream I've been holding in since that damned phone call.

When my throat is raw, I feel Ilarion approach from behind me. I hate how so much of me is comforted by his closeness. I'm not allowed to feel that. Not from him. Not anymore.

Not ever, whispers the guilt in my mind.

I scream again. And again. Until, eventually, I'm all screamed-out. The tears have ebbed enough to let me see straight. I stand up and turn around to face him. The skies hang above us, dark and dense, promising thunder and lightning, but no rain.

The rain has only ever been good luck for us.

That's how I know there won't be any.

72

ILARION

The sudden shift in her demeanor is alarming. She blinks at me as if there aren't any tears still glistening in her eyes or smeared down her face. She talks as if I can't hear the rough aftermath of her gut-wrenching screams and wracking sobs.

As if I didn't just watch her fall the fuck apart.

My god, what I'll do to never witness that again.

But if there's one thing Taylor is always consistent with, it's being a glutton for inflicting pain and torment on herself. Which is how I know the answer before I even ask the question.

"I assume you have a plan?"

She sniffs and wipes her nose with the back of her hand. "Yes. But you're not going to like it."

"No shit."

She tenses but stands her ground. "It's the only way."

"No," I disagree, "it's not the only way. But you're too self-destructive to see anything else."

"If it was a choice between Celine and me, what would you do?" I see that flash in her eyes, that *knowing* she thinks she possesses. She's so sure there is only one path.

I take a step forward and she backs up immediately, terrified of getting too close to me. I hate that even more than the bullshit she keeps spouting.

"You," I answer. It's impossible to keep my own torment out of my voice, but maybe it's time she fucking hears it. "I would choose you."

"That's a lie."

"It's not." I shake my head, but I don't look away. "That's my truth. And I'm not scared to let Celine know it, either. Fuck, she probably already knows it. And you know what? She won't hold it against me. Maybe you and Celine aren't as close as you think you are."

Her expression twists. "You don't know anything about my relationship with my sister."

"I know enough."

"Right." Taylor nods. "You already told me. She doesn't trust me around her boyfriends, is that it? Is that what she told you?"

"No, that's not it." I know she's not going to ask, so I tell her. "Your sister *loves* you, Taylor. She thinks the world of you. Which is probably why she thinks you're so much better than she is." She furrows her brow as I continue. "She's not scared that you're going to steal away the men she wants; she's scared that the men she wants will want you instead of her."

Taylor's eyes go wide. "That's insane."

"Is it?" I ask. "It's happened to her twice now."

"No, it hasn't," Taylor says firmly. "Because *this* isn't happening now."

"Fucking hell, Taylor, don't you see?" I am literally baffled by how completely blind this woman is. Those beautiful eyes see nothing, even and especially when it's all right in front of her. "Celine doesn't *want* a man who'd rather be with you. She wouldn't want to be with me if she knew how I feel about you."

Taylor chews on her cheek. "We don't know that."

I momentarily wonder if I can bang my head against the Hummer hard enough for any of her so-called logic to make sense. "Do you want to be with me, knowing I wanted to marry your sister?"

She scoffs. "Absolutely not. I've been chanting that since Day One."

I nod. "Right. So what makes her any different?" I see her hesitate, and a glimmer of hope is on our horizon—or at least it's the dawn of her *finally* understanding. "How is she *so* different from you that she wouldn't feel the same way you do? How come you get to turn down a man who was going to be with someone else, but she can't?"

I revel in the frustration that rolls across her face and balls her fingers into fists. My point has landed.

Fucking *finally*.

But then she takes a step toward me, her face flaring with determination. "Do you love me?"

This time, I'm the one who wants to take a step back from her. "Taylor…"

"Why can you say everything else but that?" she demands. "Why can you claim me, possess me, and work your ass off to keep me, but you won't say that? Why can you demand that I say the words, but you're too afraid to say them yourself?"

The words are literally caught in my throat. She doesn't know how many times I've wanted to say those three damned words. Or how terrified I was when they first flared to life in the back of that damned car.

She doesn't know.

Because I just…

Can't.

Say.

Them.

Taylor nods with a sigh and smooths her hands over her sides. "I get it. I do. You think you love me and you don't want to lose me. You equate love with possession, but that's not how it works. Love is sacrifice." Her eyes meet mine. "Love is letting go."

A memory I've tried so fucking hard to forget over the years suddenly floods my brain.

Mila's tear-stained face. Blood flecked around her mouth. A fresh bruise blooming across her cheek.

"Please, Ilarion," she sobbed. "Please…if you love me…if you love me…let me do it."

I dropped to my knees in front of her, begging the only way I knew how. "It will eat you up from the inside out, Mila," I pleaded with her. "It's not an easy thing to look a man in the eye and pull the trigger."

"I want to watch him die. I want to watch that poisoned soul leave his body."

"You don't know what you're asking."

"I've had years—fucking years—*to think about what to ask when the time came. I know what I want."*

"Let me do it for you," I said. "Let me carry this—"—

"I'm stronger than you think," she insisted. "Please, Ilarion. If you love me...let me do it."

"Ilarion."

I blink, and I'm staring at Taylor, not Mila. As different as the two situations are—"night and fucking day" doesn't even begin to cover it—it doesn't feel that different. It feels like I'm being asked to prove my love, all over again.

"What's the plan, Taylor?" I ask.

She shuts her eyes. "She loves you. Benedict knows that she's your fiancée. You need a wife. All three things suggest that marrying Cee is the right thing to do."

"And where does that leave you?"

"When she's recovered, I will tell her that…that I'm pregnant."

My eyes harden as I understand where she's going. I hate it now with a thousand times more white-hot intensity than I did the first time around, when I already fucking despised it. "You still want to pass off the baby as someone else's?"

"It's the only way," she says again, as if repetition will make it tolerable. "You will have a niece or nephew, not a daughter or son. You'll still get to see them grow—"

"But I won't be able to claim them as mine."

"No."

"That baby in your belly is my heir."

She shakes her head. "Make heirs with your wife, Ilarion. This baby has to be mine and mine alone."

"You think it's going to be easy? To watch *my* child grow and act detached from it all?"

"You do pretty well already."

She might as well have slapped me across the face. "What the hell does that mean?"

Taylor runs a hand through her hair, and for a moment, the gesture distracts me. I want so badly to touch her hair, to run my fingers through it. To just hold her and forget this whole conversation ever happened.

"I don't mean it to be cruel." She smiles at me sadly. "You're just really good at not expressing your emotions. You're practiced at hiding how you truly feel." She lets out a crazed little laugh, but I don't know what's so funny. "You and Cee actually have that in common. It's how we landed in this mess, isn't it?"

Stop pointing things out. Stop making sense. Stop fucking seeing *me, goddammit!*

"This city might just be too small for all three of us, Ilarion," she adds softly. "After the baby's born…after the…the *wedding...*" Her voice sticks on the final word. "After that, I'll leave."

My blood runs cold. A fleeting image of a future without Taylor in it flashes before me, and I want to vomit.

But, as she said, I'm very good at pretending. "Where to?"

"Not far." She shrugs. "Just one or two states over. Iowa, maybe. I always thought it was pretty out there. But it doesn't really matter where. Just far enough that we don't have to see each other all the time. But not so far that we can't visit now and then."

I grind my teeth. "You've got it all worked out, don't you?"

"Ilarion—"

"No."

"'No'?" she repeats. "What are you saying?"

"I'm saying that your plan is short-sighted and idiotic. What happens if the baby looks exactly like me?"

"I'm willing to take that risk if it means preserving Cee's feelings." She shakes her head. "I've made my decision."

"Then allow me to make mine," I snarl. "When Celine has properly recovered, I'm going to sit her down and tell her the truth."

Taylor's eyes go wide. "No—"

"I'm going to end our engagement and allow her the opportunity to meet and marry a man who truly loves her the way that she deserves to be loved."

"Please, Ilarion, don't do this."

"And under no fucking circumstances am I forfeiting the right to my own child," I add in a menacing growl. "That is *not* happening. If you want to move states, you go right ahead. But our baby is staying with me."

"You can't do that!"

I lean in. "Watch me."

"My sister—"

"*I don't give a damn about your sister!*" I shout before I can stop myself.

Her eyes cloud over for a moment. "I don't care what you give a damn about."

"Clearly."

"The only thing I care about here is Celine. As long as she wants the marriage to continue—"

"She's not going to want to marry me when she knows the truth."

"Ilarion, please, you can't tell her."

"To protect you?"

"I'm not worried about me. I want to protect her!"

"You want to lie to her!" I exclaim. "What kind of fucking sister are you?" Hurt and doubt pool in her eyes, but I don't give her a chance to respond. I grab her arm and haul her back to the Hummer. "Get the fuck inside and be quiet. We're done talking."

She's quiet when I get into the driver's seat and lock the doors. Tear after tear rolls down her cheek. It rips me apart inside to pretend I don't notice.

"I don't know what she ever saw in you," she whispers hoarsely. "I don't know what I saw in you."

I don't respond. There's nothing to say, really—it's a mystery to me, too. Voicing it out loud is just her way of inflicting the kind of agony I know she's enduring.

Pain has a lot in common with misery.

They both love company.

73

ILARION

Mila and Dima are both in the foyer when Taylor and I enter.

"Where's my father?" Taylor asks immediately, rushing toward Mila.

"He's in the medical wing with Celine," she replies. "He's a little worse for the wear, but otherwise, he's doing good."

Taylor's back goes rigid. "They hurt him?"

"He's okay, Taylor," Mila reassures in a comforting tone that I haven't often heard from her. "Just focus on that, okay? He's a tough man. The only thing he wanted to know is if you and Celine were safe."

Taylor frowns. "Did he ask about Mom?"

Mila sighs. "Of course he did."

"Did you tell him?"

"He was…not in the greatest state of mind when we found him," she admits. "So no, I didn't tell him about Fiona. I figured you might want to."

"And Celine?"

"She's still groggy and disoriented from all the drugs. She hasn't really asked much of anything."

Despite herself, Taylor glances over at me. Then she seems to remember the fact that she currently hates my guts, because she turns away almost as fast. "What does Dr. Baranov say? Is she expected to recover?"

"Based on his initial tests, she'll be okay," Mila assures her. "She's going to need a little physical therapy where her limbs are concerned. Just to regain her strength. But she's going to be just fine."

Taylor's breaths come out heavy and labored. One after another, faster and faster, like a train rushing down the tracks with its brakes cut.

"Hey," Mila interrupts, grabbing her by the shoulders and giving her a shake. "You need to calm down."

"I…I have to tell them… I have to…"

"Do you want me to come with you?" asks Mila.

"No!" Taylor shakes her head, though she sounds uncertain. "No. I'll… I have to do it myself."

She gives Dima a passing nod and goes upstairs, taking the steps two at a time. The moment she disappears through the passageway, Mila and Dima turn to me.

"What the hell happened between the two of you?" Mila blurts. "You might as well have walked in with your fists raised. I'm guessing Celine's miraculous recovery didn't feel so miraculous?"

"Taylor is relieved her sister's okay." I say it as diplomatically as I can and try to avoid the rest, but I can't stop my jaw from clenching. It's been doing that since our last leg home.

Dima arches a brow. "But…?"

I don't respond. I don't know where to even begin to explain the insanity. The shitshow I'm buried neck-deep in.

Mila's eyes go wide. "Ilarion—"

"I was willing to break off the engagement and come clean with Celine." Sticking to the facts is easier than voicing the pain. "She's not."

"Shit," Dima hisses under his breath. "How's she going to explain the baby?"

"Some random one-night-stand." I want to punch a wall just saying that out loud. "All I get to be is an uncle and a goddamn mysterious, nameless, one-night-stand."

"This is ridiculous," Mila spits. "It's a waste of three people's lives."

"You know how Taylor can be." I shrug, even as I'm boiling inside. "She's fucking stubborn."

"So are you," Mila scoffs. "But in this case, you happen to be right."

"You can talk to her." Dima turns to my sister. "Talk some sense into her."

Mila frowns. "Me? Why me?"

"Because the two of you have a special bond. Don't think I haven't noticed."

"You're her fucking toffee Santa Claus. *You* talk to her!"

"Enough." I hold up my hands to silence them. "There's no point in talking to Taylor. I've already made my decision and I've informed Taylor of what's going to happen."

"That's not going to end well," Mila warns gently.

"No, I don't expect it will." I sigh. "Now—the mission. Tell me everything."

Mila and Dima exchange a glance.

"What?" I snap.

"Celine has been asking for you nonstop since she woke up. You don't want to—?"

"I'll give Taylor some time alone with her family and then I'll go up there. First, I need to know where we stand with Benedict."

They exchange another meaningful glance. I fucking hate when they do this nonverbal shit in front of me.

"The alarms were ringing when we left the extraction site," Dima explains wearily. "He would almost certainly have been informed shortly after. The warehouse where Archie was being kept was heavily guarded, but neither Benedict nor his brother were there."

"So they weren't expecting it."

"They didn't have a goddamn clue."

That is the first thing to bring a smile to my face in what feels like ages. I wish I could've been there to see Benedict's jaw hit the floor when he realizes that he just lost his only source of leverage.

"He's going to try to get to Celine," Mila suggests.

"Or you," Dima adds.

I roll my eyes. "I fucking wish he'd try."

"Excuse me, sir?" I turn to see one of my security guards at the entrance with a solemn frown. "A car approached the gate a minute ago. They threw out a body and drove away."

I glance toward Mila and Dima. Then the three of us rush headlong to the front gate.

74

ILARION

When they roll the corpse onto its back, I see a face I recognize: Oleg, a low-level intermediary for the Bratva. His eyes are lifeless, his throat slit wide, his shirt soaked in blood.

"Search him," I instruct my men. "There's a message in this."

Dima pushes the guards out of the way and starts patting down the body himself. Just inside the left breast pocket of his suit is exactly what I was expecting to find. He hands it to me.

I tear open the seal and read through the contents. It's fairly predictable, but I don't doubt its sincerity. It's practically carved into the paper with a furious pen. I can almost imagine Benedict's face as he scrawled the note.

I will destroy you and everything you hold dear. I will burn your Bratva to the ground and I will dance on top of the ashes and laugh.

But before I do any of that, I will first come for everyone you love.

I will flay that fucking right-hand man of yours, cut him up into dozens of tiny little bits, and scatter them to the wind.

I will take your sister, solder a collar around her neck and cuffs on her wrists, and she will spend the rest of her life spreading her legs for me and carrying my bastards.

And as for that pretty little fiancée of yours? I will give her the death I once reserved for you after I've fucked her to pieces. She will scream so loud that no matter where you are, you'll hear it.

But don't worry, my friend: I won't kill you.

I'll just make you wish I did.

I pass the note over to Dima and Mila and they read it together. Dima's face twists with disgust. Mila's is iron, but I know her well enough to see less stoic emotions churning beneath the surface.

As ironic as it is, something about Benedict's letter calms me. Maybe it's the fact that of all the people he mentioned, Taylor wasn't one of them.

If only the bastard had a fucking clue.

"He certainly has a flair for the dramatics," Dima calmly says, crushing the letter in his fist once they've read it.

Mila looks at me. "He's going to be a threat to all of us until he dies, Ilarion."

"I know," I assure her. "Which is why he's going to die. Soon."

75

TAYLOR

I race up the stairs, but when I get to the medical ward, I pause. My hand trembles over the doorknob before I finally bully myself enough to push it open.

They don't realize I'm there at first. Dad's hunched back obstructs Celine's face. He's clasping her hand in both of his and murmuring something in that soft, calm voice he used to use when we were kids.

It's amazing how quickly that voice transports me. Back to a time when I still had a mother. Back to a childhood when there were no secrets between my sister and me.

Long before I carried her future husband's baby in my belly.

Dad's scent is still cotton and soap, despite the fact that he's in new clothes that are definitely not his. They're too fitted, too bland.

But he smells like my father, and that's all that matters.

"Dad?"

He doesn't hear me. He just goes on talking to Celine, so I try again.

"Dad."

Cee hears me first. As she frees her hand out from underneath Dad's, I frown, wondering what I just walked in on. There's a look in her eyes that bothers me.

He catches on a moment later. He swings around and leaps up, almost toppling the chair he's sitting on. "Taylor! Thank God—you're okay!"

"Of course I'm okay," I say. "Are you okay?"

He sighs and his hands go limp on my shoulders. "I've been better."

It's not like Dad to admit something like that, no matter how true. I look past him to my sister. The motorized bed is helping her sit upright. She's lost weight, same as Dad, but unlike him, she's wearing a smile.

"Heya, kiddo," she croaks through a voice dusty with disuse. "Where've you been?"

I lunge over to take the seat Dad just vacated. "Hi," I breathe, taking Celine's hand and holding onto Dad at the same time. "You have no idea how happy I am to see you're awake. Are you okay? How do you feel?"

"Like I've been sleeping for a hundred years," she jokes. "But Dr. Baranov says that's just the drugs."

"You look good."

She laughs weakly. "Don't lie to me. I look like a donkey's ass."

"Nonsense," Dad chimes in. He clamps onto Celine's wrist so the three of us form a tight circle. "Where is your mother? I've been asking about her, but no one seems to have an answer."

I tense up. They're both holding onto me, so they feel my fear ripple through them.

"Taylor?" Celine frowns. "Why did your face just do that?"

I have no idea what my face just did, and I'm not interested in asking, either. "Dad, why don't you sit down?"

He shakes his head even as he goes pale. "I'll stand. What's going on?"

I open my mouth to explain, but instead of the calm, coherent lie I planned on telling, a broken sob comes out. "It's… She…"

"She was hurt, wasn't she?" Dad's voice bristles with rage. "Your mother was hurt in the crossfire between two very dangerous families. Families that we should stay far away from!"

I haven't heard him like this in a long time. Maybe not ever. I knew he wasn't exactly a fan of Celine's engagement, but something had been holding him back.

And I'm guessing that something was Mom.

"Dad…" Celine swallows and winces. "I'm sorry. I should have told you who Ilarion really was. But I just wanted you to get to know him first, before I—"

"Wait," he interrupts. "Are you telling me…you…you *knew* he was a Bratva don when he proposed to you?"

Her hesitation is all the answer he needs.

"Goddammit, Celine!" he cries, throwing his hands up in the air. "Did I teach you girls nothing?"

"You taught us only to be scared!" Celine hisses. "I didn't want to be scared anymore."

"Sometimes, it's justified!" he yells back at her.

"Stop!" I interrupt, unable to take the fighting anymore. Don't they both realize how lucky we are to be here at all?

"Sometimes, it's more important to be safe than happy," Dad snaps.

"That's a ridiculous thing to say. Mom disagreed with that, too, you know. She would have—"

"Mom's gone!"

The room falls deathly silent. Celine opens her mouth to ask a question I can't run from. But then she closes it again. Finally, after a long moment… "What do you mean?"

I blink and a tear rolls down my cheek. Dad understands me before Celine, because he slumps into the chair and stares at me with blank disbelief.

"No…" he murmurs. "No. No."

Celine looks at Dad, and then back at me. "Taylor, what do you mean?" Her voice grows frantic. "Where is Mom?"

I grab her hand. "She's gone, Cee. I… I buried her over a week ago."

"B-buried?" she stammers, her eyes trembling with horror. "No, no… That's not possible."

"If it's any consolation, it was…" *It was horrible.* "It was her choice."

"No!" Dad jumps back up on his feet. "How dare you say that? How *dare* you even suggest that she wanted to…to…"

But his words fade as he looks at me. He knows it's true. She told me she'd been suffering for so long. I don't doubt she'd told Dad even more than that.

"She suffered these last few years, Dad. You know that. She wasn't happy, and for some people, happiness means more than safety and stability. It did to her."

Fuck. I can't have Ilarion and those issues rearing up in the middle of this. But the moment I say the words to Dad, I can already feel myself eating them right back.

He shakes his head. "It's not possible," he says. "She wouldn't just… Not without…"

He keeps mumbling to himself. More denials, more rejections. My heart feels like it's breaking all over again, but I blink away my tears and turn to Celine.

"I know this is a shock—"

"It's not a shock!" Dad yells, even though I'm not even sure he's listening. "It's not a shock, because it's *not true*!"

Celine and I both flinch, but we don't take our eyes off one another. "Cee…"

"It's okay, Tay," she says gently. "I know. I'm so sorry you had to do it alone."

She gives me a tug with her fingers. It's the lightest of touches, but it's enough. I end up with my face on her shoulder, sobbing against her neck.

When I finally come up for air, Celine's cheeks are wet, too, and Dad is still pacing in the far corner of the room, shooting glares at Celine and I as though he's mad at both of us for accepting that Mom is gone. Like our acceptance is what really killed her.

He jerks to an abrupt stop. "Tell me what happened."

I swallow and say all the words I've been dreading for so long. "She was shot at the engagement party and taken to the hospital. She had a private room. The best care. When I saw her, she was talking, she was breathing, she was stable and doing okay." Dad opens his mouth to interrupt, but Celine holds up her hand and he falls silent. "I sat with her for a while. I spoke to her… She was tired of fighting, Dad. She was tired of simply surviving instead of living. She was done."

His chin wobbles. He looks paler than ever before.

"She asked Ilarion to look after you, and then I left her room. A few minutes later, the alarm went off. The doctor ran in, the nurses ran in, and… Well, it doesn't matter. They said she did it herself."

Dad drops right back down into his chair. He's so limp, so damn near lifeless. Like we'll have to scrape him out of that seat with a shovel.

Celine is quiet, but her breathing is steady. "It's so weird," she murmurs. "It's like I've woken up in the wrong world. Some horrible alternate reality."

"… Payback…" Dad mumbles to himself. "For…all my sins…"

Celine and I exchange a glance. "Dad?" I venture. "I know this is a lot, but—"

"We have to leave," he blurts. He jumps to his feet. "Right now."

"Dad," Celine groans, "I've already told you: I'm not going anywhere. I need…I need to talk to my fiancé."

My whole body twitches, but this time, neither Celine nor Dad notice. I struggle to my feet and walk to the door. "Come on, Dad," I say gently. "Let's go. Celine needs some space."

He shakes his head, but he lets me pull him along.

"I'll tell Ilarion you're asking for him," I say to Celine before I leave her room with Dad shuffling his feet behind me.

We've just cleared the medical wing when Dad suddenly grabs my hand. I turn to him, expecting anger, but he looks more panicked than mad.

"Taylor, I need to tell you something—"

"There you are!"

Dad drops my hand as Mila rounds the corner toward us. Her smile is pleasant but distant, though it grows even colder as she looks at my father. "Archie. We have a special room ready for you. I'll take you there now; I'm sure you'll want to rest after everything you've been through."

I want to talk to Dad, but I'm not sure if having a conversation right now will be good for either of us. He looks nervous as he glances at me. "Honey, we…we should talk."

"And we will, Dad," I assure him. "But right now, you need to process. You've been through a lot and you need some time. Don't worry—I'll be here."

"Come on, Archie," Mila says.

He looks between us and frowns. Then he does something I don't expect: he grabs me and pulls me in for a hug. He's even skinnier than he was last time I saw him—I can feel the ridges of his spine poking through his borrowed clothes—but he's real. He's warm. He's breathing.

Mom might be gone, but at least Dad's still here.

"I love you," I whisper in his ear.

He pulls back, but both his hands stay on my shoulders, like he's silently begging me to meet his eye. "I'll see you soon, okay?" His eyes are bright. Almost too bright.

Then he plants a kiss on my cheek, releases me, and slumps off down the hall with Mila. She turns the corner first, but Dad hangs back just long enough to glance over his shoulder at me. His expression is not one I recognize; it's calculated and alert.

It's…unlike him.

He places his hand over his pants pocket. He pats it once and points to me.

Then he's gone.

I stand there for a long time before I glance down at my own pocket. When I stick my fingers inside, I'm stunned to find a piece of paper. His handwriting is as familiar as my own.

South entrance. Midnight. Be there, and bring a bag.

Don't tell a soul.

Our lives depend on it.

76

ILARION

"A-are you sure?" Dima says, looking at the list of targets I've just given him.

I've been holed up in the den since we returned to the house. The medical wing should have been my first stop, but I decided that Taylor deserved that first meeting more than I did.

That's what I told myself, at least.

Truth is, I just don't want to fucking go up there.

"I'm sure," I reply without missing a beat. "Benedict is not going to expect an attack so close on the heels of a Zakharov victory. He's licking his wounds and regrouping. I'm going to attack him while he's down. And I'm going to stomp on his fucking throat."

Dima looks up at me. "This list is…ambitious. We're going to need every single man we have."

"That's why they're all arming up as we speak." I close my eyes and picture what's happening. Across the city, in rundown bars and nondescript apartments and dusty warehouses, Zakharov men are pulling arms from locked trunks and tucking knives into their sheaths. They're gathering, one by one and two by two, a trickle turning into a river turning into a fucking typhoon.

We're going to hit the Bellasios like a goddamn natural disaster.

And when we're done, there won't be a trace of the Italian bastards left.

I open my eyes and see Dima still watching me warily. "Go get ready," I tell him.

He frowns. "You're not coming?"

"I'll meet you at the primary target. But I have to…*deal*…with a few things here first."

Mila walks in just then. Her face looks drawn, but her eyes are laser-focused. "I put the old man in a room downstairs," she says. "He didn't seem particularly chatty. Kinda on edge, actually. Definitely not grateful that we just saved his ass." Her thorniness isn't hers alone; we're all more on edge with Archie in the house.

"He didn't say anything at all?"

"Pretty sure he's expecting to speak to you. But I think you should go and see Celine first. She's been asking for you." She bites back a scoff. "She's the only one of them who actually wants to see you."

I grit my teeth. "I'm going up to see her now. You're with Dima. He'll fill you in."

"Wait," Dima interrupts as I turn to leave. "Are we all going tonight? I mean, we have Taylor and Celine to consider. Not to mention the old man."

"A small contingent of soldiers will be left behind here to make sure they're alright," I explain. "But as you said, this will require all hands on deck. The Therons will be safe behind a locked door."

With that, I leave them behind and trudge up the stairs.

Every step is harder than the last. I feel like I'm walking to my own doom. But when I arrive at the medical bay and open the door, Celine is asleep. Her closed eyelids tremble and flutter with chaotic dreams.

I'm ashamed how relieved I feel that I can stave this conversation off, if only for a little bit longer.

But the feeling is real. It's churning in my gut and there's no denying it. One way or another, someone's heart will be broken tonight. It's the only way it can be.

So, with a bitter sigh, I turn my back on the woman I was meant to marry and ascend one more flight to talk to the woman I wish I could marry instead.

77

ILARION

Taylor is pacing when I enter. The tracks in the carpet say she's been at it for a while. I watch her bare toes trail through the lush nap of the rug before I drag my gaze up her legs, past the belly growing a life we made, and to her face.

The soft smirk playing at the corners of my lips curdles into a frown when I see her eyes. She looks up at me, her hands clasped behind her back. But the effort to keep me from seeing that they're shaking makes her whole body shake instead.

Her lip quivers worst of all. "I told them," she croaks. "I told them about Mom."

Fuck. "I'm sorry, Taylor."

"Are you?"

I don't answer. What would be the point? I knew from the start I'm not the hero in her story. If she wants to make me the villain—so be it. That's her choice.

She bites her bottom lip as though she's trying to stop herself from saying something she knows she shouldn't be telling me. "Did you see Celine yet?"

"I tried. She was sleeping."

She looks relieved to hear that. "She's weak, Ilarion. And I just told her that our mom is dead. I don't think she can handle much more. So if you—"

"I'm not planning on telling Celine anything tonight," I reassure her. "Dima, Mila, and I have business outside the mansion."

"Why do you say it like that? 'Business.' So…cryptic." She swallows. "I don't like when you say stuff that way."

I sigh and adjust the clasp of my watch out of mindless habit. I debate the best course of action, but in the end, how could I choose anything but the truth?

"We're hitting the Bellasio compounds. We can't risk retaliation. One night of hellfire and the Bellasio threat will be gone for good. One clean sweep."

"'Clean' is a funny word for killing a lot of people," murmurs Taylor.

I incline my head in acknowledgment. "Everything comes with a cost."

She snorts. "Tell me something I don't know." Her eyes go glassy as she stares at a blank stretch of wall for a long, silent moment.

I cross the distance between us until I'm only inches away from her. Only inches, but it feels like miles. She looks up at me, despite herself, and I watch as her expression brimmers with vulnerability.

"Ilarion," she says softly, "I won't betray my sister again."

"And the alternative is what? Betraying yourself?"

"I don't see it that way."

"You love me."

She flinches. "I—"

"Go ahead," I growl. "Deny it. Lie to me and deny it." I lean in closer. "You do it pretty well already."

She sucks in a sharp breath, then glances up at me through her long lashes. All I want to do is pull her to me, kiss her until she surrenders. Kiss her until she fucking breaks.

"Ilarion—"

"Say it."

She flinches. "I love you," she concedes softly. "Or at least... I want to. But I can't."

"Yes, you can. You came before her. You were the first. You were...the *only*. It was always you, Taylor. Only ever you."

She shakes her head. "I was just a random accident. She's the woman you proposed to."

"Stop stealing my choice."

Taylor pauses. Then blinks at me. "What?"

I flex my fingers against my palms, letting the sting of my nails biting my skin remind me I can't touch her the way I'm craving. "You keep acting like you're allowed to deny me my choice. Like I'm not allowed to make my own fucking decisions."

I'm not a man who spills his secrets or his heart and soul out like some lovesick sap. But I *am* a man who might not make it through the night. I've planned and schemed and I'm confident in the path I've chosen.

But there's always that very slim chance that death is waiting —and if I've learned anything from this shitshow, it's that it's foolish to gamble with fate.

Better be honest while I still can.

"Have you even considered, for one goddamned second, how things would be different if you'd just told me your name?"

Her eyes widen.

I nod. "Exactly. You chose for me then. You took away my options. You stole my ability to make an informed decision when it came to Celine."

"That doesn't make a diff—"

"The hell it doesn't!" I keep my voice low for the sake of Celine downstairs, but it's still just as harsh as a yell. "What? You think I would've even glanced at her sideways if I knew who her sister was? You're going to look me in the eye and tell me you honestly believe that had I known Taylor Theron was the same woman who stole my fucking heart from the backseat of my car, I would just call it a 'whoops' and marry some total stranger I can't even bear to be near?"

I'm very aware I sound insane. I'm very aware the floodgates are wide open and I'm pouring out more than I have in a lifetime of buried emotions.

But *my-fucking-god*, this beautiful woman drives me up the fucking wall.

And if the floodgates are open, it's because she's been chiseling at them for weeks with her stubbornness.

One day, when I'm no longer questioning my sanity, I'm going to bask in pride for our child. I couldn't ask for a better heir or a better mother to raise him. Or her.

If that kid is half as iron-willed as either of us, she'll be a force to reckon with.

Taylor hiccups on a sob she refuses to let out. "I do love you, Ilarion. But it's too late. I fucked up. And now, I'm not allowed to love you. One day, I'll forget enough that I… I won't care anymore."

It's like she's plunged an icy knife right into my heart. And instead of simply telling her how I feel, instead of saying the three easiest words in the English language that my tongue just won't work out, my expression darkens.

It's far easier to pretend like I'm not dying inside.

"Unfortunately, for you, that's not going to matter."

She frowns. "What do you mean?"

"As of tomorrow, Benedict Bellasio will no longer be a threat to us. You and your father will be safe here until then. At that time, Archie will be free to move back into his own home." I draw in a ragged breath before I finish, "But you will remain here."

"Ilarion—"

I silence her with a glare. "When Celine has recovered, I will tell her about us, and about the baby."

"It will break her."

I bark out a laugh. It's harsh and it's cruel and it's full of the truth she needs to hear. "You just know so much about everyone, don't you? She's not as fragile as you believe her to be. She's not as fragile as you *want* her to be."

That one lands like a sucker punch to her soul. *Good.* I'm not loving the way my words make her cower in on herself, but I'm definitely not loving the fact that I even have to say them.

I may be pissed right now, but I'm not an asshole. Well… not always.

"I will make sure she's comfortable and provided for. I'm not just kicking her to the road."

"She won't want your money."

"I'll give it to her anyway."

Taylor sniffles and folds her arms over her chest. "We can't. *I* can't, Ilarion. I'm sorry."

"Even though we love each other?" I demand. At least, I meant it as a demand, but all it sounds like is a desperate plea.

She blinks back her tears and smiles sadly at me. "It figures that you would only be able to admit you love me now that you can't."

Stop telling me what I can and cannot do. "We can raise our child together, Taylor. We *will* raise our child together."

I can see it on her face: she wants that. She wants it more than anything. But she's scared and stubborn, and the chaotic storm of her life is roaring too loud for anything to make sense.

"Ilarion, please. Listen to me. You can tell Celine the truth. You can keep me here under your roof...but I can't be with you."

I lean in, a fraction of an inch away from pressing a kiss onto her stubborn mouth. I let my lips linger, feeling the warmth coming off her body, tasting the phantom kiss on her breath.

"We'll see," I say at last.

Then, as painful as it is, I walk away.

78

TAYLOR

When Ilarion is gone, I drop into the window seat. My fingers claw into the thick fabric of the cushion, trying and failing to tether me to reality. I can't quite breathe right, and no matter how hard I try, it's becoming increasingly obvious that I won't ever be able to breathe here.

Not in this house. Not with my sister's shadow hovering over me.

I force myself to straighten up. Ilarion says he's the one with no choices, but I don't have many, either. All I can do is face the situation head-on. To stop hiding from the truth.

And the truth is, I'm having his baby.

The truth is, I love him.

The truth is, if I stay here, I'm going to cave. Maybe not today or tomorrow, but one day.

Because I know in my heart that I will never love another man the way I love Ilarion Zakharov.

I pull out the note my father slipped into my pocket. I've memorized the words already, but I read them again anyway. Then I glance up at the time.

Forty-six minutes to midnight.

Through the window behind me, I see Zakharov men amassing. Clusters of shadows joining clusters of shadows. When I squint, I find Dima in the middle of one patch of darkness. A moment later, Mila joins him. They bark orders, pointing and gesturing, then the trickle of the exodus begins.

I feel a tingle on my skin as I wonder what midnight holds for me. What midnight holds for them, too.

Tomorrow's sun is going to rise on a different kind of world.

I wonder where I'll be then. Do I trust my father enough to let him lead me blindly into the rest of my life?

I know Archie Theron. My dad is paranoid to a fault and fiercely protective. In my heart of hearts, I already know what he's going to tell me.

We have to leave as soon as possible.

Ilarion can't be trusted, and even if he could be, his lifestyle is too dangerous.

We're all at risk if we stay close to him.

All things I already know.

I tear myself away from the window and step into the bathroom. The idea was to splash some cold water on my face and shock these lurid thoughts of my system. But instead, I stand in front of the mirror and stare at my reflection for a moment.

My cheeks are pale and gaunt. I look *afraid.* My eyes dip down to my belly. It's getting to the point where I'm starting to feel pregnant. Which means I'm going to have to tell Celine and Dad soon—before I start *looking* pregnant.

I pull my hair back and tie it in a ponytail. But the adrenaline rush of the cold water doesn't last longer than a second or two.

I check the clock. Nineteen minutes to go.

By the time I head back to the window in my room, I see that the gates are closed, the trucks have disappeared, and all is quiet in the courtyard. The butterflies have gathered in my belly.

I don't bother packing. I just grab the same bag I took with me to the mountain. It's filled with all the clothes I never got a chance to wear.

I sling it over my shoulder and follow the staircase down to the ground floor. Then I take the kitchen exit out into the gardens, creeping slowly, keeping an eye out for any stragglers or wandering security. I wind through the gardens until I find the path that will lead me to the south gate.

Like everywhere else, it's quiet here. Stones shift underfoot, but the night air is dead still. Not even a breeze to ruffle the hedges.

I round a bend and see it standing there. The gate. The boundary between the life I wanted and the life I'm going to get.

It's simple iron, painted jade green. There's no chorus of angels waiting to usher me through. No Zakharov guards, either, which strikes me as odd. It just stands there, eerily alone.

But there's no turning back now.

I open the latch and pass through.

At first, I don't see anything. Just the darkness of night and a lot of trees. Then: a burst of light in the distance. The flash of headlights, there and then gone again.

A signal.

I dart through the trees until the car materializes from the darkness. It's a shabby Honda with a dented hood. Ilarion wouldn't be caught dead in it. I slow to a walk just as the driver's side door opens.

"Taylor."

"Dad!" I gasp when I realize that there's blood on his collar and flecks of it down his shirt. "What's happening? What the hell is going on?"

"We're leaving," he says. He eyes my bag. "Good—you packed. Let's go."

I take a deep breath, steady my nerves, and deliver the first line of the speech I practiced in the dark of my bathroom.

"No."

79

TAYLOR

Dad does a double-take, glancing over my shoulder before dropping into a hissed whisper as if the trees might be eavesdropping. "This is the only chance we're going to get, Taylor. We have to take it."

"Not until you tell me what the hell is going on," I say. "How did you even get past the guards? Why is there blood all over you? And where's Celine?"

He looks at me silently for long enough that two things strike me at the same time. One is that the first two questions that I asked probably have the same answer. The second is that, all of the sudden, he looks very different from the man who raised me.

That man was scared, trembling, badly shaven, underfed.

This man is alert, aware, watchful. And *calculated*. There's purpose in his expression and in his stance, and when I glance into the shitty little Honda he's brought to the party, I realize there's a gun lying casually on the passenger seat.

"Fucking hell," I whisper. "You have got to be kidding me."

Dad shakes his head sadly. "You never used to swear so much."

"Considering the way this night is going, I think I'm pretty *fucking* justified!"

"We don't have much time, Taylor." He rakes his fingers through his thinning hair. They leave behind more blood smeared on his scalp.

"Then talk fast. There were guards at the gate, weren't there?"

"Yes."

His voice doesn't waver, not even for a second. I can only stare at my father in disbelief, wondering if it's even possible. Wondering if I've just been blind this entire time or if maybe living with Ilarion has convinced me that everyone has dark secrets.

"Dad…"

"Sweetheart, it had to be done. They would have set off the alarm, and I had to do what was necessary to get you out of here."

"Are they dead?"

"Yes."

I shudder. He didn't hesitate. Didn't blink.

"You don't go from a family man to a cold-blooded murderer in the span of a few hours. So tell me, Dad. Who are you? Who are you *really*?"

He grabs my hand. He holds it tight, the way he used to do when I was a toddler and it started thundering outside and I wondered if the world was ending.

"I am your *father*, first and foremost," he says.

"And?" I loft a brow. "What else?"

He takes a breath. "Up until recently, I was also a *vor* for the Zakharov Bratva."

I rip my hand from his. Because as much as the dots are rapidly connecting, I still did not see it coming.

"Are you telling me…that *you* worked for…Ilarion?"

"Yes."

"He's a Bratva don."

"*Pakhan*, but yes. And before that, his father was the *pakhan*. He's the one who recruited me, seventeen years ago."

Seventeen years ago. I would've been three. My father is saying he let go of my hand during that thunderstorm that terrified me so much and went skipping off to join the fucking Russian mob.

I turn my back on him for a moment, scrambling to fill in the blanks. There's so many that I can't focus long enough to ask the right questions. "Did Mom know?"

"No," he says softly. "I didn't want her to worry."

"So the whole travel agent thing…?"

"Was a cover."

"Fuck," I breathe, turning back around to face him. "This is insane."

"I'm sorry, sweet—"

I shake my head and hold up a hand. "Don't bother with apologies. They won't help."

"I don't need your forgiveness, Taylor. I just need you to get in the car."

"Why?" I demand. "I don't know who the hell you are. Why should I trust you?"

"Because I'm your father. And because I still need to protect you. And, most of all, because Ilarion Zakharov is a dangerous man."

"From where I'm standing, so are you."

"Taylor—"

"You worked for him. You…oh my god," I gasp, as another part of the puzzle snaps together. *"You knew who he was when Celine introduced him to all of us."*

He swallows and nods. "Yes."

"And he knew you as well."

"Yes. He did."

I exhale sharply. "So he must have known who Celine was. Which means the only reason he got involved with her was because…"

"I defected," Dad fills in. His voice dips low with regret.

"'Defected.' That's a nice word. But what you mean is that you betrayed him. You…" *SNAP.* Another puzzle piece. This one hurts like he slugged me in the stomach. "You chose *Benedict Bellasio?*"

He closes his eyes, and for a moment, I see the man who raised me. The suburban father who worked long hours at the travel agency and watched White Sox baseball in the evenings while he massaged his sick wife's feet.

"I've made a lot of mistakes," he says at last. "And now, I'm trying to fix them."

But I can barely hear him over the *snap-snap-snap* of more puzzle pieces falling into place one after the next.

"He proposed to Celine to keep you loyal," I whisper to myself. "He wanted you to be a double agent. Except that Benedict Bellasio stormed his property and stole you and Celine away."

To his credit, he doesn't bother denying any of it. "Benedict thought I had defected back to Ilarion. His engagement to Celine…it didn't look good for me."

"I sense a 'but' coming."

"I managed to convince him that it was a coincidence. Ilarion happened to meet my daughter by chance, the two fell in love, their feelings for one another were genuine. He bought it."

"So, as far as Benedict Bellasio is concerned, you're still on his team?"

He gulps. "Yes."

I back away from my father slowly. "I'm not going with you. Fuck Benedict Bellasio. You may have sworn your loyalty to him, but I will not. That motherfucker killed my mother and—"

His eyes widen. "My god, Taylor! I'm not going back to him! I'm not going back to anyone. I don't care about any of that anymore. The politics, the mind games, the fucking death. No. It's done. The only thing I care about is keeping you girls safe. We're leaving the state. The country even, if we have to."

I consider that for a moment before I release a breath that comes out as a half-sob, half-laugh. "This is ridiculous. All of it. My father's in the Russian mob—wait, no: he *was* in the Russian mob, before he became an Italian spy." I cackle madly, feeling more and more unhinged. "My sister's engaged to man he betrayed, and I'm fucking carrying his baby!"

"What?"

His voice snaps like the wind. I turn to him with the laughter bubbling wildly in my throat. "Oh, this really is the night for big reveals, huh, Dad?"

A beam of moonlight through the branches catches his face and turns him pale as a ghost. He splutters, "Y-you're pregnant?"

"Four months along."

Another puzzle piece snaps into place. The biggest, heaviest one yet. The fucking centerpiece.

"The night that he and I met…" I close my eyes and let out a breathy laugh. I need to, before I drown in a flood of tears. "Of course. Ilarion was in the neighborhood—to meet with you. That was why you were so jumpy and paranoid. *You knew he was coming.*"

"Taylor, we really have to—"

"You thought he would kill you," I muse. "He turned out to be too smart for you, huh, Dad? He realized that the best way to hurt you would be to take your daughters. I don't think even he realized how brilliantly things would work out."

"Did he force himself on you?"

I laugh again, every bit as unhinged as the first. "No, Dad, Ilarion Zakharov did not *force himself* on me. In fact, he was the person I ran to after you hit me. Remember that?" I tilt my head to one side. "Remember how you slapped your own daughter for trying to be an independent, grown adult? It's almost poetic that she'd run straight into the arms of the guy you screwed over." Another realization hits me, and I laugh even harder. "Oh my god. Your first grandchild is the heir to the Zakharov Bratva." I giggle. "Congrats!"

If I'm being cruel, I'm far past caring. I've carried so much heavy guilt over that night, and it turns out it's all my father's fault. My father, *vor* to the *Zakharov Bratva*.

For seventeen. Goddamned. Years.

Which means he's not only known Ilarion this whole time; he's known Ilarion *and* Mila since they were children.

They've always been a part of my life; I was just never allowed to know about any of it.

"You're a totally different person to me now."

He shakes his head sadly. "I'll just have to live with that. But I can live with anything if it means you girls are safe."

"Touching," I whisper. "But somehow, it still doesn't make up for all the lies."

"We can sort through all that later, Tay. The only thing I need to know now is, do you trust me enough to come with me?"

I glance back at the house. "You keep saying 'girls,' but Celine's still in there."

His face sours into a grimace. "We have to leave without her."

I turn back to him. "What?"

He nods again. "She won't leave him."

"Did you tell her everything you just told me?"

"Everything." He jangles the car keys in his hand. "Including the fact that the only reason Ilarion chose her was to get back at me, to control me, keep my loyalty. She still chose to stay."

My hand flutters over my belly. "She really is in love with him…"

I meet his eye for a split second. In some ways, I'd made the decision a long time ago. But hearing Celine's choice makes it easier.

I glance back at the mansion one more time. It's only right now, right when my world has been shaken harder than that stupid snow globe I stole from the cabin…that I finally realize Ilarion was right.

I don't know my sister as well as I thought. Hell, I don't even know my own father, apparently.

Or maybe I clung to some imagined *idea* of them. Of people who do things out of love and not out of selfish desperation at the cost of others' happiness.

But Dad wanted more than his wife and children could give him. He tainted our lives with fear and paranoia, lying to us every single day, because he chose to pursue something being a *vor* gave him.

And Cee…

My stomach churns at the thought of her. She doesn't care about Ilarion's happiness, or Dad's, or least of all mine. She lied to me and forced me to carry the blame for something that happened years ago.

I don't want to think it, but I know that if she finds out —*when* she finds out—she'll cling to Ilarion that much harder, because she simply doesn't care about anyone's happiness but her own.

Tears sting my eyes. I wanted so badly to be loved fiercely by the very same people who have done nothing but leech my loyalty dry.

And the one person who actually does love me, fiercely and protectively…

Is the one person I already turned my back on forever.

I look at my father, where he's gone to sit in the driver's seat of the car. I barely recognize him now, but it's easier to think of him not as my dad, but as someone from Ilarion's world who knows what to do.

Because I have to face it—that's exactly who my father's been my whole life.

I open the passenger door and give him a nod.

"Alright. Let's go."

80

ILARION

I once had a dream about standing atop the ashes of the Bellasio empire.

That is the closest I'll ever come to a real-life premonition.

I stand on the elevated road that overlooks the Bellasio mansion and watch as it burns. Plumes of smoke and ash claw at the sky above like a corpse's gray fingers.

And all I can think is, *Nothing has ever looked so beautiful.*

Mila and Dima join me. "Well, it's done," Mila says, surveying the ruins of the estate with an apathetic frown. "Every property he owns has been hit. Along with the men who guard them."

"Not *every* property," I mutter.

Mila glances at me. "We hit every property on your list."

"Yes, but Benedict and Gregor were not in any of them," Dima fills in for me. "Which means—"

"There are more," I finish for him.

Mila throws her hands up. "Does it even matter?" she protests. "So yeah, there'll be smaller locations. Safehouses. Little fucking shacks out in the boondocks. And there will be a few Bellasio rats here and there hiding in them. But who gives a shit? We've hit his power base."

"That does not make him powerless." Then I exhale. "But it sidelines him. For now."

Mila raises both her brows. "Does that mean you're going to let him go?"

"Hell no. Not until his corpse is cooling at my feet."

She shakes her head. "Then I don't know what the point of tonight was. All we've done is give birth to a desperate man with nothing to lose."

"Which is exactly why I intend to keep looking for him."

"He's going to find a burrow to crawl into," warns Dima. "He won't be easy to catch."

"Ah, but I have a secret weapon," I remind the two of them. "I have Archie. The man was a double agent for long enough. He'll be able to tell me of any other locations that we might be overlooking."

Mila spits on the ground at our feet. "Surely even Benedict isn't stupid enough to use any safehouse that Archie knew about."

"He won't have a choice. He's out of options, and even if he has somewhere farther afield to run to…no one can run that fast." I turn my back on the smoldering ruins and face the line of trucks waiting for us.

"So Archie is the big hope," Mila says in disgust. "Can we even trust him? He betrayed us once. What's stopping him from doing it again?"

I smile cruelly. "I have his daughters. Both of them."

Then I descend the hill to my victorious army.

Mila and I climb into the Hummer in front of Dima's. We drive away from the fire, leaving it as an orange glow against the night sky behind us.

As the silence settles, I glance at my sister. Her face is a mask of steel. She stares into the middle distance ahead of the truck as we eat up road with a careful blankness. I know how hard she's fought to keep her mind that blank. That empty.

The past can't hurt you if you don't let yourself remember it.

"Mila?"

"Hm?"

"Is this what you want to be doing ten years from now?"

She scowls. "Have you asked Dima the same thing?"

"Dima has a life."

She tenses. "What does that mean?"

"It means he goes out. He fucks, he drinks, he fights. And one day, he's going to find a woman and he's going to settle down with her," I say as gently as I can manage. "Unless…unless you do something about it."

Her scowl hardens long past the point of being believable. "I… I don't know what the hell you're talking about."

"I think you do."

She pointedly turns away from me and crosses her arms over her chest. "I'm not having this conversation with you, Ilarion."

"I've seen the way you look at him. I know what's keeping you tethered to this Bratva, and it sure as hell isn't me. It isn't loyalty to the cause or love of the game, and God knows it isn't for the sake of family tradition. It's for him. Admit the truth, Mila."

"Shut up."

"Mila—"

"Shut the fuck up!"

I fall silent. The sound of the engine churns all around us. Mila picks at her nails again and again until I hear a hiss of pain and look down to see she's torn one clean off. Blood trickles onto her pant leg.

"Mila."

"There's no point, okay?" she says in a broken rasp. "I can't…I can't be with him the way a man wants a woman to be with him."

"I want to see you happy. You haven't been happy in a very long time." I cast a quick glance at her. "Except for when he's around."

She sighs, and her eyes flutter closed. "I haven't been happy since the first moment *he*…touched me."

It's been a while since she's spoken of it. The air in the car feels electric now. A lethal charge in every breath.

"I wish you'd told me sooner. I wish I could have stopped it."

"You loved him."

"I loved you more." I gently nudge her. "I still do."

She gives me a small smile. "I know that. Thank you. But what happened is a secret that I intend to take to my grave. And if I were to be with Dima, I would need to tell him the truth and…I just can't do that."

I leave the conversation there. I'm not about to force her to face her trauma. I know what that can do to a person.

81

ILARION

I drive through the gates of the Diamond and park behind Dima. Mila and I are just walking into the house when Dima skids to a stop at the head of the staircase. His eyes are wide with panic.

"I just went in to check on Archie, to prep him for our talk. But…he's not there."

My spine goes rigid. "Taylor?"

Dima just shakes his head.

Mila turns and rushes back out of the house to convene with security. I race upstairs. Dima follows me back to Taylor's room.

Her scent still lingers in the air, but it's already fading. It won't last much longer. As my heart pounds harder and harder against my ribs, I check the closet for any trace of what might've happened.

Her black duffel bag is gone.

"Fuck," I growl. "*Fuck!*"

I'm standing in place in the closet, fists knotted and shaking, when Mila surges into the room a moment later. "He took down three guards," she says. "They left through the south gate."

"Celine?" I ask Dima.

"I checked on her. She's still in the medical wing. Asleep when I got there."

"They left her behind?" Mila gasps.

"No." I turn toward the window. In the distance, I can just make out the glow of the Bellasio blazes. "No, neither Archie nor Taylor would have willingly left her behind. Celine chose to stay."

Mila frowns. "Archie wouldn't have protected you. He would have told both of them who he was—the connection between the two of you. He would have told Celine why you chose to propose to her in the first place."

I nod and give the only explanation that makes any sense: "She doesn't care."

I badly miscalculated everything. This whole goddamn mess started with a simple oversight and one slip of a miscalculation. Now, the wrong woman is in my house pledging blind loyalty to me while the perfect woman of my dreams is lost in the wind.

"But Taylor…" Dima says. "Taylor cared."

"Taylor's not thinking of me." I say that, but something deep inside refuses to believe it. Dares to say it *knows* not to. "She's thinking only of Celine."

And how Celine will react when she finds out about our baby.

That's when I punch a hole through the closet wall. *"Fuck!"*

"Ilarion," Mila intervenes, moving into my line of vision, "it might not be too late."

I think about it for a split second. Should I let Taylor martyr herself despite what she really wants?

Or should I find her, drag her back and force her to accept what she really wants?

Taylor told me that to love someone is to let them go. But no one ever taught her what I learned years ago: that loving someone means allowing them to face their demons. Love is doing what's best for the other, even at the risk of destroying that love in the end.

And *god-fucking-dammit*, I love her.

So there's only one thing I can do.

"Find her."

TO BE CONTINUED

Ilarion and Taylor's story continues in Book 2, ***DIAMOND ANGEL****.*
Click here to keep reading!
www.amazon.com/dp/B0C7JD1X23

Printed in Great Britain
by Amazon